# OTHER WORLDS WERE POSSIBLE

## *JOSS SHELDON*

First published in the UK in 2023.

Cover design by Marijana Ivanova.

Edited by Alice Ilunsford, Daniela Costa, Jordan Tate and Geraldine Nyika.

Proofread by Sadia Khan.

"Part of what I mean by the myth of normal is that we assume the conditions of broader society are healthy simply because we're used to them, even when they're not healthy at all."
**Gabor Maté**

"The assumption that what currently exists, must necessarily exist, is the acid that corrodes all visionary thinking."
**Murray Bookchin**

"The struggle of man against power, is the struggle of memory against forgetting."
**Milan Kundera**

"The world of hunter-gatherers, as it existed before the coming of agriculture, was one of bold social experiments, resembling a carnival parade of political forms... Many of the first farming communities were relatively free of ranks and hierarchies... A surprising number of the world's earliest cities were organized on robustly egalitarian lines, with no need for authoritarian rulers... Human beings, through most of our history, have moved back and forth between different social arrangements; assembling and dismantling hierarchies on a regular basis... How did we get stuck? How did we end up in one single mode? How did we lose that political self-consciousness, once so typical of our species?"

**David Graeber and David Wengrow**

# UNCLE CROW'S LAMENT

The *Tale of Uncle Crow* had been rattling around Sunny's mind...

It was a well-worn fable; one he had heard on innumerable occasions, whilst sitting beside the campfire, chewing on barbecued meat. That yarn was always recounted by the oldest member of their clan, who always swore blind that the subject was their very own uncle; a man not much older than themselves. The other elders must have known this was not the case. Yet they never doubted the truth of the story itself; a story they had first encountered at that impressionable age, when the young believe almost everything they are told.

The story had once been true. Of this, there was little doubt. But it had been embellished by the whimsy of time. It was impossible to say how much of the tale had actually happened, how much had been forgotten, which bits were correct, and which bits had been re-remembered, re-imagined and re-invented; intentionally or by accident, in the recent or distant past.

The story was so simple, it barely merits such

an introduction. But it was spinning around Sunny's head with such ferocity, it was only natural that Sunny ponder these things, *as well as* the story itself.

Uncle Crow had a big belly, or a big smile, or a big mouth. What was big, had a habit of changing. Sunny, for his part, never had a fixed image of Uncle Crow in his mind. If he had been with his mother, that legendary ancestor might appear to him with his mother's peculiar eyebrows; the ones which took an unpredictable turn as they reached their outer limits. But if he had been with his sister, Harmony, that character might appear with *her* marbled eyes; cerulean, turquoise and teak. Uncle Crow could look like a mighty warrior. He could run with a rhythm that matched the wind. And he could look like a gawky teen, with limbs which moved in contradictions. He could be tall or short, stocky or lithe; a fact which said as much about Sunny, and his volatile imagination, as it did of Uncle Crow.

On this particular occasion, however, the image which appeared in Sunny's mind did not have his sister's eyes *or* his mother's eyebrows. It did not look like a warrior *or* a teen. *This* Uncle

Crow was the mirror image of *Sunny*.

The resemblance was uncanny. Here was the scar Sunny got as a boy, when he had insisted on going hunting with the grown-ups. He had struggled to keep pace, tripped, and lacerated his ankle. Here was Sunny's oversized nose and his broken chin; the two features which dominated his face to such a great extent, that they hid most of his eyes and mouth. Here were the tattoos which covered Sunny's skin; his loincloth, his only item of clothing; and his legs, which were the second longest in the clan. His torso was not in proportion. It was not especially narrow, but it was a little short. This imbued Sunny with a mildly comedic appearance; something akin to a dog on stilts.

Why did this Uncle Crow share these features with Sunny? And why had he appeared at this specific time?

Uncle Crow may have looked like Sunny. He may have looked different in every possible way. No-one could say for sure. All they knew was this: Uncle Crow was a great hunter. Nobody doubted the fact that he was the greatest hunter the Eagle Clan had ever known. A few people had gone so far as to claim that he was the greatest hunter *the world* had ever known; an opinion which could neither be confirmed nor denied. Yet such trivialities had never prevented the clans-folk from falling for the superlative; describing Crow's abilities as "Marvellous", "Exceptional" and "Wonderful"; remarking on how he was almost certainly better than any hunter a rival clan had ever produced; insisting that he had mastered his craft, and was, dare it be said, pretty much perfect when it came to his ability to hit any target, from any range.

"Why, haven't you heard? Uncle Crow once downed two antelope with a single arrow!"

"No, it was three!"

"Three antelope with one *broken* arrow."

"No! They were buffalo. Uncle Crow killed three buffalo with a single broken spear."

"And, what was that? His back was turned? Uncle Crow killed three buffalo, with a *blunt* spear, without even spotting those creatures?"

"No! Surely it cannot be true?"

"But yes. This was the mark of the man."

***

When he was still a child, Crow's successes had been welcomed with warmth and appreciation...

Young Crow was a prodigious talent, but he had a lot to learn. He could spend days in the bush, and still return empty-handed. On those rare occasions when he *did* return with food, his kinfolk celebrated, and complimented his achievement. When he shared that meat, he was received with appreciative gestures; with cheesy grins, stomach rubs, and even the occasional wink.

Young Crow was a quick learner. By the time he reached Sunny's age, he was bringing home more meat than anyone else, feeding half the clan. Yet his unprecedented generosity was not met with any additional gratitude. If anything, he was met with *less* appreciation than before. His kinfolk still rubbed their stomachs, whenever the meat was tasty. But the winks had become a thing of the past. The smiles were a little too stony for comfort.

As Crow moved into his prime, there could be no doubting the matter. He was the most successful hunter anyone could recall. Thanks to Crow, everyone was able to eat meat for both lunch *and* dinner.

But his peers no longer *rubbed* their bellies, to show their appreciation. They *hugged* their bellies, to comfort themselves from the stomach pains this meat induced. The cheesy grins went the way of the cheeky winks. Uncle Crow had not seen one for so long, he began to suspect that they had been nothing more than a figment of his imagination.

It had become the norm. Like the clouds, which brought the rain, which nourished the grass. The grass did not give thanks to the clouds. And his kinfolk did not give thanks to Uncle Crow.

Things moved ahead, as things have a habit of doing...

In one of those mythical years, in which the sun shone for just the right amount of time, and the rains fell whenever they were called; the valley bloomed, animals feasted upon the new growth, multiplied, and filled the plains. Uncle Crow took advantage, hunting more animals than anyone had hunted before.

The clans-folk gorged themselves, eating far more meat than was good for their health. They became bloated. They retched. An elderly woman keeled over and died, mid-sentence, whilst addressing her peers. A toddler's corpse was discovered beneath a tree.

A consensus began to form: This was an abomination, and a single man was to blame.

That evening, the clans-folk held a meeting. Uncle Crow pled his case: He had only tried to help. He was providing them with the very food which kept them alive. Had he not always been there for them? Should they not be grateful? So what if he brought home a little too much? He had not forced anyone to eat that meat. His peers should have shown a little restraint. They should take personal responsibility for *their* actions.

His kinfolk did not interrupt Uncle Crow, even when they disliked the things they heard. They maintained a dignified silence, as tears assembled in the knuckles of their eyes, and as their brows crumpled into furrows. Members of their tribe *always* remained silent whilst their peers were speaking, granting them the time they needed to plead their case. They only ever made a decision once they had listened to everyone's point of view. And even then, a vote had to be held, and the result had to be unanimous.

In this case, the vote was unanimous at the first time of asking. Uncle Crow was invited to enter into a voluntary exile.

Crow respected the group's decision, agreeing to this request without a word of complaint.

And yet, in an unpredicted turn of events, the clans-folk *did* heed Uncle Crow's advice. They did take a little more "Personal responsibility". Or perhaps it was *collective* responsibility. Rather than rely on a single hunter, they each hunted a little; sometimes alone, and sometimes as part of a group. They never secured quite as much meat as in the days of Uncle Crow. But that never seemed to matter.

***

The Eagle Clan did not measure time using seconds, minutes and hours...

They could not help but notice the difference between daytime and night. They knew of the seasons, solstices and lunar-cycles. But they had no need for such things as "Weeks" and "Months". They rose a little before the sun, when the air was at its coolest. They fell asleep as the moon approached its zenith. They hunted if they were moved by a desire to hunt. They fished if they felt like fishing. They gathered plants whenever they appeared. And they repaired their huts whenever it took their fancy. No-one ever told them what to do, and no clock ever told them when to do it.

But if had they used such units, it could have been said that Sunny had recalled *The Tale of Uncle Crow*, on no fewer than five occasions, in what had been a little under an "Hour". An image of that legendary hunter was reappearing in his mind's eye, on an increasingly regular basis.

But why?

It started three days before...

Sunny had awoken before dawn, jumped to his feet, and tiptoed out of the circular hut which he shared with eight other people; avoiding the bark-less wooden pole in the centre of that abode, stepping over the bodies which were strewn across the earthen floor, and slipping out through an opening in the wall; a head-high bamboo structure, which was interwoven with strips of banana leaves.

Sunny had collected a spear from the clan's communal store, and wandered into the bush.

Things had not gone as smoothly as he might have envisioned...

On that first day, Sunny had only spotted a single animal. Impelled by an inebriating cocktail of excitement and nerves, he had tangled his gangly legs; rustling one too many plants, and kicking one too many pebbles; alerting his prey, who bolted from view.

Too proud to return empty-handed, Sunny had slept in the wilds, and tried again the following morning. This time, he failed to locate a single target.

On the third day, he believed his perseverance had finally been rewarded, when he backed an antelope into a cave. He thought he might die, when that animal readied itself to charge; bowing its head, exposing the points of its antlers. And he thought he might triumph, when he pushed through his fear; lunging forwards, bracing his knees, and thrusting his spear into space.

Neither of these things had come to pass. The two combatants had danced a tango; passing without touching, making a sound, or leaving a mark.

What was Sunny to do?

He needed another plan. And, in one of those rare moments of inspiration, or luck, or destiny; he remembered, or found, or was discovered; by a nomadic clan, who had erected their camp nearby. Perhaps Sunny had spotted the smoke, which billowed out from their fire. Or perhaps he had smelled their food. He was so drowsy, overcome by hunger and thirst, that he could not be entirely sure how he found those people. Nor could he remember how he had ended up by their fire, clasping a bowl of pigeon soup.

That meal, and the sleep which followed, had set Sunny straight. Come dawn, he was back on his feet, raring to go, and determined to complete his mission.

As he was leaving the camp, he noticed five oxen, who were tied to a tree. He must have been mesmerised by those animals, because he was oblivious to the person who approached him from behind:

"Pretty impressive, right?"

Sunny jumped. His heart missed a beat, and his nose missed a breath. He had to thump his chest back into action, and gulp down a mouthful of air, before he was able to form a response:

"*Aah... Aah-ooh...* Yes! Yes, yes."

"Why don't you take one?"

"Eh?"

"What's ours is yours?"

"But... It's just... Well, I couldn't."

"Consider it a gift! Take it now, and re-gift us whenever you're ready."

"Really?"

The woman nodded.

Sunny shrugged.

It had never been his intention to take another clan's animal. He would have preferred to hunt one himself. But these were particularly fine oxen. And he could always hunt a different animal, sometime in the future. He could use *that* to settle his debt.

Sunny reached a conclusion: He would have been stupid *not* to accept that ox.

He trod back into the camp, spoke to the elders, received their blessing, chose the fattest ox, and led it back to their clan's Small Camp.

It really was a splendid animal; so shiny it sparkled, as tall as most men, with horns like an eagle's wings. Sunny supposed it might provide enough meat to feed his peers for half a lunar-cycle.

He daydreamed as he walked, envisioning the claps and cheers which would greet his arrival. Allowing his imagination to roam free, he saw people emerge from their huts, burst into song, lift him, throw him, and catch him as he fell:

"Amazing, Sunny!"

"What a fine animal."

"Wow, Sunny, you're the best!"

"You're a hero."

"Please will you have sex with me?"

He knew, deep down, that he was unlikely to receive such a welcome. But he still expected a little praise and a modicum of respect. He could have never predicted the sheer indifference with which he was met.

There he stood, as proud as a sunset; with his chest puffed, and his hands on his hips; with the animal before him, and the camp before them both.

And *nothing*. No-one came to meet him. No-one said a word. At first, no-one even glanced in his general direction.

After several moments had passed, a couple of elders finally turned towards Sunny, almost unwillingly, as though it was the greatest of all possible burdens. They did not say a word, or react in any other way. They merely looked him up and down, before returning to face each other. One nibbled the piece of wood he had been chewing since daybreak. The other nodded, as though to agree with her friend, who was yet to voice an opinion.

Sunny was happy to wait. He knew there wouldn't be a procession. That was a flight of fancy. There wouldn't be any hollers or hurrahs. But he was certain that a few people would smile. Someone might offer a word of praise. Someone else might pucker their lips or clap.

As the moments rolled by, his certainty gave way to doubt, which gave way to dejection. This was a fine animal. Its meat would feed the clan for several days. Why was no-one coming to greet him?

He broke.

Calling out to the two elders, he implored:

"Come and see this miraculous beast. Come and wonder at its stupendous thighs, astonishing rump, and eye-boggling hulk. Dearest auntie and beloved uncle: This is the finest catch of the season. Come and feel its bounteous meat. There's enough to satisfy us all. I mean... I couldn't possibly take a share, until the elders have taken theirs."

Nothing.

"Come! Come and look at its muscled limbs. Come and see its opulent coat. Come and feel its sturdy bones."

Nothing.

Supposing he had little to lose, Sunny led the ox between the two rows of huts which gave shape to their Small Camp; the place they called home during the dry season. He had already jinked his way through the clan's allotment; a hotchpotch of plants, which skirted around the southern end of this encampment, blurring the border between their home and the scrublands which lay beyond; an unnervingly flat expanse; dusty, dry, yellowish, amber and bronze. Now he was strolling down this avenue, which had formed organically over the course of a hundred generations. None of the tiny flowers, which filled the grasslands to the north, could be found on this earthen track. It was a perfect desert; hard-packed, impeccably smooth, without a crack or dent in sight. A visitor might have supposed it had been designed this way. But the clans-folk had never maintained this space, unlike the fire pit which took pride of place at the opposite end of the lane. A few of the elders *did* take care of that circle; the place where the clans-folk roasted their meat and held their parliaments. They swept that space every morning and most afternoons.

Sunny came to a stop in the shade of one of the twenty-six bulbous trees which lined this road. They were all alike; emerald spheres, which towered above their podgy trunks; balancing precariously, as though they might tumble at any moment. Those trees provided a certain symmetry to the camp. There were two of them between each hut. And they served a purpose; supplying the shade which cooled this place when the heat became too much to bear.

There were only two seasons in this region; a *rainy season*, and a slightly longer *dry season*. The rainy season was characterised by daily showers. They did not last for long, but they were intense; pounding the ground, churning the earth, and flooding the land. The dry season was oppressive. The air was so dry, it glistened. The heat could cook an egg. The tribes-folk had evolved to tolerate these temperatures. But they were still grateful for the shade these trees supplied.

Sunny took a breath, allowed the shadows to stroke his skin, and gazed along the lane.

Something caught him by surprise: There were people in almost every hut. They seemed to have stopped what they were doing, just to stare at him. Or at least, Sunny *felt* they were staring at him. In the days which were to follow, he would question if this had really been the case. But in that moment, he had no such doubts.

He led the ox a little further up the lane, reached the silent couple, stopped, and addressed the woman, who was called *Aura*:

"Dearest Auntie Aura: Feast your eyes upon this."

Aura lifted her face, revealing a maze of tattooed lines; bluish, bruised and blurred. Every adult in their tribe had facial tattoos, but Aura had more than most. Her face was a leathery canvas, confused by a mishmash of patterns, which had been drawn by an array of different artists, over the course of hundreds of seasons. It took quite an effort to work out which line belonged to which pattern, and to focus on that design, whilst ignoring the surrounding fuzz.

Aura was wearing the type of loincloth which was worn by almost everyone in their tribe. It was made from two pieces of antelope hide, which had been stitched together with boar sinew, such that the front piece covered her genitalia, and the rear piece covered her buttocks. She wore her hair in the style which was common among a few of the local clans; tying it into plaits, before combining those plaits into a bun. Her neck was decorated with ivory pearls, and her wrists were adorned with eggshell beads. But the rest of her body remained as naked as the day she was born, covered in nothing but these bluish tattoos.

Whilst her attire made Aura look like any other member of her clan, her features marked her apart. Her face was longer and thinner than any other face Sunny had ever seen. Her teeth were skew-whiff. They pointed outwards in different directions, and met her gums at different angles; they were different shapes, shades and sizes. Time had not been kind to Aura's body. But she still retained an unflinching femininity. People said that she had been a wondrous beauty in her youth. All the men had desired her body. And, since she was a generous person, she had shared it with anyone who had asked.

"Oh, that?" she finally replied, with an almost aggressive form of disinterest.

"Yes, Auntie."

"That old bag of skin and bones?"

"Well... Auntie... Can't you see? This is a fantabulous beast!"

"Beast? It's *beastly*, that's for sure. All I see is limp skin and withered bones. Its own mother must have been ashamed of the wretched thing."

Sunny tried to suppress a frown. Surely Aura was mistaken. She was old. She was probably losing her sight.

He changed tack, turning to address Aura's friend, a man named *Sparrow*.

Sparrow was also wearing a loincloth. His hair was also plaited, and his skin was also awash with tattoos. But despite these things, Sparrow and Aura could not have looked less alike. Though they were a similar age, time had been gentle with Sparrow. His teeth were still aligned, white, and well-proportioned. His face was neither too long nor too short, too wide nor too narrow. Yet it was hard to imagine that he had ever been handsome. There was nothing wrong with Sparrow's appearance. Everything was where it was supposed to be. But it lacked character. It was scientific, not artistic; too average to catch one's attention, too blurry to pique one's interest, and too plain to inspire warmth or love.

"Beloved uncle: What do you say?"

"Bag of bones. Worthless. You must have burnt off more energy, dragging this creature home, than you'll ever get from the crumbs of meat on its shrunken carcass."

Sunny stalled:

"But... It's just... Well, I wanted to share it. Won't you do me the honour?"

"What would I want with that?"

"To eat it, uncle."

"Eat what? I'd have to eat its horns, because there's certainly no meat on its body."

Sunny froze.

It was probably for the best. It would have been disrespectful to argue with his elders. And he could still share this gift with the other members of their clan.

He bowed his head, backed away, and continued down the lane.

But he could not let the matter rest.

Hungry for validation, he paused outside the next hut, waited for a person to appear, and boasted once again:

"Auntie! Feast your eyes upon this

tremendous creature. It'll fill our bellies for twenty dusks and twenty dawns!"

Sunny had been addressing *Kitten*.

Kitten was a similar age to Sunny's mother. She had borne no fewer than fifteen children, although only three had survived past infancy. Her losses weighed heavily in Kitten's eyes. Yet there was an inescapable sense of defiance in her demeanour. Kitten's shoulders were aggressively square, and her breasts projected forwards, as though intent on poking anyone who approached.

Kitten scoffed, generating so much mucus, she was forced to spit it out:

"*Tut, tutty-tut-tut, tutty-tut*... That sack of guts will barely feed the members of a single hut. Don't you know that we are many? What, have you forgotten your Auntie Aura, and the people with whom she shares a hut? Or your Auntie Butterfly, and the people with whom *she* shares a hut? What about that hut, where Health is the matriarch? Or that one, where Mountain lives with her children and grandchildren? So many huts, with so many people in each. And you have the gizzards to arrive here with such a tiny amount of meat? Huh?"

"But... I mean... Haven't you seen this animal's mountainous height? Just look at how far its body extends. Dearest auntie: Gaze your eyes upon its gargantuan, humongous, super-colossal chest."

"Size? It's big, but there's no *fat* on the thing. It's all carcass and air. Are you blind? Can't you tell the difference between a proper animal and an old wreck like this?"

"Oh."

"I'm surprised at you, Sunny Boy. For how many seasons has the sun shone upon your head? You should be old enough to hunt properly; to bring home *real* meat; to know the difference between a good animal and a bone-bucket like this."

"Oh."

"Of course, we'll eat it. But it won't fill us. It won't give us the energy we need to hunt. We'll traipse off to sleep, dejected, with hollow legs and rumbling bellies."

Blown back by the savagery of Kitten's response, Sunny opened his mouth to say "Sorry". But he barely emitted a sound. He turned, paused, and tried to apologize again. He failed, accepted defeat, bowed his head, and trudged away; heading back to the hut in which he slept, where he greeted his mother:

"Mother kindest: Don't you think we could feed just a few people with this ox? It's just... Well, there's got to be *a bit* of meat on these bones."

Sunny's mother took her time; pondering her son's question, as though mulling over a mouthful of berries, some of which were sweet, and some of which were sour.

She eventually deigned to respond:

"You know our tastes, chick-i-lick. We love meat. In fact, we love *fat*. When we see a skinny animal like this, out there in the bush, we almost always let it go. We save our energy for a worthy creature. A creature who's dripping in fat. You know the sort. The kind of animal whose meat is layered with white fat, which turns into a clear, thick oil when it's cooked. The sort of fat that slides down your throat, lines your stomach, and gives you roaring diarrhoea."

Sunny could not disagree. His people *did* like fatty meat. This was why he had selected this particular ox. It possessed more fat than any other animal they had captured since leaving their Big Camp, at the end of the rainy season.

Why could his peers not see this?

"No doubt, its bones will be good for soup. But there's no *fat* on the thing."

Sunny pinched the ox's belly.

"What's this?"

"It's a little fat, but not much. Lovely: I worry that this animal will cause a fight. You serve up something like that... There'd be so little to go around, one person is sure to accuse another of taking all the prime cuts. A few people will go hungry, whilst others will eat. And then what? Smoke in a beehive! You'll have provoked a riot."

Sunny thought better than to disagree. A single person might have been mistaken. But he had heard the same opinion from *four* different people. They could not all be wrong.

And yet, no! They *could* all be wrong. This *was* a fine creature. It was jacketed in layers of fat. He had done well to get it, and his kinfolk should have been grateful.

That was when it hit him...

That image of Uncle Crow appeared in his mind's eye, replete with his mother's unpredictable eyebrows. There it was, providing more meat than anyone else. And there it was again; cast into exile, chided and disparaged, in much the same way that Sunny was being chided himself.

No-one had called him "Uncle Crow". At least, they had not done so out loud. But Sunny was almost certain that they were calling him an Uncle Crow, in the subtext of their speech; in the hidden meanings, which lurked between the lines; all the more powerful because they were left unspoken, and so remained unpolluted by the inadequacy of words.

Perhaps those people were envious. Sunny very much doubted that they had ever returned with such a majestic animal, back when they were as young as him. He doubted that they had *ever* returned with such a catch.

Did they know that he had been gifted this ox by another clan?

Surely not.

Then what?

Sunny could not be sure.

But of one thing he was certain: This image of Uncle Crow. This semi-mythical character had not just appeared to him once. It had appeared again and again, with increasing regularity; transforming in shape and appearance, until there could be no doubting the matter: Sunny was no longer seeing an abstract Uncle Crow. He was seeing an image of himself.

# SHAMING THE MEAT

The ox moseyed around for an unspecified number of days, that no-one seemed inclined to count.

As though obeying an unspoken law, the animal never ventured beyond the camp's invisible boundaries; remaining between the two rows of banana-leaf huts, stopping to eat the grass which surrounded the fire pit, and avoiding the windbreaks, made from reeds and grasses, which protected the clan's possessions: Their stone-bladed hunting-spears, wooden thrusting-spears, and the barbed-points they used to spear fish. Their arrows, whose tips were covered in poison. Their bows, clubs, rabbit traps, fish traps, fishing nets, blades, and water vessels. The baskets and cords they had made by weaving plant fibres together, the stone anvils they used to crack nuts, the pot they had made from clay, the sewing needles they had made from animal bone, the digging-sticks they had made from antlers, and their burins; the stone flakes, with chisel-like tips, which they used to decorate these objects.

Whilst the members of the Eagle Clan did

own a few personal possessions, such as their loincloths and beads, the items kept in this store were held in common. People borrowed them whenever they wished to use them. But they returned them once they had finished; treating this store as though it were a *library of things*.

The ox moseyed on; indifferent to Kitten, who had gathered some yams, which she was sharing with her hut-mates; and indifferent to Aura's nephew, *Buffalo*, who had gathered some bananas, and left them for anyone to take.

Unseen and unheard, the ox observed a group of children, who were playing *Grown Ups*; pretending they were adults, and thereby learning *to be* adults. The younger children were hunting butterflies with bows and arrows they had made themselves. The older children were hunting small mammals. In time, they would join the adults; hunting alongside their elders, whilst maintaining this spirit of play.

None of this was organised. There were times when the children were content to do nothing. They were comfortable, living in the moment; unafraid of boredom, happy to daydream; to stare at the distant hills, or observe the dust motes as they danced between shafts of light. If they wished to do something, they did not nag their mothers. They invented a game; drawing shapes in the dirt, nursing the dolls they had made from sticks, and picking berries from nearby bushes; experiencing the world first-hand.

The ox meandered on, reaching a cluster of children who had just built a model camp, filled with replicas of the huts in which they lived. In building this camp, they had taught themselves how to build *real* huts.

Now they were playing inside that camp, re-enacting the events they had observed, and mimicking the adults' behaviour; holding mock debates, deciding when to hunt, and where to gather wood.

It was an education...

Left unsupervised, these children could get hurt at any time. Harmony still had a scar which skirted around the ball of her thumb, because she had tried to catch a flame when she was still a toddler. But this painful experience had taught her to respect the power of fire. She had never been burnt again.

Most lessons were not nearly so harsh. The youngsters learned through a process of observation and exploration. They only ever asked for advice when it suited them, and they never had to endure a lesson which had been imposed upon them by an adult.

It worked. In the same way that toddlers learn to walk, and infants learn to talk; through a mixture of play, trial and error; so the members of the Eagle Clan learned to hunt, fish, gather, navigate, build, debate and negotiate...

They discovered the habits of hundreds of different mammals and birds. They worked out how to track game, by spotting the most elusory of clues. They learnt how to make spears, arrows, blowguns, darts, snares and nets. And they began to master these weapons; setting traps for small animals, hunting by themselves, and as members of a group.

They began to gather. There were tens-of-thousands of plants in their region, but most were inedible or poisonous. Only a few hundred were good for human consumption, and by the time they came of age, the clan's children could identify them all. They could name twenty-nine different types of edible mushrooms. They knew where each one could be found, on what hosts they might grow, and when they would be ready to harvest. They knew which mushrooms *not* to eat. They knew which roots, tubers, nuts, seeds, fruits and leaves were the most nutritious, and which could be used as medicine. They knew how to dig, peel, roast, grind, mix and sift each of their favourite treats.

In time, these children would discover how to cook, make fires, predict the weather, treat injuries, care for the sick, raise babies, play music, tell stories, perform dances, perform rituals, and maintain diplomatic relations with other clans.

They were never cajoled into learning these things. It simply happened, just as soon as the moment was right.

***

The ox remained in a stationary position for most of its days, only setting its legs into motion when it felt it had no other option; begrudging the inconvenience, even though no-one had compelled it to move.

Nobody deigned to slaughter that animal, until it had been three days since the clans-folk had eaten any meat. Only then did an elder, named *Serenity*, take it upon himself to perform the fatal deed; slitting the ox's throat with a blade they had fashioned themselves, using a hard cobble to strike flakes from a triangular rock. Unprompted, several of his peers emerged from their huts. Two youngsters, named *Pilgrim* and *Blue*, took the blade from Serenity, and used it to remove the ox's leg. It took them a while to complete this task, although this was of little concern; they had all the time in the world. When they were done, *Health*, the group's medicine woman, wandered over, blessed the meat, used the same blade to score its skin, turned that utensil around, and used the blunt end to pound some medicinal herbs. She rubbed those herbs into the flesh, and passed the joint over to Sparrow, who had already prepared a fire. Aura and Harmony took over. They turned the meat and managed the fire, whilst *Mountain* and *Setting Sun*, the clan's eldest members, observed proceedings from afar; ready to offer their advice, should ever the need arise.

When their meal was almost ready, the community began to gather. They mixed the ox's intestines with the contents of its stomach, took a dollop each, and used it to wash their hands. Then they turned their attention to the stomach itself; cutting its lining into tiny squares, and eating them raw.

Acts like these helped the clans-folk to maintain a rich balance of bacteria, which protected them from disease. No member of the Eagle Clan had ever suffered from allergies, diabetes or cancer. They had never even heard of "Obesity" or "Autoimmunity".

When it was ready, the group removed the roasted meat, laid it out on top of some banana leaves, and squatted down to dine; forming circles, helping themselves to a few shreds of fatty meat, chewing them slowly, before returning for another portion.

Sunny waited for the others to dig in. He took a little for himself. And then it struck him: No matter how hard he tried to deny the facts, he could not ignore the quality of this food; the meat's marbled flesh, the layers of fat, and the crispy skin, which had crackled and fizzed upon the fire. *He had been right all along*. This *was* a splendid animal.

Sunny took a great deal of pleasure from observing his kinfolk, as they devoured the meal, with inflated cheeks and dizzy eyes. Their happiness made the hairs on his arms stand on end. But the feeling was bittersweet. Sunny had not forgotten the reception he received when he returned with this ox. A kernel of anger still nestled in his stomach. And now it was germinating; transforming into a seed of irritation, a shoot of vexation, a growth of fury; bursting forth, compelling Sunny to speak in a manner he had not intended, and which he would later come to regret:

"Beloved Uncle Sparrow! Didn't you say that this animal was a 'Worthless bag of bones, possessing nothing but a few measly crumbs of meat'? And now you chew down upon the largest of mouthfuls, before helping yourself to a second serving, and then a third!

"And you, dear Auntie Kitten: Didn't you say it was a 'Sack of guts, barely sufficient to feed the members of a single hut'? Can't you see how many people are eating right now?

"And you, dear Auntie Aura: Why on earth and the ancestral realm, are you eating an 'Old bucket of bones'? Have you pooped out all your pride?"

Sunny silenced himself before he could challenge his mother. But it was far too little, and far too late. Wishing to avoid a confrontation, his peers had stood up and walked away. Sunny had been abandoned; left here alone, insulting the breeze. A swarm of flies could be seen feasting on what remained of the roasted meat. And the fire was collapsing into ash.

\*\*\*

Sunset had come and gone by the time anyone talked to Sunny.

He was approached by Serenity; an elder who possessed an irrepressibly melodic pair of eyes. They were not *hypnotic*. You did not lose yourself in their gaze. But they were *metamorphic*; so placid, they inspired you to relax in their presence. Serenity was almost always the first person to attend the scene of a fracas. His mild persona served as a natural tonic; soothing his companion's annoyance, and dulling their grief.

But Serenity knew all too well that his ears held a greater power than his eyes; that the grieved must be heard, before they can begin to heal. And so he looked into Sunny's eyes, raised his eyebrows, and waited for the youngster to speak.

Sunny did not produce a sound. His mouth had landed him in enough trouble already. But when Serenity placed a hand upon his shoulder, and performed an empathetic nod, he supposed it would have been rude to prolong the silence:

"Beloved Uncle: It's just... Well, it's just that I feel... I feel that too many people take. Not enough people give... And... I mean... It's the *takers* who're accepted... Uncle Serenity: *The givers are insulted*..."

Serenity looked almost sorrowful, as though he was attempting to suck the pain out of Sunny's eyes.

He waited for Sunny to continue:

"Take Sparrow... Didn't you see how he tore into the meat?... You know, I don't wish to say rancid things about a beloved uncle. But... Well, I've watched on as he's gorged himself on the fruit my mama spent a whole day collecting. And yet I've never seen him gather any fruit himself. I've never seen him hunt... It wouldn't be so bad if he made an effort. If he tried and failed. I'd understand that... But he just takes and takes. He never gives thanks. And it's just... Well, he's always the first to criticise. He did call the ox a 'Bag of bones'. I didn't make that up. And... Well, he wasn't eating bones tonight!"

Serenity took a deep breath, inhaling Sunny's angst.

It had the desired effect, up until the point at which Serenity closed his eyes. Breaking off eye-contact, left Sunny feeling exposed; helpless, alone, and riddled with fear.

What on Mother Nature's green earth had he done? Would his kinfolk ever forgive him? Or would he be exiled, like Uncle Crow?

Serenity did not answer these unasked questions. He simply sat there in silent contemplation, for an uncountable number of moments; only revealing his eyes once he sensed that Sunny was ready.

A smile wafted across his face.

"Sunshine: Sparrow wasn't always like this."

Sunny waited for more.

"He used to hunt as much as could be expected. He wasn't particularly proficient. He could go for months without downing a target. But he tried his best, and he kept us entertained; providing companionship; telling stories and jokes. Whenever another hunter was successful, Sparrow would rush to their side, congratulate them, and help to carry their meat."

"Oh."

"Sparrow's sister's son was his greatest happiness and joy. And, unlike Sparrow, that boy *was* a talented marksman.

"Sparrow accompanied his nephew whenever

he went to hunt. You should've seen the size of Sparrow's smirk, whenever the lad hit his mark! It didn't matter if that kill was small or scrawny. Sparrow was like the parrot who wore the rainbow!"

Sunny waited for more.

"Child: Sparrow's nephew was killed by a snake, right there, in front of his eyes. Sparrow tried to protect the boy. But by the time he got close enough to strike, it was already too late. It wasn't Sparrow's fault. There was nothing he could've done. But he blamed himself nonetheless."

Sunny bowed his head.

"After that, Sparrow never went hunting again."

Serenity allowed his story to linger, gazed into Sunny's eyes, and waited to see if it had the desired effect.

But Sunny did not sound entirely convinced:

"Oh... Yeah... I suppose that explains it... Well, it explains why he doesn't *hunt*."

Serenity closed and reopened his eyes.

"But it doesn't explain why he doesn't *gather*?"

Sunny nodded.

"Okay. Allow me to explain... Now, Sparrow's lover had a daughter; a girl with a butterfly heart. You know the type? The sort of person who likes to flutter away on their own, even when they're young, and not yet educated in the ways of the world... Once upon a time, when that girl was still younger than you are today, she went off to collect berries... Sunshine: You know what berry collectors are like? They feel a need to check every berry they find, to be sure they're the sweet ones... And this is what came to pass: That young girl tasted a berry she had never seen before. It was poisonous, but she didn't feel any ill effects. And so she ate a second berry, a third and a fourth. She ate almost as many as she collected.

"Only when she had filled the basket, and begun her journey home, did she start to feel a little queasy. But she persevered without complaint. She didn't collapse until she had reached the edge of our camp.

"Sparrow came running, looked at the girl and gasped. For it was at that very moment, that the girl took her final breath. Sparrow was helpless. He couldn't do anything but watch, as her spirits escaped from her body, and floated back to our ancestral forest."

Serenity shook his head in solemn contemplation.

"Child: Every life that's lived is a story. Some people like to tell theirs. Others prefer to keep theirs to themselves. But behind every action, there's another action. Behind every character, there's a lifetime of tales; tragedies and comedies alike."

"I... I..."

It did not feel right to push for more. Sunny had been insensitive enough already. And Sparrow *did* help a little, in his own individual way. When the clans in their tribe gathered to form their Big Camp, in the rainy season, Sparrow helped in the fields; growing tobacco and harvesting coffee. He also grew cassava, on the fringes of this camp, albeit with limited success. Farming was inefficient. It required a great amount of clearing, weeding, fertilizing, watering and picking. It was nowhere near as productive as hunting or gathering. And so Sparrow only ever produced a small crop; a fact which gave Sunny the false impression that he barely contributed at all. But Sparrow did what he could, given his circumstances. And the cassava he grew did provide a degree of insurance; something which clan-members could eat on the days when they were unable to secure any other food, and something they could trade with the neighbouring clans.

Sunny would have been happy to bring this conversation to an end. But Serenity could sense that he needed to unburden himself a little more.

"Go on," he said. "Let it out."

"Okay... But only if you insist."

Serenity nodded.

"It's just... Well, you've explained why Sparrow doesn't hunt or gather. Thank-you, uncle. But... But none of this explains why he insults the people who do."

Serenity chortled so loudly, the noise jolted hundreds of birds from their branches; creating a cloud of feathers and beaks:

Aah-ooh. Ah-ah-ah. Chuck-a-chuck ooh!

"What's so funny?"

"Our sweet, sacred, ancestral mothers! *Ho ho ho*. Sunny: How long have you lived with us?"

"Since I entered the mortal realm."

"Since you entered the mortal realm? And you still don't know our ways?"

Sunny frowned.

"Haven't you heard us call the greatest animals the worst names? If someone were to slay a giant buffalo, single-handedly, and drag it back here alone; we'd call that thing a 'Rat'. The hunter would probably call it a 'Mouse', just to pre-empt his sistren's sneers... The person who kills a falcon, might complain of its feathery, good-for-nothing wings. 'So much to pluck! So little meat!'... The person who hunts a boar, might criticise its unappetizing smell, inedible tusks, and the hairs which get stuck in your teeth; anything to divert our attention from the quality of its meat.

"If we miss a target, our friends might laugh at us for the rest of the day. But if we kill an animal, things are sure to be even worse.

"When we ask for help, carrying a creature we've killed, our friends will come to collect it. And as soon as they see the animal, they'll say: 'What? You dragged us all the way here *for that*? If we'd known it was so skinny, we'd have stayed at home.'

"Child: When this happens, you just have to nod, agree and apologize. Then you must watch on, as everyone takes their share. And still, they complain! It's 'Too gaunt', 'Too old', 'Too small', 'Too thin'.

"The insults are compliments, when you come to think of it. The more someone insults your meat, the better it must be. The ancestors know it to be true: Up is down, and left is right... If someone returns to camp and says, 'I've killed an animal, but it's so small, I don't know if we should even bother to fetch it'; then you know that a mighty fine feast awaits."

Sunny could not deny it. He had seen this several times before. Yet somehow it felt different when *other* people were involved. That was fun and games. When *he* was the butt of the joke, it was another matter entirely. Sunny had spent four days in the wilderness, alone, without food; risking attack, sunstroke and dehydration. The insults had dented his pride.

"But why?"

"'Why'? *Why!* Sunshine: Surely you must know?"

Sunny shook his head. No-one had ever told him, and he had never asked. He had learnt almost everything he knew through a mixture of observation and imitation; watching his peers and copying their behaviour. As a technique, it was pretty efficient. It had taught him *how* to perform an abundance of different activities. But it had not always taught him *why* things were done the way they were.

"By the good earth, that explains it!... Sunshine: We're an egalitarian bunch, wouldn't you say? No-one really bosses anyone else around."

Sunny nodded.

"And why do you think that is?"

"Because we don't allow them?"

"*Because we don't give them the means*!... Imagine there's one hunter who's better than the rest. It's not hard to do. Uncle Crow may be the stuff of legends, but there's usually an individual, each generation, who returns with enough meat to feed half the clan... Child: Let's say we dollop sunshine upon their head. We inflate their ego. What do you think will happen?... They'll stomp about like an elephant. They'll tell us to 'Do this' and 'Do that'. And if we refuse, they'll withhold our meat, and we'll starve... Before you know it, that person will have bribed a bunch of their friends with the prime cuts. Then *they'll* start making demands; saying 'Do this' and 'Do that', on behalf of the Uncle Crow... Whoosh! Mother

Nature's lightning! A whole hierarchy will have emerged."

Sunny tensed his cheeks.

"Sunshine: There are two wolves who live within us. One is good. It's joy, peace, love, hope, humility, kindness, empathy, generosity, truth and compassion. The other wolf is evil. It's anger, envy, greed, self-pity, resentment, lies, pride, ego and arrogance.

"To be the best people we can be... To be the best *clan* and the best *tribe* we can be... We must nurture the good wolf, and suppress the evil one.

"This is why we shame the meat. We say it's worthless, in order to constrain the hunter's evil wolf; to obliterate their pride, greed and arrogance; before these dangerous traits have the chance to ravage us all.

"This is how we keep would-be-bullies in their place, and remain an egalitarian sort of clan."

Sunny nodded. It was all becoming clear:

"And this is why we share?"

"Exactly! Sparrow does his part. He's the clan's *griot*; the spreader of news, singer of songs, and teller of tales. He tries to grow vegetables too. Okay, he's hardly proficient. But he always shares the cassava he grows."

Sunny had one final question:

"Beloved uncle: Why hadn't you told me any of this before?"

Serenity could barely repress a smile.

"*Ho ho ho*. Why, sunshine, because you never asked!"

# SISTER-O, BROTHER-O

His conversation with Serenity should have soothed Sunny's mind. Yet that image of Uncle Crow had appeared yet again. It was gate-crashing his thoughts, refusing to leave him in peace.

Sunny tried to keep himself busy. He collected some firewood, sharpened a spear, helped to repair a couple of huts, fashioned a flute from a length of bamboo, and played that instrument until his ears began to ring. Yet no matter what he did, he could not escape from that image of Uncle Crow.

Something was amiss. But it was not rational. Sunny knew why he had been mocked. He was comfortable with Serenity's explanation. If anything, the insults were a compliment; confirming that he *had* returned with a splendid supply of meat.

It had to be something emotional. Perhaps it was *remorse*. Sunny had not caught the animal himself. He had borrowed it from another clan. He had hidden this information from the people he loved the most. Perhaps it was *anxiety*. He doubted his ability as a hunter. He worried that he might not be able to re-gift his debt. Or perhaps it was *embarrassment*. He had been a fool not to understand why the ox had been mocked.

Whatever the cause of his malaise, Sunny was pretty certain that he needed a physical fix. He needed sex. And he knew just who to ask.

Her name was *Hope*. Her face was so lithe, her eyes almost touched her ears, and her chin seemed to swallow her jaw. It had been tattooed during a coming-of-age feast. Two V-shaped lines dominated her forehead, one inside the other. Egg-shaped patterns decorated her cheeks, and a grid of blueish lines covered the region which began below her lower lip.

The elders had far more tattoos than Hope. The women who drew those images, tended to add a new design once every ten or twenty solstices; soaking a thin length of sinew in a mixture of lampblack, urine and graphite; attaching that thread to a needle made from bone, before drawing it through the skin, just beneath the epidermis.

Hope, who was still young, remained a relatively blank canvas. But there were dots on all her major joints; her shoulders, elbows, hips, wrists, knees, ankles and neck. These had been added during a second rite of passage, held to celebrate her first kill. Members of their tribe believed that spirits lived inside animals' joints. When an animal was killed, these spirits were released. Tribes-folk drew dots on their own joints, to ward off these lost spirits; preventing them from entering *their* bodies, and controlling *them*.

Hope had taken Sunny's virginity four seasons before; beckoning him with a curl of her finger, before leading him into one of the cabins which lay hidden beyond the periphery of their camp. Anyone could use those cabins, although they were mainly frequented by adolescents. Adults were more likely to have sex in one of the huts; hanging their loincloth on the door, to let others know that they did not wish to be disturbed.

Promiscuity was not frowned upon. If anything, it was encouraged. Tribes-folk shared their bodies, in much the same way they shared their spears, berries and meat. Had they regularly refused requests for sex, they might have been considered selfish, or even shameful.

The members of their tribe had no concept of

marriage. They did not believe that a woman could belong to a man, or that a man could belong to a woman. Very few things belonged to anyone. Relationships did form, for love or pleasure. But they ended when the love ran dry. Lovers were not compelled to stay together for the sake of their offspring. Children were raised by their mothers, and by their mothers' relatives, but not by their mothers' lovers.

The clan was strictly matriarchal. The eldest woman in a lineage was the matriarch of a hut. Her children, and their children, resided in that hut until the day she died. If one of them gave birth, they *all* helped to raise the baby; forming a parental team.

As well as his mother, Sunny had a grandmother and two uncles; all of whom had helped to raise him. But he also considered *Pumpkin* to be a guardian of sorts. That man had been his mother's main sexual partner, back when he was conceived. And he considered *Life* to be his secondary guardian, since that man was also having relations with his mother. Their tribe believed in *partible paternity*; that a foetus could be formed using sperm from different men; that a baby could inherit skills and attributes from *each* of their mother's lovers.

Sunny regularly turned to Life for advice about hunting, because he was a talented huntsman. Pumpkin had taught him how to make spears and arrows. And so Sunny *had* inherited skills from these men, albeit through nurture rather than genetics.

As well as his four father-figures, two of whom had passed away, Sunny also had two siblings. But he considered every member of his generation to be a sibling of sorts. His kinfolk were so promiscuous, he must have shared at least a little genetic material with everyone else in his peer group.

He certainly looked upon Hope as a sister; a close confidant who had always been there for him. A few seasons his senior, she had taken it upon herself to teach him what she knew about sex, in much the same way that Sunny had taken it upon *himself* to show the younger children how to set traps and throw spears.

Hope was so satisfied with her work, that she returned to Sunny whenever she had a desire for sexual gratification. This time, however, was a little different. This time, Sunny had *gone to her.*

Sensing his need for affection, Hope felt

compelled to help.

She had one request:

"Let's go somewhere different. The watering hole, perhaps."

Enticed by the call of the unknown, Sunny acquiesced.

Hope took him by the hand and led him on; skipping through the long grass, flicking dew onto his knees, and disturbing the lizards, who were quick to shoot for cover.

The watering hole was a bluish-grey beacon, surrounded by grasslands, which were surrounded by wilderness and hills. A great distance from the nearest stream, it was only ever fed by rainwater. During the rainy season, it expanded to form a glorious lake. Petals, blossoms and ferns jostled for position on its banks. But it began to shrink as soon as the rains receded, becoming little more than a puddle. It was not much to look at. It was not much to smell. But it served a purpose: There were no other sources of water in this vicinity. The clan's ancestors had dug a few wells, to make this land habitable for humans. But animals had little choice. They *had* to visit this pond. It was the only place they could find a drink. Left exposed, their feet buried in the mud, those animals proved easy targets for a patient hunter. This is why the clan established their Small Camp in this location: It was the perfect place to hunt.

And now, for Hope and Sunny, it was the perfect place for sex.

They lay down among the reeds, a good distance from the water's edge, and began to nibble each other's eyebrows. Eyebrow-nibbling was fairly common in their tribe. Lovers had been known to become so aroused, during foreplay, that they had bitten off entire chunks of skin. Indeed, you could always tell if someone was in the grips of a passionate relationship, just by glancing at the space above their eyes.

Members of their tribe did not kiss. The closest they ever came to such a thing, occurred when mothers chewed food for their infants, before passing it from mouth to mouth; a loving act, but not a *sexual* act. Lovers retained that exquisite desire to explore their partners' bodies, and connect in intimate ways. But they did this by nibbling eyebrows, stroking flesh, and smelling each other's skin. Friends greeted each other by performing nuzzle-sniffs, rubbing noses or patting arms.

Hope and Sunny took their time; nibbling each other's eyebrows, and inhaling each other's scent. They had not undressed. But Sunny could access Hope's bosom, which was already exposed. Her breasts were *always* exposed. Members of their clan only ever covered their loins.

Sunny stroked and sucked Hope's nipples, in the way she had taught him. Then he approached her legs; massaging her thighs with his cheek, kneading her calves, sniffing her soles, and tickling his face with her toes.

He waited for Hope to tug his braided hair; the signal she had developed to tell Sunny that she was ready for him to return up her body.

As soon as they were lying face to face, Sunny began to stroke Hope's cheek, neck and ears. He repeated this routine until Hope gave him a second signal; removing her loincloth, and shunting him down onto her genitalia.

She circled her finger upon Sunny scalp, directing the patterns she wanted Sunny to copy with his tongue.

This foreplay lasted far longer than the sex itself; an act which began when Hope pulled Sunny up from her groin, and ended soon after they had climaxed.

Their post-coital embrace lasted for longer than everything which had come before. Sunny would have been happy for it to last forever. High on endorphins, his mind was finally clear; free of that image of Uncle Crow.

But whilst Sunny may have been happy to remain in this state forever, someone else had other plans...

The sky darkened. Sunny could not avoid the transformation, which had turned the reeds from green to grey. But he felt little desire to investigate. He was happy to exist in the moment, enjoying Hope's body as it breathed in time with his own.

"Good day-o."

This greeting shook Sunny to his core. It was not the words which disturbed him. It was the *voice* in which they were delivered. That voice was both strange *and* familiar. It was as warm as could be expected from a member of his own clan, with the elongated "O" sound which only they used. Yet it was primmer and more powerful than any voice Sunny had ever heard before. It was a confusing accent; both comforting *and* disturbing, cosy *and* caustic.

Sunny felt compelled to break off his embrace, and look upwards, just to see what sort of a person might speak with such a contrary kind of rhythm.

The image which met his eyes was just as confusing. This man's facial hair was almost identical to Sunny's. It stretched down from his sideburns, and skirted around his mouth, without filling the spaces between. This man's shoulders were the same width as Sunny's. They had the same roundness. They connected to his neck and arms at all the same points. His skin had been decorated with the very same tattoos. He wore the very same type of loincloth. His body looked eerily familiar. And yet he wore it in the most peculiar manner. He stood proud, tall and brash; lifting his shoulders as high as they would go, pushing them forwards; not allowing them to waver, falter or droop. And, what was more, he appeared to be maintaining this posture without exerting any effort. He must have been holding himself this way for so long, that his body had fixed itself in place. He had probably forgotten what it was like to stand in a natural fashion.

"Day... Good," Sunny replied, stumbling over

his words.

"Day good," the man repeated.

Sunny covered his groin:

"Do... Do we know you?"

"Perhaps."

Sunny cringed. It was not just this man's voice, appearance and posture which were making him queasy. It was his speech as well. What sort of person said "Perhaps", when you asked them if you had ever met?

The stranger must have sensed Sunny's anxiety, for he did not respond with an additional comment, but with an action; reaching behind his back, and removing a peculiar device: A long shiny tube, which was attached to a triangular piece of wood.

Sunny had never seen anything like it.

The man tried to explain:

"A *gun*."

"A what?"

"A *gun*."

"Oh... I mean... A what?"

"A..."

The man's use of this alien word had only added to Sunny's nausea.

"A gun. This can kill the biggest prey, from the

greatest distance-o. Yes, brother. This is a fact."

Sunny did not believe a word. Whatever this thing was supposed to be, it was certainly no good for hunting. It did not have a sharp end or a blade. It did not appear to contain any arrows, darts or poison.

"You don't believe me? You think I'm a rascal? A giant mouth, all pubic hair and no snake?"

Sunny was about to refute this allegation. But his head was already nodding. He *did* think this man was fibbing; that he was all "Pubic hair and no snake".

"Ah, brother! If I were in your position, I'd think the very same thing. Only a fool would trust a stranger. And not just any stranger. A strange man, who makes strange boasts, about a strange gun. And what is a 'Gun'? And who is this man?... Brother, you're wise beyond your seasons. You're right to have such doubts. Yes. This is an indisputable fact: You're a big wise man, with the most beautiful of lovers."

Sunny had been so mesmerised by this man, he had completely forgotten about Hope, who had covered herself and slunk back into the reeds.

"Yes-o. Big wise man. He has his doubts. Very

clever. Very wise."

The stranger smiled, revealing a tooth which twinkled like a star.

"You need proof? Big wise man needs evidence? He cannot believe a stranger? He must see the facts with his eyes?"

Sunny noticed that he was nodding again.

"And you think I'll just put on a show?... Brother, what would be the point of that? What's in it for old Hunter?"

Sunny frowned.

"Confused-o? You don't get your brother? Why, we must agree like men! We must make good, like leaves and wood."

Sunny waited for more.

"Brother, let's talk facts: I'll show you how to use this gun. I'll show you how to kill the largest beasts in the valley. But if it works as I say... If it's an undisputed fact... Then, my brother, you'll be honour-bound to take it. You'll have to use it whenever you hunt."

Sunny laughed. It was a minuscule laugh, which barely tickled his throat. But it was a laugh nonetheless; cocksure and condescending. Sunny did not believe this man would be able to kill a single thing with this spear-less, point-less, poison-less device. But he was ready to be entertained; to watch on as this stranger succumbed to failure.

"Okay then. Prove it works and I'll take it."

"Ah! Good choice. A *wise* choice, from a big wise man!"

With that, the stranger swung around, wedged the wooden triangle into his shoulder, and pointed the tube towards the sky. He looked along the length of that pipe, and pulled something round, which Sunny had only just noticed.

Bang!

The noise took Hope and Sunny by so much surprise, they jumped upwards and backwards together. But even from this new location, a body-length away, they could not help but observe the scene.

A bird had exploded above them, sending feathers in every direction. What remained of its body was floating to earth, at a much slower rate than made sense; as though Mother Nature's laws had been thrown into confusion by the sheer peculiarity of this event.

"Ah! Wait just here, my brother. Yes. You'll see. This is a fact."

The stranger, *Hunter*, turned and sprinted away. He vanished, and then he reappeared, holding the mangled remains of a bird:

"You see the power? Wow! Shredded-o! My brother, this thing could kill an evil spirit! With this gun... Brother... You'll be the boss of the jungle! An ancestor among men!"

Sunny was impressed. His eyes bulged so much, they began to turn purple.

"And now, big wise man. Now, you must take this gun. A deal is a deal."

Sunny tried hard to repress a smile. He still felt a pressure to re-gift his debt to the neighbouring clan. With a weapon like this, that task would be a doddle. He would be able to shoot an animal which was just as big as the ox. His debt would be cleared, and his mind would find peace.

The stranger passed Sunny the gun, before rooting around in a bag; handing over a handful of shiny balls, a few scraps of material, and a sack of powder.

"Now, these *shots* are scarce-o. I'll give you ten... You wrap them in this cloth... Like this... Then you ram them down this tube. The *barrel*... See?... And this, the *gunpowder*, goes on here...

"Now, use five of these shots to get animals for Hunter. No teeny ones. Just big, big beasts. Big animals, from a big man. The size of a buffalo. The size of an ox... This is the deal... The other five shots are for you. A gift-o. A present from one brother to another."

"But..."

"A deal is a deal."

And with that, the man disappeared.

Sunny was startled. Had he really just taken on an even bigger debt than before? Did he really owe this man *five* animals? Five! What had he done?

He held his face between his knees, allowing his oversized legs to swallow his undersized torso; hiding his broken chin, gigantic nose, and almost all of the tattoos on his face.

Hope could not help but smile.

"Oh, Sunny. Mister 'Big Wise Man'. Mister I'm In Big Trouble Now. Mister Silly, Silly Boy."

# A DEBT OF GRATITUDE

Five days had passed, and Sunny was back where it had begun; here, on the border of the neighbouring camp, staring at the oxen. They were tied to the same tree, eating from the same pile of grass, chewing with a sideways motion.

The intervening days had been eventful...

At first, Sunny had not dared to use the gun; hiding it among the reeds, and hoping his problems would disappear. His mind had been riddled with doubts: What would his kinfolk say, if they knew he had borrowed the ox from another clan? What would he do, if their gun stopped working? What would happen, if he wasted all their shots?

It was Hope who helped him around. She grabbed him by his wrist, and led him into the bush, for what he assumed would be a sexual encounter. He was sorely mistaken. Hope pushed him away, when he tried to nibble her eyebrows. She pointed at the gun, and told him in no uncertain terms: "You must kill the five animals, return this thingy, and end this whole caboodle. No good will come of this. No good at all."

She handed Sunny a bow and arrow, slapped him, called him a "Mister Silly Boy", called him a "Mister Big Wise Man", stared into his eyes, softened a little, quaked a little, sniffed his hair, nuzzled his cheek, told him she loved him, and shoved him away: "Hurry! Go, Mister Silly Boy. Go! Go! Go!"

Sunny went.

But things had not gone according to plan.

Sunny stalked a golden antelope. Or perhaps it was a buff antelope. It was so far away, it was impossible to tell.

But Sunny had no such doubts when it came to the gun itself. Hunter, the stranger, had made it look so easy to use.

He poured a little gunpowder into the barrel, wrapped one of the balls in a scrap of cloth, rammed it into the powder, added a little powder to the flintlock, and cocked the hammer. He stood in the same erect fashion that Hunter had adopted, pressed the gun's heel into his shoulder, took aim, inhaled, and squeezed the trigger.

Bang!

The trigger contracted the spring, which pulled and released the hammer. The hammer's flint struck the frizzen, shaving the iron, and creating enough sparks to ignite the gunpowder.

The shot flew towards its target.

The antelope bolted.

Not only had Sunny missed, he had scared off every other animal in earshot, and wasted one of their shiny balls.

He dusted himself down and headed towards the neighbouring camp. There was no point remaining here, without a single animal in sight. Even if he did shoot another target, he would struggle to drag it all the way to that encampment.

It was late when he arrived, so he slept a short distance away, within a patch of trees.

He awoke early the following morning, and caught sight of a second antelope. This time, he was not so arrogant. He bided his time, waiting for the animal to approach. He controlled his breathing, allowed his pulse to drop, and only pulled the trigger when he was certain the moment was right.

Bang!

He missed again.

Something similar happened the next day: He missed a goat, wasting the third shot, and leaving them with just seven.

But the day after that, Sunny finally hit his target: A buffalo. As far as Sunny could tell, it was almost exactly the same size as the ox he had borrowed.

Confident his debt was about to be cleared, Sunny hid the gun among the exposed roots of a gnarled old tree, removed the shot from the buffalo's skull, stuck an arrow in the wound, peppered the buffalo's body with the rest of their arrows, marched into the camp, and asked the clans-folk to help him carry the buffalo.

The reception he received was mixed...

The meat was insulted. But he considered this a compliment. Indeed, it was Sunny who had started the ritual; declaring that the animal was, "So hollow, it might as well be a ghost," and claiming, "You'd find more meat on a cat who'd starved to death."

It was the response he received from Songbird, the woman who had loaned him the ox, which caught Sunny by surprise.

"Impressive legs," she said, running her eyes across the buffalo. "They're the same size as the ones on the ox."

Sunny should have probably looked at the

buffalo and passed comment himself. But his eyes were fixed on Songbird, pulled in by her gravitational field. Songbird was almost as old as his mother, but she must have been at least three times the size. Sunny felt compelled to stare at her thighs, which were quite possibly the roundest things in the world, and at the space where he had expected to find her knees. He knew it was rude. But he was unable to avert his gaze, no matter how hard he tried.

He stared at Songbird's spherical neck and round mouth, whilst she appraised the animal:

"Impressive legs. Hmm... They're pretty much identical to the legs on that ox... Impressive rump. Near enough the same size as the ox's rump... The same quality. Hmm... The same depth of fat... Impressive tail... Impressive head... Impressive ribs... The same! Everything the same!... How dare you? Thunderous skies and stony mountains! Giant cliffs that never crumble! The same, the same, the same!"

Sunny could barely whisper a response:

"It's a buffalo... A different animal... You gave us... You gave us an *ox*."

"Do you take me for an unhatched egg? The bird who fell off the branch? The fish who was scared of water?... I can see it's a different beast. Similar, but different."

"I'm trying to clear our debt."

"Upon the fluffiest cloud! Why would you dream of doing such a thing?"

"Because I owed you..."

"How dare you? How very dare you? What kind of cold, heartless exchange did you think this was? Do I look like a whore? Did you think you could just re-gift me, and then dump me, without so much as a second though? Two eggs for two eggs? A chicken for a chicken? And then *puff*! Our relationship is dead before it was even born?... Who, what and why??? *Who* do you think you are? *What* did we do to insult you? *Why* are you acting like such a boulder?"

"I... I... I had a debt. I felt a duty to re-gift you... Dearest auntie: One must re-gift one's debts."

"*One... One must...* I've never heard such chicken poop, in all our starlit days. If you hate someone, *then* you re-gift them. You wouldn't wish to be in your enemy's debt... If you never plan to see a person again, if you trade with a stranger or someone you don't trust; *then* you clear your debt. But your own kith and kin? You maintain debts with the people you love."

Sunny frowned.

But Songbird was not done:

"Does a person re-gift their mother for the milk she gifted them in infancy? For the space they were gifted in the maternal hut? For the loincloths they were given as children? For all the affection they've ever received?... Do friends keep tallies? If someone cooks for you on ten occasions, do you insist on cooking for them exactly ten times? Not nine or eleven? Do you count every little item you take from the communal barbeque, and make a mental note to re-gift every rib and fillet; not a morsel more, and not a morsel less?"

Sunny shook his head:

"No... But..."

"But what? Are we not friends, tribes-folk, kith and kin?"

Sunny was unable to form a reply.

"Well then. We don't clear our debts. We stay indebted forever. And we allow our debts to bond us."

Sunny nodded.

"We can under-gift or over-gift, give more or less than we received. So long as one of us remains in the other's debt, we must maintain our relationship. But we shouldn't ever *settle* our debts, unless we wish to *sever* our relations."

Sunny frowned.

Songbird continued:

"Here. Come with me."

She led Sunny to a patch of dusty earth, which had been enclosed by a fence made from sticks. Then she lunged at a gaggle of chickens, who ducked, dived, and ran back through her legs. Songbird's head followed the chickens, forcing her buttocks into the air. But she had the last laugh, when she grabbed a cockerel, held it up by its shanks, and passed it over to Sunny.

"Take this... Good... So now you owe us a chicken."

"Oh... And I'll have to return, to give you something *smaller* than a chicken. Or... You know... To give you something *bigger*?"

"Exactly!"

Sunny still looked confused.

"But why are you so keen for me to return? I mean... You barely even know me."

Songbird grimaced; insulted not just by the question, but by every syllable which had emerged from Sunny's mouth. Her cheeks withdrew into her face. She grunted, took

Sunny's hand, and pulled him into a tent.

Unlike the Eagle Clan, who lived in huts made from leaves, wood and bamboo; Songbird's *nomadic* clan lived in tents, which were easy to disassemble and move. Their tents also contained a bark-less central pole, and an earthen floor. They were also empty inside. They did not contain any possessions, furniture or decorations. But they were teepee-shaped, with walls made from hides. And they were small. Whilst up to ten people could sleep in the Eagle Clan's huts, it was rare to find more than five people in one of these tents.

As soon as they were inside, Songbird whipped Sunny's loincloth away, fell to her knees, and took his penis in her mouth.

It was like nothing Sunny had experienced before. His member stood to attention without a moment's delay. He felt his ejaculate coming fast and strong; sending fireworks up his urethra, before exploding into Songbird's mouth. He had never cum so quickly. He had never felt so aroused.

But Songbird refused to allow him to bask in this post-coital glow.

"Understand?" She asked.

Sunny nodded with a tad too much glee. He reckoned he must have looked like an overstimulated puppy.

"Impressive!" Songbird continued. "Now you do me."

She got to her feet, wrapped her arms around Sunny's chest, and fell backwards; forcing Sunny to fall on top of her ample frame. Then she thrust his head between her legs, where he repaid the favour, but not the debt.

***

His conversation with Songbird helped Sunny to see things in a whole new way...

Yes, he was supposed to provide Hunter, the stranger, with five large animals. And yes, it was unlikely he would settle this debt. But none of this mattered. Hunter would remain a creditor. He would have to reappear, from time to time, to ask for a little more meat. These liaisons would form the basis of a new friendship. Hunter might even bring Sunny another gift; something as mysterious as the gun. Sunny might discover the truth behind the man: Where had he come from? Why were they both so similar, and yet so different? How had he discovered the gun? And why did he hold himself so erect?

Such thoughts added a skip to Sunny's step. He had eaten a big dinner the previous evening, to recover his strength, before spending the night with Songbird; falling asleep long after the sun had set, and experiencing a dreamy sleep. This was the norm. Fewer than one-in-fifty members of their tribe ever suffered from broken-sleep. They rarely took naps. They enjoyed a small amount of high-quality rest; sleeping on the hard-packed earth, or mattresses made from straw. They remained wide awake the rest of the time.

Sunny did not eat breakfast when he awoke, about an hour before sunrise; the coldest part of the day. Sunny *never* ate breakfast. Their tribe did not even have a word for that meal. Sometimes, they ate a handful of berries, midway through the morning. But, more often than not, they were happy to subsist on one or two meals a day.

He splashed water on his face, freshened his breath by chewing a scented twig, and brushed his teeth using a second twig, which he had frayed apart at one end. It might not have been the most effective method, but it was all that was required. Sunny's tribes-folk did not consume many carbohydrates or sugars. The tobacco they smoked at the Big Camp could turn their teeth a little brown. But their mouths contained very few bad bacteria. So there was little need for them to brush with a high intensity. Less than one percent of their teeth showed signs of decay. And such damage was usually so minor, it could be filled with a dab of beeswax.

After cleaning his teeth, Sunny caught the chicken, which he had dropped whilst being pleasured. He collected the clan's arrows, which had been removed from the buffalo's side. He said "Goodbye", and headed home; collecting the gun on his way, and allowing his mind to wander.

The landscape here was also dominated by scrubland and grassland, which rippled out towards the horizon; interspersed with the occasional huddle of trees, some rocky outcrops, and a couple of greyish cliffs.

It felt particularly hot and dry today. The effect was all the more intense, because Songbird's clan had set fire to vast swathes of this savannah. There was method to the madness: Burning the old growth killed off invasive plants, and gave new shoots the room they needed to grow. It would not be long before these ashen fields were filled with splashy flowers, which would sustain the region's pollinators. Luscious grasses would also appear, enticing animals for the clans-folk to hunt.

The clan's fires served another purpose: They removed the dead leaves, which allowed sunlight to permeate the soil and heat the earth. This encouraged microbial activity, producing the nutrients which fed the new plants. And, because those fires removed this foliage in a *controlled* manner, they reduced the chance of wildfires, ignited by lightning, which could have been catastrophic.

Sunny was familiar with this practice, because the Eagle Clan burned the greenish expanse which stretched out from the north end of their camp, surrounded their watering hole, and reached the nearest hills. He was familiar with this route, because he had passed this way three times since the last full moon. But he was still caught off guard by an unfamiliar sight: A man. And not just any man. A man who was completely covered in cloths!

Sunny had to blink himself back to sanity, before he was willing to accept the evidence his eyes were supplying. Despite the heat, this individual was wearing not one, but two different cloths upon his torso: A white cloth, which featured a vertical line of beads. And a beige cloth, which had tubes for each of his arms. In place of a loincloth, the man was wearing leg-cloths, with tubes which reached his ankles. Atop his head, was what appeared to be a straw basket. And on his feet, were what looked like the remains of an animal's hide, which had been cut into strips, and rebuilt in the shape of his feet.

Why had he wrapped himself up in so many cloths? Sunny could only think of a single explanation: This man must have possessed an abnormally large penis. He had no choice but to wrap it around his body, using these cloths to hold it in place.

And why did this man smell so bad; of cloves, musk and mould?

Only once Sunny had considered each of these things in turn, did he notice something more peculiar than the stranger's attire: His skin. This man was an albino! Every atom of colour had been washed from his face, and he did not appear to have a single tattoo, even though he had clearly come of age.

If he was not an albino, he was almost certainly a spirit; a lost ancestor, who had been trapped in the mortal realm.

Sunny's interest got the better of him; compelling him to tiptoe forwards, silently, and take up a position within the man's shadow. From here, he observed the valley in the same way as the man, mimicking each of his motions.

Only when the man turned, did Sunny turn. And only when he lifted a stick, did Sunny notice the contraption by his side. That three-legged frame was supporting a white cloth.

Sunny watched on as the man took a stick, and ran it along that cloth. His eyes filled with wonder, as a grey line appeared behind the stick.

Sunny continued to stare.

The stranger gazed through a golden tube and consulted a golden disk, paying close attention to every river and mound. Then he took two more sticks, which he used to draw lines in different colours.

Sunny was struck by something magnificent: The lines on the cloth matched the vista before him! A blue line followed the course of each stream. A series of concentric lines replicated the lay of each hill. Sunny was able to follow the route he was taking, from Songbird's camp to his own, both of which were marked with an X.

"Criss-cross," he whispered. "Home."

The man squealed like a startled pig. He jumped far higher than Sunny had supposed was possible. For a moment, he thought the man might have actually jumped out of his skin.

Upon landing, the man grabbed hold of himself, checked that he was still inside his body, and made sure that his organs had landed in the correct positions. He checked that his legs were still attached to his feet, that his feet were still supported by the ground, and that the ground was where he had left it.

He took a breath. Then he pivoted, turning his torso towards Sunny, whilst keeping his feet in the same position.

"Blah! Blah-di-blah, blah blah. Blah-blah-blah."

The man had spoken total gibberish. The noises he made did not even come close to forming real words. Yet each noise was different. Each sound flowed into the next, with the rhythm of an actual sentence.

The man rubbed the sweat from his palms, looked Sunny up and down, softened a little,

JOSS SHELDON | 87

calmed a little, pointed at the valley, and then pointed back at the cloth.

But something was awfully peculiar. The man was pointing with his *finger*!

To Sunny, this gesture seemed utterly insane. His people only ever used their fingers to point when they were referring to the *time*. They might point upwards, to speak of *noon*. Or they might point at a segment of the sky, to signify the *portion of time* when the sun could be found in that space; arcing eastwards, to refer to a section of the morning; or swooping westwards, to refer to the afternoon. They never pointed their fingers across the land. When they wished to draw someone's attention to another *location*, they puckered their lips, and shunted them in the appropriate direction.

Sunny showed the man how it was done; scrunching his lips towards the valley, before shunting them back at the picture.

The man nodded.

Now this was a gesture Sunny *could* understand. Members of their tribe also nodded to say "Yes". They shook their heads to say "No". Sunny figured these things were probably universal. They were learnt in infancy, when babies turned their heads to one side, away from their mothers' breast, as if to say "No" to the milk they were being offered. Children exaggerated this gesture as they grew; moving their heads to *both* sides, over and over again. They moved their heads the opposite way, up and down, to signify the opposite thing: A "Yes".

Sunny nodded.

The man nodded back. He exhaled, allowed his arms to hang loose, and spoke in a calmer tone; accentuating his gobbledygook:

"Blah, blah-di-blah. Survey, blah-di-blah."

Sunny tapped his lip. He had picked up a single word: "Survey". It was not a real word. It was the kind of thing an infant might say, when experimenting with speech; combining random sounds, in the hope they might form a word. Could this man be an oversized infant? Surely not! Infants did not wear so many cloths. They did not draw with magical sticks.

"Survey," Sunny repeated.

"Survey!" The man exclaimed. "Blah, survey, blah."

Sunny took one step back, and then another.

The stranger turned around, but Sunny had faded from view.

***

It had not been his intention, but it was not in his nature to say "No" to a gift from Mother Nature...

A short distance from home, Sunny came across a stag. Under normal circumstances, he might have let it be. He was alone. Killing such a creature usually required a team effort. And the stag was too far away to shoot with a bow and arrow.

But Sunny had a gun. And he needed to get five animals for Hunter. He supposed he should kill the stag, if only to reduce that debt.

He removed the bowstring, bound it around the chicken's legs, and used an arrow to pin it to the ground. He hid in the long grass, steadied his breathing, steadied his pulse, took aim and shot.

Bang!

For a brief moment, he thought he had missed. *Again.* But the stag did not bolt. It remained rooted to the spot, frozen in space and time; refusing to be rushed, only deigning to fall when *it* was ready. And even then, it did so at an unfeasibly slow rate; tipping onto its side with a motion which was so surreal, it rendered Sunny incapable of joy. He could not quite believe his success. It took him several moments to accept the situation, and several more to approach the stag.

As soon as he reached that animal, he sensed that someone was drawing near.

Moving as quickly as he could, he stuck his fingers in the bloody wound, removed the shot, and stuck an arrow in the hole.

He stabbed a few more arrows into the animal's body.

"Nice archery."

"Thanks, auntie."

It was Kitten who had appeared.

"It had to be, mind. The thing is so small, it'd have been easy to miss."

"Yes. I've seen rabbits who were bigger than this."

"Rabbits? Most rats have more meat."

"Most beetles too."

Kitten blushed pink with pride:

"Come, Sunny Boy... We can't carry this thing on our own. Let's go for help."

Sunny nodded. He forced a smile. But this was far from the result he had desired. If his kinfolk ate this animal, he would not be able to gift it to Hunter. He would still owe that man five animals.

And there were only five shots left to fire.

# THE PRODIGAL SON

Sunny had used their remaining shots...

Having learnt his lesson, he had ventured further from their camp. He had achieved a modicum of success, downing an antelope and a boar. But his other three shots had missed their target. Sunny had killed a large flightless bird, using one of their spears. But he still needed another two animals, in order to settle his debt.

Unsure what to do, he went to the toilet among a patch of trees; pondering his options as he pooped. When he was done, he washed his behind; pouring water from an old coconut shell, which he held in his right hand, whilst using his left hand to direct the flow.

He re-emerged onto the path, feeling refreshed, only to find himself standing in front of another image of Uncle Crow. Only this Uncle Crow looked less like Sunny, and more like Hunter.

"Hello, brother-o."

It even sounded like Hunter. Sunny had to stop, and rub the confusion from his eyes, before he resumed his journey home.

He walked straight into that Uncle Crow.

"Brother! Be calm. Be steady-o."

"Oh... It's... It's really you?"

"*It's really me.* Aren't you happy to see your brother?"

"Oh... Of course, err... 'Brother'."

The optimist in Sunny was genuinely happy to see Hunter. He supposed the stranger might have been content with the three animals he had killed. He hoped that Hunter might have brought another gift; something just as wondrous as the gun.

Hunter jolted forth, burying Sunny in a full-body embrace; hugging him so hard, his ribs creaked, and his lungs squeezed out of shape. Sunny was left with little choice but to endure several breathless moments. But still his optimism persisted. If Hunter was this happy to see him, then this rendezvous was sure to be a positive affair.

"I've got three animals for you!" he boasted, forgetting he was two animals short. "Come. Hope and I dragged them into a thicket, to protect them from the sun."

Sunny could not discern a reaction. Hunter neither smiled nor grimaced. His eyes refused to betray his thoughts.

It was excruciating. Sunny had busied himself for days, to get meat for this man. He deserved a reaction, *any* reaction, good *or* bad. And yet there was nothing. Sunny might as well have been talking to a tree.

He allowed the moment to linger; gazing upon this statuesque man, who did not appear to breathe.

He waited a while, and then he waited a little longer.

Hunter sprang into life.

"Ah! Three animals? Now then, let's see what we've got."

Why did he not react like this before?

Sunny used his lips to point the way, but it was Hunter who marched ahead; adopting a pace which was far too quick for comfort, and a silence which was tinged with fury.

They reached their destination. Sunny pulled back the branches, held them aside, and beckoned Hunter to enter the grotto beyond; a leafy space, which glistened in various shades of green.

"Nice antelope, brother-o," Hunter began, squatting down to pinch its skin. "Wow!"

It was a good start.

"But this boar is turning bad. And this bird is too small to count."

It was not the response Sunny had desired.

Hunter tensed his cheek.

"You owe me four more animals."

"Two."

"Four... How many shots do you have?"

Sunny lowered his gaze.

"Do you have any?"

Sunny shook his head.

Hunter tutted:

"Oh brother. *Tut-tut-o.*"

"It means..." Sunny was a little nervous to even make the suggestion. "It means you must return, to collect the rest of the meat... We're going to see each other again."

Hunter guffawed:

"Ah! Brother! I'll return for my four animals. This is a fact... Now, take these shots... These are for an additional five animals. Yes. I'll return for my *nine* animals. And yes. We'll be the best of friends."

Sunny stalled. If he had already cleared his debt, he would have rejected the shots and powder which had been placed on his palm. He did not appreciate the pressure. But he was

Hunter's debtor. What choice did he have?

"So... So, you don't mind that I was a little short this time?"

"Mind? You're still learning-o. I'm sure you'll do better, the next time around. So long as there's a chance you might succeed, then everything will be just fine."

Sunny nodded.

"And if you can't get me any meat, you can always use something else to settle your debt. That girl, perhaps. *Hope*? Ah! Factually! Hope. Yes, my brother, she'd cover the debt."

Sunny did not reply. The idea of using a person to settle a debt, seemed so preposterous, he could barely believe his ears. And so he *did not* believe his ears. He supposed he must have misheard, or misread, or misunderstood this stranger. He dismissed the comment and nodded again.

"I do need a small favour-o."

Sunny nodded a third time.

"Tonight, I plan to address the clan. I suspect that a few people will greet me with open arms. But others might not be so kind. Some of my words will be welcomed, but others might cause offence. What I need is an ally, a brother; a big wise man, who'll support me when the time is right... Sunny, I think you're the man for the job."

Sunny was still nodding. But a darkness had appeared in his eyes. Hunter had not threatened him. He had not uttered an aggressive word. Yet Sunny could not help feeling that he had been warned. There seemed to be a subtext to Hunter's speech, in the comments which lingered, unspoken, in the gaps between sounds; inside every comma and full-stop. Perhaps it was a figment of his imagination. But Sunny was certain that Hunter was saying something he had not felt a need to voice: "Do as I say, or I'll tell your clans-folk what you've done. And then I'll take Hope away."

***

Hunter was not a soothsayer, with the ability to see things before they happened. He had predicted that a meeting would take place, because *all the clans* held meetings, pretty much every single night.

The clans-folk gathered around the fire, soon after the sun went down. They barbequed meat and chatted amongst themselves. Sometimes a person might stand to address the group; telling a tale, or spreading the news which had reached them from another clan. They might play music, sing, dance, or perform a show.

When the circumstances dictated, these meetings could evolve into parliaments. One person might suggest an idea. A second person might suggest another. The group would throw these ideas around, discussing their pros and cons, before voting to make a decision.

They could also evolve into trials...

The Eagle Clan had no chief, police, judiciary or prisons. If someone was suspected of committing a dangerous act, it was up to their victims to raise the matter. The accused would mount a defence. Then their peers would conduct a vote, to decide if their behaviour had posed a threat. If the vote was unanimous, a second vote would be held to decide the culprit's fate.

The clans-folk did not *impose* punishments, in a vindictive fashion. They *suggested* "Protections", to safeguard the group's wellbeing. If the defendant did not believe a protection was just, they were invited to propose an alternative. Their suggestion would be put to the vote. This process was repeated, until an agreement was finally reached.

If there was one thing that defined these parliaments, it was the courtesy which was granted to the speakers. There were no interruptions; no heckles, jeers, cheers, tuts, claps, moans or groans. The silence continued even *after* a person had sat down, when they were given a few moments to compose their thoughts, lest they should think of something to add.

So, when Hunter reappeared that night, riding on horseback, there *was* a clan meeting, and he *was* allowed to speak.

His arrival inspired an eerie silence to descend. This could not be fully explained by the fact that it was the first time anyone had seen a horse. The clans-folk had seen more majestic animals. But no-one had ever seen a human *sitting atop* such a creature. What was more, the horse appeared to be content with this state of affairs; trotting wherever Hunter dictated, and stopping on Hunter's command. A second horse seemed happy to carry some sacks.

Kitten's jaw fell open. It swayed a little, as though it had become disconnected from the rest of her skull.

Sparrow's eyebrows rose so far up his

forehead, it was a wonder they did not merge with the rest of his hair.

Between them, the bonfire blazed gold and bronze; stabbing flames out into the ether, spitting sparks in every direction. The elders sat on the logs which surrounded that fire. The other adults squatted, or sat cross-legged on the ashy ground.

Hunter dismounted the horse, stepped forward, and addressed the clans-folk:

"My family-o! How good it feels to be back among the ones I love."

It was not entirely clear if his approach was welcome. Hunter had taken the group's silence as an invitation to speak. And, now that he had begun, no-one dared to interrupt.

"How I've missed this sweet aroma; the burnt meat that smells of honey, the crispness of the night sky, the flavour of steamy breath. I've travelled far and wide. I've missed many, many moons. And I've discovered an indisputable fact: Nothing is so sweet as home."

Hunter looked at each person in turn; staring into their eyes, smiling, and revealing that shiny tooth.

"But we cannot survive on sweetness alone.

Honey doesn't bring back the dead. The syrup of human kindness won't moisten droughts or conquer disease... My brethren: We can be so much more. Yes, it's a fact. In the Faraway Lands, the people live forever! I've gone there and seen it myself."

Hunter performed a sanguine nod, brought his finger to his lip, and turned to face Kitten.

"Imagine that! Imagine a world in which mothers didn't die in childbirth. Wow! A world in which babies weren't taken from their clans. Auntie: I know your pain. I feel it as though it were my own. But this is a fact: Another world is possible. In the Faraway Lands, they have medicine that can cure any disease. Take this medicine from me. Give it to your children. They'll never die in your arms again."

Hunter closed his eyes, allowing a Buddha-like serenity to wash across his face. He took a deep breath, gazed upon the scene afresh, and turned to Sparrow's sister.

"Medicine-o. But powerful. Stronger than all the herbs in the forest. This is a fact. If you had the medicine I'm offering now, your daughter wouldn't have succumbed to those berries."

He nodded, in a contemplative fashion;

attempting to display his sorrow, but failing to disguise his smugness, which revealed itself in the upturned corners of his mouth, and in the grungy hollows of his eyes.

He turned to face Sparrow.

"Ah, Sparrow! Uncle! Oh, how I've missed you. And oh, uncle, how I've agonized over your loss. Your own nephew! Your sweet boy, snatched away at such a tender age. What a tragedy! What misfortune!... Surely, you'd like to take precautions, to prevent such a disaster from reoccurring?... Yes, uncle, it's a fact. Another world is possible. I've seen it with my own eyes, in the Faraway Lands, where no-one is eaten by snakes. In the Faraway Lands, they have 'Guns'. Deadly weapons-o. Fantastical machines, which can kill a snake from a thousand paces. Wow! My uncle: Allow me to give you such a weapon. Allow me to help you to save your other nephews."

Hunter surveyed the people who had assembled before him. Everyone was so silent, so serene, he supposed they must have been hanging on his every word.

He was sorely mistaken. The clans-folk had only remained silent, because this was their custom. The silence continued a little longer, to give Hunter an opportunity to add to his previous remarks. It was only when he gestured with open palms, that the clans-folk dared to rustle a little; repositioning themselves, looking from side to side, and waiting for someone to speak.

Sparrow went first:

"I've got no desire to possess one of these crazy weapons. I'm happy with the spears and bows we've always used; weapons which have served us for millions of lunar-cycles... It's sad when a nephew is taken. But this is the law of the prairie. We humans take far more lives than are taken from us. And I've little doubt that our nephew is in a better place, over there in the ancestral forest."

Members of their tribe believed that people's spirits lived on after death; returning to their clan's ancestral forest, from where they kept a watchful eye on their descendants; protecting them from harm, and exposing their misdemeanours.

The group fell silent, to allow Sparrow to speak a little more. When it was clear he had nothing to add, Kitten stood up, cleared her throat, and turned to address Hunter:

"*Tut, tutty-tut-tut, tutty-tut*... What? Didn't you know that I have three beautiful children? I'm blessed! How dare you pity me, Hunter Boy? Do you really think I wanted twenty boys and girls? Where would I put them? Haven't you seen the size of our huts? Huh? Aren't you aware that if weakling children survived, our population would grow too large? It'd be unsustainable. Diseases would ravage the group. We'd kill too many animals, destroying the very ecosystem which sustains us... No, your hocus-pocus concoctions aren't any use to us."

There was a certain logic to Kitten's response. Hunter's plea had reminded her of the *Fable of Old Auntie Rabbit*. That legendary ancestor had raised no fewer than twenty-five children. The exact number varied, depending upon who was telling the tale. But whatever the number, the storytellers all agreed on one thing: Auntie Rabbit's offspring were a burden upon the clan. Almost every adult had to carry one of her infants, whenever they moved between camps. And when they grew into adults, they came to dominate the clan; voting as a bloc, and almost always getting their way. Their peers waited for things to improve. But their patience wore thin, and they eventually took their revenge. They castrated Auntie Rabbit's sons, and they gifted her daughters to rival tribes.

Ever since those days, the members of their clan had taken precautions to prevent the emergence of another Auntie Rabbit. Mothers breastfed their children until they were eight solstices old, to reduce the chance of another pregnancy. They performed abortions; consuming a mixture of poisonous leaves and herbs. They had even been known to practice infanticide; abandoning their babies in the clan's ancestral forest. This was a *solemn* act, accompanied by chants and meditations. But the clans-folk did not believe it was a *permanent* act. They believed that they were only destroying the baby's mortal body; that its spirits would live on forever. They might even return to the world of the living, encased within another baby.

Kitten had something to add:

"And as for your pride, Hunter Boy! 'Wow' indeed. Boy: You're in love with the smell of your farts. Your evil wolf must have killed and eaten your good wolf."

Sparrow's sister agreed with a nod. She did

not trust Hunter, and supposed his medicine was actually a type of poison.

Hunter seemed slightly ruffled. He still stood perfectly erect, with raised shoulders and an inflated chest. But his arrogant sheen had begun to fade. His pupils seemed a little less sharp. He still spoke with a bombastic voice, but his speech sounded a little forced:

"My brethren, this is a fact: The things I've said are just the tip of the buffalo's tusk. Wow! Uncles and aunties. Wow! The things I've seen in the Faraway Lands!... I've seen buildings the size of a thousand huts. And sturdy too. Powerful enough to withstand a million storms... I've seen stories written down in code, passed from one person to the next, and performed on gigantic stages... I've seen ways of travelling-o. My brethren: *I've travelled myself.* I've sat in these things they call 'Trains'; giant tubes which whoosh you across the land at the speed of gazelles. I've sat in their 'Ships'; floating camps, which can cross the widest of waters... Wow! These are the undisputed facts. And you can have this for yourselves. Just say the word. Accept my cargo, and your lives will be transformed forever. Yes, my uncles and aunts. You just have to believe in the future. It's going to be so much better than the past."

The group fell silent.

Hunter took this as an invitation to continue:

"Perhaps you're unconvinced. Perhaps you're not ready for homes that can withstand typhoons. Perhaps you're not ready to travel the world. This is fine, my brethren. As fine as a colourful bird... But please just take one gift. Take these blankets. They'll keep you warm when the winds blow cold and the rains fall heavy on your head. Or take this gun. Use it to protect yourself from snakes. Or use it to hunt. You'll kill more creatures than you've ever killed before."

A silence ensued, which was eventually broken by Serenity:

"By the good earth, we don't wish to 'Kill more animals than we've ever killed'. We aren't Uncle Crows, with bottomless bellies that can never be filled. The ancestors know that our stomachs are already full. We have all the things we need."

Serenity did not continue. It was not in his nature to say ten words, when five would suffice.

Hunter looked around in search of support;

attempting to look friendly, but failing; appearing more desperate than he had intended, with bulging eyes and sallow cheeks. He only changed his appearance, for the briefest of moments, when he panned around to Sunny; shooting the youngster a glare which was so sharp, so piercing, that it lifted Sunny to his feet.

"Err..." he stammered. Sunny was not a confident speaker. He had attended thousands of meetings, and taken part in hundreds of votes. But he had never addressed the group himself. "I... Umm... I think we should... Err... Accept the... You know... The potions. I mean... Well, yeah... The potions."

No-one said a word. But Sunny could feel the onslaught of his kinfolk's soundless protests. Buttocks were repositioned and fingers were rubbed against thumbs. Sunny was certain that his mother had made a tutting motion, without making the sound of an actual tut.

"I... Umm... It's just... Well, let's say Hope was gifted a child... Well... Umm... I'd like it if that child got to live... Like, in the mortal realm... Like, with us... Umm... Yeah."

The air seemed to soften. A few members of the clan must have empathised with Sunny's point of view.

But one of the elders, a man who everyone called *Dusk*, was not among their number. Dusk was a peculiar-looking chap. It had been said that Mother Nature used up so much skin and muscle, whilst making his oversized head, that she had run short of materials whilst she was making the rest of his body. Dusk's torso could barely support his head, and his legs could barely support his torso. Although no-one ever mentioned these things out loud. Dusk was an elder, and so was treated with respect.

"If the ancestors deem it right, they'll allow the child to live," Dusk responded, after the customary pause. "And if they deem the child unworthy, they'll call it back to the ancestral forest. This is the natural order. It'd be foolish to challenge Mother Nature."

There was a brief moment of silence. But the clans-folk knew it would not last for long.

As if compelled by a collective instinct, they turned to face Dusk's rival, a man known simply as *Dawn*. They were expecting him to disagree. And with good reason: Dawn almost *always* disagreed with Dusk. Their squabbles were so routine, it would have felt strange had one of them *not* challenged the other. Even their bodies disagreed. Dawn went to considerable lengths to buff up his chest, which had the effect of making his head look *too small* for his body.

No-one could be entirely sure why Dusk and Dawn did not get along. Rumour had it that they were brothers or best friends; inseparable partners, who had fallen out over a girl. That woman had stopped having sex with Dawn, who had grown envious, confronted his erstwhile buddy, and stabbed him in his leg.

This explained the large gash which extended from Dusk's buttock down to his knee. It explained his wide, wobbling stance. And it explained the hostility.

But this story made little sense. The girl could have had sex with them both. She could have alternated or abstained. Dusk and Dawn could have made a pact. They could have cut her out completely, or insisted that she sleep with them together. And who was this mysterious woman? And where was she now?

The story was believed, or at least accepted, because a more believable alternative had never been aired. Dusk and Dawn did not discuss the matter, and no-one could remember the truth.

The truth did not particularly matter. It was the *animosity* that affected the group. Whenever Dusk or Dawn aired a view, their peers turned to face their adversary, instinctively, *expecting* them to disagree. Their bickering could delay the decision-making process by a matter of days. But what could they do? It was pretty normal for clans to contain members who did not get along. Some personality-types seemed destined to clash. Squabbling clans-folk had even been known to go separate ways, joining different clans. But it had never come to that with Dusk and Dawn. Their disputes had always been solved. And, it was generally agreed that this was a good thing. It was Mother Nature's way of challenging them; forcing them to consider alternative points of view, before settling upon a compromise; reaching the best of all possible solutions.

Such a solution would have to wait.

Dusk had just suggested that they leave their babies' fates to Mother Nature, and Dawn was readying himself to disagree:

"It was Mother Nature who sent us this brother! The ancestors are known for their ability to adapt. They've always used every tool at their disposal. Who are *we* to look a gift bird in the anus?"

The momentum was beginning to shift.

Sunny had already voiced his support, making the case for Hunter's medicine. And now Dawn was supporting Sunny.

Keen to drive home his advantage, Hunter interceded, a little sooner than custom would have permitted. He threw his arms to the breeze, and smiled from cheek to cheek:

"Ah! There we have it! This distinguished elder gets it. And this fine young man gets it too. There can be no escaping the facts: The children are our future. Yes. Just look at this boy. Ask yourself: What kind of world would you want for him?"

No-one answered.

The silence floated in mid-air; in the eyes which turned to Hunter, Sunny and Dawn; on the leaves which rustled in muteness, and among the flames which danced in front of the jet-black sky.

Hunter looked confident, then confused, then calm.

"Ah!" he said. "My brethren: You're ready to vote. Good-o. Who's in favour?"

No-one lifted their hands.

Hunter glared at Sunny, who felt himself raising his finger, tentatively; as though he was not raising it himself, but allowing an invisible creature to lift it on Hunter's behalf.

Hunter stared at Hope and then Dawn, neither of whom moved a jot.

"All those against?"

Almost everyone lifted their hands.

"Ah," Hunter concluded. "A split vote. Well, my uncles and aunts: We must resume these discussions tomorrow."

No-one disagreed. They remained there in silence, for a while, before resuming their conversations; leaving Hunter on the edge of the circle, abandoned, without so much as a shadow by his side.

# AN ECHO FROM THE PAST

Hunter spent the night alone, in one of the cabins which were usually reserved for sex.

But this was not the only place he resided that night. He also took up residency in Sunny's mind, plaguing the youngster's thoughts, and inspiring a flurry of questions: Who was this man? Why did everyone treat him with so much cynicism? None of the elders were alarmed when he called them "Auntie" and "Uncle". They seemed to know the man. But how?

And what did his peers think of *him*? Were they judging *him*, because he had voted for Hunter's proposal? Did they consider him a traitor? Or a rebel? Or a fool?

\*\*\*

It was already dawn, and Sunny had barely slept. The sun lay flat across the horizon; red, amber and gold. The grasslands to the north were fresh with that curious form of dew; the kind which appears even when the air is dry. A few small birds were visiting for the first time this season, although they were only tweeting half the notes in their songs.

"Mother kindest: You know him, don't you?...

Hunter, I mean. The man from last night."

His mother inhaled, allowing a meditative peace to form around her eyes. Her skin glowed, both absorbing and reflecting the light. Her cheeks did not soften or harden, form a smile or a frown; refusing to reveal her emotions.

Sunny waited for a reply which never came. He repeated his question a second time. But it was only once he had waited a little longer, and asked a third time, that he finally received a response.

"He called you 'Brother-o', didn't he?"

Sunny nodded.

"Well?"

"He called everyone 'Brother'. Or 'Sister', 'Auntie' or 'Uncle'."

"Terms of endearment... But with you, maybe... Maybe he was being literal."

"Oh... You mean..."

His mother raised her eyebrows.

"It's just... Well, you're not old enough to be his mother."

His mother rolled her eyes.

"He's your nana's grandson. Let's not split grasses."

Sunny was taken aback by his mother's

condescending tone. He had to make an effort to steady his legs, before deigning to push for more:

"So... Why haven't I ever met him? I mean... Why haven't I even *heard* of him?"

"He left the clan before you were born."

It was like getting juice from a sunbeam!

"Oh... Yes Mama... But *why*?"

His mother dropped her head. She waited, realised that Sunny was determined to receive an answer, accepted that he deserved one, sighed, and mumbled as she spoke:

"Because he poured shame upon our hut. Upon all your aunties and uncles."

It was personal. But why? What had Hunter done?

Sunny did not ask. He placed his hands on his mother's shoulders, pulled her close, hugged her gently, and held her until she spoke:

"He... Chick-i-lick... Your brother was the closest thing we've ever known to a real-life Uncle Crow. He... He was a great hunter. He could spot a bird before anyone else, throw a spear, and kill it as it flew; all within the blink of an eye. He never missed. But... But he grew so arrogant! He demanded we move here, there, everywhere; to barren lands, and to lands used by other clans... Lovely: If he'd had his way, he'd have brought us into conflict with our neighbours. He'd have started a war. And for what?... The boy was a broken arrow. He'd already succumbed to greed."

Sunny held his mother close. He could feel her pain, as it seeped into his chest.

"It's okay... I've heard enough... Mama: It's okay."

But his mother had found her flow:

"One day, Hunter killed five large animals, all by himself. He dragged them home, without asking for help. He shared them, of course. But there was far too much meat and fat. Most of it went to waste. And for what?... After that, he demanded that we move on. 'I've hunted all the animals in this region,' he proclaimed. Only his tone was a little too boastful. Too brash. So the clan held a trial and cast votes."

"He was banished?"

"Yes, chick-i-lick. He was invited to remain in a voluntary exile, until three summer solstices had passed. The terms of that protection have lapsed, which is why he was permitted to speak. But..."

His mother choked on her words.

"There's more?"

"Yes... You see, the clan didn't only invite Hunter to go into exile... You know, we have a special way of keeping order: Every member of a hut is held responsible for every other member of that hut. We all have a duty to keep our aunts and uncles, sisters and brothers in line. This is how we prevent bad things from happening... So, if one of us misbehaves, we're all considered responsible, because we've all failed to control that individual."

His mother fell silent again.

Sunny tried to finish the story:

"Oh... You mean... What you're saying... You were *all* invited to go into exile?"

A tear appeared in the corner of his mother's eye. She sucked it back into its socket, wiped her hands on her loincloth, and then placed them on Sunny's head. She looked at her son, mustered her strength, and spoke with calm determination:

"We were abandoned. Whenever we approached, our sisters turned their chests and bent their ears; moving away, ignoring our pleas, ignoring our very existence."

The tear reappeared.

"Our blessed ancestors above! It was the toughest season of our lives. We only had four adults to hunt and gather. Some days, we found far too much food to eat, but there was no-one with whom we could share it. On other days, we starved and withered away... Sunny... Chick-i-lick... Your sister returned to the ancestral forest."

Sunny's mother took a deep breath.

"Lovely: Those times are behind us now. We were welcomed back into the group. You were born. The sun danced on our foreheads as before."

His mother dropped her shoulders. The air returned to her lungs. But Sunny could sense there was more to this tale.

"And... Well, you've not forgotten? Is that right? You worry that history might be revisiting us once again?"

His mother's face relaxed for the first time in days.

"When you saw me return with the ox, grinning like the monkey who'd caught the moon... Well, you thought I was becoming a second Hunter? You thought I'd disgrace the hut? That we'd be forced to perform another protection?"

His mother seemed to nod, without actually moving her head.

"Oh, Mama. I promise you this: I'll never allow that to happen. Never... And Mama, you must make me a promise too. You must warn me if I begin to err again."

His mother hugged Sunny with tender intensity, only loosening her grip to pepper his face with the most delicate nose rubs she could muster.

She had the final word:

"Sunny: I feel... I worry that you've already begun to err... At yesterday's meeting... Lovely: I think you know what you did."

Sunny nodded. He knew exactly what he had done. And he knew what he had to do to make amends...

*** 

Sunny was the first person to arrive at the campfire that evening.

He rubbed a sharpened stick along the indent he had created within a piece of wood. A light smoke appeared; wafting, hesitantly, as though it was disinclined to move. Sunny took a fistful of dried grass, and held it above the smoke. A couple of sparks appeared, flickering on and off. He waited a while longer, before blowing on the grass, which began to billow and blaze.

Sunny placed this smouldering creation in the middle of the fire circle, arranged some twigs just above, waited a little, blew a little, and then waited a little longer. When the structure caught fire, he added a slightly larger set of sticks, waited for them to succumb to the flames, added some bigger sticks, and then some logs.

He stepped back, admired the fire, clapped his hands, and helped himself to a drink. The clan kept a supply of water for their evening meetings, which they stored in the giant eggshells they had taken from a variety of flightless birds, in various places, at different times. They buried these vessels beneath the earth, to keep their water cool.

Sunny's body was brought to life by the contrasting sensations, produced by the heat of the fire and the coolness of the water. His skin pulsated: *Thud. Thud. Thud.*

It would have been wrong, however, to attribute this sensation solely to the fire and water. His heart raced, and his muscles spasmed, because he had also just spotted Hope.

Hope appeared different, although it was impossible to say how. Her face was just as lithe. Her body was just as slender. Every part of her was present and correct. Perhaps she smelled different. Sunny could not be sure. But there was something. Something that pulled Sunny in; which made him want to jump inside Hope's body, and reside within her skin. He wanted to talk to her without making a sound. He wanted to hold her without needing to touch. He had never felt anything like it. And he had no idea how to respond.

Hope sat by his side.

As though she had sensed his state of mind, she did not say a word. She did not touch or look at her lover.

Sunny could not have wished for anything more intimate. The iciness faded, and his body warmed from within.

The iciness suddenly returned. Only now, it was all-encompassing. The cold was both within and without, surrounding him and penetrating his body. Sunny checked the fire, supposing it must have been extinguished, and was surprised by the intensity of its flames.

The chill had come from an entirely different source: Hunter. That prodigal son had galloped through the grasslands, flattening the tiny flowers, before coming to a sudden halt.

He had changed. He was no longer wearing a loincloth. He was dressed like that ghost, or spirit, or albino; the person who Sunny had spotted whilst returning from Songbird's camp. The only difference, so far as Sunny could tell, was that Hunter's cloths were a murky shade of brown.

Now Sunny did grab hold of Hope. And now she embraced him back.

Hunter looked at them, grinned, and waited for a greeting which never came.

***

At first, it felt like nobody was going to join them. Then everybody arrived at once.

They came bearing food, which they cooked on the fire; toasting mushrooms, roots and yams. Sparrow brought a cassava, but it would be a while before it was ready. It had to be grated, its liquid had to be expressed, and its remains had to be oxidised before they could be cooked. There was very little meat that night, just a couple of frogs and wrens. This was not uncommon. Hunters may have spent countless evenings, boasting of their prowess in the bush; of all the times they had downed buffalo, boar or antelope. Such tales served a purpose. When the elders spoke of each species, its habits, and how it could be hunted; they passed on their knowledge to the younger generations. But if you had pushed them on the matter, they would have been forced to admit that they had only ever shot a handful of gazelles, and ten or twenty antelope. Their successes were real, but they were rare. As on this evening, most meals only included a few morsels of meat. Around ninety percent of the clan's calorific intake came from plants. Around a quarter came from tubers, corn, bulbs and roots. Even though these foodstuffs were rather small, they tended to be bunched together, so a large amount could be gathered in a single outing. Grasses, fruits, seeds, nuts and edible leaves could be found throughout the year, in spots which were known to the clans-folk; either because they had always been found in those locations, or because someone had noted their presence during a recent expedition. Gatherers *always* returned with food, and their hauls were fairly consistent, whereas most hunting trips ended in failure. The clan's very survival depended on their gatherers, most of whom were female; not on the hunters, most of whom were men.

Indeed, this was why Sunny had been so keen to return with an animal, and why he had accepted the loan of an ox. *He wished to prove his worth.*

It also explained why he had been so excited by Hunter's gun. That weapon had the potential to revolutionise their diet. With a device like that, he and his fellow hunters might be able to provide their fair share of food, for the first time in the clan's history.

Sunny sensed he was not alone; that a number of the other hunters had also wanted access to a gun. They had not rejected Hunter's offer because they were indifferent to Hunter's *rifle*. They had rejected it because they did not wish to be in Hunter's *debt*.

***

By the time they had cooked, eaten, and engaged in idle conversation, Sunny had almost forgotten the man who was looming above them, sitting atop a mysterious animal, wearing far too many cloths, and possessing way too much braggadocio.

Hunter cleared his throat:

"Ahum!"

It sounded more like a shout than a normal bodily function. That noise rattled up Hunter's windpipe, projected itself over the fire, bounced off the hills, rebounded back, and fell flat at the feet of its maker.

The silence was instantaneous.

Hunter smiled, revealing his sparkly tooth, which reflected the fire.

"Welcome back, my uncles and aunties. Welcome back to our humble abode."

He panned around.

"I think we got off on the wrong foot, and for that I offer my humblest apologies. My brethren: There *is* another world. It *is* a bright, fine thing, with medicine and meat, sturdy huts and dazzling art. But you love *your* world. It's only natural. Most people support the status quo, whilst it remains the status quo. And who am I to shake things up? You love your lives. Why would you change your ways for me?"

He looked at the crowd, to see if anybody wished to answer.

"Because of the facts! That's why. Because

change is on its way. Change is going to kick you in the eggs, whether you like it or not. Yes, uncles and aunts. The Sons of Empire are coming. I've come here to warn you. I've come to *protect* you from them."

The silence was orchestral; a cacophony of scrunching brows, popping eyes, and the mutest of all possible murmurs.

"It's an indisputable fact. You need to know what you're up against. It's a greater force than anything you could imagine. Yes. A million Uncle Crows are on the march."

Hunter paused for effect.

"The Sons of Empire have conquered all those who've stood before them... Ah! In one battle, one-hundred-and-sixty Sons took on *eighty-thousand* natives. And do you know what happened? They vanquished every last one, without losing a single man... Wow! Just wow!

"What? You doubt me? Doubt away! It still remains a fact. And facts are crocodilian. They'll eviscerate you if you ignore them... Believe it. The Sons of Empire have impenetrable armour. Your arrows won't ever pierce it... They have deadly weapons-o. Their rifles can destroy whatever protective cloths you wear... They're what they call 'Patriots' and 'Religious fanatics'. They have these abstract ideals. Crazy beliefs, the likes of which you couldn't begin to comprehend. And they're prepared to die for these made-up concepts!... They have these things they call 'Books', which imbue them with the experience of a thousand battles... And their horses! My brethren: Their horses can appear out of nowhere. They can surround you at unimaginable speeds, picking you off before you have the chance to call for help. They're unbeatable. When under threat, their horses simply retreat. They regroup, and they come again. Yes. Uncles and aunties: The Sons of Empire are coming. And they're going to crush you all."

Hunter had patted the horse, whilst boasting of the species' prowess. And now he was patting it again; pausing, allowing the clans-folk to consider his claims, before illustrating his point with a tale:

"Factually! I've seen such things with these very eyes. I've witnessed a Son of Empire approach a camp like this, and spray leaden fire from his gun. Wow! He killed so many people! The survivors piled up the bodies, to make a protective wall. Their river turned red with blood."

He nodded solemnly.

"Don't think they wouldn't do the same to you.

"But, my brethren, you're in luck. The Sons believe they've already conquered this valley-o. They say this land is already their land, and its people are already their subjects."

Sunny scratched his head with such ferocity, he might have drawn blood.

He struggled to understand why anyone might think they had conquered his clan, simply because they had vanquished an unrelated people in another place. He had never heard of a "Subject". It did not sound like any word in their tribe's language. And he could not understand how the land could belong to these "Sons of Empire". A person's body belonged to them, as did their loincloth and beads. But land belonged to nature; to every plant, bird, animal and insect who made it their home. Their tribe had a kind of unspoken agreement, acknowledging that the Eagle Clan were guardians of this land. But they would have been happy to share it with a visiting clan. They had used other tracts of land in the past. Only a psychopath would think the land could belong to them. The very idea was met with a collective gasp.

"*They say this land is already their land, and its people are already their subjects.* If you fight them, they'll kill you. If you welcome them, they'll force you to adopt their ways. But take my treats; this gun, these shots, this horse... And then... And then, you might just survive."

Hunter nodded with smug satisfaction:

"No-one else will offer you a gun. I'm taking a big, big risk. Wow! If anyone found out, I'd surely be killed... Yes, it's a fact: I'm doing this because I care.

"The winds of progress cannot be tamed, but you can protect yourself from their thrust. So please, take these precious gifts. If you refuse, you'll be slaughtered or enslaved. But if you take these things, there's a chance you'll all survive."

Hunter nodded with even more self-righteousness than before. Only this time, he did not continue his speech. He waited for a response. And, when none was forthcoming, he pushed for an answer, asking: "Well? What do you think?"

It was Serenity who replied, after the customary pause:

"If your intentions were as honourable as you suggest, you'd only need to speak softly. Yet yesterday you resorted to bribes, and today you've dealt in threats... Child: It's better to have a little less thunder in the mouth, and a little more lightning in the hand."

Another hush ensued.

This time, it was Kitten who broke the silence:

"How do you know so much about these watermelon heads? What, are you a 'Son of Empire' yourself? A Mister Coconut? Furry on the outside, but hard beneath the hair?"

Hunter grinned. He was happy to have provoked a reaction.

"I once lived like you, without a care in the world; floating on the wind, living for the breeze; hunting, gathering, and sitting around the fire. Ah! Those innocent days! But, alas, I was cut adrift. Puff! As quick as a ray of light, I found myself clan-less and alone. It was tough. I had to find my own food, make my own fires, and build my own camp, *every single day*. It was exhausting-o. I needed release. And release came, when I reached the Endless Ocean. Stood there, gazing out across those waters, I caught sight of a colourless man. Brethren! You wouldn't believe my surprise. Wow! I thought he was inside-out! I'm not afraid to admit that I was scared. Shocked! My brethren: I couldn't move a limb!

"But that man was not nearly so alarmed. He walked by, without so much as a second glance. It was only when he returned, a little while later, that he looked me up and down. He offered me food, and ushered me aboard his giant canoe; a thing so large, it contained a hundred huts. A thing with enormous wings, which propelled us across the water.

"I was grateful for the companionship and the adventures which came my way. But I'd be lying if I said things were easy. They forced me to cook, clean, tie ropes, hoist wings, and carry their precious treasure. I accompanied them on their missions, set up their camps, helped them to wage war, and acted as their guide and translator. Factually: They kept me busy day and night. Wow! It was a big, big education.

"Yes, uncles and aunties: I went and saw the world. I saw huts made of stone and huts made of wood, huts with walls so thick they could repel an ancestral attack, and cross-shaped huts with coloured windows. I saw tracks which went on forever, and a camp which was built on top of rivers. I tasted the delicacies of a hundred different peoples. I was wowed by plays, poetry, stories and songs; the likes of which you couldn't begin to imagine.

"Uncles and aunties: I was gone so long, I'd forgotten my home. Factually: My memory only returned, when I walked the very same paths I'd travelled all those seasons before.

"We fought battles, claimed land, and moved on our merry way. But then I recognised our valley-o. I thought of you. And I was overcome by a sense of... Of... Well, nostalgia, I suppose. And... Yes, I suppose it must be said... I felt *remorse*. I'd abandoned my people, to live a better life. I felt... I felt this insatiable need to make amends. To give something back. To clear my debt to the ones who'd ushered me into this realm.

"So here I am, laden with gifts. I only ask that you accept them. Allow me to clear my debt."

The fire spat sparks in arbitrary directions.

Kitten spat as she spoke:

"*Tut, tutty-tut-tut, tutty-tut...* Your story

makes about as much sense as an elephant who's lost its trunk. What? You were forced to leave the clan because you were a big bossy man? And you became a teeny-weeny small man, who wiped the arses of these albino ghosts? And you accepted it? And you want us to believe that you're happy with this arrangement?... Why, Hunter Boy? Because you got to gaze upon a hut made of stone, from afar, and then move on? Because you listened to a new song and ate a new meal?... No... The sun could set in the north, and it'd make more sense than this."

Kitten paused, believing she was done, only to think of something else:

"And you even helped them to kill people like yourself? It's treachery. Your story whiffs of rotten fish. Hunter Boy: You've lain with wolves, and you've caught their fleas."

Kitten finished, for good this time, and awaited Hunter's response. But Hunter was in no mood to rush. He was happy to play tricks with the silence; sucking down the aromas of charcoal, ash, burnt food and dried grass; gazing out at the silhouettes of distant hills, as they melted into the moonlight; and at the tops of ill-defined trees, whose borders were fuzzy with movement. He waited for a bird to land nearby, investigate its surrounds, have second thoughts, and take flight. And he waited for an animal to yowl.

"Auntie! Auntie Kitten! Ah, how I've missed our little mouse-and-eagle chats. Why, you haven't changed a jot. I suppose you never will. This is your blessing, and this is your curse. Yes, auntie: Your blessing and your curse."

The clans-folk waited for Hunter to answer the question. But their visitor just repeated these words, "Blessing" and "Curse", until they sounded like distant echoes.

A drop of rain shook Hunter back to life:

"It's an 'Elephant who's lost its trunk'? Ah! Maybe in the present-o. But we're walking into the future. Change *is* coming, and there's nothing you can do to stop it... Yes, I'd prefer it if the Sons of Empire weren't so strong. And yes, I'd prefer to maintain our ancient ways. I'd prefer it if meat rained down from the ancestral realm, pre-cooked and seasoned to perfection. But such things aren't to be. The Sons *are* coming. They will see, and they will conquer... I've chosen to be by their side; to be on the side of the conqueror, not the conquered; to be a winner, not a loser... And yes, Auntie Kitten: I may have worked my way up from the bottom. I may have performed degrading tasks. But I'm rising to the top. I'm one of the Sons' 'Representatives'. They're rewarding me with land, with power, with everything I've ever craved."

Hunter's conclusion was said in such a low hush, he appeared to be talking to himself:

"Resistance... Is... Futile..."

He repeated this phrase three more times, staring into his chest; adopting a voice which was so quiet, his words seemed to melt into silence.

Kitten whispered her response in a voice which was almost as solemn:

"It was you, wasn't it? It was you who slaughtered that clan? It was you who caused their river to turn 'Red with blood'?"

Hunter did not deny it. He just muttered his old refrain:

"Resistance... Is... Futile..."

He bowed his head, took a breath, waited, waited a little more, shook himself alert, and resumed his address with a renewed sense of vim:

"But all is not lost-o. My brethren: I come bearing gifts. I come with guns! Take them and flee. Make a life for yourself in the deepest depths of the bush. Yes! The other clans won't be so lucky. No-one will offer them these things. You must take these splendid gifts. You must protect yourselves and flee."

Hunter believed he had said enough. He had presented the "Indisputable facts", and given the clans-folk a day to mull them over. He was confident they would see sense.

"A vote! Raise your hands if you wish to be safe!"

No-one moved.

Hunter scowled at Dawn.

But Dawn just shrugged:

"I've had a night's rest, and it's helped to clear my mind; to see things for what they are... I've decided to unite with the rest of the clan."

Hunter turned to Sunny, scowling at him in the same manner as the previous day.

But this time, Sunny kept his arm by his side. His mother's words were still ringing in his ears. And he did not appreciate the pressure which Hunter was applying.

But neither did he like the idea of being

shamed. So he stood up and explained his predicament, before Hunter had the opportunity to expose him:

"Dearest aunties and beloved uncles... Sisters and brothers... I've got a confession to make... There's a... There's a reason I voted for Hunter's proposal: He said if I didn't, he'd tell you what I'd done...

"It's just... Well, it'd be better if you heard it straight from the parrot's beak. This secret is too heavy to carry.

"You see... Well, Hunter approached me a while back. He showed me the magic bow, with its magic arrows. And... Well, I was awed. But, you see... I thought it was a gift... Well, as soon as I took that magic bow... That *gun*... He put ten shots in my hand, and said I had to give him five large animals. And... Well, I only managed to kill three, and only one was to Hunter's liking... So he gave me another ten shots, and said I owed him *nine* large kills. Now I'm in his debt and at his mercy.

"This is why I voted for his proposal."

The group looked far from impressed. A transgender woman frowned so much, the lines on her forehead seemed to push against her skull. A young man bit the insides of his cheeks, forcing his lips to pucker and crease.

After the customary pause, it was Serenity who cross-examined the defendant:

"You accepted a gift from an outsider, without seeking the group's blessing?... Hmm... Dangerous. Very dangerous... Sunshine: You know what we say?... One finger cannot lift a pebble. A canoe doesn't progress, when everyone rows in different directions."

Sunny winced. He had not considered his behaviour to be "Dangerous". People often took things from other clans, in much the same way that he had borrowed an ox. But those clans were members of the same tribe. Sunny had no idea that the very same acts could be considered "Dangerous", when an *outsider* was involved.

"Yes, the ancestors know it to be true. Strangers can threaten our very existence. And so the clans-folk must scrutinise their proposals, as a collective, before they can be approved."

Sunny nodded. It made sense. But how was he to know?

"Your actions weren't only wrong. They were *dangerous*... Now, we have several protections, to shield us against such dangers: We could invite you to withdraw from clan meetings. We could invite you and your hut-folk to enter into exile. We could even ask you to return to the ancestral forest."

Death? That seemed a little extreme.

"Child: Justify your deeds."

Sunny could not.

But this time, he was not alone. Hope was rising to her feet, and she looked defiant; like a threatened animal, caught in a fight-or-flight situation; scared, but determined to save her life. Her eyes blazed red, reflecting the fire, and her chin jutted out like a weapon.

"I was with Sunny. And I'll say this, with a hand on every spirit within me: The boy didn't act with malice. There was no talk of a debt when he took this gun. Hunter spoke as if it were a gift, just as he spoke of gifts tonight. Sunny was foolish to fall into his trap. The boy is a Mister Simpleton, a vole among hawks, a squirrel-brained sloth. He's a numbskull, a blade of grass, an empty coconut. But he isn't a Mister Malicious. He isn't a Mister Dangerous Threat."

Sunny did not know if he should be grateful or insulted. It must have involved a great deal of courage for Hope to speak out on his behalf, going against the prevailing mood. Hope was younger and smaller than almost everyone at this meeting. And she had come to his defence, whilst even his own mother remained mute. Yet she had humiliated him. Were her insults really necessary?

After another moment of silence, Sparrow concurred:

"The boy is like the buffalo who chased its tail, believing it to be a snake."

The slurs rebounded around the circle:

"He's the chicken who tried to hatch a stone."

"The spider who got caught in its web."

"The star who forgot how to twinkle."

"The fish who drowned in water."

"The bird who fell off its branch."

"The ant who got lost."

Sunny was beginning to understand. *This* was his protection. He was being humbled; brought back to earth, to restore harmony within the clan. Sunny had thought he could have the most powerful weapon, and use it to get more meat than anyone else; to become the clan's most prolific hunter. His kinfolk were putting him back in his place. It was like when they insulted the meat, to keep a hunter modest. Only now, *he was the meat.*

But this did not resolve Sunny's predicament. He still had a debt to re-gift.

When the insults faded, and everyone turned his way, he made a new proposal:

"If... If we can get the meat *together*... The nine animals... Then the debt would be cleared, and we'd be rid of this man for good. But... Well, I cannot do it alone... I mean... Perhaps I could, over the course of many seasons. But if you were all to help me, we could be rid of him in a twinkle."

Sunny noticed that his mother was smiling.

Serenity tipped his head; a gesture which seemed as good as a question.

"I mean... This is the lesson I must learn? We help each other out of scrapes. We act as a collective?"

Almost everyone seemed to nod, apart from Dusk, who looked as though he was about to protest. He had pressed his palms to the ground and lifted his buttocks, such that they only just kissed the earth. Dawn looked like he was readying himself to disagree with whatever Dusk had to say. But Dusk bit his lip, Dawn's face relaxed, and the group exhaled together.

A vote was taken, and it was agreed that the clans-folk would unite to re-gift Sunny's debt. A second vote was held, and the clans-folk agreed never to accept gifts from Hunter again.

But it was Hunter who had the final word:

"You people are too sceptical, too stuck in your ways, and it's going to cost you dearly."

He took a rifle, laid it down on the ground, and placed a few shots by its side.

"You don't believe me? No? Then take these. I'm not asking for anything in return. Factually: I only asked Sunny for that meat, so I'd have a reason to visit again. Keep your meat. Keep these shots and this powder. You're going to need them. Ah, yes! Ingest my words: The Sons of Empire are coming. The... Sons... Of... Empire... Are... Coming..."

# OUR ENDLESS NOMADIC DAYS

The drop of rain which landed on Hunter's palm, may have been the first in several lunar-cycles, but it was not to be the last.

The clans-folk understood what it meant: The rainy season was upon them. Their leafy shelters would no longer keep them dry, and animals would no longer visit the watering hole. It was almost time to leave.

They dismantled their huts, bundled up the posts and bamboo, wrapped them in banana leaves, and stored them in the branches of a leafy tree, high above the ground. They filled their water vessels, packed their possessions, and headed in the direction of the tribe's Big Camp.

They ran from the rain. But they also ran from something else: They ran from Hunter, from his threats and bribes, and from the things of which he spoke. For whilst they questioned what he had to say, they were in little doubt that he spoke in half-truths. Sunny had told them about the surveyor. The Sons of Empire *were* coming. They did pose a mortal threat.

***

It took the clans-folk several days to walk to the Big Camp; their home for the rainy season...

Two adults led the way, to protect the band from a frontal attack. The first, *Landscape*, had appointed herself a kind of de facto leader. She did not act like a petty tyrant, nor did she claim to possess any mystical powers. She only ever made unilateral decisions on the rare occasions when the clan was confronted by a sudden threat; when there was no time to form a parliament and hold a debate. Even then, her peers could ignore her orders. But Landscape was skilled. She was an expert navigator, who could read the land far better than anyone else. Even though she knew the route, she still took great care to check their position relative to the North Star; viewing that beacon through the gaps in her fingers, to make sure they were still on track. Landscape had a knack for finding the most appropriate places to cross the streams and bogs, which popped up in different places each year. She was known for her ability to sniff out the best spots to hunt, gather, find water and sleep. Landscape had fallen into this role by dint of skill, rather than any desire to lead. And she would fall out of this role, just as soon as they reunited with their tribe.

Behind Landscape and her companion, the clan's two geriatrics headed up the main group. Bent-backed and a little unstable, Mountain and Setting Sun set a sluggish pace; swaying from side to side, and stopping at regular intervals. They had to be carried whenever the path became too rocky or steep. But they were not considered a burden. Even though their hunting and gathering days were behind them, and even though they rarely made a fire or cooked, they were treated with the utmost respect. They were walking encyclopaedias; repositories of knowledge, able to answer the questions that no-one else could. When the clans-folk came across a fruit or berry they had never seen before, they consulted Mountain or Setting Sun, who always seemed to know what it was, and whether it could be eaten.

The clan's youngsters followed the elders. Then came the young mothers, holding their infants, and the other adults, who were carrying the clan's possessions, including their two new guns. A couple more hunters trailed this group, to protect the clan from behind.

Almost everyone gathered food as they went...

There were two schools of thought where such food was concerned. Some people, including Dawn, claimed that the ancestors had chosen this route because it passed by so many fruit trees and berry bushes, which had been there since the day Mother Nature gave birth to the world; when humans still had giant butterfly wings, and serpents still had legs. Others, including Dusk, believed that this idea was too good to be true. The members of their clan walked in a fairly straight line. They did not bend one way to visit a tree, and another way to visit a bush. Dusk argued that the clan had taken this route even *before* those plants existed. He believed that their ancestors had eaten whatever fruit and berries they could, and gone to the toilet by the side of the path; depositing the seeds from the food they had consumed. Those seeds had sprouted, and grown into the plants which now lined the route; bearing a variety of dates and satsumas, as well as two types of currants which only appeared at this time of the year, four lunar-cycles before the summer solstice.

The group was split, no opinion won out, and the debate rumbled on.

***

After traversing the contours of several hills, the clans-folk followed the lay of three seasonal streams. They set their traps, caught some small fish, ate those fish, speared some larger fish, and only moved on after a day of rest; arriving at the border of the *Great Expanse*; a yellowish plain, where sand danced atop the earth, and only a few plants had proved stubborn enough to survive.

At first glance, one could have mistaken this place for a waterless void, incapable of sustaining a pilgrim for much more than a day. This assumption was almost correct. The members of their clan could survive for *three* days before reaching water. It helped that they were acclimatised to their environment. They were experts at controlling their body temperature, by regulating their sweat. But it also helped that they knew exactly where to find their next drink.

Deep beneath the earth, there was an aquifer filled with *fossil water*; the remains of the snow which had melted towards the end of the previous Ice Age. That water could be accessed via a network of wells, which had been dug by the clan's ancestors, over the course of several lunar-cycles. It was hard labour. But their efforts were rewarded with a form of immortality, because the water sources they created were named after *them*. When their descendants cut across this desolate expanse, zigzagging from one well to the next, they repeated their names as they went; travelling from *Parrot's Well* to *Daybreak's Well*, and so on; stopping there to drink, and refill their vessels, whilst giving homage to the person who had dug that well.

They used some other methods to gather water...

Whilst here in this desert, they dug up cold stones from beneath the ground, just before sunrise, and waited for the dew to form on their surface. Whenever they visited a forest, they rose early to siphon the droplets which appeared on the larger leaves. They followed the lay of the land; knowing that water always sought the lowest point, and that if a seasonal stream were to form, it would do so in these natural valleys. They looked for the greenest vegetation; a sure sign of water. They tracked the birds, and the trails left by animals. And they stopped at two oases; relaxing in the shade of the surrounding palms, and using their nets to catch fish.

The clans-folk, therefore, were equipped to survive in this inhospitable terrain. They had filled their water containers, and were picking a path from one well to the next; using the baskets they had made from reeds, to carry the ferns and cattails they gathered en route, and the meats they had smoked before leaving.

The two strangers they encountered were not nearly so prepared...

Although the members of their clan would never know it, these explorers had been part of a much larger expedition, which had set off with twenty-three mules and twenty-six horses; six wagons, filled with enough food to last them for many solstices; some tables, chairs, rockets and a Chinese gong. But their wagons had come apart almost as soon as they reached the desert, and they had been forced to dump most of their supplies; loading what they could onto their animals. Most of their companions had perished during the days which followed. Several of their animals had been killed for their meat. Now just two men remained. And, judging by the state of their lips, it appeared that it had been days since either had drunk any water.

Sunny's companions stopped short, staring at these men from a safe distance. It was almost impossible to know what they were thinking. Perhaps they were scared, or shocked, or confused. Judging by the tilt of their heads, and the furrows in their brows, it seemed that they were more curious than anything else. Sunny's peers had been thinking about the Sons of Empire, ever since Hunter had addressed the group. These mythical creatures had been the subject of several conversations. And now here they were in the flesh.

Yet these stumbling, bumbling wrecks did not resemble the kind of menaces of whom Hunter had spoken. They looked even frailer than the group's two geriatrics. They wore something peculiar on top of their heads, presumably because they had lost all their hair. They did not appear to have earned a single tattoo. And they smelled of monkey urine.

"They all have that aroma," Sunny explained. "Uncle Survey smelled the same."

It was hard to know how to respond. These men might not have appeared particularly *fearsome.* But they represented something *fearful.* They were not members of their own tribe, or one of the other tribes who resided in the neighbouring regions; people who looked and acted in a similar fashion to themselves. These strangers looked completely different. They wore different things. They came from an imaginary place, an unfathomable distance away. They represented a group of imperialists who had only been a *theoretical idea* up until this point; a concept spoken of in stories. Yet here they were in the flesh; a *physical reality.* There could be no avoiding the truth: The network of neighbouring tribes, which extended as far as the imagination would allow, were no longer the only tribes in existence, with the sole way of life on earth. Their entire world had become claustrophobic; cramped by the presence of a whole new set of people. It was difficult to breathe, impossible to move, and the idea of speech seemed utterly fanciful.

This explained the current standoff; a timeless sort of impasse, that could have lasted for moments, or days, or seasons. The Eagle Clan had little desire to measure time. They lived from event to event. And this present event had left them at a loss; paralysed by an infinity of doubt, and unable to form a response.

The impasse was only broken by Landscape, who tiptoed forwards, stopped, had second thoughts, remained in her new position, tiptoed forwards again, and stopped again; repeating this ritual several times, before arriving in front of the strangers.

She reached over her shoulder, removed a canteen made from an animal's bladder, unfastened the leather tie, and passed it to one of the strangers.

He drank the water.

Landscape's behaviour was unsurprising. It was their tribe's custom to offer hospitality to anyone they encountered. This was why they had allowed Hunter to speak at their camp. They took an entirely different approach to trade; to debt and obligations. But where *hospitality* was concerned, there was little doubt in their minds: They were obliged to be generous.

The man said something indecipherable.

Others followed in Landscape's footsteps, stepping forth, offering the water they had been carrying in an assortment of coconut shells, bamboo tubes, hollowed-out gourds, and goatskin satchels; donating what little food they had, and using their lips to point towards the nearest oasis.

The strangers drank all the water they were given.

There was a brief pause. And then one of the men performed a strange gesture. He clenched his fingers into a ball, whilst pointing his thumb in an upwards direction. Sunny was unsure how to react. Pointing upwards meant *midday*. But it was already late in the afternoon. The man's hand had formed a fist. But Sunny's instincts told him that this stranger was not angling for a fight. His eyes looked humble, despite this peculiar *upward-thumb*.

The other man made a different gesture. He connected his thumb and forefinger, to create an O, whilst fanning his other fingers, to create a K. Members of their tribe used a similar signal, whenever they wished to have sex. But these men did not seem particularly horny. Their groins were not bulging. And Sunny could not imagine why anyone would wish to have sexual relations with a person who looked quite so meek. That seemed a little perverted.

The strangers withdrew their hands and

smiled.

Sunny smiled back.

The strangers stood up, spoke a little more, without making themselves understood, pointed their fingers towards the oasis, pointed their *lips* in that same direction, smiled again, spoke again, and then ruffled around in their sacks.

Bang!

The explosion was so loud, so sharp, so sudden. Sunny's clans-folk had never experienced anything like it. They sprung up, instantaneously, and sprinted off at full speed; carrying their geriatrics, infants, and most of their possessions; forgetting their pot and a few other items; not turning back, not checking to see what had caused that blast, and not stopping until they were out of sight; hidden behind a ridge and a solitary bolder.

Those crazy strangers! Perhaps Hunter had been right all along. Why on earth and the ancestral realm would they wish to assault them with such a noise? What had the clans-folk done to offend them?

These questions would inspire several conversations, during the days which followed. Some people said the blast had been a threat.

Others said it was the result of an attack which had gone wrong. Some people said the strangers had wanted to eat them, or steal their skin, or turn them into rocks. Others said it was a strange, foreign way of saying "Thank-you". No-one guessed the truth: That it had all been a dreadful accident. What kind of person would produce such a noise *by mistake*?

The debate rumbled on, without a middle, and without an end.

***

Sparrow's stomach rumbled on...

The gunshot had spun him into a state of shock. He had still managed to flee in fear, along with the rest of the clan. But as soon as he had come to a stop, he had bent double, gagged on the air, and vomited over his toes. His peers had rushed to his aid, helping him to regain his composure. But they had given little more thought to the matter. Sparrow did not mention his other symptoms. And he did not appear to need assistance, until he was seen clutching himself, shivering, and turning a paler shade with each passing moment.

Was Sparrow undergoing a metamorphosis, transforming into a Son of Empire? His skin was certainly fading. His body was shrinking, and he had an overall aura of weakness. Perhaps this was why the stranger had fired a gun. It was a form of witchcraft; an act of psychological warfare, which would turn them all albino.

Sunny kept his thoughts to himself, whilst Health got to work. The clan's herbalist inspected Sparrow, and pondered his symptoms, before declaring that his kidneys were still suffering from the aftereffects of shock.

She dispatched a couple of search parties to gather bombax.

The first group returned soon after, bringing a basketful of leaves, which Health turned into a tea. The second group reappeared much later; carrying some bark and fruit. Health burnt the bark, mashed up the ashes with the fruit, and fed the concoction to Sparrow.

Sunny was not surprised. Health *always* knew which plant to use, no matter the ailment. He had seen her use ginger to soothe respiratory complaints, spear grass to fight off impotency, turmeric to combat inflammation, devil-pepper to treat hypertension, clove basil to stop diarrhoea, papaya seed to kill parasites, and aloe vera to heal skin disease. Health had learnt these things by observing her mother; a woman who also carried a supply of herbal aspirin, which she made from meadowsweet; an antimalarial, which she made from cinchona; and a good supply of neem, an anti-inflammatory, which she used to heal everything from fungal infections to liver complaints. Had it been necessary, Health would have known just how to use acanthus to treat syphilis, amaranth to treat abdominal pains, and dogbane to treat filarial worms. She knew how to extract all the active ingredients; how to make infusions, lotions, charcoals, snuffs, poultices and gruels.

But such things were never enough on their own. Members of their tribe believed that ailments were not only physical. They also had a *supernatural* cause. They might be inflicted by a jealous ancestor. Or they might be a lesson from Mother Nature; a way of reminding a person not to neglect their spiritual, social or moral duties. Because of this, illnesses had to be cured by *spiritual means*, as well as by medicine; through divination, incantation, sacrifice, exorcism or libation.

Hence, just as soon as Sparrow had consumed the bombax, Health took the clan's diving rods; a flat set of bones, bound together with leather; and hurled them at one tree after another. She continued until she found a tree that satisfied her; remaining there for quite a while, slashing and thrashing its trunk.

Only once she had finished communing with the spirit world, did she return to the group. She declared that the ancestors had accepted her pleas, and would allow the medicine to take effect, so long as they sacrificed a rabbit.

This inspired a brief but heated discussion...

Dusk insisted that they set their traps, retreat and wait:

"Positively! It's the only method we've ever used to catch rabbits."

Hearing his rival's voice, Dawn was propelled into a vertical position, by a force he could do little to withstand. He held four fingers to the side of his head, and flicked his palm towards his peers; the gesture they made when responding to a stupid remark. And he spoke with uncharacteristic speed:

"Negatively! We can't afford to waste time, sitting about, doing nothing, hoping for our traps to fill themselves. We must attack those rabbits with our spears."

Rather than take sides, the clans-folk agreed to do *both* these things. And, when neither method was successful, they settled down for the night, telling stories beneath the moonless sky.

They tried once more the following day, failed again, fell asleep again, awoke on the second morning, found a rabbit in one of their traps, offered it up to the ancestors, and checked on Sparrow.

Sunny, for his part, was far from convinced. He had enjoyed Health's theatrics. When she bounded from tree to tree, he had clapped and stamped along. But he could not be sure if it had made the slightest difference.

Perhaps another factor was at play. Sparrow had needed *time*; time to rest, recuperate, and allow the medicine to take effect. Perhaps this was why Health had demanded a rabbit. It was a stalling tactic, designed to give Sparrow the time he needed to recover. Or, then again, perhaps it was not.

One thing was clear: The colour had returned to Sparrow's cheeks. He no longer looked like the strangers they had met in the desert.

Health picked some grass. She fashioned it

into a talisman, to ward off evil spirits; tied it around Sparrow's chest, and declared that they were ready to depart.

***

The clans-folk wandered for several days and several nights...

They discussed the gunshot, Sparrow's illness, and Dawn's ridiculous plan to hunt rabbits with spears. They talked about the bushes, streams and trees; recounting ancient tales they had heard a hundred times before, and new stories which they invented as they spoke.

At the midway point of their journey, they stopped off to visit their ancestral forest. This was the place their spirits went to exist, once their bodies had succumbed to death. It was a sacred place, the closest that mortals ever came to the ancestral realm. And it was a bountiful place. It contained the plants they used to make the poisons they daubed on their arrowheads, and the plants they believed were *selectively* poisonous; causing liars to vomit, without affecting honest folk.

They spent seven days in this place, making offerings to Mother Nature, singing hymns in praise of the dead, performing ghost dances, asking the ancestors for protection, and gathering a variety of plants. If someone had died during the dry season, they would have preserved their bodies, and brought them here to rest; hanging them from a branch, and leaving them for the eagles to eat. This act enabled their spirits to escape from their corpses. But no such deaths had occurred in the previous season. And so the clans-folk took their time. They only departed once everyone was ready; following Landscape and her companion, stopping whenever they fancied a rest, trekking for several days, before reaching their destination...

# STONE CIRCLES, TRIANGLES AND SQUARES

Entering the Big Camp was like stepping into another world...

Most of the other clans in their tribe had already been here for several days. They had pooled their resources, working together to construct this temporary city.

The clans which lived further inland had arrived first; travelling downstream in their canoes, before disembarking at the point where seven rivers converged. The clans which lived nearby had arrived soon after. But the Eagle Clan had to travel *upstream*; a far slower proposition. They were among the last people to arrive.

A few clans had erected communal tents, which were supported by wooden pillars and covered in hides. Others had erected teepees, arranging them in a circle. And some, such as Sunny's, had set up their homes in the man-made caves, which had been chipped out of the surrounding cliffs, over the course of countless generations. To reach them, one had to ascend a rocky incline, which had been used so much, the footholds had worn down into step-like shapes.

The walls of their caves were covered in art, which had been painted in a style which was aggressively unique. As if to exert their own identity, the members of their tribe did not carve the rockface, in the manner of the Northern Tribes. Nor did they depict any heroic figures; accentuating an individual's features, giving them motifs and staffs, or making them larger or brighter than their peers; as was the custom among a few of the tribes to the south. Their tribe had their own particular style. They painted flowing murals, in which everything extended out of something else, and *into* something else. There were fish, birds, bees and deer; a cornucopia of flowers, reeds, rivers and mountains; hunters, gatherers, fishers, navigators, healers, storytellers, artists, mothers, babies, children, spirits and ancestors. They were all depicted in the throes of an unceasing waltz, dancing into each other, with no beginning, nor any kind of end.

These galleries served a purpose. They were the tribe's *memory palace*. The images here might not have told the type of stories that outsiders would have been able to decipher. But they presented a mental pathway; providing visual cues, which triggered memories of events, places, routes, people and genealogies. These caves were not only a home. They were a historical picture book; one which grew larger each time the tribe convened.

The caves opened up onto a series of path-like ledges, which offered a panoramic view across the planes. From here, one could just about make out the distant remains of a line of pyramids, each a little taller than the last, and each submerged by forest; reclaimed by nature, after they had been abandoned by their makers. It was not possible to see the *Pyramid of the Sun*, the *Pyramid of the Moon*, or the seasonal lake which connected these ancient wonders. Nor was it possible to see most of the hill-like mounds which lay hidden in the forest beyond. These were smaller, older, and more numerous than the pyramids. No-one knew who had built them, or why they had been deserted. But they were a gentle reminder of a distant past, which could be seen from the clifftops, above these ledges and caves.

The city itself was neither old nor new. It was the descendent of several other cities, each of which had been created by one generation and destroyed by the next; a symbolic act, which allowed the tribe to reinvent itself afresh, without being held hostage to a history that was too permanent to control.

The debris from those abandoned cities was almost always reused...

No-one had ever seen a woolly mammoth. They had no idea who might have found a pair of their tusks. But this hadn't prevented the tribes-folk from putting them to good use; propping them upright, and using them to form the entrance to a communal tent. Several of the caves remained vacant, replaced by a newer cluster of caves lower down. Some limestone pillars lay felled. But they still displayed their artwork; showing off images of menacing animals with exposed genitalia, and beasts who had several human heads. Alongside these pillars, was a set of wooden posts, which had been erected to form a *Sacred Circle*. A gaggle of oxen and goats had been tied to these posts, which towered above the *Grand Meeting Place*; the home of the tribe's assembly.

Sunny intended to visit that parliament come nightfall. But right now, he was more concerned with an altogether different concern. Upon entering the camp, he had lost sight of Hope. It had taken him an age to track her down, and he had not been best pleased when he found her. Hope had been with another man. Someone a little taller than Sunny. Someone slightly older, with bigger teeth and eyes. Sunny did not know this person, or what he had done to make Hope smile so much. But he was all too aware of his body's reaction. His stomach felt as though it had smashed through the base of his belly, and crashed down upon his feet; stapling him to the ground, rendering him unable to move and unable to intervene.

This sensation faded with time. So what if Hope had another lover? They had spent plenty of time together during their pilgrimage. He did not own the woman. She had the right to take as many lovers as she desired. *And so did he.*

Later that day, Sunny walked through the city alone, attempting to get his bearings; to match up the position of each tent, with his memory of where they had been the last time he was here. Everything seemed the same but different; in roughly the same place, but not *exactly* the same place. Everything seemed slightly larger or smaller. The colours had faded, or were slightly brighter. The hides had been repaired or replaced. Some new things had materialised, and some old things had vanished from view.

Much to his annoyance, Songbird's clan appeared to fall into the second category. He could not find them, no matter how much he searched.

Sunny did, however, spot another person whom he recognised; a lad from the Eel Clan, with whom he had played as a child. Sunny approached that young man and said "Hello", only to realise that it was not the person he had supposed. This youth had the same build, height and shape. He wore his hair in the same manner, scrunched up into a ball. His skin was also covered in tattoos of stick-like figures, which were supposed to ward off evil spirits. But this youngster had darker, more mysterious eyes. His ears were more erect.

The lad did not voice a reply. Sensing Sunny's needs, he beckoned him with a curl of his index finger, and led him to a distant cavern; a dark, silent place, far away from the hubbub of the camp.

As soon as they entered the cave, the lad

pushed Sunny up against a wall. That act was both soft and hard; gentle enough to be resisted, as affectionate as a caress, and yet firm enough to fold Sunny into position.

The *thud-thud-thud* of a thunderstorm echoed around that rocky room, growing a little louder each time it rebounded off a surface. There was something deliciously comforting about that sound. The rains might have been gushing down, flooding the valley outside. But it was dry in here; it was cosy, warm and safe.

The lad leaned in. He paused, just before he made contact; giving Sunny a moment to resist. Then he brushed his nose over Sunny's. He waited a little, before nuzzling Sunny's cheek. And he waited again, before sniffing the roots of Sunny's hair.

Sunny was confused, but not concerned. He had not planned this. He was not entirely sure what was happening. But he had wanted a sexual encounter. It seemed that he was about to get a sexual encounter. Who was he to complain?

And who was he to resist? Hope's snub had left him feeling lusty and enraged. These emotions had overpowered him; propelling him here, and dragging him into this nervy, illicit experience.

Sunny had never thought about having sex with another man. He understood the benefit, from a social point of view. He was building a bond with a member of another clan. This was an act of friendship and diplomacy. But he was unsure of the deed itself. What was he supposed to do? Was it safe? Was it physically possible?

Sunny gave himself to the moment. He cleared his mind, threw his arms upon his partner's shoulders, flung that man around, thrust *him* against the wall, sniffed his face, and nibbled his eyebrows with more venom than ever before. The taste was exquisite. The metallic flavour of blood, and the woody texture of hair, formed a cocktail between his lips. But the boy's face was a mess; all saliva and detritus. Sunny could not stand to look. And so he jolted downwards, burying himself in the man's chest, and sucking his nipples in the manner that satisfied Hope.

His partner winced, gasped, composed himself and smiled.

He waited for Sunny's consent, before taking Sunny's penis in his hand.

He tried to be tender, and he tried to be firm,

but he could not inspire an erection, no matter how hard he tried.

Sunny closed his eyes, to hide from his shame. But his partner just gave him a silent embrace, laid him down on the ground, removed his loincloth, and rode him as though he were a woman.

The agony! Sunny felt violated. The most private entrance to his body had been torn wide open, and a foreign object had been thrust inside his personal sanctum. It took a great effort not to scream. He bit his lip so hard, it removed a layer of skin.

The discomfort departed, almost as quickly as it arrived. Sunny felt stretched, his anus burned, but there was pleasure in the pain. His prostate was being pounded, in an almost aggressive manner, but it was also being massaged; triggering a sensation which reverberated through his body, sparking every nerve-ending, and covering his skin with fizziness and wonder. Sunny felt like a born-again virgin, doing something which was both new *and* familiar. It was far more intimate than any sex he had experienced before. He was opening himself up to another person, in a whole new way. And it was far more euphoric. He did not cum, nor did he form an erection. But he felt sexy, fabulous and queer.

*** 

The evening's parliament had already begun by the time Sunny took his place alongside the members of the Eagle Clan, on the grassy slopes of the Grand Meeting Place. In the centre of that basin, the *Sacred Circle* was occupied by the tribe's *representatives*. One delegate from each clan was sitting on the ground. These men and women, who had been elected by their clans-folk, would make decisions on behalf of the tribe. Only they were allowed to vote, and their votes had to be unanimous if they were to pass.

Sunny was not alone. Almost every adult in the tribe was watching from this bank. They were not just passive observers. They were permitted to make speeches, contribute information, ask questions, argue in favour or against the motions, and propose motions of their own. They could not vote themselves, but they could persuade the representatives to vote one way or the other.

The Sacred Circle was shrouded by a fog of smoke. Sunny supposed that the representatives must have been here for quite a while, smoking themselves into a state of tranquillity. This was the norm. Members of their tribe believed that tobacco helped to appease the passions and sharpen the intellect, enabling smokers to dissect even the most complex of issues. Back in the time of the *Early Ancestors*, tobacco (and coffee) had only been used by shamans, who took highly concentrated doses, to induce the altered states of consciousness which were required to commune with the spirit world. These days, however, tobacco was consumed by almost everyone. The tribes-folk went to great lengths to produce that crop, planting massive quantities on the plains above the cliffs, and harvesting it towards the end of the rainy season.

By the time Sunny arrived, the delegates were already discussing the temporary security force, which was being formed to maintain order in the camp. No such force existed at any other time, and this one would be abolished as soon as the camp was abandoned. If an individual or clan did not approve of such an arrangement, they were free to leave. But so long as they remained, they were obliged to follow the rules which were being established tonight.

Sunny spotted their clan's representative, Serenity, who was sitting with his back to the clan, focusing on the only person who was standing: An elderly lady named *Bear*. Bear was a rotund individual, plumper than any member of the Eagle Clan. Even her cheeks were pudgy. And they seemed to glow. Her skin was reflecting the fire, which was splashing out ribbons of amber light.

Like the other members of the tribe, Bear wore a loincloth. But hers was made from a single length of fur, which also covered one of her breasts. Unlike anyone else, two streaks of ash had been smeared across her chest; they extended down from her shoulders, before meeting around her navel. Sunny understood what this meant: Bear was tonight's chairperson. This explained why she was standing. And this explained why she was addressing the tribe:

"We propose that no individual or clan shall be allowed to hunt alone, whilst the representatives are arranging a tribal hunt. No individual or clan shall be allowed to keep their own supply of meat or hides. These items must be handed to the Women's Council for redistribution. No individual or clan shall be allowed to send war parties, or arrange migrations, that have not been approved by the representatives."

If anyone had opposed these proposals, they would have taken this opportunity to speak. Such objections were not uncommon. Tribesfolk experienced three different systems of governance; whilst living in their Small Camps, in this Big Camp, and whilst living as nomads, journeying between the two. Each society had its own customs, each of which had a habit of evolving from one season to the next. The tribe was flexible; willing to debate and amend its rules.

It would not do so tonight...

Bear's comment was met with a prolonged silence, which she took as a show of support. She was not particularly surprised. A fairly similar set of guidelines had been adopted at every Big Camp, for over a generation. They were only being put to the vote tonight, to regain the group's consent. From this day on, everyone would be expected to obey these rules, because they were *their* rules, which *they* had approved at this meeting.

The proposal was passed with a show of

hands.

Bear closed her eyes, to contemplate the significance of this vote. She waited for the emotion to fade from her face, slowed her breathing, and allowed her chest to inflate with a grandiose rhythm.

She only spoke when the moment was right:

"We propose that a security force be established, to ensure these rules are followed, and to maintain order during hunts, festivities, ceremonies and parliaments. This force shall have the right to cane, insult or exile any individual or clan who endangers the wellbeing of the tribe."

This was also an old proposal. A similar motion had been passed at every Big Camp that Sunny could remember.

It was met with silence and voted through.

Bear continued:

"Now we must select the security force itself. I propose we don't choose a clan that has wielded power in living memory. We should exclude the Hawks, Cranes, Eagles..."

Again, Bear's proposal was met with silence. And again, there was an uncontested vote. No-one wanted a single clan to form a dynasty.

"I propose the Sharks."

This time, a voice *did* break the silence, after the customary pause:

"Proposition opposed!"

It was Summit who had spoken. Tall and long-limbed, with an extended neck and narrow face, Summit was Shark Clan's representative.

"It'd be an honour to be your security force. But we're a humble clan, no better than any other. We're poor hunters and mediocre gatherers; a motley band, whose tents are a little shabby, and whose children are skinnier than most. What right do we have to guard our aunties, uncles, cousins, nieces and nephews; most of whom are more honourable than ourselves?"

It was just the type of response Bear had envisioned. She would not have wished to empower a clan which actually coveted power. She had selected a clan she supposed would be awed by the role; who would act humbly, out of a sense of duty, and not for personal gain.

It was a pantomime. And Bear was happy to play her part:

"In that case, we'll have to appoint the Rabbits."

The Rabbit Clan's representative shook her head.

"I see. Okay then. It'll have to be the Frogs."

The Frog Clan's representative shook his head.

Bear threw her hands in the air.

"What's a poor chairperson to do? Sister Summit: I beg of you. For the good of the tribe, in the name of the ancestors: Please guard our precious camp."

Summit bowed her head, paused, slowly lifted her gaze, and beseeched the group:

"Will any other clan volunteer?"

There was silence.

"Blow the mountains over! I suppose we don't have a choice."

A vote was held, and the Sharks were elected.

*\*\**

Sunny struggled to pay attention...

The representatives were arranging a hunt, deciding when to meet and where to go; who would act as spotters, spearers and messengers. But Sunny's thoughts kept drifting back to that afternoon's encounter.

What had they done? Was it even sex? How could he play the part of a woman, when he was clearly a man? When he enjoyed playing the part of a man? He had not even formed an erection. Yet the whole thing had felt so illicit, so exciting and wild. Should he tell Hope? Would she be jealous? Would she want to join them? Would she even care?

The representatives agreed upon a plan which Sunny did not quite catch.

Everyone exhaled.

It seemed the assembly was about to disband. And Sunny, for his part, was relieved. He was tired of these formalities, and keen for the dancing to begin. But when Bear asked if anyone had something to add, Serenity rose to his feet.

"We were approached by an exiled brother," he said; looking around at the gathered masses, before turning back to face the other representatives. "This man delivered a grave warning: A strange and dangerous people are on their way. Their skin is the colour of sand."

Bear nodded, whilst responding with a single word:

"Wogies?"

This comment split the tribe. A handful of clans hummed in agreement. But Serenity frowned; opening his palms, to invite an explanation.

"Ah, yes, I suppose they must be *Wogies*...

"You don't know the story?... No?... Okay then. Please allow me to explain... In Ancient Times, back when our ancestors had only just lost their wings, our tribe was flown to these lands in the beaks of giant birds. When we arrived, two tribes were already here. The first, the *Zogies*, were a warlike tribe who we vanquished in battle. The second, the *Wogies*, were a peaceful tribe, whom we enslaved. They were, as you put it, 'The colour of sand'. And they were knowledgeable. They taught us how to cure hides, weave baskets and build canoes; how to hunt, fish, farm and gather.

"Esteemed sisters: Those were happy days. But they weren't destined to last. Our ancestors, you must understand, allowed themselves to get carried away. They forced the Wogies to perform too many tasks... Things became so unfair, so unjust, that the Wogies eventually snapped. They couldn't stand to be enslaved any longer.

"After the Grand Feast, which brought the Big Camp to a close, those slaves made a dash for freedom. Our ancestors tried to catch them. But they'd become so fat and cumbersome, they were unable to maintain the chase. We never saw the Wogies again."

Bear paused before concluding:

"It appears that the Wogies must have returned, after all these generations. They must have come to reclaim this land."

Serenity scrunched his lips. He was almost certain that Bear was mistaken. But he was loath to confront such a respected individual, in front of her peers, without any evidence to support his hunch.

"You may be correct. You usually are. But, by the good earth, one thing is certain: If these strangers are Wogies, then they've changed beyond recognition. They're no longer a peace-loving tribe. They've killed hundreds-of-thousands of people. And they plan to come for us; speeding along, atop animals they call 'Horses', and shooting this thing they call a 'Gun'."

Kitten passed a rifle to Serenity, who held it aloft; turning three-hundred-and-sixty degrees, so that everyone could see.

A question rang out from the banks:

"It has no sharp point, no blade, no arrows. What threat could it possibly pose?"

Having anticipated such a challenge, Serenity

beckoned towards a thicket. After a few moments of hushed suspense, Sparrow, who had made a full recovery, emerged with a bearded goat.

He had acquired that animal from the Dog Clan; exchanging it for three spears, and a promise to provide a fourth. The Dog Clan was the only clan in the tribe that kept a herd of goats, which they moved from place to place. Each clan was individual in this respect. Songbird's clan kept oxen; moving them about in a similar fashion. Other clans kept chickens or guinea fowl; leaving them in their Small Camps, whenever they moved about. Some clans managed orchards or grew crops. Others bred fish or frogs.

Sparrow led the goat into the circle.

Serenity lifted the rifle to his shoulder, pointed its muzzle towards the goat, and gazed along the barrel.

Bang!

The explosion was unlike anything the tribes-folk had ever experienced. It inspired a collective gasp. A couple of people screamed. Most shuffled backwards, involuntarily, unaware of their own reactions. But very few people looked away. Their eyes remained fixed on the goat, whose head exploded in slow-motion; spraying various amounts of blood, in a multitude of directions. The goat's body stood firm for the briefest of moments. Then its knees buckled. It seemed it might regain its composure. Then its legs crumpled, and its body slunk to the ground.

Serenity turned towards the direction from which the challenge had come, gave a look which seemed to say, "Does that answer your question?", waited for a response which was not forthcoming, waited a little longer, and then addressed the rest of the tribe:

"These aliens aren't like us. Their skin is the colour of sand. They sit high on their horses, and slaughter their enemies using these guns. The ancestors know that this is true. The Sons of Empire... The *Wogies* have already killed hundreds-of-thousands of natives; people like you and me. They believe this land is theirs."

After the appropriate period of silence, Bear stood to respond:

"So, what do you suggest we do?

"If they attack us, we may have no choice but to defend our homes. Still, let's not forget the past: When I was a youth, we waged war on the

Western Tribes. And do you know what happened? People said we'd 'Won' the war; we'd proved we were great warriors, capable of vanquishing any foe... Esteemed sisters: I remember a different story. I remember the day a brother died. I remember the pain in our great auntie's eyes, when she took her final breath. Almost half our tribes-folk perished. And for what? That war didn't bring peace. We endured many more skirmishes during the seasons and solstices which followed. Nor did it improve our lives. Things returned to the way they'd been before.

"Brother Serenity: We endure such conflicts every generation or two. Our grandmother told me of a similar war, with a Northern Tribe, back when she was a child. Her mother spoke of clan-on-clan battles. If war comes, we might have to fight. But we'd be wise not to court a conflict.

"Honourable tribes-folk: We've always had two freedoms. The freedom to disobey aspiring Big Men, and the freedom to abandon those Uncle Crows... It seems we cannot disobey these Wogies. They'll wage an unwinnable war. And neither can we flee. If we do, they'll chase us on these *horses*. If we hide, they'll find us, or we'll starve... So, what are you actually proposing? Are you asking us to perform a ghost dance? Are you suggesting we make an offering to Mother Nature?"

Serenity nodded at the last suggestion, before gesturing towards the goat.

Bear continued:

"Have you even seen these wonderful Wogies?"

Serenity nodded again.

"And did they kill you?"

Serenity refused to be ruffled by such a question.

"If they let *you* live, what makes you suppose they intend to come for *us*?"

This time Serenity did respond:

"Why has anyone ever come for us? They want our land, trees, animals, sisters and brothers."

Bear thumbed her chin:

"And these strange aliens you met, did they take your sisters or brothers?"

Serenity shook his head.

"Why ever not?"

"They were weak. The poor things hadn't drunk in days."

"Esteemed brother: You say they're a threat, with the power to kill hundreds-of-thousands. And then you tell us they can't even care for themselves? Even a baby knows how to drink."

Bear allowed the semblance of a smile to form along the edges of her cheeks. She folded her arms, leaned back, and gazed out across the crowd.

"So, Brother Serenity: What do you propose we do, to protect ourselves against this 'Threat'? These Wogies? These descendent of peaceful slaves? These people of whom we know so little; just the tales you've heard from an *exile*?"

Serenity closed his eyes, opened them slowly, and whispered his response:

"I don't wish to propose a motion. I'm just a humble messenger, gifting you this information."

# THE HUNT

Their tribe contained somewhere between fifty and a hundred clans. The exact number varied, because the clans tended to split whenever they grew too large, and whenever factions began to form. People moved from one clan to another. Some found lovers at the Big Camp, and decided to join their clans; an act which prevented inbreeding. And clans also disbanded; when their members struggled to reproduce, when they succumbed to attack, and when they suffered from fatal diseases.

Each clan was named after a mammal, amphibian, reptile, fish or bird. These were known as the clan's *spirit animals*. The clans loved and protected these creatures. They performed rituals, to ask Mother Nature to defend them. And they attempted to create an environment in which they might flourish.

The clans also believed that their spirit animals *took care of them*. Whenever a member of the Eagle Clan spotted an eagle overhead, they felt strangely reassured. They believed that their ancestors' spirits lived on within those birds; that they were watching over them, and protecting them from harm.

The neighbouring tribes were also split into clans, which all bore similar names. Whilst relationships between these *tribes* could be tempestuous, there were times of peace and times of war, relations with these sister *clans* tended to be good. Should Sunny's clan ever come into contact with another Eagle Clan, they would welcome them with open arms; sharing everything they owned: Their food, their land and their bodies. The love-making could go on for days. The members of one Eagle Clan were essentially married to the members of *all* the Eagle Clans. It was only natural for them to partake in sexual relations.

The clans retained some individual features...

The Eagle Clan did not care for any livestock, but the Dog Clan raised goats. The Dog Clan only captured small animals, like rabbits and fish. The Eagle Clan targeted larger animals, such as boar and antelope.

The Eagle Clan lived in banana-leaf huts. Others lived in mud huts, teepees, caves or tents.

In some clans, the men all hunted and the women all gathered. In others, the roles were reversed. In most, the roles were mixed;

everyone did the tasks they enjoyed the most.

A few of the clans kept pets; the orphaned offspring of the creatures they had hunted for food. They treated them in much the same way they treated their children; feeding them, lavishing them with affection, and taking them wherever they went. But different clans cared for different pets. A couple had adopted showy birds. Others had adopted small primates. They cared for dogs, cats, pigs, chickens and goats.

Each clan had its individual quirks. But each clan was a part of a greater whole: The tribe. When they convened, here at the Big Camp, their members shared their knowledge; speaking of their customs, practices and skills. Sometimes, they inspired other clans to imitate their ways.

There were other reasons for the clans to unite. Together, they were strong. They could repel attacks from rival tribes. And they could launch successful hunts, on a scale that would have been impossible within their tiny groups...

*** 

The ground was wet with rain. The air smelled of pollen and molasses.

By the time Sunny arrived, the clan's best weapons had already been claimed. He was given the only remaining spear. Its stone blade was smaller than most. The flint had been sharpened so many times, over the course of so many seasons, that it had gradually worn away. But the handle was sturdy, and a new leather strap had been used to bind the spearhead to that pole.

Sunny was grateful for the weapon, although he would have preferred a bow, like the one his uncle had managed to wangle. The lad he met the previous day, had both a spear *and* a bow. But Sunny thought better than to complain. A few members of their clan did not have any weapons at all. One clan only had ten spears between them.

There was inequality here, the likes of which Sunny rarely experienced in the dry season. But that inequality of *property* was too small to provoke an inequality of *power*. People with two weapons could not give orders to people who did not have any. When it came to the hunt, everyone had to perform their task together, as *equal* members of a team.

The hunt began with a process of reconnaissance. A few people had already spotted a herd of buff antelope, a little further to the north. Their presence had been verified by the members of a different clan, who had found hoofprints and faeces.

The plan was to surround the entire pack of that large, ox-like variety of antelope, and drive them over a cliff. Unlike more aggressive kinds of antelope, this particular breed was not known to fight back. Its members tended to *flee* from danger. They were a herd animal, who did not scatter when under attack. And so they could be manoeuvred as a group; pushed towards the cliffs together.

But first, they had to be located...

A team of elders and adolescents went to gather plants, and to fish in the rivers; to ensure the tribes-folk would have something to eat, even if the hunt was unsuccessful. A few clans remained in their temporary city, to protect it from attack, and to babysit those children who were too big to carry, but too small to hunt. And a second set of clans were positioned along the bottom of the cliffs. Should a herd of antelope be forced over the precipice, the members of these clans would be responsible for spearing any animals who survived the fall.

Everyone else marched to the place where the

antelope had been spotted, before spreading out across the plains. They dispersed a few sighters, to locate their prey, and settled down to wait.

The Eagle clan had been allocated a position among a brambly grove, where a cluster of trees provided cover from the sun and rain.

They had been paired with the Parrot Clan.

Sunny recognised a few individuals from that clan, whom he supposed must have been representatives at previous camps. But the majority of these people were strangers to him.

The elders, however, appeared to be on familiar terms. They chatted about a long-forgotten drought, a battle with another tribe, and what they dubbed, "The Time of the Immortal Hawks".

To while away the time, a few of the women, including Sunny's mother, began to play *patolli*...

Most of the females in the Eagle Clan, wore necklaces strung with beads they had carved from the eggshells of giant flightless birds. Most of the women in the Parrot Clan, wore beads they had made from bone. When they played Patolli, each woman staked six of their own beads, in the hope that they might win six of their opponent's.

To play, each contestant threw five wooden tokens. Their score was determined by the number of tokens which landed with the marked-side facing up. If three tokens displayed such a mark, the player moved their bead three squares around an x-shaped leather board. The aim was to circumnavigate the entire board, landing on your opponent's home square, without overshooting that target. Every time a player achieved this goal, they were allowed to take one of their opponent's beads, and add it to their necklace. But if a player landed on a square which was marked with an O, they had to give that bead to their opponent. And if a player landed on one of the four shaded squares, and their opponent then landed on top of them, their opponent got to keep both beads.

To win, players needed a small amount of skill and a large amount of luck. Much of it came down to the roll of the tokens. Although, watching on, Sunny reckoned that there must have been a certain technique when it came to throwing those pieces. His mother seemed to roll an awful lot of fours and fives.

Although Sunny did not know it, cheating was

relatively common. Anyone who could cheat *without being caught*, was afforded a great deal of respect. But anyone who was caught, could expect a torrid time. Fights had been known to break out when a cheater was exposed. People had been killed.

The games played on this day proved a peaceful affair. Most participants won as many beads as they lost. But the effect was clear for all to see: By the time the sun began to set, the majority of the women had lost around half their beads. They had won around half of their opponents'. Their necklaces now contained a fairly even mixture of bone and eggshell beads.

Sunny supposed this had been the intention all along. The clans had not wished to do anything so grubby as to trade; to barter, or to put themselves in each other's debt. But they had wanted to exchange their beads. Games of chance, such as patolli, provided a social means by which this could be achieved; through gambling rather than trade. It had also helped to pass the time, which was just as well, since the sky was turning from pink, and the spotters had still not located the herd.

\*\*\*

They had better luck the following morning...

Once again, the tribes-folk rose at dawn. They were delayed by a storm, waited for the rains to pass, and then headed to their allocated positions. Only this time, the sighters *did* spot the buff antelope, who had strayed a little further than the tribes-folk had anticipated. A messenger was dispatched, to ensure the clans beneath the cliffs were in the correct position. And two more messengers were dispatched, to inform the nearest groups along the line. These clans sent their own emissaries, to alert the next groups along. Before long, the news had been relayed down to the furthest outposts, and everyone had come together; forming a chain which contained over two-thousand individuals.

That chain advanced in single file.

Sunny, who was caught in the middle, had no choice but to follow the lead of those on either side. He had taken part in similar hunts, during the previous rainy seasons, so he knew they were effective. Yet he felt a little helpless. He had no say in proceedings; no option but to surrender himself to the process, for the overall good of the hunt.

Although he could not appreciate it from

such a distance, the tribes-folk at the top of the chain had headed north, going well beyond the antelope, before turning back towards the cliffs; bending the cordon around the herd.

Hoot!

That sound, created by blowing through a ram's horn, was the signal for the tribes-folk to advance. Everyone reacted, almost instinctively; perhaps because they had done this so many times before, or perhaps because they had become a machine; a singular entity, propelled by its own momentum.

They jogged in a slow and steady fashion.

It took quite some time before Sunny saw the herd. And even then, he did not make a sound. His peers were still silent. Who was he to act alone?

The antelope were clearly aware of the humans who had surrounded them. The tribes-folk were an obvious presence; holding their weapons in their right hands, whilst using their left hands to grip their neighbour. But those animals did not seem overly concerned. The hunters were a good distance away. They had slowed to a walking pace. The antelope maintained their distance, meandering towards the cliffs, without feeling a need to panic.

A young antelope bolted, and the others gave chase.

The tribes-folk responded; pursuing their prey, whilst attempting to maintain the cordon. They might have gone faster, but their pace was set by the tribe's slowest members; a few of the older adults, a man with dwarfism, and a woman who had Down syndrome.

The buff antelope ran beyond the limits of the cordon.

The fastest sprinters, positioned at either end of the line, sprinted free of their peers. They were not as quick as their targets, but they held out their spears and maintained a steady formation, whilst the antelope veered from left to right; zig following zag following zig.

The antelope screeched to a halt, as soon as they reached the clifftop. Their hooves clung to the ground, causing their torsos to overshoot their legs. The momentum almost carried them over.

The tribes-folk closed in, encroaching a single step at a time. Now they had reassembled. Now they had closed the gaps. Now they had squeezed in so tight, half the hunters were forced to move back.

A single voice called out to the valley:

"Are you in position?"

"Yes!"

"Yes!"

"Almost... Wait for it... Yes!"

The first voice counted down:

"Three... Two... One..."

On what would have been the count of "Zero", the hunters burst into motion; dashing towards their prey, waving their weapons, and screaming at the top of their lungs.

It was electrifying. Sunny was both petrified *and* invigorated. Scared of the sound, which was primaeval, hellish, infernal and raw. And buoyed by the adrenaline of the chase; that fight-or-flight impulse, which accompanied every hunt, and which would surely secure them the food they needed to survive.

Sunny hurried ahead at a pace which put undue pressure on his gangly frame. His lanky legs struggled to find the space they required, pinned in too closely beneath his smallish stomach. He almost stumbled each time his feet made contact with the ground. His chest overshot his hips, or lurched backwards, or swayed from side to side.

He froze, stopping dead in his tracks, as everyone else rushed by.

Sunny had been paralysed by a sudden bolt of empathy. He was making eye contact with a lone animal; a creature who, like himself, was neither a child nor an adult, but somewhere in between. He felt that antelope's fear; surrounded by an onrushing army, with nowhere left to run; aware that its final moments were upon it, that there would be no escape, no hope, just the deep dark call of the abyss.

As that creature turned from the spear which was darting towards its head, Sunny felt an urge to turn. As that creature tumbled over the ledge, Sunny tumbled to the ground. And as he heard the hunters below, stabbing the animal through, he felt a stabbing pain in his chest.

*** 

The camp fizzed with tension.

The previous night, they had shared what little food the elders and adolescents had found: A few fish, a decent amount of fruit, and a small number of leafy vegetables. Some of the clans had eaten the food which remained from their journeys. But the others had called on the Dog

Clan to sacrifice their goats.

Each time such a proposal was made, the Dog Clan protested; casting the single vote required for the motion to fall. They were offered the first share of the tribe's hunt, extra meat, and all the hides they could carry. But still they voted "No". They said they might reconsider the request after a few more days, but they did not wish to be rushed.

Most of the tribes-folk accepted their decision. The Dog Clan had caught, domesticated, bred, fed and transported those goats. They retained the right to decide their fate.

But a few individuals were so hungry, their stomachs had overpowered their sense of duty to the tribe. They had stolen a goat, led it beyond the pyramids, killed it, and roasted it at what they supposed was a safe distance.

They would have gone unnoticed, had the wind not changed direction. But the wind *did* change direction. The smoke wafted back towards the camp, and the Shark Clan was sent to investigate. They found the perpetrators, returned them to the Sacred Circle, bound them to the wooden posts, and beat them with a branch. When they were done, they rounded up the other members of their clans, and caned them as well. They were considered responsible, because they had failed to control their peers.

By the time the Shark Clan had finished, their victims' backs were drizzled with blood. The mood was sombre. There was a collective acceptance that their behaviour had been wrong, and that a protection had to be performed. But the spectacle had left a bitter taste. The tribes-folk were unused to rough justice, even here in the Big Camp. So they remained a little shaken, even though they knew there would be no repeat of the previous night's events. The tribes-folk had killed three-hundred antelope, enough to feed them for twenty or thirty days.

Sunny washed his hands in a pile of intestines, and sat down to eat some food. He stared into the fire, whilst thinking about that caning, and about that poor creature, who had looked at him with such fear; as if to say, "Spare me, I'm just like you."

Did the meat he was eating come from that same creature? It seemed unlikely, but it remained a possibility. What right did they have to take that animal's life?

Sensing Sunny's pain, Hope squatted down by his side. It was the first time she had approached him in days.

She did not speak. Perhaps she could not find the right words. Or perhaps she had understood that no words were needed.

She took Sunny's hand; an act which inspired his legs to spasm. He dropped a chunk of meat, threw his arms around his lover, and held her tight; whilst their clans-folk finished their meals, and whilst several returned for another serving.

Sunny felt the warmth of Hope's love. Her embrace heated him from within. But he also felt vulnerable. This woman retained the power to lift him up, and the power to dump him down. She had avoided him for days. She might do so again.

He came to a sharp realisation: It was not good for him to be so emotionally dependent on a single individual. Hope had other men to whom she could turn, whenever it took her fancy. Sunny required a similar society of lovers.

The following day, he searched for the person he still called "The lad"; finally finding him in an abandoned cave, at the far end of the cliff. That young man was dancing with his kinfolk, performing a ritual to honour their ancestors.

The lad introduced himself, saying he was called *Beetle*, before explaining his clan's traditions: The Eel Clan honoured their ancestors, just like everyone else in the tribe. They lay their dead to rest in a tomb; a tradition which was practised by a few other clans. What marked them apart, was the way in which they decorated those corpses with bracelets and headbands.

Anyone who died during a full moon, was given the *special treatment*. Their bodies were adorned with headdresses encrusted with teeth, and topped off with a pair of antlers. The members of the Eel Clan danced for these lucky totems, each time the Big Camp convened. They gifted them with flowers, and asked for their protection.

Usually, the Eel Clan only performed these ceremonies a few times a season. But they had been visiting their tomb once a day, ever since Serenity had made his speech; chanting affirmations, and striking yoga-like poses; imploring their ancestors to protect them from the Wogies.

Beetle took Sunny by the hand, and led him to a newer, more secluded cave. The cavern they had used before, had been filled with antelope. Their carcasses were being stored in that cool dark place, to stave off decay.

Beetle and Sunny repeated their previous encounter.

Sunny still struggled to explain the sensation. It was nice to be held; to share an intimate embrace with another person. The moment of release felt pretty divine. But he could not form a full erection, no matter how hard he tried. His stomach did not react to Beetle in the way it reacted to Hope. It did not spin, or whizz, or whirl. The whole experience was fairly *nice*, and that was good enough. But it was not *spectacular*. It was not life-affirming. It was not divine.

***

Beetle and Sunny met up in that cave, every day or two, for almost an entire lunar-cycle. They appreciated each other's company. They enjoyed each other's touch. And they both felt a need to escape from the throng of the camp.

That cave was their sanctuary; a place where they could be alone. Until one afternoon, when their solitude was interrupted...

Three condescending tuts reverberated around the cave:

*Tut.* Long pause. *Tut.* Longer pause. *Tut.*

Those tuts turned into echoes, which transformed into a series of disembodied words:

"You shall not lie with a male as with a female.... Leviticus Eighteen... If a man lies with a man as with a woman, both of them have committed an abomination. They shall surely be put to death... Leviticus Twenty."

Sunny had recognised all the words apart from "Leviticus". But the speech seemed laboured, as though the speaker was taking special care to select each individual word, before considering the next. And there was something else: The tone. It was drenched in condescension. Whoever was speaking, was standing in an elevated position, raining down words from above, drenching his speech in spittle and scorn:

"The unrighteous will not inherit the Kingdom of God. Don't be deceived! Neither the sexually immoral, the idolaters, the adulterers, the homosexuals, the thieves, the gluttons, the drunkards, the foul-mouthed, nor the swindlers, will inherit the Kingdom of God. Flee from sexual immorality! Every other sin a person commits is outside the body. But the homosexual sins against his *own* body!

"Don't you know that your body is a temple of the Holy Spirit within you, gifted to you by God? You are not your own, for you were bought with a price. So glorify God in your body... Corinthians Six."

That voice! It was making his head pulsate.

In the first place, he did not appreciate the interruption. Sex was supposed to be a private affair. Who was this man to intercede? And, in the second place, why was it any of his business? Sunny had not done anything wrong.

Yet that voice had an effect which Sunny could not shrug. Sunny felt... He had to pause before he could define the emotion which was tickling the gaps between his fingers. He thought it might be regret. But why? He had not harmed another person... It could have been remorse. But he quickly dismissed the notion. Why should *he* feel remorse? He was the innocent victim of an unwanted intrusion... No. It was something else: *Shame.* Sunny felt ashamed of what he had done; not for any rational reason, but simply because this man *had made him feel ashamed*. And he felt hatred: Hatred for this man, with his patronising voice, which had generated this negative emotion.

Sunny leapt to his feet, still naked, and bounded towards the exit.

Now he was blinded by the whiteness of light. Now he saw the silhouette of a man. Now he formed a fist. Now he pulled his elbow behind his shoulder. And now he froze.

His soles pressed into the dust, and his muscles turned to stone.

The man in question looked even more peculiar than he sounded. Sunny had been in little doubt before. The man had spoken the tribe's language. He could have been an exile, like Hunter. He could have been a member of their own tribe. Or he could have been a multilingual member of a neighbouring tribe. But no! This man did not only *sound* different, he *looked* different too. He was dressed from head-to-toe in a strange black cloth. A cross-shaped piece of wood hung from a cord around his neck. And his skin was pinkish-red. It did not feature a single tattoo.

This man was not like them. He was not like

Hunter. He did not even look like the explorers they had met in the desert. His tone was condescending, yet his appearance was comely. His posture was stiff, yet he had a kindly face. Sunny still wanted to thump the man, but he could not bring himself to do it. What threat did he pose? All he had was his words. And his words were a complete and utter shambles.

Sunny returned to get his loincloth, dressed, and tutted in the manner that this man had tutted at him.

He departed without a second glance.

\*\*\*

Several days rolled by, before Sunny saw that man again.

In the meantime, he had sex with both Hope *and* Beetle. He took part in several hunts, two of which were successful. He helped to paint a mural, which depicted their encounter with the Wogies. He carved patterns into the posts which formed the Sacred Circle. And he transformed an antelope horn into beads.

Sunny was not an especially proficient artist. He spent more time chatting than doing anything productive. But he assisted the more talented artisans, whenever they asked for help;

sharpening chisels, mixing paints, and heaving columns into position. It was a social affair. Sunny did his bit.

The next time he saw the stranger was only in passing. That man was using one of the tribe's communal toilets; a deep pit, surrounded by a banana-leaf wall, and covered with two bamboo planks. Toilet-goers sat on those slats, and pooped through the gap in-between.

Sunny could not stop himself from staring. Nor could he stop himself from investigating that man's stool. He had expected it to be pinkish white, to match the stranger's skin. But he was surprised to discover that it was the same as his own; tubular, stinky and brown.

If Sunny had been unsure before, there could be denying it now. Despite this person's appearance, he was not an ancestor. Ancestors did not poop. This man really was a human. He cleaned his anus with a cloth, instead of using water, which seemed rather unhygienic. But he *had an anus*, which meant he must have been real.

*\*\*\**

The third time he saw that stranger, a few days later, Sunny was back on the banks of the

Grand Meeting Place. He was choking on the smoke; bored with the representatives, who were planning another hunt.

Sunny was keen for these formalities to evolve into storytelling, and then into a kind of party. Griots, such as Sparrow, were usually given the chance to tell a tale or two, once the discussions were done. It would not be long before they broke into song. Sunny had brought a flute, so he could play along. Members of the other clans had brought a variety of instruments, the likes of which Sunny only ever heard whilst he was here in this pop-up city. Together, they would form an orchestra, whose music was improving with each passing night. The people who did not play, might begin to dance. Others might mix things up; playing a little, singing a little, and dancing a little; changing tact whenever it took their fancy.

But such festivities would have to wait.

The tribe's meal had been delayed by a rainstorm, this meeting had not begun until everyone had received some food, and it was already getting late. Five stars were twinkling, intermittently; as though competing for attention, or trying to convey a message. The sky was navy. The sky was mauve. The sky was black.

Bored of the representatives, Sunny had allowed his mind to wander; to distant places, and events in the distant past; when the arena fell into a static hush. That hush was so coercive, it clasped Sunny's shoulders and shook him to attention.

That alien was *here* in the open, halfway around the Sacred Circle.

A few people gasped, presumably because they had never seen anything like it. Others tutted. Perhaps they had also been accosted, in much the same way as Sunny. Word had begun to spread of a series of similar encounters. Some people had rejected the talk of the "Red Man" in their midst. Others feared the bad omens he might bring. A few people were excited at the prospect of encountering such an exotic individual.

Now here he was, adorned in the same body-cloth, and wearing that same peculiar smile; that look which was almost smug, almost righteous, almost patronising; but not quite any of these things, or anything else which Sunny was able to describe. To Sunny, that man could only be defined by his otherness, which blurred his physical features. And anyway, there was really no need to describe his face. If you had called him the "Red Man", everyone would have known who you meant. This person was one of a kind.

The silence rippled around the arena; rustling the leaves, which had not been heard since this meeting began, and crackling the fire, which simmered beneath the remains of a few antelope.

Bear opened her chest to the visitor:

"Ah, esteemed brother: We've been awaiting your appearance... Come, do tell. We've been told that your people believe this land is their land. That they intend to spray leaden fire, and send us back to our ancestral forests."

The Red Man narrowed his eyes, crossed himself, and smiled; projecting his words without deigning to raise his voice:

"Firstly, allow me to thank you for your hospitality, and for this opportunity to speak. My name is Father Ralph. I'm a missionary from the Christian Church, here to spread the gospel of our Lord Jesus Christ.

"I shall answer your first question with a single word: 'Yes'. We've already claimed this land. But please don't be offended. Whilst we're small in number, we've conquered bigger territories than this. We've vanquished far larger tribes than your own. For we serve the one true God... Amen to that!... Our God is divine; all-powerful and all-knowing. With him on *our side*, your tribe never stood a chance.

"You ask if we wish to kill you?

"No! A thousand times 'No'! Blessed children of Christ: We don't wish to kill you. We wish to *save* you. We wish to lift you out of the darkness, and bring you into the light; to raise you up from your childish ignorance, and deliver you into salvation.

"This is the white man's burden. We come in God's name, to save your souls from damnation, so that you might enter paradise, which we call 'Heaven', and exist in eternal bliss.

"In the Lord's name, let it be said: Once you come to realise the errors of your ways, you'll understand the good we've done, saving you from yourselves."

Sunny could not help but notice the change in Father Ralph's speech. It had found a rhythm. The missionary still paused between sentences, to savour the taste of his self-righteousness. But he no longer stumbled between words. Perhaps he had rehearsed this lecture to the point of perfection. Or perhaps had mastered their language.

Sunny was impressed. But Bear was unmoved. Sunny could tell as much from the way she puckered her lips, revealing the pinkish skin inside her mouth, and by the way her eyes meandered towards the stars.

But Bear shielded her disapproval from Father Ralph; maintaining a gracious smile, whilst speaking in a kindly voice:

"Our esteemed brother: We're already in paradise. Look around you! We're surrounded by the people we love. We have a wonderful community, all the food we can eat, and all the time in the world. We have art, walks, conversation, stories, sport, music and sex. Why would we need your... What did you say it was called?... Okay, yes: Your 'Heaven'?"

A short silence ensued. Father Ralph must have understood the tribe's custom.

Bear gestured for him to respond.

"It's not 'Our' heaven. It's *everyone's* heaven. And you need it, because your so-called 'Ancestral forests' don't actually exist. God will punish you for this heresy. As it is written: The cowardly, faithless and detestable; the murderers, perverts, sorcerers, idolaters and liars; they shall be taken to a lake that burns with fire and sulphur, where they shall endure a second death, and be tortured day and night.

"But there is hope! For God is good and God is love. Let Jesus into your heart, follow the righteous path, and you *shall* be saved. You shall enter heaven; a place where the gates are made of pearl, the streets are lined with gold, and everything is illuminated by the divine light of the Lord. Hallelujah, praise the Lord!"

Upon hearing these revelations, a hand shot up so quickly, it propelled the body to which it was attached; lifting that person to her feet.

This woman, named *Protectress*, was different from her peers. Whilst they took great pleasure from eating meat, she only ate fruit, leaves, tubers, excrement and ash. Whilst her peers loved to engage in idle conversation, Protectress liked to disappear into the wilderness, to commune with nature alone. She had a habit of falling into epileptic trances, speaking in tongues for several days. She wore her hair long, or short, or replaced it with feathers. Sometimes she made herself look like a man. Sometimes she walked around naked. She had been known to fast for days, balance on her head for entire nights, and perch upon a branch like a bird.

Protectress's behaviour was unique. Very few people claimed to understand her. But she was one of their own. Her clans-folk loved her, and were happy to accept her quirks. There was a general belief that she was mentally ill, but that her illness had come about because she had been touched by Mother Nature. She was even revered. In times of trouble, the members of her clan turned to Protectress for guidance; asking her to call the rains, or lead them to fertile land. Things were a little different in the Big Camp. The security forces had beaten her, when she was younger. But even they now accepted her ways.

Having leapt to her feet, Protectress was standing as tall as her crooked back would permit. The people behind her were staring at the peg which had been clamped to her anus. Her malformed arms were flailing about, and her eyes were gazing in different directions.

She had won the group's attention:

"I'm familiar with this 'Heaven' of which you speak. I've frequented that place on no fewer than one separate occasion. And yes, I'll admit, it seems like a fine old camp. There are, as you say, a few sets of pearly gates. The pathways are so spangly, they could blind an arthritic goat.

"Skip-bop, da doo-bop. *Screech!* Doo-wop, di doo-bop.

"But glimpse beneath the surface! Glimpse, glimpse, glimpse. Ooh jiggedy! You'll be aghast at what you'll find. This heaven is a cold, heartless void! There are no discussions, debates or votes. Skiddly nope! The people in this 'Heaven' are slaves to a tyrant they call 'God'.

"Skiddly-doo, bee-bop, shoo-wop.

"I couldn't cope in that ghastly place, and neither could you. It's a wiggly-woggly-Woggy place. It's not for freedom-lovers like us."

Father Ralph's brow crumpled into furrows of red and pink. He had played out this scene in his mind, on twenty or thirty occasions. He had imagined a plethora of different reactions, and worked out a way to respond to each. But he had not anticipated a response like this.

He fired off his reply without pausing for the customary period:

"Blasphemy!... Holy Moly!... Goodness gracious... What a... What a dang notion!... You cannot possibly... You cannot possibly have been to heaven! Heaven is... Heaven is for the dead."

Protectress *did* wait in silence, before agreeing with Father Ralph:

"Yes. Heaven is for the dead. I was dead when I visited. Dead, dead, dead."

"You're not... You're not dead."

Pause.

"I came back to life."

"Preposterous!... People... We... Cannot... Die... We cannot die and come back to life."

Pause.

"Can't we?"

Father Ralph thought better than to reply. He was still keen to introduce Jesus; a man who *had* risen from the dead. And he sensed that no good would come from arguing with a woman who was quite clearly insane.

He turned to Bear.

The chairperson had recovered her calm. Even from a distance, Sunny could tell that her face had softened. Her eyeballs had expanded. Her cheeks were soft and airy:

"Let's say, for argument's sake, that you're correct. This heaven *is* a fine place. We should all wish to enter... What would you have us do to gain admittance?"

Bear's welcoming tone had the desired effect; encouraging Father Ralph to relax.

The missionary closed his eyes, crossed himself, and rediscovered his rhythm:

"We ask that you invite Jesus into your hearts. Love the one true God, creator and master of the universe. Follow his commandments. Don't worship false idols; these 'Ancestors' and this so-called 'Mother Nature'. Don't engage in sin. Choose a partner, and commit to her for life. Cover your shameful bodies. Rest on the Sabbath. Love your neighbours. Love your enemies. Praise the Lord."

Pause.

"And if we don't do as you say?"

Pause.

"If you accept my olive branch, God will save your soul. You'll find bliss in the Kingdom of Heaven. And I'll do everything I can to ensure you're protected on earth. No sword shall be swung in anger, and no shot shall be fired in vain. Our conquering army is good and pure. They wouldn't kill a fellow Christian.

"But if you're stubborn, if you resist, then I'm afraid you'll be on your own. I'll pray for your souls. But the righteous may slay you. Your souls might burn in eternal hellfire."

Pause.

"Bribes and threats?"

Father Ralph did not respond. But it was clear what Bear was saying: This outsider was no different from Hunter, who had also tried to entice them, before giving up and resorting to threats. Sunny had disliked Father Ralph from the get-go. He disliked him even more now. This man was a wolf in sheep's clothing. He might have *spoken* of love. But he wanted them to abandon the very things they loved the most.

"A promise of protection."

Bear responded with her right hand; holding her fingers flat, and clapping them against her thumb, to make them look like a chattering mouth.

She opened her palm, held it aside her ear, and flicked it away; the gesture the tribes-folk performed, whenever they heard a lie.

And she left it to Serenity to respond:

"I spoke before of an imminent threat. The Wogies *are* here. They *do* have the power to kill us all... Now, I don't claim to like this man. But if he can save our lives... If he can act as a mediator, and prevent a war... Then, sistren and brethren, we should open our ears to his mouth."

Pause.

"Esteemed brother: Do you trust this man?"

Pause.

"Certainly not."

Pause.

"So this might be a trap?"

Serenity nodded.

"And you think we should walk straight in?"

Pause.

"Sistren and brethren: I think it's our least bad option."

Bear thumbed her flabby chin, turned her torso but not her hips, and gestured towards the other representatives.

"Is there anyone here who wishes to commit to a single lover for the whole of their mortal life? Even if it makes them unhappy?... For the good of the tribe, we should be able to reject unhappiness. Yet if we were to bow to this man's commands, such a thing could never happen. We'd be locked into miserable relationships. We'd grow exasperated. We'd start arguments, fights and wars. We'd *destroy ourselves* from within.

"Esteemed sisters: This 'One partner for life' malarkey is quite clearly a TRAP!"

Sunny noticed that almost everyone was nodding. The auditorium glistened as their heads bobbed up and down, reflecting the firelight in a thousand different directions.

It was left to another representative to have the final say:

"We spoke in private... Yes, I see you remember... You told me that this 'God' character, this 'One True God', came down to earth; revealing herself to one set of people, at one specific time.

"Please explain to our gathered tribe: Why on earth and the ancestral realm would she behave in such a fashion?

"If this spirit mother could reveal herself, why didn't she do so in full view of everyone; descending in triumph, with pomp and majesty? Why didn't she visit every tribe? Why didn't she visit *us*? And why did she visit *your* people, of all the people in nature? What makes *you* so very special?

"Brother stranger: Each tribe has its own beliefs. Yet you, in your arrogance, claim that only yours are righteous. That we must obey *your* rules, or be damned forever.

"What vanity! Your ego is the size of the moon!"

# OF LOVE AND LOINCLOTHS

The camp had expanded a little, and then it had fixed itself in place. What had once felt wondrous, now possessed the odourless air of the mundane.

Parallel to the cliffs, a wide avenue divided several clusters of teepees, tupiks and marquees. Pathways had formed between these temporary homes; battered into position by a thousand forgotten footsteps, misshapen by the rains, and reinvented with each passing storm.

At one end of that avenue, the Sacred Circle was fully decorated. Its posts were covered in images of hunters, beasts, fishes, plants and spirits. The surrounding slopes were brown with earth. The grass had been flattened, the ground was pockmarked with footprints, and the fire pit was white with ash.

Alongside the avenue, opposite the cliffs, a field was being used to host the *Tribal Games*. These were taking place every day, now the city was fully built, and the tribe had ample reserves of food. The most popular game was called *chunkey*. Players took turns to launch logs at a rolling sphere, whilst running as fast as they could; attempting to land their poles within a whisker of that moving target, without making any contact. Tribes-folk also played a ball game, and a version of lacrosse. They wrestled, boxed, held spear-throwing contests and archery competitions. Large crowds gathered to watch these spectacles. They gambled thousands of beads, and smoked copious amounts of tobacco.

Beyond this arena, beneath the caves which were being used to store meat, was the tribe's communal store. This was by far the biggest structure in the camp. It loomed high above the other tents, casting a shadow which engulfed the avenue.

That tent was filled with an abundance of different things...

The buff antelope from the first hunt had all been eaten. But their remains had been repurposed and placed in this store. The largest antlers had been turned into pickaxes and mattocks. The remainder had been converted into headdresses, which would be used during spiritual ceremonies. The teeth had been made into beads.

The tribes-folk had not only hunted antelope.

They had killed hundreds of gazelles, a good number of wild boars, and a few of the frailer buffalo. They avoided the stronger buffalo, because the risks were too great. Those animals had been known to turn and attack the hunters.

Sunny had helped to hollow out the bigger bones, converting them into containers and flutes. Other people had shaved the smaller bones into slices; fashioning them into needles, bodkins, fish hooks and barbed spears. Together, they had tanned the hides; massaging fat into the leather, before drying those skins, and cutting them into shape; making loincloths, tent coverings, satchels, and the slings they used to carry their babies.

These items had been deposited in the communal store, along with a little meat, which had been dried, smoked or salted, in preparation for the clans' onward journeys. There were baskets filled with maize, manioc, beans and gourds. A small team had grown these foods on the wetlands. There was also a great deal of tobacco. Members of *every* clan had united to grow that crop, on the plains above the cliffs. It required an enormous amount of energy to process tobacco, the tribes-folk did not take it lightly, but the rewards justified the effort. Rumour had it that they had learnt how to produce tobacco from a distant tribe, who farmed it *all year round*. Although no-one could recall meeting such a tribe, nor could they understand why anyone would wish to toil for so long, to produce a single plant, when Mother Nature provided so many.

Next to this tobacco and meat, was a heap of groundnuts, and an even bigger pile of raw coffee. The ancestors had planted a coffee orchard, countless generations before. A small band of tribes-folk helped to pick, peel and dry the beans those trees supplied. Sparrow was among their number.

This communal store was bursting at the seams. And, now that the rainy season was drawing to an end, its contents needed to be shared.

Almost everyone had a wish list. If people had been allowed to help themselves, everything would have all been taken, and the latecomers would have been left with nothing.

To solve this dilemma, the tribes-folk elected a Women's Council. Anyone who wanted an item, was invited to petition this panel.

Sunny knew exactly what he wanted: A new loincloth. When he had joined the queue, he had been pretty sure he would receive one. But now, after waiting for most of the day, his mind was riddled with doubt.

He stepped inside.

The smell of leather hit him immediately. But it quickly dissolved into a potpourri of disparate aromas; a combination of nuts, bone, cinnamon, cardamom, and a scent he was unable to name. He was sure he had come across that fragrance before. But in here, it seemed more pronounced. It clogged his nostrils and filled his throat.

Sunny cast his gaze along the line of ladies, who were squeezed together on a modest bench. Almost all of them were shorter than Sunny. Most lacked his physique. Yet despite this, he felt they were looming over him; dressed in a cloak of maturity, which made him shrink in their presence.

It was the first time Sunny had ever addressed this council. In previous seasons, his mother had petitioned them on his behalf. He was unsure if he should speak, and only did so after an uncomfortable pause, during which one woman smacked her lips, another sighed, a bird entered the tent, flew around, tried to escape, conceded defeat, and perched on top of a pile of nuts.

"This loincloth is wearing thin. Look at these holes... Yes, just here... They're small, but they're growing. And... You know... This fur is wearing thin. And it's become an effort to strap. It used to be the perfect fit. But I feel... And I feel I've outgrown it."

Sunny had intended to stop. But he was disturbed by the ensuing silence. And so he found himself speaking again, much to his own surprise:

"Dearest aunties: I helped to hunt the animals who provided this leather. It's just... Well, I helped to tan their hides. I'm particularly taken by one such loincloth, which I've tried on already... That one... Yes, that's correct. That one there... I only ask that you give me this single loincloth. I've helped to make several, and I'm only asking for one."

A small pause ensued. Only this time, the silence did not last.

A councillor lifted her chin.

Sunny thought this woman was called *Tobacco*, but he could have been mistaken. He had seen her on one of the ledges near their caves, but they had never spoken. The woman scared him. There was something in her eyes, with their tiny pupils, that made him want to run. Her shoulders were in constant motion, shuddering and jolting, but her breasts never seemed to move. She had shrivelled skin and scrawny arms, which was not so strange. But her frail appearance clashed with her booming voice.

"And you think, just because you helped to tan and cut this leather, that you have some sort of ancestral right to keep it?"

Sunny shook his head.

"Tell us boy!" She elongated the word "Boy" for an unreasonable amount of time. "Boi... oi... oi... oi... oi... Did you help to gather any nuts?"

The rains came gushing down, pounding the tent, beating a discordant rhythm; all drums, cymbals and bass.

Sunny shook his head.

"Then, by such logic, you shouldn't be granted any nuts... Yet, I'd bet our last bead that you'll eat them. Someone will come in here on your clan's behalf, claim those nuts, and share them with you at your camp."

Sunny bowed his eyes.

"Why so glum? Don't be ashamed boyo. The nuts are for everyone."

Sunny raised his chin, but stopped short of nodding. He was a little too confused to respond.

"Boyo: We'd all like a new loincloth. Or some beads. Or some nuts... Don't you think that *our* loincloths have stretched? Don't you think that they're also covered in holes? Or scuffs? Or stains?... What makes *you* so special?"

Sunny could not answer.

Tobacco nodded towards a woman who was named *Rainbow*. Sunny knew this for a fact. She was his mother's friend; someone who had cared for him as a child, and who was wearing beads his mother had carved.

Rainbow adopted a compassionate but stern tone; scrunching her raggedy eyebrows, and shunting her lips as she spoke:

"Your request is not unreasonable. But neither is it essential. Your loincloth has seen better days, but there's still some leather around the holes... Sunny of the Eagle Clan: We may be inclined to accept your appeal, once the moon has grown and shrunk. Wait until the eve of the Great Feast, and then return with your representative. If they deem your need great enough; if they're willing to petition on your behalf, prioritising your request above those of your peers; then we'll have little choice but to accept. And if there are loincloths leftover, when we're packing down this store, then I think we'd struggle to say 'No'. But now is not the time... Go, child! Go enjoy the camp. You're a sunrise of a lad. That loincloth suits you fine."

***

Life meandered on...

The rains came, and the rains receded. The tribes-folk still hunted, and they still roasted meat. They also cooked some of the vegetables from the store; making soups, porridges, stews and broths.

These meals evolved into meetings. The representatives smoked themselves into a state of tranquillity, before planning the Great Feast, arranging hunts, and discussing any new information which emerged. Sometimes, Sunny waited for the dances which followed. Sometimes he left; going off alone, with Hope, or with his newest lover: A girl named *Desert Dew*.

On a couple of rare occasions, the

representatives were forced to dish out justice...

A child was forgiven for taking a chunk of jerky from the communal store, after claiming that he did not know it was forbidden. But an older man was caned for the very same offence. A woman was accused of slothfulness, but made a valiant defence; saying she was about to give birth, and did not wish to endanger the baby. That case was dismissed. But two men, who had hunted without the tribe's consent, were cast into a three-day exile.

Talk inevitably turned to the Wogies...

New reports had emerged. According to some sightings, or perhaps they were just rumours, the Wogies had killed several members of *rival* tribes. But this was no hardship. The enemy of their enemy was a friend. The Wogies might have claimed a portion of their rivals' land. But again, it was not *their* land. *They* were no worse off. There was a general fear that their tribe might be next. If the whispers were to be believed, the Wogies had already occupied the coastline. They had spread epidemic diseases, wiped out the local tribes, and erected camps in that fertile zone. Now they were casting their sights inland, following the rivers which would lead them here.

The paranoia grew with each passing day. But the tribes-folk could not agree upon a response. There was nowhere to run. There was nowhere to hide. If these Wogies were as fearsome as the reports suggested, then little good would come from engaging them in battle. They might merge with the other tribes; forming a super-tribe, which might defend itself through sheer weight of numbers. But this had never been done before. They talked about sending a diplomatic mission. The Wogies' messenger, Father Ralph, had seemed amiable enough. But they struggled to decide what terms they might offer. The tribes-folk could conceive of welcoming these strangers, allowing them to do their thing, and even sharing a portion of land. But they were not prepared to abandon their way of life; to betray Mother Nature, submit to a tyrannical god, or commit to a solitary lover. Such things felt like a fate worse than death. Rival tribes had attacked them, killed them, and set up camps in the places they used to live. But they had never done anything as invasive as this.

Father Ralph was becoming a legend. The missionary had remained in the camp, sleeping in a private tent, in the shade of a billowy tree; preaching to little groups, and conversing with individuals. He had not attended the parliament again. He appeared to have given up on his attempts to convert the tribe en masse. But if the rumours were to be believed, he had won a few converts. Some people said he had persuaded a couple of *clans*; bribing them with material wealth, and offers of protection.

Sunny supposed the whispers were probably true. He had experienced another lecture himself, albeit through no choice of his own. Father Ralph had approached him from behind, spun him around, and clasped hold of his shoulders; launching a verbal tirade, from which Sunny could not escape.

Most of that talk was a blur. Sunny distinctly remembered one phrase: "The wicked liberty of the savages". But he had not been able to decipher its meaning. How could liberty be "Wicked"? Father Ralph had said that he wanted to *liberate* the tribes-folk. But if this was the case, then why was he mocking the liberty they already possessed?

Perhaps Sunny had misunderstood. His peers rarely spoke of liberty in such an explicit manner.

In the same way that they breathed, without thinking about the air; they were free to do almost anything they chose, but they did not give much consideration to this freedom.

Father Ralph had used some other words which Sunny could not understand: "King", "Laws" and "Nation". The missionary had to borrow these from a foreign language, because they did not exist in the tribe's.

Try as he might, Sunny struggled to grasp these alien concepts. A "King" seemed to be an egotistical version of an Uncle Crow, who lived in a faraway place; someone who needed to be ridiculed, shunned, exiled or killed by his clan. The king's "Laws" sounded like a fanciful kind of wish list; a series of things the king wanted others to do for him. Sunny had no idea about the "Nation" this "King" appeared to bully. As far as he could tell, a "Nation" was a bit like a tribe. But Father Ralph knew the word for tribe, and had chosen not to use it. There must have been a reason. But Sunny could not figure it out.

Sunny listened intently, as Father Ralph spoke of these fantastical things; nodding whenever he supposed it might be appreciated. This seemed to do the job. It made the missionary happy, and saved Sunny the hassle of producing an actual response.

That all changed when Father Ralph asked a question:

"Blessed child of Christ: Do you know how the world was created?"

Sunny beamed. Everyone knew how the world was created!

"Of course," he replied. "Mother Nature pulled the planets out of her primal void... First, she gave birth to a mysterious race of fish-people. Then she destroyed their habitat, to make space for us. I mean... This was at the *Dawn of Everything*; back when the skies and the earth hadn't been pulled apart, when animals could speak, and it was still possible to invent new things; things like cooking, sunsets and people."

Father Ralph frowned. It was an elongated sort of frown, which reached down from his forehead to his chin. It was open-mouthed and toothy, scented with overtones of magnolia and sulphur.

"What a jape! No, it was *God* who created the world."

"Oh... Is 'God' the Woggy word for 'Mother Nature'?"

"Not exactly. No. God is a *man*."

"A man gave birth to the world? How peculiar! I've never heard of a man giving birth."

"God can do anything! He's omnipotent. He isn't an emotional woman, like your so-called 'Mother Nature'. No, blessed child. God is *divine*."

This made little sense to Sunny. For him, acts of nature, like storms and earthquakes, *did* seem pretty emotional. Although he did not believe that women were any more emotional than men. He had emotions himself.

But Sunny thought better than to express this opinion. He did not wish to provoke their guest; the agent of such a violent and unpredictable foe.

Taking Sunny's silence as a sign of accord, Father Ralph adopted a theatrical tone; projecting his voice, as he spoke of "Original Sin", "Redemption", "Praying", and a plethora of ancient characters: *Abraham, Isaac, Moses, David, Jesus* and *John*.

"Are these your ancestors?"

"By Jove, I suppose they are."

"We love our ancestors too. We also ask them for protection."

"Then that's something we have in common. We're all God's children, after all."

Sunny supposed that Father Ralph had a point. He might have looked a bit peculiar, with his pink skin and superfluous cloths. But his face was human enough; smallish, round and graceful. He had the same kind of globular skull as any person Sunny had ever met. Father Ralph also rolled his eyes, when he thought someone was being foolish. He spoke a language that seemed to contain nouns, verbs and adjectives. Sunny was almost certain he had spotted Father Ralph humming along to their music. And now there was this: His people also had a creation story, a set of special ancestors, and a collection of myths. Perhaps they *were* alike.

Father Ralph must have noticed the transformation, because he shuffled forwards into Sunny's personal space; leaning over the youngster, burying him beneath his shadow. In the days which followed, Sunny would forget most of this conversation. Those words; "Pray", "Nation" and "King"; had been so foreign, they had entered through one ear and departed through the other. But Sunny would remember Father Ralph's final question, even though he was confused by the word "Law", and even though he thought that a yoke was a part of an egg.

"So, my child, do you agree? Will you submit to the yoke of the law of God?"

Sunny stared into Father Ralph's eyes; hoping the moment would pass, or that something would interrupt them.

When he felt he had no other choice, he performed a tentative nod. His head felt so heavy, it took a great deal of effort to lift. He did not allow it to drop *too* quickly, because he was worried his body might follow; causing him to stumble forwards. But that simple, painful nod, had the desired effect. Father Ralph beamed, revealing the yellowest set of teeth Sunny had ever seen.

"Then you must stop this Juju mumbo-jumbo, with your charms and your spells and your symbols. It's unholy nonsense. And you must refrain from laying with that fellow. Find yourself a good woman, and commit to her for life. Find the light of God. Allow his radiance to illuminate your soul."

Sunny was about to say "No". What right did this man have to make such a request? He felt he was under attack. And tribes-folk had a duty to resist such attacks, lest their perpetrators grow strong and seize control of the group.

But then he thought of Hope; her smell, the way she walked, and the way he felt whenever they touched. Would it really be so bad, to commit to her for life?

A warm fissure of delight scurried across his ribs.

Caught between emotions, Sunny was unable to react. Father Ralph released his grip, grinned in an ostentatious manner, nodded, and strolled away.

***

The following morning, Sunny was shaken awake with a newfound clarity of mind. *He had to be with Hope.* No-one else satisfied him like she did. No-one else made his arms feel light and airy. Yes, he still wanted to have sex with other people. But he would give that up for her. Perhaps Father Ralph was onto something. Perhaps it would be worth the sacrifice; forgoing a few lovers, but keeping Hope to himself. Life would be an explosive mix of energy, thrills and sex.

He just had to get Hope alone, to propose the

idea. But this was easier said than done, because Hope was nowhere to be seen.

Sunny processed some hides whilst he awaited her return; stitching satchels with feverish intensity. It was a cathartic pursuit. Sunny channelled his nervous energy into his art. But it did not seem to while away the time. Sunny kept checking the sun's position. Yet that star refused to move. He arched his neck, discovered that it was where he had left it, stitched a little more, and then checked on the sun again. If anything, it had moved *backwards*.

Sunny succumbed to exhaustion. He returned to their cave in a daze, stumbled through the opening, collapsed, and fell into a dreamless slumber.

***

The sun *had* moved by the time Sunny awoke. It had moved so much, that he looked for it in the wrong place.

The shadows had turned, and the leaves no longer glistened.

Sunny rubbed the sleep from his eyes, stretched his arms, and wobbled his shoulders. He rose to his feet, shuddered, and left the cool embrace of the cave.

He spotted Hope. She was sitting with her friends, on the ledge outside their caves, laughing to the point of tears. But to reach her position, Sunny had to walk past Serenity. And as soon as he got close, that man stepped out; blocking the path, before speaking in a meditative voice:

"Let me see this loincloth."

Serenity whipped the garment from Sunny's hips and lifted it to his eyes. He did not seem particularly impressed, at first; rolling his lips and scrunching his lashes. But he took his time. He combed the fur, pulled the leather, and contemplated the matter.

His eyes bulged.

"Sunshine: You know we can't carry too many nuts. Our Small Camp is further than most. But for this very reason, we must demand more than our share of cured meat, to sustain us on our journey. And we also need some satchels. These are our priorities."

Sunny understood. Serenity would probably lead the clan's contingent, when they appealed to the Women's Council. It was normal for the clan's representative to adopt this secondary role. And whilst Serenity was sympathetic, he had more pressing concerns.

Sunny did not mind. He had made peace with the council's decision. His loincloth still did its job, a few of his peers wore worse, and his request had not been rejected outright. He might get still get a loincloth, if any still remained on the eve of the Great Feast.

Right now, he just wanted to get dressed. He was embarrassed, standing there naked in front of his peers, cupping his genitalia. And he was impatient. He wished to push through this conversation, run to Hope, and tell her how he felt.

But that would have been disrespectful.

Serenity was still speaking:

"Some of our sisters have asked for antlers, to dig up roots. Their need is small, but we must prioritise their request, because they haven't appealed for several seasons."

It was infuriating. Sunny's request had been denied. He understood this. He *accepted* this. So why was Serenity speaking? It was out of character. That man was usually so efficient with his speech.

"If all these requests are granted, and if the council is favourable, we may ask for another loincloth. I can see that yours needs to be replaced. But we can always make you another one, back at the Small Camp."

Sunny nodded. He could not be upset. Serenity had been so reasonable. His tone had been irresistibly smooth.

And there was cause for optimism. Sunny *would* get a new loincloth, one way or another.

He smiled, pressed his forehead against Serenity's, exhaled, and turned to face Hope. But she and her friends were nowhere to be seen. Sunny supposed they must have sought shelter inside a cave, or perhaps a marquee. The sky had turned black, and the rains were starting to fall. It would be difficult to find her, and impossible to get her alone.

He flicked his tongue against the top of his mouth, stepped onto the lip of the ledge, and allowed the waters to wash over his skin.

***

Sunny did not see Hope till nightfall, when he was taken by nerves, and could not muster the courage to speak. Perhaps it was because she was surrounded by her closest friends. He did not wish to embarrass her. Or perhaps that was just an excuse.

The following day, Sunny looked for Hope soon after he awoke. But she had already left the camp.

Serenity approached.

"Child: We're going to the Women's Council. Would you like to come?"

Sunny performed the most cursory of nods. He would have preferred to search for Hope. But it was unlikely he would have found her. It would have been rude to reject his elder. And there was little else to do. There were no more satchels to stitch. The tobacco had been dried, the coffee had been roasted, and the preparations for the Great Feast were already complete.

They descended the step-like rocks in silence. They snaked between the tents and the mud-caked tarpaulins, which smelled of decomposing straw. And they emerged onto the main boulevard, where the last remnants of grass now sparkled with morning dew.

They reached the communal store, greeted a few of their clans-folk, and entered without much of a wait. Sunny supposed they must have had an appointment.

His thoughts turned to Hope: Why had she left so early? Was she avoiding him? Did she have another lover? Did she know what he was planning to ask?

Sunny knew it was wrong, yet he could not help feeling jealous. He shuddered at the thought. What on earth and the ancestral realm had he become? Did he even want to dedicate himself to a single woman? It conflicted with all their tribe's traditions. Had his mind been poisoned by Father Ralph? Surely not! It *would* be good for them. His mother only slept with one man, Pumpkin, and she seemed fairly happy. They might not have sworn an oath, but they acted as though they were exclusive. And if it could work for them, then it could work for him and Hope.

Sunny broke free from these daydreams and doubts. He observed the scene before him, and was surprised to discover that the women were nodding as one. It felt like they were nodding *at him.*

A few helpers bundled up some sides of dried meat.

Sunny had lost track of the conversation. He had lost track of time. But, as far as he could tell, everything was going smoothly. Serenity had received the meat for their journey, as well as the antlers his aunts had requested. Now he was asking for a few items he had not mentioned before: Some decorative arrowheads, nuts and coffee. He was given these, along with a bundle of tobacco, which no-one had even mentioned.

He tipped his head towards Sunny:

"And this young man would like a loincloth."

Tobacco nodded in a manner which verged on the sarcastic.

"Ah, yes. It's you, boyo... Oh yes, I remember this one! He helped to tan the leather, so he feels he's owed a piece. Upon Mother Nature's face! Yes, sisters, I remember *this one.*"

Sunny felt an urge to protest; to deny the connection. He had tanned the hides to help the tribe, not for personal gain. He felt he should get a new loincloth, because his old one was wearing thin. The two things were unrelated.

He pinched his lips. It was not his place to speak. And he sensed that Tobacco was trying to incite a reaction. It was in his self-interest *not* to object; to stay humble, and accept whatever happened.

Tobacco turned to Serenity:

"You think this boyo deserves it?"

Serenity nodded.

Tobacco threw her hands in the air.

"I don't know what things are coming to! Back when I was a tattoo-less girl, we'd have never gifted a loincloth to someone who was already wearing one. We'd have never ceded to a boyo with such bendy logic... Does a butterfly need two pairs of wings? Does a frog need to tweet? Would you gift daylight to the sun?... But, alas, I suppose it's a measure of the times... Ho humph... If no-one has any objections, I suppose he can have that tatty old good-for-nothing cloth in the corner... Yes, that one there. The one no-one else would take... Yes, yes, I know. Everyone else said they'd rather traipse about naked, than wear that scuzzy thing. But it's all he deserves. Force it upon the boyo, even if he protests. Let it be a lesson."

Sunny hesitated, before extending his hand, tentatively; unsure if he should accept an item which had been described in such derogatory terms. If it was as bad as Tobacco suggested, he would stick with the loincloth he had.

It was only when Sunny gripped the cloth between his fingers, lifted it to his face, performed a double take, doubted himself, and checked it again; that he finally accepted the truth. This was the loincloth he had requested. The one which was the perfect fit.

He frowned.

Tobacco winked. She almost smiled. Then she scowled, and bid him depart with a violent swoosh of her hand.

# THE URGE TO DESTROY IS A CREATIVE URGE

Sunny squandered a couple more opportunities to get Hope alone. Overcome by nerves, he had panicked, stalled, stuttered and traipsed away.

Perhaps it was for the best. He would see a lot more of his lover once they had left this seasonal city. There would be far less competition for her attention.

A trumpet-like sound filled the valley:

Hoooooo. Hoomph-hoomph-hoomph. Huk-huk-huk, huk-huk-huk, hoooomph!

That noise rebounded off the cliffs, accosting Sunny's ears for a second time. It was joined by the sound of several other instruments, producing a cacophony that could only mean one thing: The Great Feast was underway.

Over in the Sacred Circle, the setting sun was perfectly aligned with the largest pillars. It shone through the biggest pair, and hit the central totem, creating a shadow which dissected the tallest pillars on the opposite side. The rising moon could be seen through that gap, as it peeped up over the horizon.

This was the summer solstice, the longest day of the year. The rainy season was almost over. But before the clans could depart, they had to gift homage to Mother Nature.

A twinkle flickered in Sunny's eye; the reflection of a flame, held aloft on a club-like torch. That beacon was probably located on the opposite side of the avenue. But it could have been a smaller flame, positioned nearby. It was impossible to tell.

A second flare appeared. Then, a third. They glistened in the half-light of dusk; kissing the sky, blurring its pastel shades, disappearing, reappearing, appearing to vanish, then returning to life.

Now there were a hundred flames. Now there were a thousand. The camp glistened, as though awash with fireflies and stars.

The longer you looked at those splashes of light, the blacker everything else became. There was only lightness and darkness, the fire and the abyss.

Still the horns rang loud:

Hoomph-hoomph-hoomph. Huk-huk-huk.

Only now, they were met with a beat: The *chuck-a-chuck* rhythm of a thousand stomping feet. Sunny had already joined in, without realising what he was doing; pounding his soles as hard as he could, keeping immaculate time.

His arms were raised above his head, flaying like branches in a breeze.

If he had looked out at the camp, he would have seen the reflections of a thousand other limbs, each moving like his own; catching the light, succumbing to the shadows, and reappearing in different positions. But Sunny was not looking outwards. He was looking *inwards*; melting into the beat, swaying; trance-like, rhythmic and free.

Now he was amidst the teepees. Now he was in the central avenue. Now he was aside the Sacred Circle; marching around and around and around.

He could not recall how he had arrived in this place. He could not recall how he had found himself with a piece of meat in one hand, and a pipe in the other. He did not particularly care. He had given himself to the moment; eating as others ate, smoking as others smoked, stomping in time with their feet; flowing rather than moving.

The aroma of melted fat wafted above their

heads. Still, the horns rang loud. Only now, they were accompanied by the ding of clapping hands.

A young girl perched atop the central totem. Adorned in the finest pelts, she would have looked like a mythical creature, had she not also been wearing beads.

Unelected, small and feeble; that girl was controlling the crowd with a bison's skull. Whenever she raised that object, the people beneath it parted. Whenever she jabbed it in a certain direction, the adults rushed that way.

This was the upside-down world of the feast: The first were last, and the last were first.

The young girl was not alone. Almost every child was wearing a pair of antlers. The smallest children were wearing the largest ones. The woman who had Down syndrome was inside the Sacred Circle; running about, setting the pace for the others to follow. The man with dwarfism was skipping a different path.

Those two seemed different. The man flashed red, then yellow, then white. The woman grew taller and taller, until her head had pierced the clouds. Sunny might have questioned the evidence of his eyes. He might have deduced that their food had been laced with magic mushrooms. But Sunny was not *questioning* or *deducing*. He was *feeling*; allowing a warmth to bubble up within him, as the pillars grew feet, and marched alongside the crowd.

Those pillars were jogging. They were running. They were launching themselves towards the sky, returning to their original positions, hooting and clapping along.

More food appeared in Sunny's hands.

Protectress, the priestess who had challenged Father Ralph, began to rub herself against the totem. She was naked, purple and green.

She was chanting a traditional prayer:

"Ancestors, oh ancestors: We thank you for your protection.

"Mother Nature, our mother: We thank you for your fruit."

These words could be heard long after Protectress was done. Perhaps they were repeated by the crowd. Or perhaps they were echoes, which were reverberating off the blare of claps and horns.

"Protect us when we leave, leave, leave. Feed us forever more.

"Skip-bop, da doo-bop. *Screech*!"

***

On they marched. Around and around and around. The sky was yellow. It was amber, magenta and cerise; a different colour each time you looked.

Sunny found himself atop the tallest cliff...

Beneath him lay the image of a woolly mammoth, which had been cut into the chalk beneath the earth. That image was so large, it had to be viewed from up high; a gift to the ancestors above.

Sunny *could* believe his eyes. This was no hallucination. And now it made sense: Hope had left early each morning, to help create this art.

There was more...

Beyond the distant mounds and pyramids, stood two giant figurines: A woman and a man, both made of wicker, and both dressed in a coat of flames. Several spirits were dancing by their feet. Their bodies were formed of fire, and their faces were made of smoke.

At first, Sunny supposed they could not be real. They were double the height of most people. But then he saw someone he recognised: His dead uncle. He spotted someone else: A woman who had died during childbirth. And now he understood. Their ancestors had returned for this special occasion, when Mother Nature was allowed to break her rules.

Sunny blinked. When he reopened his eyes, he was back at the Sacred Circle, marching around and around. Only now, a torch was in his hand. He was setting fire to the pillars; stepping back, watching on as they succumbed to the flames; rushing forwards, and pushing them over.

The camp's refuse was thrown on top of the fire. Everything had to go.

Sunny was eating.

He came to his senses. The man with dwarfism was no longer flashing in different colours. The woman with Down syndrome had returned to her normal height. Sunny's mind was clear. But his body longed for completion.

He ran free from the crowd, and the crowd ran free from him. Everyone turned together, at the same time, as though compelled by a collective urge.

Sunny headed towards the camp.

He launched himself feet-first at one of the larger tents, rebounded off its side, and crashed down upon his elbow. Cringing with pain, he watched on as someone else performed a remarkably similar act.

Now they were jumping *together*; hugging onto the pole, as it tumbled to the ground.

Now they were trampling the tarpaulin.

As the Sacred Circle burnt in the distance, consumed by fire and flame; so the tents came down around them. *Everyone* was acting together, destroying *everything* they had built.

Tomorrow, this camp would be little more than dust. But tonight was about this moment; killing this city, so the clans could be reborn anew. For nothing was permanent. No social order was ever fixed. Every system had its time; a time to grow, a time to rule, and a time to be destroyed.

# THE MORNINGS AFTER THE NIGHTS BEFORE

The next world had usurped the last...

Those tents which had not been toppled, were dismantled the following morning. Their tarpaulins were bundled into packets, and their poles were stored in the caves. Several clans had already departed. Several more were about to leave.

Sunny wiped the sleep from his eyes, dazzled by the sweetness of sadness; melancholic at the thought of leaving, but excited for the adventures which lay ahead.

The sky was cloudless, which made the air feel dry, and allowed the sunrise to spill across the vista; eggshell, vanilla, plum and baby pink.

It all seemed so ephemeral. If a great city could vanish overnight, then why not the stars and the moon? Why not the earth beneath their feet?

These thoughts evaporated from Sunny's mind the moment he spotted Hope.

She almost smiled. She almost winked. As though playing a game; as though she knew how Sunny felt, and was happy to exploit it; she neither smiled nor winked. She stopped short on the cusp of a greeting, allowed her face to freeze between emotions, and allowed her feet to come to a rest. She stood still for half a moment, before retreating into a cave.

Sunny laughed. He was happy to play along; certain he would have Hope to himself, shortly after they had departed.

A bird tweeted a single note, the elders descended the cliff, and the others followed. They passed through the remains of the camp, traversed the valley, and arrived at the riverbank; where they rested, built some rafts, and readied themselves for the day.

***

It would not have made sense to come this way whilst making their outbound journey. It would have required an almighty effort to paddle *against* the current. But things were easier now they were heading *downstream*. They could board their rafts, sit back, and go with the flow; covering a distance which would have taken several days to walk.

Come nightfall on the third day, they reached their ancestral forest. It had been their intention to deposit the corpse of an elder named *Delight*;

the only member of their clan who had died at the Big Camp. Delight's body had been preserved and stored in an empty cave, in anticipation of this moment.

The clan's ritual had not changed for as long as anyone could remember: They bound the cadaver's wrists on either side of a branch, leaving their body to dangle. They prayed. And they waited for the eagles to arrive, consume the person's flesh, and free their spirits; enabling them to return to the ancestral realm, here in this holy forest.

This was sacred ground. The other clans were well aware of this fact. Even the neighbouring *tribes* respected this place.

It came as a ghastly surprise, therefore, to discover that this vast space was now barren. Stumps pockmarked the landscape for as far as the eye could see. Even the bushes and plants appeared to be withdrawing. It smelled all wrong; a little of sap, and a little of sawdust. Small birds were hopping from stump to stump, disorientated; vainly attempting to find their former homes, or their young, or anything which might guide them.

As if of one mind, everyone followed

Landscape, their de facto leader; tiptoeing forwards; inspecting the scene with their fingers, noses and eyes.

Their soundlessness swallowed the hum of the wild.

Sunny squatted down beside a stump, ran his finger along the cusp, and was surprised to find a series of jagged marks. This forest had not succumbed to Mother Nature; to a storm, or flood, or fire. Each tree had been felled by a peculiar type of blade.

His stomach contracted.

Sunny had been struck by something so obvious, he was embarrassed not to have noticed it before: The trunks and branches had all disappeared! Only the stumps and leaves remained. But why? Surely no human would have deliberately destroyed an entire forest, just to use its wood. Why would anyone need so much? The members of their clan had been known to fell a single tree. They had used the wood from a few trees at a time. But a whole forest? How could a person fall victim to such a debilitating bout of greed?

Spotting his kinfolk, who were disappearing into the distance, Sunny sprang to his feet and gave chase. But as he made his way, he noticed something new: Several saplings had been planted in the spaces between the stumps. They were aligned in an almost perfect grid. And there was something else. Sunny did not realise it at first. But the more he looked, the more he could not help but notice a peculiar thing: These saplings were all the same!

What sort of monster would cut down a beautiful forest, and attempt to replace it with such an abomination? Did the people who planted these saplings not understand that trees grew best when surrounded by *different* trees? That the decaying leaves from some plants, provided nutrients for others? That different plants attracted different insects? That these insects ate each other; ensuring that there were never too many pests, and that no individual species was attacked by *all* the pests? Forests were a varied and wonderful ecosystem, in which every agent played its part. But this? This desert of identical saplings was an aberration. Mother Nature was bound to reject it.

Sunny reached his mother, who was shaking her head.

"Rubber."

Sunny frowned.

"Rubber? Mother kindest: Rubber?"

"Rubber... All rubber... Rubbery, rubber trees. They're not even that great. Too sappy. No fruit... Rubber... All rubbery, rubbery rubber."

Sunny paused to think. But his mind drew a blank.

"I don't understand."

"Rubber."

"Rubber?"

"Rubber... Sappy, sappy rubber."

The other members of their clan were reacting in different ways. Some were also muttering. Only they were stumbling over the tops of different words: "Gone". "War". "Obscene". Others were smacking their lips, tutting, grinding their teeth, or clutching their ears. Some were going from stump to stump, trying to make sense of it all. A few were crying. One person was on her knees, running her fingers through the soil.

Sunny fell into a slow, trance-like state; swaying in figures-of-eight, despite his ongoing attempts to stand still. It was all he could do. Their clan had a fable for almost every calamity they could imagine; for ambushes, raids, murders, abductions and war. But Sunny had never heard a tale about anything quite so perverted as this. It could only mean one thing: Nothing like this had ever happened before.

How were they supposed to react?

***

By the time Sunny came to his senses, the sun had already set. His peers had gathered, and Serenity was breaking the silence:

"Sistren: We must make a decision. We can hang Delight here. Or we can take his body to another wooded area. A *new* ancestral forest."

Sparrow replied with violent words, but a passive voice; as though he felt a need to speak, but lacked the energy to fight.

"Don't get too big for your feet, you old power prigger. You jelly-lipped tyrant. You authority whore and stealer of words."

Kitten echoed her companion:

"Brigand! *Tut, tutty-tut-tut, tutty-tut...* Don't you think we can't see your inverted spirits; inside-out and attempting to flee? Oh yes, Serenity Boy. Your wooden neck and golden tongue are as visible as the sun, now we've emerged from the city smog."

Such comments were not a slight on Serenity

himself. It was the clan's *custom* to ridicule their former representative, whoever it happened to be, soon after they left the Big Camp. This served a purpose: It humbled that individual, reminding them that they were just a regular member of the clan, without any special powers.

Yet Sparrow's and Kitten's insults were missing the pizzazz of days-gone-by. They were going through the motions; mocking Serenity out of a sense of duty, without the jovial spite which usually accompanied their words.

Sensing that Dawn was about to propose an alternative to Serenity's motion, *Dusk* got ready to object. Sensing that Dusk was preparing his own proposal, *Dawn* got ready to object. But neither Dusk nor Dawn presented a motion. And so neither felt the need to respond.

A vote was cast, and the result was unanimous: The clans-folk agreed to take Delight's body to the nearest patch of trees.

*** 

The new day was welcomed with silence and sloth...

Barely a word was spoken. What was there to say? Everyone knew what they had seen. It was too late to save their forest. Perhaps one day they would return, remove the saplings, and plant a variety of trees. But that mission would have to wait.

They trudged ahead.

It was only once the sun had passed overhead, and begun its slow descent, that the conversation resumed afresh...

Some said it was the ancestors who had torn their forest to shreds; destroying their home, so they could move to a new location. But that did not explain the saplings. Why would the ancestors want so much rubber?

Others claimed that a typhoon must have been to blame. But that did not explain what had happened to the missing trunks and branches.

A consensus began to form: This was the act of an outsider. Someone so profane, they had no respect for the dead. Someone so ignorant, they thought they could plant a forest which only contained a single type of tree.

Who would do such a thing?

Hunter was a deeply troubled individual. But he was no fool. They had met a couple of simpletons, on their way to the Big Camp. But those men had been far too feeble to commit such an atrocity. Father Ralph had some peculiar ideas. But he had been in their camp all along.

It must have been a *group* of these Wogies; an entire army of this strange and foreign tribe. Those people really were a threat. They were not content with conquering the living. They wished to conquer the dead! They were not just waging war on their *people*, but on their *land*; on Mother Nature herself.

No! It was too far-fetched to believe. There must have been a more reasonable explanation. But what could it possibly be?

\*\*\*

Time was the greatest healer...

Yes, they had borne witness to something horrific. And yes, they were facing a mortal threat. If a group could destroy such a sacred place, if they could attack Mother Nature, then who knew what else they would do?

But six days had passed, and the clans-folk had not experienced anything untoward. Their shock was beginning to thaw.

They had set up camp in one of the two oases which dotted their route. It was lusher than before. But the plants were still coarse; a dullish shade, with tough leaves and spiky flowers.

Sunny respected them, for surviving in these inhospitable surroundings. But he did not particularly *like* them. They were too fearsome to love. Sunny's feet were sore, and he was growing impatient; longing for their final destination, where the trees would be laden with blossom, and the flowers would be vying for the eye's attention.

But they would not reach their Small Camp for at least a couple of days.

Sunny nodded at Hope.

She rolled her eyes, turned away, waited for a reaction, turned back, and took control; beckoning *Sunny* with her finger, before placing her hands on her hips; waiting for Sunny to approach *her*.

She grabbed his wrist, and dragged him behind the nearest mound; walking so quickly, that Sunny struggled to maintain the pace. He got his feet in a tangle, almost tripped, and almost stumbled over the debris:

"I... I..."

Sunny knew what he wanted to say. He had practised his speech, in his mind, on what might have been a hundred separate occasions. But now he had Hope alone, he could barely even speak.

"I... I would like... I think we..."

"Shut up!"

Hope shoved Sunny to the ground, with more ferocity than Sunny had experienced before.

"You've got no other girlfriends or boyfriends here, Mister Sunny Loverboy, so you thought you'd come back to old Hope? Eh? No choice. Miss Hope or Miss Nada. And, after nine long days, you supposed you'd settle for me?... What, Mister Lothario? You can't speak? Did the serpent eat your mouth? Did you think you could just give me a nod, and then I'd come running? Eh? Mister Big Balls? Mister Snake Charmer? Mister Sower Of Fertile Seeds?"

Sunny was confused. Was this a game? Did Hope genuinely believe that *he* was the one who had taken several lovers, rather than spend time with *her*?

"I... I..."

"Don't make excuses! You owe me. You owe me big time... What? You thought you'd get away with it? Eh? Creating a harem? Abandoning the one who taught you everything you know? Eh? Mister Little Boy In A Big Man's Body? You've got an awful lot to learn!"

Hope ripped the loincloth from her hips, squatted over Sunny's head, and brushed her vagina up his face; beginning at the point of his chin, proceeding as slowly as she could, before reaching the tip of his scalp.

She smelled of ginger and cloves.

Hope repeated the action, ever so gently, ever so many times. Whenever she sensed a movement, she shunted Sunny's head; thwacking his face with her pelvic bone, pressing his skull down into the dust.

She released the pressure, and began the process afresh.

Sunny could not be sure if he was being caressed, attacked, rewarded or abused. It took a good while, before he even noticed that the force had increased. It took him even longer to realise that Hope was no longer going up and down, but following a circular path around his bulbous nose.

She locked onto Sunny's lips, thrusting back and forth.

Sunny took the hint. He extended his tongue, running it between her labia, before focussing on her clitoris; sucking, blowing, sucking and...

Hope came, emitting a sound that was more

angst-filled than ecstatic; a sort of hushed, primaeval yelp.

She rose to her feet, reattached her loincloth, kicked some dirt past Sunny's face, turned and stormed away.

Sunny had no idea what had happened.

***

Sunny had almost given up on his previous plan. He could have Hope to himself, whenever they were away from the Big Camp. Surely that was enough?

Why did he even want to be exclusive? It was not the way things were done. Whilst he had refused to accept it before, he supposed he must have been manipulated. Father Ralph *had* played tricks with his mind.

Dinner was almost over...

The members of their clan had spent the afternoon catching fish in the oasis's pool. They had returned the ones which were still growing, and the ones which looked pregnant. But they had kept around twenty fishes, roasted them, and eaten them along with some oranges. It made a pleasant change from their previous meals; a fairly monotonous combination of berries and dried meat.

Hope sat down beside Sunny, and squeezed his thigh.

"I'm with child."

"Oh... You... But... Well..."

"Eh? Have you lost the ability to speak? Mister No Tongue, No Teeth, No Words?"

"I..."

Sunny nodded.

"Is that it? Aren't you going to congratulate me?"

"Yes! I mean... Whoopee! I'm as happy as the sun on a cloudless day."

"But no more sex till I give birth."

"No... More... Steady your smoke... No more, *what*?"

"No more sex. Just stuff like we did before."

Sunny nodded. He was happy for Hope, although he was flummoxed by his own imperceptiveness. How had he not noticed this before? Hope's midriff had clearly expanded. She would probably give birth within four or five lunar-cycles.

Sunny was excited to meet the baby, although he was not entirely convinced by this chastity clause. That did feel a little extreme.

His thoughts were cut short by an eruption of

noise:

Ewww! Oi! Ewww!

At first, it sounded like the type of roar that could have only been created by a prehistoric monster. Then their ears adjusted and the noise evolved; becoming more volcanic, like an explosion which had emanated from deep beneath the earth. It took them quite some time to realise that this cacophony had erupted from the mouth of one of their peers. Pumpkin was both shouting *and* gasping for air; creating a noise that was both loud and choked, squealed and strangled:

"Ancestor on earth! Ancestor on earth!"

Pumpkin was standing between two of the surrounding mounds. He appeared to be dragging something heavy, but it was too dark to discern the details. Sunny hoped he had hunted an animal. They had not eaten fresh meat for days. But the hellish nature of Pumpkin's yelps, suggested that this was unlikely.

"The dead alive! The living dead!"

The clans-folk waited for Pumpkin to explain.

When it became clear that he had nothing to add, Landscape approached her friend, somewhat tentatively; stopping after every few steps, considering whether she should continue, peering back in search of support, before completing another few steps.

Sunny was the fifth person to stand. Or perhaps he was the sixth. He was the second person to reach Pumpkin. And he was one of the first to understand the cause of that man's delirium: Pumpkin really had returned with something that looked like an ancestor. This was peculiar, since they had always considered their ancestors to be spirits; entities which had no physical form. And this thing, whatever it was, had an unmistakable outline. It occupied space, and must have weighed a lot. Pumpkin looked exhausted from the effort he had expended, dragging it back to this place. But this thing did not seem particularly human. It was other-worldly; shadowy, gaunt, and far too pale to be real. It had no eyeballs, only sockets. Its skin was far too tight.

Pumpkin's peers appeared to agree. Some nodded, in the most pensive of fashions. A couple shuffled backwards, two toe-lengths at a time. One turned around to flee; returning to the collective embrace of the group.

Kitten tutted:

Tut, tutty-tut-tut, tutty-tut.

Her neighbours turned to face her, searching for an explanation.

But Kitten felt no need to explain.

Tut, tutty-tut-tut, tutty-tut.

Sunny looked up at Kitten, and looked back down at the "Ancestor on earth". His peers were doing something remarkably similar, apart from Pumpkin, who was staring into the darkness.

Tut, tutty-tut-tut, tutty-tut.

A lone voice finally asked the question which everyone else was thinking:

"Auntie Kitten: Why do you tut at the ancestor?"

Kitten attempted to tut, and then to answer. But she was overcome by so much scorn, that she emitted more of a splutter than a tut, spraying saliva into the ether:

"*Tut... Splutter... Mist... Tut...* Ancestor? Have you completely lost your beads? Ancestor? Ancestor, this big fat hairy tuchus!"

They waited for more.

The leaves glistened in the moon-splashed light.

A bird whistled two solitary notes.

But still, Kitten remained silent.

"Not ancestors?"

"What? Have we taught you nothing? Or have your minds dropped out through your buttocks?... Since when did ancestors have bodies?... *Tut, tutty-tut-tut, tutty-tut...* This ain't no ancestor. This is quite clearly a tut-tutting corpse!"

After a moment of reflection, a few people crept forwards. Sunny supposed they must have believed Kitten. If this was not an ancestor, then there was no reason not to approach.

Health was among their number. She had set fire to a bundle of dried sage, which she was wafting above Pumpkin's head; producing a crackling sound, and some pearly layers of smoke. This age-old ritual was performed to cleanse the air; to unburden the clans-folk of their stress. It appeared to be having the desired effect; dissipating the terror which had lurked in Pumpkin's eyes, and relieving the tension which had caused his shoulders to crumple.

Seeing the transformation, judging it safe to advance, Sunny approached the corpse. He explored it with his eyes, before using his fingers; stroking its shoulder and pinching its arm.

"The Desert Woggy."

"The man we tried to help."

It seemed so obvious. It was a wonder it had not occurred to him before: This man must have died in the days which had followed their previous encounter.

If only he had not fired that gun and scared them all away! They could have escorted him to safety. He would still be alive today.

The conversation rumbled on:

"These Wogies aren't so tough after all. Huh! They can't even go for a walk without dropping dead like unwanted leaves."

"We'll be okay. They may destroy our forests, but they'll never replace us. They don't even know how to live!"

# HOME, SWEET AND SOUR HOME

The clan had two sorts of stories...

Most were allegorical. It did not matter if the details evolved. Who knew? Perhaps Uncle Crow had once been a woman: *Auntie Crow*. Perhaps that person had a different name: *Auntie Owl* or *Uncle Hawk*. It was the *moral* of the story which mattered: Successful hunters had a duty to remain humble, to maintain harmony within the group. The fable was just a mechanism; a medium through which this message was conveyed.

But there was a second type of story. These were retold with such rigidity, they might as well have been scripted. The details were always the same. Almost every word was identical, whenever the tale was told.

This gave the impression, rightly or wrongly, that these stories were not fables. They were oral histories, which recounted *real events* from the past.

One such story referred not to an individual, an Uncle Crow or Auntie Rabbit, but to a group: *The First Ancestors*...

According to legend, the First Ancestors had lived in a time of plenty, when fruit juice flowed in the streams, the flowers were always in bloom, and the trees bore new fruit each morning. But what was particularly special, for a clan so devoted to hunting, were the animals who lived in that epoch. They were more varied than any set of creatures there had ever been.

Among these fabulous specimens, was an animal called a *woolly mammoth*. This beast was a colossus; double the height of most people, and almost two-hundred times the weight. Hunting a woolly mammoth was easy. The First Ancestors only had to chase it into a pit filled with spikes. And the rewards were great. A single animal could provide enough food to feed a clan for an entire season.

There was just one issue: Left out beneath the sun, their meat would soon decay. This problem was not insurmountable. The clans-folk could have dried or salted their food. They could have stored it in a cool, dry place.

But why go to all that bother?

To save themselves the trouble, the clans-folk gorged on that meat whilst it was fresh, and abandoned whatever remained. They kept the hides and tusks, but only if they needed them right away. Then they went out to hunt, killing a second woolly mammoth, and then a third; eating as much as they could, and abandoning the leftovers.

Life was easy for the First Ancestors. But their behaviour had consequences. They hunted so many woolly mammoths, that their numbers began to dwindle. It became more difficult to track them down. In time, they killed the very last one.

Still, there were other animals to eat...

When the First Ancestors arrived in their region, it was home to about twelve different types of large, flightless birds. Some were nearly three times as heavy as a human. The largest laid eggs which were a hundred times larger than a chicken's. There were flightless geese and an array of primates, each of which tasted delicious.

These creatures had never seen humans before.

They looked at the First Ancestors. They did not see any sharp teeth, piercing claws or poisonous stings. And so they saw no reason to flee.

The First Ancestors had their fill; walking up

to their prey, and stabbing them through with their spears.

But the good times were not to last. They killed so many creatures, their populations rapidly decreased. Within twenty or thirty generations, they had gone the way of the woolly mammoth.

The absence of these species had a catastrophic effect on the ecosystem. With fewer large animals, the smaller animals flourished. They ate all the fruit and nuts.

The First Ancestors could no longer find fruits to eat each morning. They had to trek to find that food, and they had to wait for it to come into season. The excess fruit did not fall into the rivers, flavouring them with juice. The clans-folk had to make do with plain old water.

Things would never be so good again.

***

The clan remained at the oasis for several days.

This had not been their intention. Other clans might have rested for many nights, whilst travelling between their camps. Some clans did not even have a Small Camp. They moved from one hunting ground to the next. But the Eagle

Clan rarely stopped for more than a couple of nights in any location. Having left their land fallow, to allow it to recover; they were keen to discover what plants had regrown, what small creatures had come to eat those plants, and what larger animals had been attracted by this prey.

Indeed, they had been getting ready to leave, when they realised something was amiss. Pumpkin had not moved. He was still wedged inside the crevice, slumped down aside the remains of the Woggy's corpse.

No-one dared to approach.

Someone said Pumpkin had been murdered. The whole thing had been an elaborate ruse, in which the Woggy had pretended to be dead, waited, and then slaughtered Pumpkin as he slept. Another person said that Pumpkin must have been possessed by the Woggy's spirit. His body was alive, but the Woggy was inside, controlling his arms and eyes.

The truth was more mundane: Pumpkin had broken his leg, whilst dragging the corpse. This explained his fiendish screams.

The clans-folk took great pride in caring for the sick, disabled and elderly; nursing their peers back to health, and feeding anyone who was unable to feed themselves. It was in their own self-interest. One day they would be ill. *They* would require this kind of assistance.

That morning, there had been two schools of thought...

The first argued that the clan should go ahead, leaving Pumpkin with Health and a couple of helpers. They would erect their camp, and return for the others once Pumpkin had completed his recovery.

In normal circumstances, such a plan would have been approved. But these were not normal circumstances. The members of their clan were still shaken. A strange people were in their midst; a people so malign, they had waged war on a *forest*. Who knew what else they might do?

The alternative school of thought called for the clan to remain together; to provide a united front against this weird and wicked foe.

This idea had won out.

The clan had remained in this oasis for nine more days, giving Pumpkin's bone the time it needed to set. But the clans-folk had already consumed all the larger fish, the oranges, dried meat and edible plants. Search parties had been dispatched, to locate more food. But they had not ventured far, and had always returned by nightfall.

Sat around the fire, their conversations had inevitably turned to the First Ancestors...

When Sunny first heard of that group, as a child, he had assumed that their story was one of crime and consequence. The First Ancestors had committed the crimes of gluttony and sloth. As a consequence, the tribes-folk now had to dedicate a great deal of effort, searching for food to eat.

But now Sunny understood that there was more to the tale. It was a call of duty, commanding them to protect their natural environment.

The First Ancestors had been irresponsible. But their descendants had learnt the lesson. These days, they usually only killed the oldest and frailest animals. They left most of the females, and they never hunted youths. They burnt the prairie, to encourage new plants to grow. They rarely cut down trees. And they dispersed seeds; assisting Mother Nature, rather than overwhelming her.

These Wogies, however, had not learnt this

lesson. Like the First Ancestors, who had killed *all* the woolly mammoths, they had taken *all* the trees in a forest. That place was also extinct.

If the Wogies continued to behave in such a manner, Mother Nature would surely make them suffer.

\*\*\*

Sunny was still thinking of the First Ancestors when they eventually departed; travelling at half their regular pace, taking turns to carry Pumpkin on a stretcher they had made from bamboo.

He supposed he was not alone. The entire clan was quieter than normal; more pensive and downcast. Even the scenery seemed subdued. The mountains slouched beneath a blanket of clouds, and the hills were blurred by mist. The greenery looked less green; more like moss than jade. The earth had lost its spring.

\*\*\*

Several days had passed, and they had almost reached their destination, when they were surprised to observe a radical change in the terrain. Had they not seen something similar, when they arrived at their ancestral forest, they might have been paralysed by shock. As it was, they advanced together; veering off the path, retreating into a copse of trees, and inspecting the scene from that hidden position.

Sunny climbed one of the taller trees, to get a better view.

Before him lay the plain which surrounded the watering hole. In normal circumstances, that seasonal lake would have been full to the brim; catching the sun's light, and glistening in convergent lines. It did contain a little water. But it was surrounded by a tapestry of channels, which were transporting water around the adjacent land.

Sunny was mesmerised. He could not help but stare at the people who were digging those trenches; heaving a tool above their heads, holding it for just long enough to reflect the sun, before swooshing it down towards the earth. It was rhythmic. As one tool pierced the ground, the next one reached its apex. Up and down they went, up and down. The tempo was irresistible.

He fixated on this spectacle for so long, it came as quite a surprise when he panned around; spotting a second group about ten hut-widths away.

The people in this group bore an almost striking resemblance to several members of

Sunny's tribe. They had that unique type of nose, which was common in this region. It was only their behaviour that set them apart. They were down on their knees, uprooting the plants which had always grown on this land; plants which were suited to this climate, which provided food for numerous bugs, and which had roots which held the earth together; ensuring the rains did not wash the soil away.

Why would anyone do such a thing?

Sunny thought of their ancestral forest, and could not help but notice the similarities.

It took him a little longer to spot a third group, who were guiding an animal. That creature was pulling a curious device, which was parting the earth like a wave; spraying soil either side of a furrow.

A few people were following in its wake, dropping seeds, before covering them over with earth.

Sunny was impressed. He thought that their tribe could have benefitted from having such a device when they were planting tobacco.

He continued to observe this performance, before noticing the bracelets which were attached to people's ankles. Made from a similar material to Hunter's gun, they appeared to be connected; binding those people together.

Only now did Sunny notice the Wogies. One was standing amidst the three gangs; pointing here, shouting there; barking, growling and howling. Sunny thought he recognised that man. Perhaps he had seen him in a dream.

The other two Wogies were further away. They both had rifles. They were both wearing an unnecessary amount of cloth. Neither had earned a tattoo.

Sunny finally acknowledged the scene.

He had been focusing so intently on this small tract of land, that he had not yet registered the changes which had been made to the surrounding landscape. Trenches, furrows and mounds stretched out as far as the eye could see. Sunny spotted a smattering of seedlings. These dotted the land which had already been irrigated, ploughed and planted. Off in the distance, he could see thousands of lines of identical plants, arranged in parallel rows. Beyond that, there might have been a camp. Although this could have been a trick of the light, which had been smudged by mist and smoke.

He scratched his head.

Sunny was familiar with a few types of agriculture. Sparrow grew cassava. The tribe grew coffee. Sunny had even observed a certain species of ant, who worked together to cultivate yeast. It was the *scale* of this operation that surprised him. These people were dedicating every last morsel of their strength, toiling throughout the hottest part of the day; channelling water, breaking the earth, fencing it off, and guarding it with their guns. And for what? To grow far more food than they would ever be able to eat? Why go to such lengths, when the rewards were so meagre? Why overburden the delicate layer of topsoil? Why use up all the water? Why obey the one man who *wasn't* performing this arduous task? And why concentrate on just a few plants, when the valley contained so many? Having such an unvaried diet would almost certainly lead to malnutrition and disease. If the weather turned, these crops could fail. These people might even starve.

The bossy man did something with his hand, creating a *whoosh* sound which shook the leaves.

One of the natives yelped.

She silenced herself so abruptly, Sunny could

still feel the resonance of her scream long after it had been muted.

He squinted, and attempted to deduce what had happened.

Although he could not be entirely sure, he thought the Woggy was holding a stick, which may have been bound in leather. It was attached to a length of material. It could have been a rope, or perhaps it was a leash. Here, Sunny had to make a leap of logic; concluding that the man had controlled the material with the stick, sending it flying, and slashing it down upon the woman's back.

Things were beginning to make sense: These people were not toiling of their own free will. They had been kidnapped. They were being *forced* to obey the Wogies.

But how had they ended up in such a state? Why were the Wogies doing such brutish things?

Judging by his peers' responses, Sunny was not the only one who was pondering these questions. Whilst a few had fallen asleep, most were analysing the scene. Some looked confused. Some were holding their fingers in a vertical position, moving them together and apart; the gesture they performed whenever they were scared. Others looked drained. Their eyes were heavy, monochrome, and shaded with fear.

They remained in this state, among these trees, until the sun had retired for the night. Then they retreated to a safe place and erected a temporary camp.

***

The clans-folk abandoned their normal routine...

They did not create a fire, sit around that fire, talk or eat. It was not until the following morning that anyone mentioned the things they had witnessed. It took several more conversations, before they were willing to accept the reality. And even then, they could not agree upon a response.

Dawn sighed before having his say. He lifted his shoulders, as though to shrug. But he kept them raised, aside his ears; refusing to allow them to return to their natural position:

"Let it be heard: These Wogies won't surrender our land without a fight. Negatively, no! Yet we don't have the strength to vanquish them in battle... I suggest we move on. We should establish a new camp, far away from this dangerous foe."

This comment was met with a murmur of assent, which rippled around the circle; only coming to a stop once it had made its way to Dusk.

That man scrunched his nose with disdain.

"Let it be said: This is our land! It was the land of our mothers, our mothers' mothers, and our mothers' mothers' mothers. It's the only land we've ever known. I'm too old to move. And I'm unwilling to abandon our home without a fight.

"Just look at these people! Look at their cloths! They aren't like us; satisfied so long as they've covered their loins. They insist on covering their chests, arms and legs; adding a second layer, and a third. They're the First Ancestors reborn. Insatiable!

"If we were to move somewhere new, they'd surely move there as well. Positively, yes!... If we move again, they'll follow in our tracks. They'll push us into the sea, or force us into the desert."

Sunny's mother tutted so loudly, it sounded like two stones had been smashed together:

"Fight! Fight? Can you hear yourself speak? Have you completely lost your beads? Ancestors, oh ancestors: What have you done to this man?"

She waited for her face to soften; from a scowl, to a frown, to a grin; before adopting the sort of tone a mother might use when addressing a child:

"Dusk, lovely: Don't you remember what you were told? These Wogies have *guns*. They have *horses*. They've killed hundreds-of-thousands of people... What you're proposing isn't a *battle*. It's *suicide*."

Dusk remained defiant:

"Guns? We've got guns! And we don't need horses. We know the land. We could sneak up on the Wogies, shrouded by the night, and kill them as they sleep. Or we could pick them off, with gunfire and arrows, whilst hiding in the trees."

A few people nodded. A guerrilla-style ambush made more sense than an outright war. But it still seemed awfully dangerous.

Sunny rose to his feet.

He had felt a sudden urge to interject, which was somewhat out of character. Sunny usually observed these discussions in silence; digesting the elders' words, without voicing his own opinions. But this was different. This was *his time*. He was fit, strong and able. He felt a duty to defend his peers.

He tried to clear his throat; to make a noise which would win the group's attention. In this, he failed. At first, he did not produce a sound. Then, he coughed. Then, he coughed again. He raised his hand, bowed his head, steadied himself, and attempted to strike a pose.

"I wish to propose an alternative."

Everyone appeared to freeze. This was not just because Sunny's behaviour was so unusual. He had never been so bold before. It was because they could not conceive of any other options. They could fight or they could flee. What else could they possibly do?

"I propose we bide our time. You know... We glide like weightless birds, analysing the situation, waiting for the perfect moment to swoop."

Dusk rubbed the outside of his arms; the gesture tribes-folk made whenever they were spoiling for a fight.

"We spent an entire afternoon 'Analysing the situation'. What more could you want?"

Sunny closed his eyes.

He was taking control of proceedings; not rushing, not panicking; breathing slowly, and allowing the tension to build.

He spoke with steady assurance:

"We observed a few people, whilst they manipulated the land. But we didn't discover how they'd ended up in such a bind. We didn't enter the Wogies' camp, find out who was there, what they were doing, or what they planned to do next."

The silence continued.

"I propose we dispatch a search party."

No-one replied. Sunny had not offered a definitive plan. But he had not denied Dusk the opportunity for a battle. Nor had he denied Dawn the option to flee. He had only asked them to wait.

Dusk supposed that the delay might work to his advantage. If they waited long enough, they could unite with some of the other clans and attack the Wogies together. And Dawn supposed that the delay would work to *his* advantage; giving his kinfolk the time they needed to accept defeat, make peace with the situation, and say "Goodbye" to their former home.

Dawn nodded, up and down.

Dusk nodded, down and up.

Hope and Sunny were sent to investigate the

Wogies' camp.

*** 

Sunny was happy to go. This mission was his idea. He felt a responsibility to see it through to completion. He hoped it would be the making of him; the day he came of age, risking life and limb for the group. And it meant he could be alone with Hope.

Hope was not so enamoured:

"This is as stupid as a dog in a tree."

Sunny could not be entirely sure if she was serious, playful or frightened. And that, he supposed, was the point.

"What sort of person would go trudging into a ring of hungry wolves? Eh? Mister Wolf Food. Mister Please Come Here And Eat Me. Mister I'm Just About Ready To Die.

"Do you want to end up like those people we saw on the plains; chained and digging, digging and chained? Eh? No good will come of this. No good at all."

*** 

Sunny was grateful for Hope's company, despite her bickering. Hope's presence settled his nerves, imbuing him with the feeling one only tends to experience when in the presence of someone who loves them; a feeling that you are being protected, even when you are not; a warm feeling, that centres on your belly, and inspires the hairs on your arms to stand on end.

The walk was uneventful...

Hope and Sunny took great care not to be spotted. If anything, they were a little *too cautious*. They did not see another person until they had reached the cultivated land. And yet they acted as though their enemies were all around; tiptoeing forth at the slowest of speeds, ducking for cover whenever they heard a sound.

The sight of another human, inspired them to proceed with *even more* caution than before. They remained in the trees, wherever possible; crawling behind boulders, and slinking between the few bushes which had survived the Wogies' onslaught.

They eventually came to a rest, behind an earthy mound on the fringes of the Wogies' encampment. That place had been erected atop the very same land the Eagle Clan used for their Small Camp. But the huts were completely different; larger, sturdier, with roofs made from layers of something that might have been straw, or reeds, or maybe even bamboo. A few of the walls had been covered in a white substance, which obscured the material behind. Others were made of wood. Sunny supposed it was probably the same wood that had been taken from their ancestral forest.

He was awestruck. The camp was still being built. Most of the huts were half-finished. They only had two or three walls, or walls which were only waist-height, or roofs which did not quite cover the ground. The pathways were uneven. But he could not help himself from admiring the progress which had been made in such a short space of time.

Hope was terrified. She was struck by the overwhelming permanence of it all. People who went to such lengths to construct their huts, might wish to live in them *forever*.

They remained in that position, mute and motionless; observing the camp, trying hard not to be spotted, and trying harder to dissect the psychedelic sounds which were wafting towards them: These screams, this bleating, and that tapping.

Sunny only broke free from this paralysis when he was distracted by a twinkle of light. He looked downwards and rightwards, in the direction from which that light had appeared; searching so carefully, and so intently, that he was almost certain he had made a mistake. There was nothing there. Then a sunbeam pierced the clouds, and the twinkle reappeared. This time, he was in little doubt. He wriggled forwards in the manner of a lizard, found the object, looked around to see if it was a trap, retrieved the item, and slithered back to Hope.

"Humph!" She scoffed. "It's junk."

The item was a tubular shape. One of its ends was open, the other was flat. It was made from the same material as the guns. Only its sides were thinner. It was turning orange, and it felt a little brittle.

"We could drink from this."

"You'd cut yourself. And anyway, why would we drink from a dirty old thingamajig like that? What's wrong with our bamboo tubes? What's wrong with the coconut shells which have always served us well for a million generations?"

Sunny shrugged. He did not see the problem. They could drink this object *and* those coconut shells. But he did not suppose it was worth an argument.

"Okay... Well, I mean... We could use it for

storage. You know, to hold arrowheads and things like that?"

Hope rolled her eyes.

Sunny waited for a response which never came, looked around, and then scampered back to the spot where he had found the can. This time, he discovered a carved stick with hexagonal sides. A grey substance ran through the middle.

He returned to Hope.

"Here. You could wear this in your ear. Or you could slot it through your nose... It'd look pretty..."

Hope slapped the object away.

"I'm already pretty!"

Unperturbed, Sunny tried a third time; returning with a fragment of something translucent. It had an irregular shape, which suggested it had been a part of something else.

Sunny cut himself on its edge:

"Ouch! Mother Nature, the ancestors, and all the unborn descendants!"

Hope raised her eyebrows.

But Sunny remained defiant:

"We could use this as a blade..."

"Oh behave! Can't you see that it's nothing

but junk? The Wogies dumped it here because it's worthless... And you treat it like it's treasure! Even dung beetles have more self-respect."

Sunny supposed she had a point.

As if to prove that point, an elderly woman appeared on the other side of the mound, where she dumped some peel and bones.

"See? Rubbish! Absolute garbage. What sort of nincompoop would wish to swim in a cesspit like this? Eh? Mister Sunny, 'Uncle Crow of the Dump'. Mister Digger Of Unrotted Manure."

But Sunny had noticed something else:

"You're looking at the wrong thing."

"I know what I saw."

"Okay. What did you see?"

"I saw a woman pour rubbish on top of your precious 'Treasure'."

"And then what did she do?"

"She... Mister Milky Eyes: You saw what she did. She spun around and retreated into this err... This camp thingy... Or whatever this monstrosity is supposed to be."

"Who made her spin around?"

"Eh?"

"Who made her return?"

"No-one."

"Oh, so you're saying she was a Woggy? A Daughter of Empire? A coloniser, free to do as she wished?"

Hope did not reply.

"She looked just like us! And she walked here without being whipped. Without being chained. You know... Just like we weren't whipped or chained by Uncle Survey, the Desert Wogies or Father Ralph."

Hope scowled.

"Can't you hear that screaming? What is it you think they're doing to the people who 'Look just like us'?"

But Sunny was sure of his convictions:

"There's only one way to find out... And, you know... I think we'll be fine. If that woman can come and go, then we can too. Let's move! Let's fly like a bird with a worm."

***

Sunny had been correct. Following in the lady's footsteps, they walked past a couple of Wogies, without inspiring a second glance.

Things might not have gone so smoothly...

When they first stepped into the open, they had proceeded in the most tentative of fashions; taking a couple of baby steps, stalling, skipping, and coming to a premature halt. They would have continued in this jilted manner, had Sunny not placed his hand on Hope's shoulder; caressing her forwards, whilst whispering: "Walk as if you belong here, or these people will stop and stare."

Sunny sensed that Hope was not particularly enamoured by this command. But she did as she was asked, which was all he could have expected.

A few moments later, they arrived outside the first building; a hut which was positioned away from the rest of the camp. It was far longer than the other buildings, but a similar width.

Peering through the doors, Hope and Sunny noted the peculiar setup. There were up to a hundred people inside. The natives were spread out across the floor. The Wogies were lying atop their own individual platforms, beyond a wooden divide. Most were stoic. A few were writhing in pain.

"These must have been the people we heard screaming."

Hope nodded.

Much to her relief, they were not screaming because they were being attacked. If anything, they were being healed. But why? What had happened to them? How could so many people be ill at the very same time?

A healthy Woggy was dashing back and forth, attempting to do far more things than any sane person would ever attempt to do at once, and demanding far too much from his assistant; a native, who began to obey each order, before stopping short to obey the next.

Those two attendants were mainly caring for the Wogies; ignoring the natives, until their screams became too much to bear.

Sunny could not make much sense of their conversation. But he began to recognise a few of the words which were repeated more than the others. There was one which sounded something like "Tuberculosis", and another which sounded like "Influenza". At first, he thought they might be talking about "Chicken pox". Then he became convinced that they were saying "Smallpox". One of the words was probably "Typhoid". But it might have been "Typhus", or "Measles", or "Whooping cough".

The way these words were spoken, after so much deliberation, made Sunny suppose they were a kind of diagnosis. Yet this seemed too far-fetched to believe. He had heard tales of new diseases, which had appeared overnight. Their clan had a story about this very thing: *The Fable of Great Uncle Death*. But he had never heard of *so many diseases*, arriving together, at the very same point in time.

Hope had reached a similar conclusion:

"I guess this explains why Hunter offered us so much medicine."

"He *was* trying to help."

"Perhaps... I don't know... Anyway, let's move on. This place is giving me the worms."

\*\*\*

Hope and Sunny proceeded along a muddy lane, flanked by two rows of huts, before emerging into an opening. This square-shaped space was surrounded by a hotchpotch of half-finished buildings. A couple were two stories high. One was cross-shaped. A few were filled with supplies. Several were filled with people.

One of the huts was producing far more noise than all the others. It was packed to the brim with Wogies, who were spilling out onto the veranda; swigging a frothy drink, and engaging in a type of conversation which was unlike anything Hope or Sunny had ever encountered. These people did not appear to be talking *to* each other, giving their companions the time they needed to speak. They were talking *at* each other. Their words were jumbled up. Sentences were waging war on rival sentences. It was almost impossible to discern individual streams of speech, just the chuggedy-chuggedy din of indecipherable voices.

They backed away, retreating to a grassy spot on the opposite side of the square. They made themselves comfortable. And they observed the people nearby.

One man was asleep, in the middle of the afternoon, for no apparent reason. A second man was skipping, then walking, then skipping; whistling an offbeat tune. A third man was feeding intestines to a dog, without using them to wash his hands.

They recoiled, almost in unison; turning to face a hut which had a roof but no walls.

Sunny's eyes were immediately drawn towards a rather stumpy animal, which reminded him of a cloud. There were thirty similar creatures in a pen at the rear of that hut. But it was this first animal who grabbed his attention. A native was holding it between his legs. "Baah", it screamed. "Baah!"

Sunny gripped his own legs, awaiting the animal's slaughter. He had killed several animals himself, but he usually did so from a distance. That seemed fair. The target had a chance to get away. It would escape if it was quick, or nimble, or cunning. But this? The native had already captured these animals. He was making them wait their turn, and appeared to be cuddling them as they were killed. It was far too intimate. It was outright *unnatural*.

The native brought the sharp object down upon the cloud-like beast. But that animal did not bleed. Nor did it collapse.

Sunny had to perform a double-take, before he was prepared to accept the reality of this situation. The native was not *killing* the animal. He was *removing its fur*!

"But... The animal will be bald. Naked! Bald and naked. Naked and bald... How on earth and the ancestral realm will it regulate its temperature?"

Hope shrugged.

She was more interested in the pile of fur by the man's feet. Another man was gathering it up; placing it in a large wooden box, which was supported by four vertical circles. When the box was full, that man climbed on top and whipped a horse, who trotted away; pulling the box towards another hut.

Hope had seen horses before. Both Hunter and Father Ralph had ridden atop those animals. But she had never witnessed a spectacle which was quite as bizarre as this.

Now it was her turn to ask an unanswerable question:

"How did he get that animal... that *horse*... To pull that thingy-whatsit?"

Sunny opened his mouth to answer, but failed to produce a sound. His gaze was still fixed upon the first man, who was removing furs with metronomic regularity. His talents were breathtaking. But something was amiss:

"The... The joy... Where's his joy?"

Hope had already worked this out:

"Can't you see? He isn't a Mister Happy, doing this out of choice; because he loves the task, or because it's necessary. Why would anyone need so many balls of fur? No. He's a Mister Slave In Invisible Chains. He's being *made* to do this... Of course, there's no joy. He's stuck in a trap."

Sunny could not see a trap. The man was not tied or bound. No-one was holding a weapon above his head, forcing him to do this laborious task.

"I don't like it... It... It doesn't seem... Umm... Right? Natural? Sane?"

"Let's get out of here."

"Okay. But let's explore one of those huts before we go."

Hope sighed. This place was giving her the spiders. But she did not feel threatened. Other natives were walking around without being harassed. She supposed that she and Sunny would also be left alone.

They walked at a leisurely pace, reached one of the larger huts, and edged inside; coming to a stop after a few more steps.

That place was filled with two types of crops.

"Rubber and cotton," Hope explained.

"Cotton?... Oh... Does it taste nice?"

"I've never tried it."

"It looks a bit... *Coarse*... I mean... How are you supposed to cook it?"

"I don't think you do."

"Oh... You eat it raw?"

"I don't think you eat it at all."

"No?"

"I think you smoke the rubber."

"Oh?"

"Yeah."

Hope shuffled back through the entrance, walking on the balls of her feet.

"Let's go."

"Soon. Let's just explore one last hut-store-place... The last one, I promise."

Hope followed Sunny's lead, without a word or gesture, but with a look which positively screamed: "Oh, do hurry up! What else could you possibly want to see?"

Sunny wanted to see what was inside this modest hut, which he entered without the kind of delay which had stalled their progress before.

This place was different to the previous building. A variety of things were on display. Legs of meat hung from the rafters, and some sacks were arranged in a row. Their tops were open, exhibiting a variety of grains. But there was one particular object which piqued Sunny's interest: That strange item the Wogies wore on their feet.

He grabbed one, realised it was too big, put it back on a shelf, and selected a pair which he supposed might fit. He squatted down, shoved the first one onto his foot, jumped up and grinned:

"Look at me! I'm a big Woggy fellow, with a loincloth on my foot!"

"Humph! Loincloths are for your loins. That's a foot-cloth."

"Huh? Okay then... I'm a big Woggy fellow, with a *foot-cloth* on my foot."

Hope smiled, although Sunny could not be sure if she was smiling *with* him or *at* him. He did look mildly ridiculous. His toes, which were splayed, pointed out at the most awkward of angles. His feet overflowed the sandal's base.

Hope did not stop to stare for long. She was enjoying herself; playing with a wooden contraption, with a row of spikes on one side. She had seen a Woggy use something similar; running it through his hair, untangling the knots and straightening the strands. But when Hope attempted to do the same thing, the object got stuck. She had to yank it free, applying so much force, she detached a clump of hair.

Sunny could not help but chuckle:

Aha! Aah... Aah...

He silenced himself just as soon as he realised how loud he had been. It was reckless; an act which could have drawn unwanted attention.

As if on cue, a stranger stomped in through the gates. His eyelids were drawn so wide, his eyeballs extended beyond their sockets. His eyebrows had a turquoise hue. It was petrifying. But Sunny was not only petrified. He was also relieved. This man was a native. His face was covered in tattoos, which bore a passing resemblance to his own.

The man scowled, formed a fist, restrained himself, and guffawed:

"Hah hah!... You think?... Hee hee!.. You think that's how you hold an axe?"

Sunny had forgotten he was holding anything at all, let alone an object which was called an "Axe".

"You hold it by the other end... By the *handle*... There... That's the handle, there."

Sunny nodded, earnestly, as he turned the "Axe" around.

"I'm inclined to believe you're not a citizen of this town."

Sunny frowned. He had understood most of the comment, which was spoken in a familiar language. But had never heard of a "Citizen" or a "Town".

"Yes, I thought as much... Now, you can stay

here if you so choose. The decision is entirely yours. But if you have somewhere else to go, or if you still have a clan to call your own, then I'd suggest you flee before you're spotted. Once they've got you, there's really no escaping."

Sunny paused to consider these words.

But Hope was in no mood to dally. Before Sunny knew what had happened, she had grabbed his wrist, pulled him out of the store, and dragged him across the square.

***

They would have sped through the camp, and out the other side, had Sunny not spotted someone familiar; a woman who was standing in front of one of the smaller huts...

At first, he thought he had seen a ghost. The very sight of that person sent a shiver down his spine; pinning him to the spot, and causing his jaw to hang loose.

Hope did not stop. She charged ahead; yanking Sunny's arm, almost removing it from its socket, rebounding back, crashing into his body, and knocking him to the ground.

"Soh... Soh... Songbird?... Is that you?"

Songbird was so large, it would have been impossible to miss her. Yet she seemed smaller than before. It was a strange thing. Her thighs were about as large as Sunny remembered. They were still as spherical as any thighs he had ever seen. Her upper body was also the same size. *Every part* of her body was as large as it had always been, if not a little larger. Yet Songbird seemed smaller. Perhaps it was her attire. She was covered in cloths. Perhaps Sunny had grown. Or perhaps the world had grown up around her. Her new hut was four or five times larger than the tent she had lived in before. This "Town" was several times the size of her clan's old camp. Songbird was still a giant. But she was no longer a force of nature. She no longer possessed the gravitational field that had once attracted Sunny. She was just as *enigmatic*. But she was far less *magnetic*.

Sunny was just pleased to find someone he could trust. He jumped to his feet and followed Songbird inside.

Hope's anger was plain to see. She had placed a forefinger beside each of her temples, such that they looked like a pair of horns. But Sunny could not be sure *why* she was angry. Was it because she was impatient to leave? Or because she was jealous of this older lady?

Hope held her ground; waiting for Sunny to protest, turn around and leave. She only followed him inside, once it became clear he was determined to stay. And even then, she remained in a bitter mood; slumping against a wall, falling to the floor, twiddling her fingers and chewing her lip.

"Auntie Songbird, meet Hope.

"Hope... Our dearest Auntie Songbird."

Songbird smiled at Hope, who avoided eye-contact, scoffed and turned away.

"Ah, yes... So, Auntie... I guess this explains why you weren't at the Big Camp."

Sunny looked around the hut, and was surprised to see the sort of things which were normally kept in a communal store: Pots, containers, a beaker, some leafy vegetables and a stack of edible roots. It also contained a platform, like the ones they had seen in the infirmary.

Songbird patted that contraption.

"Come. Sit on this 'Bed'."

She patted it a second time.

"Come, come... I won't bite, unless *you want me to...*"

Sunny edged forwards. He looked to Hope

for moral support, gave up, and finally took a seat. It was not nearly as bad as he had feared.

"Hmm…" Songbird continued. "That wasn't exactly our choice… So, *no-one* from our clan made it to the Big Camp. Most didn't make it at…"

Songbird did not finish the sentence, but Sunny was reluctant to push for more. Songbird was clearly hurt. Her hands were trembling. She was not crying, but her eyes had moistened. They were reflecting the few slithers of light which had managed to creep in through the gaps in the walls.

"They took… They took my sons… They… Hmm… They tied them up, and marched them away. Someone said they were being sent to a distant 'Plantation'. But no-one told us what a 'Plantation' was… They said I should come to this town, or my daughter would be next."

Sunny stroked Songbird's thigh, granting her the time she needed to continue.

"I… Hmm… So, I think I should start at the beginning."

Sunny nodded.

"So, there was this man. He… Hmm… He looked like us. He spoke our language. But he wasn't of our mind. He…"

Sunny filled the silence:

"Hunter?"

"Yes!… *No*… So, I've met that Hunter chap. He… Hmm… But I'm speaking of someone different. Someone similar, but different.

"So, this other chap, he offered us what we called 'Cargo'. Impressive things. Enchanting, beguiling things. Things we'd never seen before. Things we could've never made ourselves.

"We saw their worth, almost straight away… Those *steel axes*! They were obviously better than our stone tools. And those *matches*! You know, it was far easier to make a fire with a match, than in the traditional way. One strike, and *Mother Nature around us*! You've got yourself a flame. An impressive flame.

"We couldn't help but be enticed. So we took their medicine. We accepted their cloths, drinks and umbrellas. We felt rich, special; showered with all those gifts."

The joy drained from Songbird's face.

"Hmm… So, we always say that 'Nature provides'. This is our way… You want a berry? You pick yourself a berry. You see it, you take it, you enjoy it, and that's the end of that. If you want a hut, you collect a few branches, and you build yourself a hut... So, that's exactly what we did: We took that cargo. We used it, enjoyed it, and thought nothing of it... But those Wogies... Hmm... Those crazy Wogies... They don't think like us. They... They said we *owed* them. We had to 'Pay' for the gifts they'd given."

Sunny scratched his head:

"Oh... Like when I tried to re-gift you for the ox, by giving you a buffalo?"

"Not exactly... Hmm... So with that, there was never any obligation. You were only really *borrowing* that ox. You could've returned the very same beast, and that would've cleared the debt. Although I rather wanted to *maintain* that debt; for you to over or under gift us. That way, you had a reason to return.

"These Wogies aren't like that. They don't care for relationships. Their debts *have to be* 'Repaid'... And you can't just borrow an axe and then return it once you're done. You have to give them something similar, but *different*... Something new... Hmm... And if you don't have anything to give, they charge 'Interest'. You have to gift *more* than you were gifted. It's a bit like a protection. If you don't re-gift them... If you don't *repay* them when they ask... Then they get all sorts of crazy. *Impressive* sorts of crazy."

Sunny thought he understood. Then he had his doubts:

"Well..."

"So, at first, we just gave them some meat... In return for an axe, we might give them an ox's leg. They were happy with that. But they kept on giving us cargo. And my sons kept on accepting it. They supposed it'd have been rude to say 'No'.

"In the end, they were unable to re-gift... To *repay* their debt. They... They didn't have anything left to give but themselves."

Sunny frowned.

"You mean... They gave themselves up as slaves?"

Sunny had never met a slave himself, but he had heard of their existence. When tribes went to war, they took prisoners, who became *war slaves*. If a murder was committed, the murderer might be gifted to the victim's clan, as a slave, as compensation for the *blood debt* which was owed. This prevented reprisal attacks. People could also surrender themselves into *debt slavery*, in order to clear their debts.

Songbird nodded.

"They thought they'd gift their time and skills, and that'd settle their debt. But no. Oh no!

"The who, the what and the why: My sons, that was the 'Who'. The what: Those *chains* and those *guns*! The Wogies tied my babies in chains, along with half the members of our clan. Then they marched them away at gunpoint. And why? Because of this cargo... This strange, impressive debt.

"Our spy followed them to the Giant Waters. She watched on as they were led into the belly of a giant canoe. The Coast People told her they were being taken to a 'Faraway Land'; that they'd never return; that they'd be slaves for *the rest of their lives*."

Sunny raised his eyebrows.

This was not like any type of slavery he had heard of before. War slaves were usually integrated into their new clans. Debt slaves were freed, once their debts had been re-gifted. But this? To be sent to another land, never to return, never to be free again? It seemed deranged.

Songbird tensed her cheeks.

"This is why I came here. I'd already lost my sons. I feared they might take my daughter. And our clan was too weak to survive. Hmm... The

Wogies took most of the adults. We were struggling to find food.

"As for the other natives in this camp... This *town*... So, each case is unique. Many came from clans who accepted the Wogies' blankets. That was a trick. Those blankets contained diseases, which killed most of the people who used them. The clans-folk who didn't die, came here to get the antidote. They stayed once they'd been cured, because their clans had been decimated. They didn't have the numbers to get by on their own.

"Some people were brought here by force. You may have noticed the slaves in chains. Hmm... Others were enticed by missionaries. The Wogies took the most fertile earth, forcing the natives to retreat to barren lands. They became hungry and weak. Then the missionaries arrived, bribed them with food, and escorted them here.

"I even believe Father Ralph sweet-talked *one of our clans*, over at the Big Camp. I've seen them walking around, aimlessly, with sullen faces and greyish skin.

"But most of these people came from different tribes, with different dialects, cultures and traditions. Similar, but different... Still, the

Wogies can't tell the difference. They're a simple bunch. Like the water that forgot to be wet."

\*\*\*

Sunny had been so engrossed by Songbird's conversation, he had almost forgotten about Hope. The last time he had looked in her direction, she had looked somewhat miffed. Her eyes had narrowed and her nose had scrunched. Yet Sunny had been indifferent.

Struck by a pang of remorse, he turned to check on his lover, a little too abruptly. This resulted in a mild form of whiplash; the disorientating type, which does no damage in the long term, but can be a little dazzling in the moment.

He need not have worried. Hope was where he had left her, sitting on the floor, glaring out into space. Sunny knew her well enough to realise this was an act. She must have been just as intrigued as he was. How could she *not* be fascinated by these revelations?

"Well..." He tried to ask a question, even though he had not yet thought of a question to ask. "Yes... That, err, explains why you came here... But... Well, it doesn't explain this... It doesn't explain this and that and this."

Sunny gestured with an open palm; presenting the bed, pots, fireplace, wood pile, vegetables and ginger.

"I mean... *You're* not a slave. Slaves wouldn't have this 'Cargo'."

Songbird smiled. It was a monstrous thing to behold; gargantuan, solid, pulsating; a joyous expression, which clashed with her sorrowful tales.

"You're right," she agreed. "Most slaves couldn't possess such things... I'm not really a slave... Not in *that* way. I'm not in shackles and chains. Hmm... Yet I'm not exactly *free*..."

Songbird's smile faded as she spoke. She looked solemn, once again, which made Sunny feel solemn himself. It was not a matter of empathy. It was more a matter of shame. He blamed himself for picking at the scars which must have taken an age to heal.

But he was keen to find out more. So, he did not tell Songbird to stop. He waited to see if she had anything else to say. And he used the intervening time to inspect one of the pots.

It was made of clay, which was not so peculiar. The pot they had lost, whilst fleeing from the Desert Wogies, had also been made of clay. It was this pot's *design* which was so unusual. It featured the image of a person, who was making love to a second person, who was attacking an animal with a spear. And there was another thing: This pot appeared to glisten.

"It's hard to explain. You can't... Hmm... So, you can't just pick the food you need. If you ate something you'd gathered, something the Wogies had planted in one of those fields, they'd say you were 'Stealing', and they'd cut off one of your hands. If you did the same thing again, they'd probably murder you."

Sunny's mouth opened wide. It became so large, it demanded to be seen; escaping from the shadow of his oversized nose and broken chin.

Could it really be so? Would the Wogies murder a person because they had eaten the food they had gathered? It was far too barbaric to believe.

"You mean they have a store? A place where a Women's Council hands out food to anyone who's hungry?"

Songbird tensed her cheeks.

"They have stores, where they store things. And they have 'Shops', where you can get food. Hmm... That food... It isn't distributed according to need. It's not *gifted*. They... Hmm... It's so strange, it's hard to explain. It took me an age to understand, and I still struggle to accept it... So, you need to do this thing they call 'Work'. You need to make something which someone else might want to use, at an unspecified point in the future. If you do this, you'll get given these beads they call 'Money'. And if you gift those beads... This *money*... Then they'll gift you something else. If you're lucky, they'll gift you something to eat."

Sunny scratched his head.

"But... Hang on... What if you don't have this money? Doesn't that mean you can't get any food? So you'd starve to death?... Or you'd go and gather some food. But if you did that, you'd get killed to death?"

Songbird nodded. But she did not appear to believe her own gesture.

Sunny continued:

"Well... Doesn't that enforce a certain type of... Of *equivalency*? Like, do you have to gift a certain number of monies, to get a certain amount of food?"

Songbird nodded with slightly more conviction than before.

"It's just... Don't these Wogies understand that it feels good to give, *without* expecting anything in return? That giving is the best thing you can receive? And that receiving is the best thing you can give?"

Songbird shrugged.

"And... Well, what about the pots? I was asking about this *cargo*. And then you told me about *food*. But what about the pots?"

"Oh, them? I used money to buy those."

"I thought this 'Money' was used to get *food*."

"And pots."

"Pots *and* food?"

"Everything! Pots, food, cloths..."

Sunny guffawed. He could not help himself. His lungs expelled the air they were holding, without seeking his permission. This caused his lips to quiver, his cheeks to shake, and a chortling sound to gurgle up from an unspecified location deep within his chest.

It was not because Sunny was opposed to alternative means of exchange. The members of their clan used one system when they were alone; combining their food, before eating it as a group. They adopted a different system in their Big Camp; establishing a Women's Council, which distributed the tribe's possessions. Sunny had practised *debt exchange*; borrowing an ox from Songbird, returning with a buffalo, and then taking a chicken to maintain the debt. Sparrow had made a *direct exchange* with the Dog Clan; gifting them four spears in return for one of their goats. And his mother had played patolli; *a game of chance*, to exchange the beads she had made for a different type of bead.

Sunny would have been happy to use any of these systems. He would have been happy to adopt the Wogies' system, if it had benefitted the clan. He had heard of a neighbouring tribe who used *wampum*; strings of purple beads, made from seashells, which might have looked like this "Money". Wampum was used to mark agreements. It could be offered as compensation. But it was never exchanged for food.

This "Money"? It was too ridiculous for words.

"So, hang on... Let's return to the moment of conception. To this... What did you call it?... This whirr... whirr... This *work*. Dearest auntie: How do you get this *work*? How do you get this money in the first place?"

"My work... So, I find clay, bring it home, and

turn it into pots, containers and beakers. The Wogies gift me money for each item I make."

"Hang on... Let's arrange our firewood in a neat and tidy stack... You make pots. You gift those pots to the Wogies. They give you this money. You give that money back to the Wogies. And they return the pots you only just made?"

Sunny howled with a kind of laughter which sounded joyful at first, but which grew more sinister the longer it lasted.

"Have I got that right?"

Songbird bowed her head.

"Not exactly."

"No?"

"Hmm... So, say they give me five 'Cents' for a pot."

Songbird rummaged about behind a pillar; retrieving a five-cent piece, which she passed across to Sunny.

He was far from impressed. The coin was less pretty than his mother's beads, and it was less useful than a pot. But he kept his thoughts to himself.

"If I wished to take that pot, I might have to 'Pay' *twenty* cents."

Sunny shook his head. His face barely moved,

either to the left or the right. Yet it managed to travel across that tiny distance, back and forth, with eye-defying velocity:

"So... Hang on... If you gift them *four pots*, they'll give you enough of this money to get *one pot* back?... You... They... Ha! They say 'Squat', and you say 'How low?'."

Songbird was too embarrassed to lift her head.

Sunny was too ashamed to speak in anything more than a whisper:

"I'm sorry. That was crass."

But Hope was not so courteous. If anything, she was more scornful than supportive. She raised her nose and scoffed, creating a guttural noise which got stuck as it ascended her throat:

"*Aargh-humph*... So tell us, Miss Work For Money For Cargo: What happens to the other three pots you made?"

"People use money to get those."

"But there's not enough money to get back *all* the thingies you make. If you make four pots, you'll only get enough money to reclaim one."

"No, there *is* enough money. There's an impressive amount of coins. It's just that *we* don't have them. The Wogies seem to get more money whenever they need it. They gift it to each other, even if they don't make things themselves. They get it from *money men*; these people they call 'Bankers'. And they get it from these men they call 'Merchants'; people who paddle across the Giant Waters, take the things we've made, take slaves, and then make a gift of this money."

Now it was Hope's turn to scratch her head.

"So... Hang on... You're saying that people get different amounts of money?"

Songbird nodded.

"Don't the people who have lots of money, end up controlling the people who only have a little? And don't the people who *make* the money, who can make an unlimited amount of these beads... These *coins*... Don't they end up with an *unlimited amount of power*? Like a gigantic Uncle Crow?"

Songbird nodded again. Only this time, Hope remained silent.

"Yes. The Uncle Crows are in charge... Field-people are gifted less money than pot-makers, who get given less than animal-fur-removers. But it's these *bankers* and *merchants*, all Wogies, who get the most. Well, them and the slugabeds they call 'Officials'. Ha! Those men all work together, as a kind of clan; using this money to 'Buy' themselves a gang of guards, who they call 'Police'. Those bullies subjugate everyone else; attacking anyone who refuses to obey the Woggy rules, which they call 'Laws'.

"I don't know who actually makes the money. Hmm... I suppose they must be the deadliest stonefish in the sea. But nobody's ever mentioned such a person... They must exist, but I've yet to see them myself."

Hope's hunch had been correct. But it was a hollow victory. She wished she had been mistaken.

"This is why I said, 'I'm not exactly free'. Hmm... I'm not a slave, not officially. But I still have to play by *their* rules. I have to do *their* 'Work' and gift *their* 'Money'. That's the who, the what and the why... Anyway, I still get to keep this cargo. So that's pretty swell."

Sunny furrowed his brow.

"Yes, about this. Did you build this hut yourself? It's not like the one you lived in before."

"Hut? They call this a 'House'."

"Oh."

"I didn't build it. I mean, me? Build this

impressive thing?... No, it's a Woggy design. A group of natives did the actual building."

"Oh... Well, if it was built by the tribe, it must belong to the entire tribe."

"So, no. Not exactly. This isn't really a tribe. It's... It's similar, but different... Hmm... So the Wogies created something they called a 'Mortgage'. I think it's short for 'Mortal Engagement'. They say that if I gift them some money every 'Month', every thirty or thirty-one days, then they'll allow me to live here. Eventually, this house will be mine."

Songbird looked to Hope and then to Sunny, attempting to gauge their thoughts. But she could not perceive a reaction, no matter how intently she stared. Her guests' faces were vacuous; frozen, deadpan and pale.

Sensing she needed assistance, Songbird reached behind a beam, retrieved a piece of fabric, and showed them the images which were drawn on one side. It looked like a code. The icons had been put together in groups, which were separated by small gaps. But Sunny could not tell what those squiggles were supposed to represent. They did not look like the murals in their caves. They did not look like birds or trees, or anything else you might find in nature.

At the bottom was a square-shaped sketch.

"They call this the 'Title Deed'. This image depicts the land which will belong to me. The land between the four corners of this house."

Now Hope and Sunny *did* respond, snickering in unison.

It was Hope who offered a reply:

*"Hee chuck-a-chuck hee-hee...* They think an individual can possess the land? The actual land? The earth beneath our feet? Mother Nature's flesh?... They think the land can be possessed; not by a tribe, not by a clan, but by a single person?... And people have to make stuff, to get money, so they can give that money back, to win the right to exist atop that land?... What else? Do you have to gift this money if you wish to take water, breathe the air, speak a word, or use the toilet?"

Songbird did not respond.

"What about birds? Do they have to get money, and then give that money back, before they're allowed to make a nest? Do rabbits need to gift money, before they can live in the burrows they've dug?"

Songbird did not respond.

"What if you don't get enough of this money? What if everyone has all the pots they need, and so they stop gifting you money for the pots you've made? What happens to this hut... This *house*?"

Songbird bowed her head.

"The bankers would take the house away."

"Take it where?"

"Take it *from me*. I'd be the one who'd have to move. The house will stay put... If you can't gift enough money to cover your mortgage, they'll say you're 'Bankrupt'. They'll make you a slave... Hmm... A field slave, in actual chains."

"Wait for just one blink of an eye... You have to make things like pots, or they'll force you into the fields, to make things like plants?"

Songbird shrugged.

"I like making pots. I made pots for our clan. And the Wogies taught me how to glaze them. They look nice and shiny, wouldn't you say?"

Sunny answered this question himself, interjecting before Hope could make another snide remark:

"Yes, they're beautiful... It's just... When we were in the camp... The *town*... We watched a man remove the furs from a clan of animals. He continued, even when he was exhausted. It didn't look like he was enjoying it anymore... And... The thing is... Surely, if you're forced to make *that many pots*, every day, there must come a point when you no longer feel any joy?"

Songbird shrugged again. Only this time, it seemed like she was making an effort.

"It's true... Before, I liked to make clay figurines. It felt like a calling... Once in a while, I might make a pot. But that was just an aside. I was applying a technique I'd learnt whilst doing something fun, to make something which had a practical use... Now, these Wogies don't care much for fun. With them, it's all pots and no figurines. They're obsessed with practicality."

Sunny nodded. He supposed there was even more to it than this. Sparrow gardened for pleasure. But these Wogies took farming to a whole new level; scarring vast tracts of land, to produce way more crops than they needed. When he was a child, Sunny had made toys which moved about atop a set of rollers. But he would have never thought to enlarge those rollers, place them beneath an oversized box, and attach that box to an animal; just to move some "Cargo". Why create so much stuff, that you had to create even more stuff, just to move it around?

Songbird shrugged for the third time.

"It's kooky, I know. Doolally. But what choice do I have? Our clan no longer exists. I don't have anywhere else to go."

"Of course you have somewhere to go! Auntie Songbird: You can come and live with us!"

"I can't. If I leave, they'll take my daughter, and send her to the Faraway Lands. The Woggy guards will give chase. They'll do everything they can to catch me. They might even murder me in the process.

"And anyway, I *do* rather like this house. This bed is ever so comfy. Hmm... If I make enough pots, I'll clear my debts, and these things will all be mine.

"Oh... And there's something else: I've heard the Wogies don't want to stay here forever. They can't handle the heat... They'll be happy so long as we keep on sending them rubber, cotton, food and slaves. So long as we keep on using their money, worshipping their God, and obeying the representatives *they* appoint. So long as we forget our history, culture and politics. So long as we forget that other worlds were possible... For me, it's a waiting game. I just need to tolerate them, whilst I'm waiting for them to leave... I know it's crazy. But I reckon it's the best option I have, to keep my daughter safe."

Sunny whimpered through his response:

"But... I mean... Dearest Auntie: I still owe you a chicken."

"No, no. Consider that debt forgiven. I don't want you to return. It's not safe for you here."

# OUR MONEY OR YOUR LIFE

The stars were already twinkling by the time Hope and Sunny reached their temporary camp.

Songbird had insisted they stay a little longer, to eat dinner, and so they had little choice but to return in the dark; stroking the rocks and trees, to confirm their location; veering off course whenever there was nothing to touch.

They returned to a heavy atmosphere...

The enormity of their situation had finally dawned upon the clans-folk. They had known of the Wogies' presence for several lunar-cycles. They had heard of their antics, and met their representatives. But they had not seen a reason to panic. The Woggy threat was real, but it was *abstract*.

Now the Wogies were *here*. They had occupied *their land*. The clans-folk had *every reason* to panic.

Sunny could not know exactly what his peers were feeling, but he could muster a guess. Judging by their faces, they were experiencing a melange of terror, anxiety, dread, confusion, consternation, and a small amount of something approaching hope, or even excitement. Their emotions were in a tangle. They did not feel a need to be consistent.

It was hard to be certain, however, because as soon as Hope and Sunny returned, their peers reacted to *them*; brushing their other emotions aside.

A few individuals, including Sunny's mother, responded with relief. They were happy that their loved ones had returned alive; unharmed and undaunted.

The majority of the clans-folk, however, had *expected* their friends to return. It was these people who accosted Hope and Sunny, as they sat by the fire; questioning them with nervous zest.

The young spies answered as best they could; speaking with one mind, when it came to most matters; explaining the division of labour, the inequality, the stockpiling of "Cargo", the "Work", "Money", "Mortgages", Uncle Crows, and the private ownership of land. They struggled to explain this last concept, and had to repeat themselves on several occasions, before people began to understand. Even then, no-one could quite grasp how a "Title Deed", covered in codes, could enable a single person to claim the exclusive rights to a portion of Mother Nature.

But there remained one issue upon which Hope and Sunny could still not agree...

"You've already seen their magic spears with their magic arrows," Sunny beamed. His eyelids opened so wide, his lashes retreated into their sockets. "Those things they call 'Guns', which can down the deadliest prey, from the opposite side of the prairie. And you've seen their *horses*; those fantastical beasts, which whisk them across the land.

"Well, I tell you this: There's more. Yes! There's even treasure in their garbage!

"Behold the eternal coconut! This could be used as a pot or beaker. Just look at the hardy material. It's made from the very same stuff as their magical spears... And this: Behold the translucent blade! As pretty as a bead, and as sharp as an eagle's beak... And this: The hexagonal ear stud! Have you ever found anything like it?"

Hope scoffed:

"I've explained all this already. That doohickey has a serrated edge. Drink from it and you'll cut your lip. You can't use that as a blade. It's not straight. And that hexagonal doodad is used for painting their funny code. Why would we want a thingy-whatsit like that? Eh? We don't need to write things down. Our memories work just fine."

Sunny was unperturbed:

"I tell you: They discarded these miraculous items, as though they were banana skins, because they have an abundance of *other things*. Revolutionary things. Things that could transform our lives. Things you can barely begin to conceive.

"We saw them take the hides from a clan of animals. A creature covered in so much fur, they looked like fluffy clouds. You wouldn't believe it, unless you saw it yourself... I reckon that's why they cover themselves in so many loincloths, and foot-cloths, and whatever-cloths: Because they can. They've got more types of cloth than there are mushrooms in the forest. Yes. They were all there, those Wogies; strutting about like rainbows, with head-cloths to stave off the sun, and bag-cloths to carry this 'Cargo'.

"I tell you: We explored their stores. Believe me sisters! These folk have so much stuff, they have to stash it away in camp-sized huts, because they couldn't possibly use it all at once. They have these things they call 'Axes', which are like our spears, but which have the biggest, strongest, scariest blades you've ever seen. They have tools which untangle hair. Hope had a fun time with one of those. They have the most beautiful pots. They even have a giant 'House' which they've filled with rubber and cotton. I mean, they had other houses we didn't even explore. Who knows what treasures they might be hiding in those?"

Hope tutted:

"*Tut tut tut*... What a load of pointless guff! If they can't use it today, why bother having it at all? And as for that useless contraption you mentioned? I'll say this, with a hand on every spirit within me: It didn't untangle this hair. *It got stuck* in this hair. It's a dangerous whatchamacallit, not for the likes of us."

Hope looked around to garner support, before locking her eyes onto Sunny's.

"Haven't you learnt anything from Songbird's sons? They were also enticed by that cargo. And look what happened to them. They were taken away, never to be seen again. They're probably dead. Possibly tortured... Is that what you want for us? Eh?... No good will come of this. No good at all."

The circle remained silent for quite some time, before Dawn began to speak:

"I'm with Sunny. It's not in our nature to leave the eggs in an unguarded nest. Let it be heard: This cargo could change our lives forever."

"Poppycock," Dusk replied. "We've lived for a thousand generations without a... What did he call it? A *foot-cloth*? An *axe*?... And did we ever complain? Were we looking for an albino saviour?... Sistren and brethren: We were happy on our own, doing *our* things, *our* way... Let it be said: We shouldn't change now, just to appease a bunch of lunatics who can't even survive whilst they're naked."

Sparrow raised his hand, stopped and waited. He savoured the silence. Then he allowed his hand to descend; an action which was accompanied by a collective sigh.

"How do you propose we get this cargo? We can't just wander up and gather it from the stores. The Wogies will kidnap us. They'll steal our hands... Are you suggesting we 'Work' for 'Money'?... And lose our joy?... Or what? That we trade the very food which sustains us, just to receive some objects we've never needed before?"

Sunny paused, to see if Sparrow had anything else to add, before offering a response:

"You're quite right. Gathering their things is too dangerous, their work is a form of slavery, and there's very little we can afford to trade. But don't you see? These people have so many wacky and wondrous ways. We've barely peeled the mango... I bet there's another solution; some unimaginable way for us to reclaim our land, or share this cargo, without resorting to either slavery *or* debt. We just need to talk to the Wogies, to discover the other options."

Sparrow thumbed his chin as he spoke:

"You're willing to return, and... No, it's crazy... You're willing to walk up to one of these Wogies... These people who've killed thousands, with these guns and diseases... These people who've chained your sisters and brothers, sent them to faraway lands, and burdened them with debt... You're willing to march up to these cloth monsters, and ask them for... For *help*?"

Sunny rose to his feet; adopting such a triangular stance, that his knees outflanked his shoulders. He inflated his chest to such a degree, that his body seemed well-proportioned. His torso aligned with his lanky legs, making him look both tall *and* balanced; not quite butch, but stronger than most of his peers; a man who was entering his prime.

He adopted a grandiloquent tone:

"I am! Dearest aunties and beloved uncles, sisters and brothers: I'm not only willing, I'm *obliged*. I tell you: I feel duty-bound to go forth. Because the future won't be like the past. These ding-a-lings *are here to stay*. They're going to change our lives, whether we like it or not.

"There are only three possible outcomes: They kill us. They enslave us. Or we come to an arrangement.

"This final option... This is the only one which floats."

Sunny's words hardly inspired an outpouring of praise. A soft, anonymous moan floated over the circle. Someone might have proclaimed: "I'd rather die, than do a deal with those lost spirits." Another person might have replied: "We could fight, or we could flee, but we should never succumb." Sunny could not be sure. His ears were abuzz; usurped by a beeping, which deafened him to this noise. His eyes were a blur. He could see people's outlines, but not their faces. He was focusing his energy on his feet, which were struggling to support his legs.

It was only when Serenity clutched his shoulders, that Sunny regained his vision.

He set his eyes upon his peers, who were holding their hands in the air.

"It's agreed," Serenity confirmed. "This operation has won the clan's consent. But first, sunshine, you must rest."

Sunny was overcome with relief. His muscles relaxed, causing his knees to buckle. His ankles bent, and his body crumpled; chest on top of waist, on top of feet.

As he fell, he saw Hope rise up before him.

She was shaking her head, shaking her shoulders, and muttering under her breath:

"Damned if I'm going. You're on your own this time, Mister Suicide Mission. Mister Please Come Kill Me. Mister I Can't Die Soon Enough."

***

Sunny did not wake until mid-morning...

His head was groggy; heavy with the residue of the previous day's emotions. But he remained steadfast; determined to complete the mission. This was *his* moment. He was coming of age; putting himself in harm's way, to protect the people he loved. Failure was not an option.

He ate the yams which his kinfolk had put aside. He rubbed noses with his mother and sister, nuzzled Hope's cheek, patted arms, and set off alone; accompanied by nothing but his thoughts.

There were regrets: What had he done? Why had he championed those needless items? Why had he volunteered to return?

There were fears: Would the Wogies enslave him? Would they force him to work? Would they burden him with a mountain of debt?

And there were doubts: Would he find a Woggy who could speak their language? Would they wish to speak to him? Did a diplomatic solution even exist?

This cacophony of questions made for an uncomfortable journey. Sunny barely looked up. He ignored the trees, which were in full bloom; the puddles, which shimmered in the midday sun; and the hills, which rolled without moving. He did not smell the sweet pollen, or the aromas of wet soil and damp moss. He did not hear the whispering of the breeze, or the scratching of bugs on bark.

He trudged ahead, only lifting his eyes when the Wogies' town appeared on the horizon.

It looked a little less majestic than before...

Sunny could not help but notice the roofs, which were incomplete or missing; the doors, which had not been attached to their frames; and the walls, which were only knee-high, or chest-high, or chin-high. Most of the pathways were covered in sludge. A few pebbles had been scattered about, in an attempt to maintain those routes, but many more were required.

It was understandable, he supposed. Their clan had been living on this land just six lunar-cycles before. The Wogies had made unfathomable progress in a tiny space of time. Yet this place felt hollow; somehow permanent, somehow inevitable, but incomplete and utterly unreal.

An infantile scream felt unmistakably real.

It shook Sunny to his senses, making him suddenly aware of his surroundings. Here were the footsteps he had made the previous day. Here were the semi-finished buildings he had gazed upon for so long. And here, opposite those huts, was Songbird's home.

Its walls appeared to be shrieking:

"Aaagh! No! Why me? Aaagh! Aaagh! Aaagh!"

Sunny had not intended to turn. He had not intended to approach that building. But he found himself creeping forwards, on the tips of his toes; squatting down behind the house, and spying through a gap in the wood.

What he saw was as grotesque as it was hypnotic. Songbird's young daughter was spread naked on the floor. Her limbs were scattered, haphazardly; bent askew at every joint. Her thighs were covered in a gloop which was yellowish and red.

Sunny could not deny the reality: A Woggy, whose leg-cloths were around his ankles, was forcing himself onto that child. Songbird was hunched against a wall, using her knees to cover her eyes. Another two Wogies were standing on either side. Perhaps they were restraining Songbird. Perhaps they were assisting the other man. Or perhaps they were forcing him to perform this gruesome act.

No. It was something even worse...

As soon as the first man was done, one of the others stepped forward. He also forced himself upon the girl, whose body was limp, and unable to resist. For one ghastly moment, Sunny thought she might be dead. For the briefest of moments, he thought it might be better if she was. Then she choked, drooled, and rolled onto her side; succumbing to a state of semi-consciousness.

The second man grunted, pulled out, and backed away; allowing the third man to approach.

Sunny vomited.

He was sure he had given himself away. His vomit was so pungent, the Wogies must have smelled it, even if they had not been alerted by the noise. Sunny could not just stand there. He had to make a decision: To confront the Wogies or flee.

His heart told him to intervene. Those men were performing a horrific act. They needed to be stopped. The girl needed to be saved.

But his head told him to flee. There was no way he could overpower three grown men. If he tried, he might be murdered, whipped or enslaved. He would not complete the mission, failing his kinfolk, who might succumb to a similar attack.

He rubbed his hand up and down his wrist; his way of accusing those men of being bracelet-wearing wenches. Then he submitted to his rational side; backing away, slowly at first, and then a little quicker; turning, running, and sprinting beyond this settlement.

He hated himself for abandoning that helpless child. And he respected himself for his restraint. He had taken the mature decision, to dodge an unwinnable battle, so he might triumph in the war.

He told himself to concentrate on the latter emotion; to be positive and march ahead. But he could not stop himself from feeling pathetic, no matter how hard he tried. His legs were weightless. His nails were scratching his arms.

One thing was certain: He was in no fit state to proceed. He needed to retreat, recuperate and recover.

***

The light had dissolved...

It could have been dusk. It could have been dawn. Sunny had experienced such a heavy slumber, the world could have turned a hundred times and he would have never known. It took him a while to recall his location, beneath a tangle of roots, within a cluster of trees. He had retreated to this position, meditated a little, fretted a little, and questioned what he had seen:

Had it been real? Why had those men behaved in such a manner? And why had he not intervened? These questions had tormented him for a while. And then they had knocked him unconscious.

Sunny had no desire to return. But he had promised to find a way out of this mess, for the sake of his kinfolk, and he was determined to find one. He was going to march into that town, approach the first Woggy he found, ask the questions his kinfolk had prepared, receive some answers, and leave at the first opportunity.

These plans fell apart, just as soon as he saw Songbird's home. He could not stop himself from entering. He was compelled by solidarity; by a duty to help Songbird and her daughter. And he was compelled by curiosity; by a desire to discover the truth.

Songbird's daughter was asleep, resting her head upon her mother's lap. And so Sunny spoke in a hushed voice:

"Are you okay?"

Songbird nodded, somewhat indifferently. It seemed she was sickened, but not entirely surprised.

And then it dawned upon Sunny:

"It wasn't... It was... The thing today. It's... It's happened before?"

Songbird responded, without making a gesture or a sound.

"Oh... Is that... So, is that her work? She has to surrender her body, *for sex*, in the same way that you surrender your body, whilst you're making all those pots?... Does she get money? Or..."

Sunny cut himself short. He had been crass, leading with such a sensitive subject, and Songbird was clearly offended. The corners of her face were gravitating towards her nose.

She ran her teeth along her lower lip, stroked her daughter's hair, sighed, and tried to ignore the question.

Then she had a change of heart.

She responded in a stilted fashion:

"Not work... A 'Punishment'... It's similar, but different. With work, you surrender your body *first*. Then you get money, which you gift for things like food. But my girl... She shared our food, *before* surrendering her body. And so she was 'Punished' *after*.

"I *choose* to make pots. But my girl didn't choose her punishment... She... She would've never chosen *that*.

"It's like... Both work and punishments are abusive. Both take your freedom and joy. But punishments are worse... They actually entered my child's body!... I... I used to like making pots. But my girl... She's just an innocent babe."

Sunny realised he was sobbing. He could not recall the moment he had begun to cry, but it must have been a while before. His tears had covered his chin, and his chest was already damp.

He could be such an insensitive brute!

He tried to reassure himself. He had gathered some useful information, about "Punishments" and "Work". But he had used Songbird, treating her as little more than a fount of knowledge. That was no way to treat a friend.

He had failed to ask the only appropriate question: "What can I do to help?"

He had still not asked that question.

But Songbird was providing an answer:

"Do stay the night, won't you? I don't think I could cope on my own."

Sunny nodded. He sat down, took Songbird's head, and placed it upon his lap.

They fell asleep together.

***

Sunny awoke, feeling reinvigorated and ready to face the day. Songbird's daughter also appeared to be in fine fettle. It would have been churlish to suppose she had recovered. But the punishment had not affected her behaviour. By the time the others arose, she had already made a pot of herbal tea. Perhaps she had suppressed the memory. Or perhaps she had been abused so many times, she had learned to numb the pain.

If anyone was bitter, it was Songbird. When Sunny explained his plan, she scrunched her nose with so much force, she almost fractured the bone. Rolls of flesh rose up, only to collapse back over themselves; making it impossible to tell where one furrow ended and the next one began.

"You're just going to walk up to a Woggy, and tell them you're not from here? That you're neither a worker nor a slave?... And you think they'll just sit you down, listen to your questions, and tell you the things you wish to hear?

"The who, the what and the why! Are you as mad as a dog with no nose? Are you a loincloth short of an outfit? Do you think you can hunt a boulder?

"They'll accuse you of 'Trespass'. And they'll concoct an impressive punishment, the likes of which no sane person would ever wish to endure."

Sunny scratched the top of his ears.

"Tress... Trespass?"

"Walking on the ground without gifting any money."

"You have to... Oh... Well, what do you suggest I do?"

"Bugger off."

"I cannot. I've made a commitment."

"Oh, Sunny of the Eagle Clan! You don't make things easy, do you?... Hmm... So, if you must insist on picking the highest mango, I suppose... Hmm... You'd need to talk to the *right* Wogies... Oh girl! Follow me."

***

After helping Sunny to find the "Right Wogies", Songbird had disappeared without even saying "Goodbye". Sunny had looked for her in every direction, searched for her a second time, and searched for her a third time, before accepting that she had vanished.

He might as well have been speaking to himself:

"Songbird?... Songbird?... Soh..."

He was back in the square, sitting on something the Wogies had called a "Bench"; sharing that platform with two familiar faces: Father Ralph and Uncle Survey.

Sunny could remember very little of the second man; just his paleness, his sketch, and the indecipherable sounds which had emerged from his mouth. Sunny had been so flabbergasted by the man's appearance, his mind had tied itself in knots. He struggled to recall the details of their original encounter.

He was calmer today; able to take a deep breath, and inspect that person's face; noting the large wart, just above his nostrils, and the strange device, which rested above that wart. Most of the material was shiny. At first, Sunny supposed it was a kind of jewellery. But there was something else: Two translucent disks were floating in front of his eyes. They were not particularly decorative. You could not see them unless you stared. And they were too small to offer much protection. Sunny could not determine if they had any practical use.

Uncle Survey was different from the other Wogies who Sunny had met. He was not vicious, like the men who had abused Songbird's daughter. He was not a fanatic, like Father Ralph. And he was not sickly, like the Desert Wogies. He was placid, pensive, rigid, and ever so clean. Sunny could not find a single speck of dust on his chest-cloth, no matter how much he searched.

"Blah-di-blah, blah, blah. Which is why, something-something to every clan. Blah, something, blah. Which is a fair deal, by the something. It's respectful of you, and us, and blah-di-blah, blah blah."

Sunny had explained their clan's position: This had always been their land. They wished to use it, just as before. And they wished to come to an arrangement which would satisfy the Wogies. But they were not willing to become slaves, endure work, take on debt, or commit to a single sexual partner.

Sunny had finished with a question: "What other options do we have?"

Uncle Survey nodded, to show he understood. Perhaps he had understood Sunny the first time they met. Perhaps *it was Sunny* who was to blame, for failing to understand this man.

It did not make much of a difference. Sunny

listened intently, as Uncle Survey replied; speaking in a slow, trustworthy voice. He recognised a smattering of words. Perhaps Uncle Survey was attempting to speak their language. But Sunny could not decipher his meaning.

He turned to Father Ralph, who attempted to translate his companion's remarks:

"What I believe Hernan here is trying to say, is that this land was never yours. It was uninhabited before we arrived. By Jove, that's it: A *people without any land* arrived on these shores, and claimed this *land without a people*."

Sunny did all he could to stop himself from frowning; making a conscious effort to look calm and inoffensive. He *was* offended. He was angry and hurt. But he did not wish for this to be known, because it might have antagonized the very people he was trying to court.

"Of course, you were around. But you were a *foraging people*. You lived in a *state of nature*. You were *a part of the land*. But you never *owned the land*. No-one has. In a 'Legal' sense, this land was uninhabited.

"You see, my sweet blessed child of Christ: 'Property Rights' are *derived from work*. One must mix one's labour in with the land, care for the land and improve it, before one can claim ownership... But you savages are lazy and carefree. You only take what's already there; coasting through life, with the bare minimum of effort, and no desire to satisfy anything more than your most basic needs. You drink water, when you could drink wine. You eat nuts, when you could eat bread. You wear hides, when you could wear clothes... You only consume one-hundredth of what might be possible, if only you bothered to work. But you don't work. You don't produce. And you certainly don't trade.

"You've never shown any industry; any desire to *improve* the land. You don't till, weed, fertilize or irrigate the earth. You've done nothing to *earn* the land. You haven't even erected any fences. You've never *claimed* the land... Genesis says: 'Be fruitful and multiply. Fill the earth and subdue it'. But you've never subdued the earth. You don't deserve to *own* it... It's true. Amen to Hernan. Amen to that."

In the days which followed, Sunny would come to regret the way he responded. He did not challenge Hernan's assumptions, even though his kinfolk *did* "Care for" and "Improve" the land; albeit in a very different way to the

Wogies. They lived *with* the land, whilst the Wogies lived *off* the land. They *preserved* the natural world, whilst the Wogies *exploited* Mother Nature.

Sunny's tribe made sure not to over-hunt or over-gather. They controlled their population, ensuring it would not become a burden on the earth. They left their land fallow, allowing it to recover its strength. They burnt their grasslands, to prevent the spread of invasive bushes. Sparrow farmed cassava. Their tribe grew tobacco. Some of the neighbouring tribes had been known to coppice and prune their trees; to weed and fertilise the places where they gathered their tubers. A few of the Coastal Tribes had created clam gardens, to encourage the reproduction of shellfish. Others had built weirs, to trap specific types of fish. They had rotas, to protect their waters from over-fishing; specifying which clans could fish in each grove, swamp and zone; and on what particular days they could fish.

But Sunny was too flustered to consider such things. Father Ralph's words had scorched his skin. His skull was pulsating. His arms felt prickly and raw.

Sunny had imagined this conversation on umpteen occasions. He had contemplated the things the Wogies might say, and how he might respond. But he had never supposed they might claim this land was "Uninhabited". How crazy was that? How insensitive!

Emotionally unstable; unable or unwilling to pause, calm his nerves, and think of the *best* possible response; Sunny blurted out the first thing that came to mind:

"You talk of property 'Rights', but not of 'Obligations'. You *work* the land, but you don't *love* the land. You've cut down an entire forest. Mother Nature cries! You've planted alien crops, in unnatural ways. And for what? To produce way more stuff than any sane person would ever wish to consume? But... Why?

"You know... Every part of this earth is sacred to our people. Every shining leaf, sandy shore, and misty forest. Every clearing, bird and bug. We respect and cherish this land. But you, the Woggy, who comes in the night and takes whatever she covets? You don't adore this earth. You don't treat it like a sister. You treat it as a foe who needs to be tamed.

"I mean... No... *I tell you*: No good will come

of this *work*. No good will come of this *ownership of land*. The earth belongs to Mother Nature. Yet you defile her. And you're sure to face the consequences. One day... Yes, one day... You'll suffocate in your excreta!"

Sunny had meant every word he had said, but he had not intended to say them. He was supposed to be appealing to these people's better nature; turning them into allies. Instead, he had aggravated them. A vein was throbbing on Father Ralph's forehead, and Hernan's eyes had turned a creamy shade of puce.

He knew it was wrong. But Sunny could not help himself. He had succumbed to his emotions. And there was no stopping him now:

"I tell you: The land doesn't belong to people. People *belong to the land*. We didn't weave the web of life. We're merely strands.

"Look: We have fables about people like you. They feature a protagonist called *Mister Perfect*; an absurd name, for an absurd character; someone we thought could never exist in real life... But... Well, then we met the Wogies.

"Now, Mister Perfect believed that everything was perfect. Not only did he believe that he was perfect himself; he also believed that his clan was the perfect clan, and his tribe was the perfect tribe. They'd conquered Mother Nature, and were living in the most perfect of all possible worlds.

"Mister Perfect was eaten by a snake.

"Maybe he was happy to come to such a premature end; eaten by the most perfect of snakes, in the most perfect of fashions. Who knows?

"Of course, his sistren had warned him about that man-eating beast. But Mister Perfect had brushed their concerns aside, saying: 'I'll wrestle that thing if it attacks me. I'm stronger than an ox... I'll flee if it gives chase. I'm faster than the light... Attack *me*? That cute little worm would be too awed by my majesty and beauty!'

"In one version of the story, Mister Perfect walked right up to the snake, who opened its mouth and swallowed him whole, or bit off his head, or tore him into tiny pieces.

"In another, Mister Perfect was on a hunt. He'd just slain a great beast; a gazelle, or maybe a warthog. He was so blinded by pride, that he didn't look around. He didn't spot the snake who'd also been stalking that creature. The snake slithered through the long grass, and bit

Mister Perfect's neck; injecting its deathly poison.

"Well, I suppose what I'm saying is that it's the moral which matters: We must control our arrogance. If we don't, it may cost us our lives.

"I'm telling you this: We once tried to help a Woggy. It's true! That man was so arrogant, he thought he could cross the desert with just one companion, without sufficient supplies... Well, he was too proud to accept our help. He shot a magic arrow, made an ear-crushing noise, and scared us all away... Things didn't work out too well for that poor fellow. A few moons later, we discovered his corpse.

"It's just... You seem like nice enough people. But you've got a bit of the Mister Perfects about you, what with your talk of caring for the land, like your way is the only way. And you're not *really* caring for it. You're damaging it on an epic scale. You risk destroying it forever.

"That's the rub of the belly. We don't inherit the land from our mothers. We borrow it from our daughters. We must protect it for them.

"Our tribe doesn't claim to be perfect. Our First Ancestors made the same mistake you're making now: They lived in a land of plenty, filled with giant animals who were easy to kill. But they hunted those animals to extinction... Well, we're still living with the consequences of that today. We have to hunt for longer than they ever did. We have to track smaller, more agile prey... Anyway, we've learnt from *our* mistakes. We know this land. We know what it needs. And it's not this work. It's not this intensive farming. It's not these forests with just a single type of tree."

Father Ralph's face had begun to soften, about halfway through this monologue. That vein still squiggled across his forehead, but its throbbing was less pronounced. Perhaps it was the way Sunny had told the fable of Mister Perfect. His words were condescending, but his tone was not malicious. His voice had grown gentler with each successive word. This had soothed Father Ralph. And it had reinvigorated him, giving him the verve he required to take control of the conversation:

"Ah! Such energy! Such lyricism! But you make a fatal error: The *merchant* may subdue nature, to produce items to trade. I believe this is what my brother in Christ was saying. *But we aren't all merchants*.

"I speak for myself, and on behalf of the

devout, when I say that there's more to work than this. Work isn't just a means to an end. For those of us who are spiritually minded, work isn't *even* a means to an end. We deny ourselves the fruits of our labour. We shun pleasure and consumption... No, for us, work is an end in itself. *Hard work is virtuous*. It brings us closer to God."

Sunny's face dropped a couple of notches. His broken chin slid under his jaw, towards his Adam's apple; stretching his face, and revealing his eyes, which had been lurking in the shadow of his giant nose. If anything, his skin became even more taut than normal. It glowed a little more, or a little less, or in a slightly different way.

Sunny had no idea what Father Ralph was speaking about, so he had no idea how to respond.

"You don't understand?... I see... Now, that's because you only live for the present. You fail to understand that this world exists to test us; to prepare us for a *future* life in heaven. We must work hard in this life, to save our souls in the next.

"As for the work itself... Dear child of Christ, that's secondary. Everyone has a place in God's master-plan. The Lord cares just as much for the lowly carpenter, as he does for his priests and politicians. What matters is that you submit. Submit to hard work. Submit to the will of God. Forgo your leisure-based society, and commit to a work-based society. Submit! Surrender your mortal body, and save your eternal soul."

Sunny paused, to allow his mind to catch up with his ears, before focussing on a single word: Heaven. He had been thinking of that place, ever since Father Ralph had mentioned it at the Big Camp. But he still had far more questions than answers:

"So, you have to work hard to get into this *heaven*, even if it destroys the earth?"

"Yes. Hard work is the ticket! It'll open the door to paradise."

"I see... And do you still have to do this 'Hard work' once you're actually in heaven?"

"No."

"Oh... Is there *any* work in heaven?"

"No. None whatsoever."

"What about *money*? Is there money in heaven?"

Father Ralph shook his head.

"No. There's no money in heaven."

"Oh... What about *land rights*?"

"No. There are no land rights in heaven. There's no land."

"So, there's no work, money or land rights?"

"Correct."

"And that's a good thing?"

Father Ralph nodded.

"So, why can't it be a good thing on earth?... I'm telling you: Our tribes-folk are already in this heaven of yours. We don't have any work or money... And... Well, we just wish to remain in this heaven, and preserve it for our descendants... Surely, we can come to an arrangement... It's just... I don't understand: Why do you want us to change our ways? Why do you want us to abandon our heaven?"

Father Ralph clutched his hair:

"Because you haven't earned it! You're stealing it!... No, no, that's not it at all... God bless you, dear child of Christ. You're not in heaven. What a dang notion! You're in the mortal realm, living the most ungodly existence."

Father Ralph looked to Hernan, who closed his eyes, in that blissful way of his, before making a speech which seemed to contain a large number of ostentatious words.

Father Ralph did his best to translate:

"By Jove, that's exactly it. Spot on! The *Colonial Company* has an... Umm... A *Royal Charter* from the king. This charter grants the company, 'The soils of all lands, countries and territories to be discovered... With the full power to dispose of every part... According to the order of the laws of the fatherland'. And a jolly good thing that is too. Amen to that! A thousand times *amen*.

"So, you see, this grant allows Hernan here to survey unowned land, map it out, turn it into the *state's territory*, divide it into blocks, and transform it into *private property*, which the company can use itself or sell on to individual citizens.

"It's the company's land. It's not your land. You're stealing this land and you're stealing a living. It's against the will of the king, and it's against the will of the Lord."

Now it was Sunny who clasped his hair.

"Who or what is this 'King'?"

"The king is our leader."

"You mean... Umm... Like a sort of representative?"

"You could say that."

"Or a chief?"

"Yes! God bless you, that's it! The king is like a chief."

Sunny had heard of chiefs. Serenity had spoken to him about the Distant Tribes, who appointed those *ceremonial* leaders, although Sunny had never met one himself. He supposed they were a bit like a chairperson; the individual who oversaw their Tribal Council. The only difference was that chiefs could be given gifts. They might keep those gifts for a while, and accrue more possessions than anyone else. But then they hosted "Potlatches", to give those gifts away. And they held feasts; sharing their food with everyone else. The inequality never lasted for long.

This *king* sounded different from those *chiefs*. He sounded more like an Uncle Crow; someone who hoarded gifts forever, and wielded power over the group.

"So, it was this Chief King who told you to leave your homes, take other people's homes, endure work, and force work upon others?"

"Yes."

"Why didn't you just call him a nincompoop?"

"Excuse me? Call him... Call him a 'Nincompoop'?... What a... What a dang notion!"

"It's just... Sometimes we come across people like your Chief King. We call them 'Uncle Crows'; these people who get too big for their loincloths. When they appear, we mock them, to keep them humble; to put them back in their rightful place. We say they're a bug-faced nutty-nut, or a crow who thinks they're a peacock. They lose our respect. And because they aren't respected, they don't have any leverage. They cannot tell us what to do.

"Why don't you do something like that with your Chief King? You know... To push *him* back into his shell?"

"Because... Because he'd put you in chains! He'd have you tortured and killed!"

"Oh golly! What a brute!... Okay then, why don't you meet violence with violence? Why don't you *kill* this Chief King?... You know, I once heard of a chief who hoarded her people's fish. Do you know what her people did? They killed her! It was as simple as that. Then everything returned to normal... Her successors made sure not to make the same mistake. Whenever someone caught a whale, those chiefs said: 'Cut it up and take whatever you like. I'll make do with the scraps.' They only held onto their chiefdoms by being humbler than everyone else in their tribe."

Father Ralph was speechless.

"Or, if you cannot kill this Chief King, you could at least send her into exile... You could disobey, criticise, depose or desert her. Then you'd all be free."

Father Ralph finally found his voice; speaking so sharply, and so suddenly, that his words merged into a scream:

"But he's our king! Our majestic majesty! We're his humble servants. Jesus, Abraham and Moses! This is what's so wrong with you freedom-loving savages. You've got no respect for your betters."

Sunny had never heard of a "Better".

"Oh... But... Hang on for as long as it takes a leaf to fall... I thought you follow this 'God' fellow. Upon Mother Nature's good face: Why do you care so much about this Chief King?"

Father Ralph almost jolted out of his skin. His eyes pushed outwards, and his shoulders bucked upwards, as though attempting to flee from their sockets.

This response did not last for long.

Father Ralph underwent a strange and

unexpected transformation: His face softened. His veins stopped throbbing. His eyes appeared to be both bigger and smaller than before:

"By Jove, I do believe I understand your confusion. The likes of Hernan and myself may appear to be worlds apart. He serves the king, whilst I serve the Lord. He cares for land, commerce, production; all that's *material*. I care for the church, souls, salvation; all that's *spiritual*.

"But, dear child of Christ, there's really no contradiction. The state and the church are united... You see, the king is the 'Chief' of *both* institutions. He's God's representative on earth, with a *divine right* to rule. Yes, that's it: God and the king are a team."

"Are you sure?"

"It's the undisputed word of God! My blessed child: You must think of the Lord as your father. He's father to all mankind. And you must think of the king as your father. He's father to our nation."

"What's a 'Father'?"

"A parent."

"A mother?"

"Yes, but male."

"Oh... A male mother?"

Father Ralph nodded.

Sunny pinched his ears. Father Ralph had mentioned something similar, back at the Big Camp. But Sunny was still struggling to grasp the concept:

"It's just... Well, men don't give birth."

Father Ralph ignored this remark:

"The king is our parent and guardian. He loves and protects us, *on God's behalf.*

"Now, where was I?... Ah, yes: So when we say that the king wills this land to become the state's territory, and then private property; we're actually saying that *God wills it.* The king is speaking on God's behalf.

"And no, we cannot just kill the king. That'd be like killing God himself. Heaven forbid! Our souls would suffer in eternal damnation."

Sunny did not know whether to frown or giggle.

"You believe this?"

"I do."

"But... Well, it's awfully convenient, isn't it? Someone bosses you about... They say: 'Take other people's land', 'Enslave yourself to work', 'When you make four pots, let me keep three', 'You'll suffer in eternal damnation if you refuse'...

And then, if you question any of it, they say it's not what *they* want, it's what *Chief God* wants... I mean, come on! You're yanking our penises."

"Excuse me?"

"Chief King is mocking you. She's ripping the loincloth from your..."

Sunny stopped himself short, once he realised what he was doing: Insulting the very people he was supposed to be courting.

"Oh... I am Sorry, I didn't mean to offend you. I'm sure we could set this straight. There's always a way. I'll just need to speak to Chief King myself; to go directly to the source of the river... Please could you introduce me?"

This time it was Father Ralph and Hernan who broke out in fits of laughter:

"*Hehe hoho haha*... What a dang notion! You?... You!... Go to... No! You cannot be serious!... You?... A savage? You wish to speak to his majestic majesty? Ha! What a jape! What tomfoolery and monkeyshine! Hallelujah! I've heard it all."

It took a little while for them to realise that Sunny was serious, and a little longer before Sunny deigned to explain:

"Well... No, I don't get it... In our culture,

people make decisions *together*. Things only get done, if *everyone* agrees... Now, I understand that your Chief King makes decisions on behalf of everyone else, like a male mother with a child. But how does she... How does *he* know what those people want, if they don't meet her... *him*... to discuss their needs?"

Father Ralph smiled:

"Because God tells him!"

"Oh, I see. Well then, please can you ask Chief God to tell Chief King that we want to remain on our land; without any of this money, work and hoarding?"

"Ah, my dear child of Christ. God already knows what you want. And he also knows what you *need*. That's why he sent us. So we can give you the one thing you truly need: The bible!"

Sunny nodded:

"Okay. Well, I'd still like to come to an understanding; to create a proposal which I could take back to our clan. A sort of *agreement to share*.

"It's like... When a hungry ant asks for food, by wiggling its antennae, the nearest ant will open its mandibles, and regurgitate fluid for that ant to eat. If an ant refused to share their food, they'd be treated as an enemy. They'd be attacked by their sisters and brothers... When a sparrow finds food, she doesn't keep it to herself. She shares it with the other sparrows.

"I tell you: Sharing is the natural order of things. We're put on this earth to share.

"When other clans pass through, we share our land with them. We allow them to hunt our animals, gather our plants, and sleep with our mothers and uncles.

"We'd be happy to share our land with you.

"We aren't even against private ownership. Our tribes-folk own their beads. It's just... Well, we expect people to *share* the things they own. If a person tried to stop someone else from using something, then we'd have a problem. We'd accuse them of selfishness and greed. We'd say their evil wolf had eaten their good wolf.

"But it doesn't have to come to that...

"If you must plant lots of stuff, I think we could come to accept that. We'll do whatever we can to heal Mother Nature. But we should still be able to gather those plants, to *share* them, without living in fear of your punishments.

"Does that sound okay? You can grow whatever you like, and we won't do a punishment on you. But you cannot steal that food from us. You must allow us to gather the vegetables you grow, without attacking us."

Hernan and Father Ralph frowned in unison. For a moment, it appeared that they were sharing a single eyebrow; a wide, furry thing, which stretched from one side of one face, to the opposite side of the other; becoming straighter, and rising higher, the longer Sunny spoke.

This illusion was only broken when they turned inwards, to face each other.

Father Ralph waited for Hernan, and Hernan waited for Father Ralph. Hernan only responded, somewhat begrudgingly, once he acknowledged that Father Ralph had lost the ability to speak.

He sighed, paused, and looked into his companion's eyes; before making a proposal, which the missionary translated; omitting a few of Hernan's words, and adding a few of his own:

"My brother in Christ: Look around you. This land is *our* land. It's been mapped! It's sovereign territory, *holy* territory, and you're nothing but illegal squatters.

"Look at the buildings! Look at the plantations! Look at these horses and guns.

"God bless you, poor innocent child. Can't

you see that you're in no position to bargain?

"And yet, we're good people. We're here on a holy mission, to bring you out of the darkness. We wish you no harm. In the name of Jesus Christ: We've come *to save you* from harm. We've come to save you from yourselves!

"So yes, we'll offer you an alternative: You can have a portion of land. It'll be your own private property, to use as you please. That's right: You can still live in your primitive huts, and hold your little meetings. So long as you don't break the king's laws, your lifestyles will barely change. You'll be an 'Aeque Principali'; an autonomous protectorate, under company and king.

"Our holy soldiers will protect you from outsiders, and our constables will protect you from your own ne'er-do-wells. You'll be given the deeds to your land, for the first time since Adam met Eve. Official documents, kept in the capital, shall declare that the land is yours.

"But you must *earn* the rights to that land, by paying a 'Tithe' to the Company. Amen, that's correct. Each year... *By the beginning of each winter solstice*... You must produce things with a certain value, which you must pay... Which you must *gift* to the crown.

"I suggest you produce grain. It's durable, portable, divisible and quantifiable. Everyone can see what you've produced and what you owe, without cause for argument or complaint. But that decision will be yours alone. See: You can still play parliament, if that's what floats your boat.

"We can even loan you some seeds and machines, to help you on your way. I expect it won't take long for you to repay the debt, and produce a surplus which you can trade for a profit. You'll be able to buy stuff like the things you see around us: Horses, buildings and clothes. You'll be rich! You'll see the value of hard work, and it'll bring you closer to God."

Sunny titled his head.

"Not sure?... Yes, it's an awful lot to digest... But, my brother in Christ: You must trust me when I say that this is a tried and tested model... Did you ever notice how a couple of clans disappeared from your Big Camp?... Yes?... By Jove, they saw the light and answered Jesus's call! They accepted an identical offer. And, whilst it's early days, it seems that they're happier now than ever before. You can visit them, if you like, and see for yourself."

Sunny's head shifted backwards, but his neck remained fixed in position.

"They're farming? They're doing... *work*... Every day of every lunar-cycle?"

Father Ralph nodded.

"Really?"

"Indeed."

"Oh... And they don't seem to mind?"

"Not at all. Hard work sets you free!"

# DREAM ON

Sunny had performed a one-man play; re-enacting the conversation with Hernan and Father Ralph. But he was struggling to gauge a reaction.

"Well, that's about it. I went, I saw, I concluded. I said I'd find an alternative solution, and here you have it. I tell you this: We don't need to fight *or* flee. We can be masters of our own *protectorate*, so long as we gift a *tithe*.

"What do you think?"

Sunny panned around the circle...

He looked at *Pilgrim*; a woman who had joined them five seasons before, after falling out with her clan. Sunny had liked her immediately, because she had the same greying ringlets as one of his favourite aunts.

He looked at *Buffalo*; an adolescent who was attending his first ever meeting. His eyes were like shallow pools. They revealed his real age. Perhaps he was too young to participate in such a discussion. But these were singular times, when customs bent like the grass.

And he looked at the older women, who were squatting in an identical manner, lined up in a perfect row. Viewed from one end, with a single glance, it was impossible to tell them apart. Their fleshy thighs repeated themselves, over and over again. But take a step to the side, and the differences were unmistakable. Each was so extraordinary, it would have been impossible to make them more unique.

A few hillocks glistened in the background; succumbing to a rainbow of oily hues, a shower of sandy sunbeams, and a cloud of polychrome dust.

The morning air was dabbed with the odours of trampled ferns and dewy ash.

Sunny was able to digest this scene, because no-one had voiced a reply. He was almost certain that his kinfolk had things to say. They might have had *more* than one thing to say. Those things might have contradicted each other. They might have made for a compelling case. But Sunny could not know for sure, because the clan had been struck by a collective bout of muteness.

Aura had clamped her hands in between the hinges beneath her knees. Sparrow was biting his lip. Setting Sun was fluttering her eyelids, attempting to refocus her vision.

"You can speak," Sunny offered, more tentatively than he had intended. "Be as honest as you like."

No-one uttered a word.

It was understandable. Their home had been taken by a murderous foe. Their land had been violated. Their ancestral forest had been turned into something grotesque. Their bellies were tormented by hunger. And their minds were tormented by anxiety and fear.

Their disquietude had crept up on them, so slowly, that its progress had been imperceptible. Everyone knew *how* they felt. Their feelings were too intense to ignore. But they could not recall *when* their emotions had overwhelmed them.

Sunny prodded again:

"What about the land? I mean, they're offering us land. It may not be *this* land... *Our* land... *Good* land... But we can make it our home. Who knows? We might even come to love it."

Sunny panned from one face to the next.

He stopped when he reached Serenity, locked eyes, and pushed for an answer:

"Beloved uncle: Surely you have something to add?"

Having been accosted such a direct question,

Serenity felt compelled to reply; answering in a voice which was so quiet, people had to turn their ears to listen:

"What do we know of this land? Will it be as wide, deep and high as our own land? Will it have a water source which will attract animals? Will it be blessed by the good earth? Will the air smell of almonds? Will its sky inspire us to smile?"

Sunny did not reply. There was no need. Serenity had cut a path through the silence, and now *everyone* wished to speak.

"They say they'll provide us with seeds and machinery," Sunny's mother began. "But they'll want something in return. They'll impose one of those things they imposed on Songbird... One of those *mortal engagements*... We'll be enslaved by their debt forever."

"What do we want with seeds and machines?" Asked Mountain. "We hunt and we gather. If we'd wanted to commit to agriculture, we'd have done it a thousand generations ago. Why on earth and the ancestral realm would we allow a foreign people to impose such a thing upon us?"

"Too right!" Aura echoed. "And they want us to produce *grain*? Grain? Of all things, *grain*?...

Don't they know that grain-based societies are prone to collapse? Have they not heard the story of Auntie Barley, whose crops were washed away by floods; who replanted them, only for them to be destroyed by a hurricane; who replanted them again, only for them to be destroyed by an earthquake? Don't they know that farming leads to over-population, and that over-population leads to war, famine and disease? Talk about putting all your eggs in a single shell! They don't know their arseholes from their belly-buttons."

"They think they're Mister Perfect," Sparrow concurred. "And we know what happened to him. He was so busy, admiring his reflection in a pool, that he became oblivious to the world around him. Yes, that's right. A serpent asked him for directions. But Mister Perfect was obsessed! He couldn't pull himself away from his reflection. The snake felt she was being ignored. She became offended, and then angry. She ate that man alive!

"Yes, you heard me: This agriculture will eat those Wogies alive. Living so closely together? What insanity! They think they're so perfect, but disease will ravage their camp. They'll drop dead in a matter of moons."

Dusk nodded his gargantuan head.

"Let it be said: We only have two options: Land or freedom... We can keep a portion of land, if we forgo our freedom; making the stuff the Wogies want, when they want it, and gifting them the larger share. Or we can flee, to avoid such brutish demands, knowing that the Wogies will surely follow."

Dawn disagreed; more out of instinct than design:

"Have you heard nothing? We thought Sunny was risking his life, when he visited the Wogies' camp. But was he harmed?... Negatively, no! He wasn't threatened *or* attacked... Let it be heard: The fact that these Wogies are willing to allocate us a portion of land, and protect us from afar, shows that they aren't as brutish as we supposed. We're being offered a bright yellow opportunity. And who knows? Perhaps life will be good, with their sturdy huts, which last forever, and their animals, which do most of this 'Work'."

Everyone turned to Sunny. It took a few moments for him to realise that they wanted him to respond. And it took him a few more moments, before he finally obliged:

"Oh... Okay... So, yes, as Dawn has said, the Wogies are apt to diplomacy. We've all met Father Ralph. We've encountered his charm. And we've seen how he seems to believe in his own sense of righteousness.

"And yes, the Wogies are offering us an opportunity to live the type of life which seems to be good enough for them. A peculiar sort of gluttonous existence.

"But there's something else. Something I forgot to mention... It's... Well, it's a little too ghastly for words... What I'm trying to say is... Oh ancestral realm! I'll just perch like a parrot and sing: They forced themselves upon Songbird's daughter. Sexually, I mean. With their man-snakes. In her... Well, you understand."

The majority of the clan did not "Understand". But they did not give voice to their confusion, since this would have been superfluous. Their *eyes* were already demanding an explanation; bulging, pointing, almost prodding; pulsating with an irregular rhythm.

Sunny buckled to the pressure, using the simplest terms he could muster:

"Three men... Big men, adult men... They stripped that girl naked. I mean, she cannot have witnessed more than a hundred full moons... A tattoo-less cub... And they had sex with that child. But not friendly sex. It was like... She didn't want it... She didn't enjoy it... She... They... They forced themselves upon her, and there wasn't a thing she could do.

"Songbird called it a 'Punishment'. It's like... I think a punishment is a bit like a protection. Only the recipient cannot refuse to perform a punishment. They cannot appeal... Songbird suffers through work. Then she gets gifted... she gets *paid* money, which she uses to get food. But her daughter shared some food, *without suffering through work*. So she had to suffer through this punishment, *after* she'd eaten."

The clans-folk muttered beneath their breath:

"For shame!"

"These inverts have no honour."

"May their spirits be trapped in a forest with no trees."

Dusk was livid. His hair had puffed up to almost double its previous volume, and his ears pointed away from his skull.

"Is this what you want? To live among people who would do such things to children? Who'd rather watch us starve than share our food?

"Positively! Dawn: You're the enemy within. Seductive but lethal. You speak of these huts and animals. And we see the appeal. But let it be said: This is a trap. These people are ravenous beasts. They'll take one thing, and then demand another. There isn't enough water or wood, upon this loving earth, to satisfy their endless desires. Why would we, a free people, wish to make ourselves slaves to such consumption? Why would we waste our mornings, putting on all the different cloths they force themselves to wear? Why would we use up our afternoons, toiling so hard in the fields? For what? To get things we've never needed, or which we could've hunted or gathered with ease?

"They may have their cargo. But this is all they have. They don't have a deep connection with nature. They aren't rich in time, freedom, relations, trust, comfort or ease. In the ways that matter, we're better off than them. They're brutes! They shackle, whip and molest. *They're the ones* who should change. It might take a while for them to adjust, but they'd be happier in the end."

For a moment, it seemed that Dusk was done. But after scratching an armpit, and after taking a breath which was so deep, he had to pause midway through; he stood up and resumed his tirade with even more gusto than before:

"If we had their possessions, we'd give them all away. If one of *our* members was hungry, we'd gift them all the food we had. But if one of *their* members was hungry, they'd give them a 'Punishment'. They'd attack a little girl for sharing the same food that we'd have given her without a moment's hesitation.

"These people don't practice mutual aid. They cannot maintain their autonomy. They're dependent on their work-punishments.

"And another thing: Can't you see where this is heading? Physically exhausted by these work-punishments, and mentally fatigued by this money-debt; the people in that camp won't have the time or energy to participate in group meetings. They'll allow a few busybodies to make all the important decisions, without consulting the community, or winning the people's consent."

A few people chortled. Others chuckled. This idea, that the members of a tribe might gift all the power to just a few individuals, seemed too bizarre for words.

Dawn had to swallow his laughter. This caused his eyes to water. He almost gagged, almost retched, and almost swallowed his tongue:

"*Cough, cough*... You think... *Sputter, sputter*... You think they'd allow a few representatives to decide how to rule *their* camp?... Sorry, their *town*... Without them there to watch, ask questions or make proposals? You think they'd permit other people to decide how much of this work they should do? And how much of this money they should be gifted?"

Dusk nodded.

Dawn shook his head, redirecting the light back onto his shoulders.

"That's *insane*! No people, at any time, or in any place, would permit other people to rule them in such a manner. It's a preposterous notion."

But Dusk was adamant:

"It's happening already! You heard what Sunny said about Chief King. Whilst we *mock* anyone who might try to become a chief, they *obey* such people. They can't even talk to Chief King, let alone suggest policies for him to enact. They're nothing but slaves, subdued by the terror they feel towards this distant, unfeeling brute."

Dawn waited a little while, to allow Dusk to add to his previous remarks. Then he shouted at the sun:

"No!!!"

This hasty reply, shot into the silence, seemed almost comical. It was forced and painfully abrupt. But it had the desired effect; refocusing the group's attention.

"No!!!... It's true: We don't wish to be consumed by consumption. And it's true that we don't wish to be ruled by others. Maybe this *is* a trap. Maybe it's not. But we wouldn't be living in *their camp*, near any of their Chief Crows. We wouldn't be living by *their rules*. We'd have our own land. We'd hold our own meetings, and grow the things *we decide* to grow... We wouldn't have to force our children into slavery, or fight our sisters, or be false friends; just to secure this money. We wouldn't have to succumb to the things this money must surely inspire: The luxury, intrigues, trickery, lies, betrayal and insincerity. The idea of having *my things* and *your things* is quite clearly inhuman. This money is quite clearly the most wretched of evils; the tyrant of the Wogies, the bane of the ancestors, and the butchery stone of the living. To imagine that one can live in a land of money and still preserve one's integrity, is like imagining that one could preserve one's life at the bottom of a lake... But let it be heard: *We wouldn't have to live in this land of money. We wouldn't have to obey this Chief King.* We could perform our own rituals, and preserve our own culture, so long as we gifted this tithe... Tell them, Sunny: Isn't that correct?"

Sunny nodded as he spoke:

"It is. This Chief King may be a brute, but he's far away, on the other side of Mother Nature's body. He probably doesn't even know we exist. And whilst the Wogies may welcome Chief Crows into *their* camps, we could still banish those figures from ours."

A few of the clan's younger members responded positively. Buffalo's eyes even glistened; catching the sun, and reflecting its kaleidoscopic rays. *Petal*, a young woman who had taken a shine to Sunny, chattered her teeth, as if to nibble his eyebrows.

Like Sunny, these young adults had been impressed by Hunter's gun, and by the sheer quantity of crops which had appeared in such a short space of time. So long as they could still make group decisions, they saw no reason to reject Hernan's proposal.

Hence, when Serenity called for a vote, the group was split. Almost all the elders opposed the motion. But Dawn and a few of the youngsters voted in favour.

The clans-folk agreed to revisit the debate the following day. Then they left to search for food.

It was not a successful mission.

They returned without any meat, ate the few greens they had gathered, chatted, and fell into a vacillatory slumber; clutching their stomachs, which shook them awake whenever they fell asleep.

***

Only one person was able to sleep until daybreak: Aura.

It was clear that she had visited another realm. Her eyes had moved in a million directions, traversing the insides of their lids; jolty, frantic and raw. Her teeth would have probably chattered, had they not been so misaligned.

She awoke with a start, bolted upright,

scrunched her lips at the moon, and shouted "Hullaballoo!":

"Hullabaloo! Dawn jiggety! The ancestors have spoken. Prawn tooting shouted at me, all night long. Squawk, squawk, tooting mohawk."

Sunny had wished to speak himself; to suggest that they visit the clan who had made a deal with the Wogies. But the opportunity had passed. Aura had monopolised the group's attention; luring them with her eyes, which were pointing in different directions, and with her lyrical half-speak, which was too delicious to resist. Even the infants had gathered at her feet, forming a semi-circle in the starlight-speckled dust.

"Abracadabra, they said. Alakazam! Go get a goat. Go get us a goat. Go! Go now! Go get us a goat! Go to the Dog Clan. Go get us a goat."

A few of the clans-folk still looked puzzled. If it were that easy, they would have "Gone got a goat" before hunger had hollowed their limbs, and their stomachs had started to rattle.

It was left to Sparrow to clarify the situation:

"So, the ancestors came to you in a dream, demanding that you take a goat from the Dog Clan?"

"Bird tweeting right, they did. What do you think I've been jib-jabbering on about all this time? Mountain mist? We'll only get out of this ziggedy ditch, if we go get that goat, and sacrifice it to the ancestors."

"Ah. Then we must visit the Dog Clan. We don't have a choice in the matter."

***

The clans-folk departed on what was known as a *dream quest*...

People had been known to travel for days, to turn their dreams into a reality. When they arrived at their destination, their hosts felt duty-bound to hand over whatever was requested. These were not *personal* petitions. The ancestors had spoken, and their wishes had to be honoured.

Clans had donated their favourite ornaments, crystals and masks; just to help realise a stranger's dream. One member of their tribe had even parted with their beloved cat, whom they had raised from a kitten, without giving the matter a second thought, or uttering a word of complaint; simply because a distant relative had dreamed that her illness would be cured if she could sleep beside that pet.

Dream quests were a means of exchange. Whoever possessed a desired item, felt obliged to hand it to the dreamer, without expecting anything in return. But that person would almost certainly experience a similar dream, sometime in the future. They would set out on their own journey, arrive at a distant location, and receive something new. Items were passed from one hand to another, in such a manner; they moved across great distances, just as though they had been traded.

But the members of their tribe seldom used such cold, impersonal logic. For them, dream quests were not economic. They were spiritual. The tribes-folk completed these missions to honour their ancestors; their mothers' mothers' mothers. They were giving something back to the women who had given them life. It was an honour, not a burden, and not just a means of exchange.

***

Very few people had ever visited the Dog Clan's camp, and even fewer could remember the route. It fell upon the clan's two eldest members, Mountain and Setting Sun, to guide the clan along. Those elders assured the group that it was not a particularly *difficult* journey, but it was rather *long*. It would take them at least three days. Perhaps it would take five, or maybe even ten. It had been so many solstices since they had last made that pilgrimage, they could not be entirely sure. And anyway, the length of the journey was irrelevant. The clans-folk had to overcome their hunger, and trudge ahead, because the spirits had demanded satisfaction.

Sunny was familiar with almost all the places they visited on the first day: The scrublands, where the sun-baked earth had cracked in several places. The hillocks that framed that wide expanse. The great swoop of canyons, ridges and ravines.

But by the second morning, he was covering new ground.

It was obvious that this land had changed, even though he had never set eyes on it before. Another ancestral forest had succumbed to a similar fate as their own. Rubber trees had usurped the land. A couple of meadows were filled with cotton which was so tall, it hid the new towns which lurked in the distance.

The clans-folk avoided those places, but the message was clear: The scale of the Wogies' ambitions was far greater than they had supposed. Their progress was far quicker. The Wogies were taking *all* the fertile land, and *all* the land near the rivers. They seemed to be avoiding vast regions, but only when the soil was poor; like these drylands, which were home to a smattering of thorny bushes, but very few edible plants, and none of the animals which might have been attracted by such a supply of food.

Still, the clans-folk needed to eat.

For this, they depended upon their eldest members; walking repositories of knowledge, who had lived through hard times, in the aftermath of floods and cyclones, and who could remember the measures their peers had taken to survive.

Whenever anyone found something that looked like it could be edible, they asked Mountain or Setting Sun if it was safe to eat. They removed every berry those elders approved. They found a few mushrooms, and a few edible roots, which they gave to their weaker members.

It was never enough to quell their ever-growing hunger. Sunny's arms felt so light, he had to check they still existed. Yet he still had to carry a child. That boy had become so weak, he had lost the ability to walk.

On the third day, they reached a mango tree. It was a weatherworn thing, with droopy branches that curled in on themselves, as though they were too ashamed to be seen. Its leaves had browned, and most of its fruit had fallen to the ground, where it had rotted or been eaten by flies. Yet there were enough mangoes for almost everyone to have two. This sated their appetites, and gave them the energy they needed to proceed.

They awoke the next morning, feeling just as hungry as before.

"Aaagh!"

It was Pilgrim who was screaming. Her mouth was stretched long; open, tall, but extremely narrow. Her tongue was rattling in the Stygian void:

"*Aaagh!* It's a lost spirit. An omen. Run! Flee for your lives!"

The commotion shook the clans-folk from their collective slumber.

They looked towards Pilgrim, allowed their eyes to follow the shape of her body, pass over her outstretched chin, catch sight of her lips, continue in the direction they were pointing, and settle on the nearest tree.

Strewn from a branch, was the largest snake Sunny had ever seen. It was longer than a buffalo, and heavier than most of the people he knew. Sunny could make out each of its individual scales. They shone in the sun's early glow; black, amber and bronze; hexagonal, three-dimensional, pulled apart by a web of white lines.

Sunny could empathise with Pilgrim's response. The snake was clearly dead, but it looked every bit as lethal as any living creature Sunny had encountered. He supposed it might even come back to life, if only to scare them all to death.

Dusk sprang to his feet. He had been intending to perform a star jump, but he was betrayed by his ageing body, and by his unnaturally large head, which had always affected his balance. He managed to raise his arms, but his legs barely parted a jot.

"Ta-da!" he sang, with thespian flamboyance. "Uncle Rock Python, at your service."

Sunny could tell that Dawn was trying hard not to respond. He was sucking his lips, gazing into the distance, pretending to ignore his rival's success.

"There's enough meat on this legless lizard to fill us up for days."

Most of the clans-folk nodded, but only in the feeblest of manners. Their faces softened, but only by a little. It took them several moments to acknowledge that they would be eating. And it took them several more moments, to acknowledge *what* they would be eating.

One of their members was not so enamoured...

Toad, Hope's cousin, tended to be a happy-go-lucky kind of child. His face was dominated by the puffiest cheeks, which gave the impression that he was always smiling, and his lips looked far too thin to accommodate negative words.

But looks can be deceiving.

"I ain't eating that blood-sucking worm. Not by sunlight and not by moonlight, during this lifetime or the next!"

A few people nodded. Some smiled. But it was Hope who took the initiative; squatting beside Toad, reducing the size of her forehead, and softening the shape of her eyes.

"Come, come. You might like it."

"No way, sunray. I hate it. It's yucky and gross."

"You can't know that, Little Mister Happy Heart. You haven't even tried it."

"I know. A boy just knows... Come on, sister. Take a look at the thing. If Mother Nature had meant for us to eat snakes, she wouldn't have made them look like *that*."

"Ah, I see. It does look rather yucky, doesn't it?"

"The worst."

"And I bet it smells pretty bad."

"Like a dozen rotten eggs."

"But it's the yummiest whatsit you'll ever eat!"

"It is?... No! Don't be a Silly Milly. You've never eaten one of them."

"It... It.. It..." Hope stuttered, struggling to respond.

And so it was left to Dusk to save the day:

"These giant worms don't live anywhere near our camps, so we don't usually get to eat them. It's been seasons since we've seen one. But back when I was a child, no older than you are today, there were times when it didn't rain. Our watering hole dried up, no animals came to visit, and we had to pack up our camp and leave. We headed this way, and ate not one, but two of these things. And you know what? Your sister shot the tail off the boar! They're scrumptious. The finest delicacy in all the savannah."

Dusk's voice cleansed the air, making everything taste of vanilla. Perhaps this is why Toad did not offer a response. Perhaps he was resigned to defeat. Or perhaps he was just so hungry, he supposed he should accept whatever was on offer.

Hope reached for Toad's shoulder and pulled him into her womb, which had grown to the size of a watermelon.

"A little frog once told me that Dusk and Dawn used to fight over the snake's bile, because they believed it gave them super-duper strength. If you want to grow up to become a Mister Big And Strong, a Mister Tall And Mighty, then you'd do well to give it a try."

\*\*\*

It took most of the morning to prepare their food. The elders all remembered the nights when their grandmothers and granduncles had cooked this variety of snake. But their recollections varied. Some said you had to place the snake inside the fire. Others said that it had to be hoisted onto a spit. Some said to cook it quickly, over a high heat. Others said they should take it slow. They all agreed that it would have been better to turn it into a soup. But that was out of the question, since they had lost their only pot.

In the end, they reached a compromise; filleting the snake, washing their hands in its intestines, and roasting its meat at a moderate height, above a medium fire.

Sunny was one of the last people to receive a portion. He chewed each mouthful ten times on one side of his mouth, and five times on the other. He paused before he swallowed, and he paused again before he took another bite; savouring the meat's contradictions; its chapped skin and silky flesh, cheerful smell and sombre flavour.

He panned around to Toad.

That child was wearing his face in an aggressively serious fashion, as though waging an offensive against his meat; chewing it as quickly as he could, before swallowing at the first opportunity.

He vomited over his toes.

But this did not deter him. Without moving, or even acknowledging his mess, Toad took another piece of meat, checked that it was cooked, and launched a second assault; going a little slower, grinding that food into a paste, but looking every bit as warlike.

He was not eating for pleasure. Like a number of his peers, he was eating out of a sense of duty. He was honouring Mother Nature, by accepting the food she had offered. He was honouring the snake, who had died so they might live. And he was honouring Dusk, who had risked his life to protect them from that creature.

It lacked the festivity of a normal meal. Even the children, with their natural penchant for disorder, were abnormally restrained; subdued by a cumbersome silence, which was far too heavy to lift.

It should have been a momentous event. They had feasted for the first time in days. Their appetites were sated, and the leftovers would feed them until they arrived at their destination.

Yet this did little to improve their mood. For the previous few days, their cravings had been so intense, they had thought of little else; wondering where they might find food, and dreaming of the moment when they'd vanquish their hunger. Such thoughts had now been banished to the darkest recesses of their minds. They had eaten so much, so quickly, they were willing to consider anything *other than* food.

Rather than ponder their next meal, they thought of something entirely different: Their perilous situation. Their beloved home was occupied and out of reach. Their options were stark. They might die at any moment.

That meal pulled a plug, releasing a tsunami of fear; asphyxiating their minds and clamping their lips. They ate in silence, walked in silence, and barely uttered a word; until the morning of the eighth day, when they reached their destination.

# DOG DAYS

They were met with the most reinvigorating of receptions...

The Dog Clan gifted them a goat, without a moment's hesitation. The elders sacrificed that animal, to turn Aura's dream into a reality. They removed its fur, roasted its carcass, and shared its meat.

On the second day, they erected their huts. On the third, the two clans hunted together. And on the fourth, they gathered dates, gourds and cacti.

The Dog Clan had lost a little land to the Wogies, but their main hunting ground remained intact. They had never hunted big game. They trapped rabbits and small birds, and they harvested meat from their goats; hardy animals, who were happy to eat whatever they could find. Their gatherers were still finding as many plants as before. And their morale was just as effusive. In fact, it was contagious. It soothed Sunny's peers, putting their minds and bodies at ease.

***

That first lunar-cycle was a joyous time;

twenty-nine days of storytelling, discussions, hunting and feasting...

Sunny made friends with *Blue*; a shiny-skinned, bird-eyed youth, whose arms were encircled by a chain of interconnected loops; tattoos which had been etched there when he was a child, to protect him from an infectious disease. Blue was one of the best fishers Sunny had ever met. He taught Sunny how to make traps, using reeds, and how to bait them; setting them on the riverbed, and waiting for a day to pass, before returning to find them full. It was a risky endeavour, now the Wogies were moving up the river, getting a little closer with each passing day. But Blue assured Sunny that, "The ends justify the means... Yes, brother, the ends justify the means... Always, brother. What good is it, avoiding the Wogies, if we starve ourselves to death?"

Sunny also embarked on a fling with an older woman; a member of the Dog Clan, who had a busy eye, and the flattest shoulders this side of the Big Camp. The affair did not last for long. The second time they had sex, Sunny spotted Hope, as she strolled through the billowy grass. She passed their hidden location, without appearing to notice. But the very sight of his pregnant lover, made Sunny feel unfaithful. His mind launched an attack on his innards, which caused his midriff to quake. He vowed never to lay with that woman again.

But the highlight of that first lunar-cycle, was the initiation ritual which the Dog Clan performed a little early, to entertain their guests. That coming-of-age ceremony was not so much a highlight because it was particularly *spectacular*. It was a highlight because it was so *familiar*. And that fleeting moment of normality, in those uncertain days, felt like the most sumptuous of comforts.

The sacred horns wailed out from their secret locations amidst the remaining trees. Heard by all, but seen by none; they hooted throughout the night, trance-like and hypnotic; a miscellany of discordant noise, that only stumbled upon a rhythm for the most cursory of moments.

The trumpeting stopped once four adolescents, two from each clan, had responded to the call. They sprinted out of the camp, scrambled up the scree, summited the highest ridge, lit a beacon, removed their loincloths, and ran through the flames; sweating off the impurities which lurked within their skin, and burning the evil spirits which lived inside their joints.

The celebrations began once they had returned to the camp...

The clans beat drums, which they had made from hollowed-out tree trunks. They performed dances, which had taken them days to choreograph and lifetimes to perfect. And they consumed magic mushrooms; giving themselves to an infusion of colour, and surrendering their bodies to the music.

The tattooing took place once the elders had returned to sobriety.

Sunny was surprised to note that the Dog Clan used a different method to their own. Rather than pull a thin length of sinew underneath the epidermis, they inserted a needle into the skin, withdrew it, and replaced it with a thin shard of wood, which they had dipped in oil and soot.

Sunny watched on, transfixed, as these tattoos were etched into skin; enjoying the process, enjoying the art; enjoying the chance to live in the moment, without a thought for the future, or a care in the world.

\*\*\*

Those were blissful days. But they were not destined to last...

By the end of the second lunar-cycle, they had eaten all but one of the male goats. Blue had moved upstream, to avoid the Wogies, and was catching fewer fish. They were still capturing rabbits. But very few birds remained. Most had flown away; searching for new homes, in a place which still had forests.

Sunny enjoyed their hunts, no matter the outcome. He loved the routine; flinging a satchel of arrows over his shoulder, picking the perfect bow, tightening the bowstring, and walking out with his friends; talking, laughing, and singing. Although the Dogs were certainly different to the Eagles, when it came to the manner in which they hunted...

Sunny would never forget one of their missions, when the members of the Dog Clan had jumped with joy, after surrounding the remains of a fallen tree. They had loaded their bows, and pointed their arrows at either end. Sunny's heart skipped a beat. He had not spotted the animal himself. But, judging by their hosts' reactions, he was certain it must have been large; a gazelle, antelope, or even an ox. One person's eyes had bulged so much, Sunny felt compelled to reach out and push them back into their sockets. Another person was smiling so hard, Sunny thought her cheeks were about to crack.

He stepped backwards, in case the target launched itself in their direction, with its head bowed and its antlers set ready for impact. But their hosts were not so cautious. They hollered. They wailed. They circled the fallen tree, encroached a little, encroached a little more, lifted their bows, and fired a flurry of arrows. A brief silence ensued. Then they celebrated; performing a fleet-footed jig, and a triumphant shriek, before swooping towards their prey.

Sunny was alarmed to see what they had killed: Two undersized pigeons. He looked around, in an attempt to assuage his confusion. Perhaps they had shot these birds *as well* as something larger. But no. All that energy, and all that excitement, had been reserved for a pair of birds who were still too young to fly.

He shouldn't have been so surprised. The Dog Clan rarely caught more than four or five birds in a day. Those birds were seldom any larger than these.

But there was no way he could have known any better, when it came to the events which followed.

A few days after this expedition, Sunny's clans-folk were hunting alone. They arrived at the same fallen tree, where they discovered another pair of birds. Recalling the Dog Clan's glee, upon making a similar find; they killed those birds, returned to the camp, and presented their catch.

They were greeted with the coldest of welcomes. The members of the Dog Clan were clearly appalled. Their mouths were agape and their jaws hung loose. But it was impossible to tell *why* they were so upset.

It was left to a liver-spotted elder to speak on behalf of her peers:

"What! Where! Why!... Why did you obliterate such a young and defenceless clan? In the name of Mother Nature's children: What could've possibly possessed you?"

Serenity played along, supposing their hosts were *shaming the meat*.

"The ancestors know that it's true: These *are* pathetic creatures. There's barely a morsel to eat between them... You've been such generous hosts, and this is such a sorry offering. We haven't come close to re-gifting your hospitality. Please, dear sister, find it in your spirits to forgive us."

But Serenity had missed the mark.

"Pathetic creatures? Barely a morsel? What... Where... Why... No! Upon our mothers' spirits. No! Don't you think we recognise these birds? Don't you think we'd have killed them, if we'd wanted to consume their fat? Don't you think we left them for a reason? Do you take us all for stones?"

No-one responded, leaving the elder with little choice but to answer her own questions.

She scrunched her brow, which caused her hairline to advance. She shook her head, as furiously as her skin would permit. And she adopted the most pained voice she could muster; annoyed by the inconvenience of having to explain something that even a child should have been able to grasp.

"After we kill a bird, we wait for the next full moon, before we even *think* of killing another member of their species. We make sure not to hunt in the same place again, until ten days have wandered by. We never empty a nest of *all* its birds. We never kill mother birds, or their last two hatchlings."

Sunny was beginning to understand.

"What you've done is unforgivable. You've not just killed these birds. You've destroyed an entire bloodline; stopping their chicks, and their chicks' chicks, from ever being hatched. You've diminished our stock of meat for several solstices to come. You've waged war on our future wellbeing.

"Shark's tooth, buffalo's tusk, antelope's horn! Unforgivable! Violent and unforgivable. Such over-hunting? You're as pestiferous as the Wogies, and just as odorous!"

***

The Eagle Clan acknowledged the error of their ways...

In a moment of sombre introspection, they admitted they had overstayed their welcome. It was the Autumn Equinox, a time when the clans usually engaged in a bout of *competitive feasting*; eating as much as they could in a single evening. But there was not nearly enough food for such an event. And their clan was partly to blame.

The Dog Clan had been more than generous, sharing everything they had, till they barely had anything left to share. If they had any honour, the Eagle Clan would say their goodbyes, pack down their huts, and move to a different location.

That night, they held a meeting.

Dawn said they should leave, because it was the right thing to do. Dusk disagreed. He said they should leave to pre-empt the Dog Clan, who were about to chase them away. The clans-folk looked to Dawn, to Dusk, and back to Dawn; awaiting a debate that never came.

The vote was unanimous.

They re-gifted their hosts the spear they still owed, following their exchange at the Big Camp. They gave them a set of arrows, as compensation for the dead birds. And the Dog Clan gifted them a pot, to re-establish a debt.

They rubbed noses, nuzzled cheeks, went to sleep, awoke, and departed before the onset of dawn.

# HELL'S BELLS

The clans-folk cruised the scrublands alone, drifting towards their former home, without ever discussing the matter.

Starvation snuck up on them again. Long gone were the times when a youngster might recoil at the idea of eating a snake. They would have devoured that delicacy twice, if only they were given the chance; consuming it with their eyes, before consuming it with their teeth.

But such meat proved elusive. The clans-folk had little choice but to eat insects; their only source of protein.

This did not require a large adjustment. The members of their clan had always eaten caterpillars and crickets. They had conversed with different clans, who ate an array of creepy crawlies. So they possessed the knowledge they needed to adapt to their new situation.

Termite mounds were a treat. A couple of infants always ran towards those earthy pyramids, whenever they came into view. They need not have rushed. Those mounds, which could be taller than an adult, took quite some time to harvest. The clans-folk had to fashion

422 | OTHER WORLDS WERE POSSIBLE

pipes from clayish mud, attach one end of those pipes to each of the mound's entrances, and place the other end in their pot. They sang, with improvised lyrics, to maintain their spirits. And they drummed out a beat with a *chooketty-hooketty* rhythm; hitting the mound with their spears, at breathtaking speed, to mimic the sound of rain. This encouraged the termites to wake up, exit their home, proceed through the pipes, and fall into the pot.

They were happy to eat those insects whilst they were still alive; opening their mouths and dropping them into the chasm. Sometimes they cooked them in hot ashes. Sometimes they turned them into a stew.

The children ate first, then the elders, and then the other adults.

They did not only eat termites...

They harvested locusts almost every night; shaking them from the trees in which they slept, before collecting them off the ground. Lots of clans ate locusts, dubbing them the "Prawns of the sky", because they contained so many nutrients.

On a couple of occasions, they came across hives filled with stingless bees. A few adventurous souls removed them from their trees, or dug them up from beneath the earth. They returned the brood to its rightful place, but retained the small brown spheres which contained the actual honey. Everyone ate that nectar together; squeezing it from those pods, before savouring its tangy flavour.

The members of the clan still gathered whatever plants they could find. They consumed a great array of moringa, ferns and nettles. It was never enough to sate their hunger, but it was enough to keep them alive, day after day, until they reached their former home...

\*\*\*

They had never intended to return. But, now that they were here, they did not intend to leave. This was *their* land; their soil, their air, their birthright. Its lure was overwhelming.

Even if they *had* wished to leave, they were in no fit state to do so, because of a couple of events which occurred soon after their arrival: Hope had given birth. And then Sparrow had died.

The post-mortem was most peculiar. The clans-folk could not find any reason for Sparrow to have stepped into the ancestral realm. He was old, this much was true. But he was healthy. He had not been sick, or displayed any symptoms, since recovering from the shock which had floored him in the desert.

Sunny's mother gave voice to the unthinkable:

"Could he... No... Could he... Could he have died of *hunger*?"

The clans-folk had never known anything of the sort. People had been born dead. They had been killed in wars and raids. They had died of diseases. They had been eaten by evil spirits, crocodilians and snakes. Sparrow's niece had died after eating poisonous berries. One of their aunts had fallen off a cliff and tumbled to her death. But starvation? It was a ridiculous notion. And yet no-one could think of a better explanation.

Confused and perturbed, the clans-folk kept their distance. They refused to touch Sparrow's body, or move it from the place he had died. Its muscles went hard. Its skin went stiff, then loose; squeezing his skull, and giving the impression that Sparrow was in the grip of terror.

It was a distressing spectacle for everyone. But it was particularly distressing for Sunny, who had always looked upon Sparrow as an uncle.

Sunny succumbed to an idiosyncratic illness. His innards danced a jig, as though they were attempting to escape from his body, because they could not cope with all the sadness which was lingering inside. Their motion made Sunny feel sick and queasy.

To overcome his grief, and find a modicum of comfort, Sunny turned his attention to Hope's baby...

He had seen plenty of babies in his short time on earth, and none had ever piqued his interest. But this was an unusual child. A gift. He could not help but lose himself in her eyes, which Hope said were identical to his own. His mother went as far as to say that the girl was, "The living image of you, lovely, back when you were born." Sunny found this a little far-fetched. He could not imagine a time when he was so small, sweet and vulnerable. Still, who was he to argue with his mother? And even he had to admit that the girl had that same domineering nose, and that same broken chin, that he himself possessed.

He gave himself to philosophical wonderment: Wasn't it amazing that a new life could take seed in a woman's womb, grow, and burst into the world? Puff! Where there was nothing, now there existed this inhaling, exhaling, noise-making, liquid-squirting creature. And she would grow up to possess a character all of her own! Wasn't her mouth, a comical imitation of her mother's, such a curiosity and a treat? And these legs! Why were they so incredibly short? Was this the way they were supposed to feel? And these eyes! These eyes which Hope said looked the same as his own. Weren't these a sign from the ancestors, that he should keep *his eyes* on the child, so to speak; caring for her, as if *he* were the child's mother?

"Aha!" he announced, speaking for the first time since anyone could remember. "We should name her *Homecoming*, for one day she'll lead us home."

No-one agreed. But, then again, no-one *disagreed*. The choice would be Hope's, and she did not seem that enamoured. But she did not have the heart to challenge Sunny, right then, when he had found the kind of happiness which had eluded him for several lunar-cycles.

She indulged Sunny for five days. She allowed him to wash the baby; a task which he took to with an almost painful form of enthusiasm. She allowed him to hold the baby to her breast. And she allowed him to take the baby to the toilet.

The members of their clan did not use swaddles or diapers. They practised a technique known as *elimination communication*; picking up on a baby's cries, squirms and expressions; taking them to an appropriate place, holding them in a squat position, and producing a vocal cue, which encouraged them to defecate. This helped mothers to control the process. They could hold their babies next to their skin, throughout the day, without a fear of getting soiled.

Sunny did not tire, even when his behaviour began to grate upon his peers. It was more of a relief *for them*, therefore, when he stumbled upon a revelation:

"For the baby! I tell you this: I must do it for her!"

Everyone turned to Sunny in search of an explanation. What was it, exactly, that he had to do for the baby?

But Sunny did not answer this unasked question. For him, it was too obvious for words.

"Yes, for her! I'll set off tomorrow, and

complete this important mission."

No-one challenged Sunny, because no-one knew what it was they were supposed to be challenging. But Sunny still felt that his motion was being critiqued. Motions were almost always contested. Why would this one be any different? And why should Sunny wait? This was an important issue. The objections had to be rebuffed, before they had a chance to be aired:

"We're hungry. We need to eat. And there are copious amounts of food, lying about in some giant huts, just half a day's walk away. And... you know... I'm telling you: It's *our* food, for it was grown on our land. We have a right to share it. Nay. We have a *duty* to share it. How dare you suggest otherwise? Why? Would you wish for another aunt or uncle to succumb to the same fate as befell our beloved Uncle Sparrow?

"It's a risk, you say? It's a risk for me. But it's a risk I feel duty-bound to take. For Homecoming's future! It'd be an honour. Open our hearts and hope to live!

"It's a risk for *you*? 'Reprisals', you say? Dearest aunties and beloved uncles, sisters and brothers: If I succeed, I'll return with enough food to last us twenty days. If I'm captured, I'll say I acted without your consent. If the Wogies find you, tell them I'm an impulsive youth, disown me, and ally yourselves with them.

"You'd never do such a thing? But you must! Lie. Cheat. Protect yourselves. Then flee.

"If you cannot find food, and if you cannot find clans to host you, then split up. Go to *different* clans, and stay with them. Do whatever you must to survive.

"Well then, it's settled. I must forage in the Wogies' stores, and gather up our food. Unless, that is, you have *any more* objections?"

Sunny looked out at his gobsmacked peers, who had never witnessed such a performance. Not only had Sunny been ranting like a madman, responding to challenges which had never been made; he had been stepping from side to side, as though conducting a debate between two halves of his psyche, neither of which was real.

It was freakish, and it was also a little scary. Sunny's torso had expanded to nearly twice its previous size. Perhaps he had inhaled, filling it with an incredible quantity of air. Perhaps it had grown by an imperceptible amount each day, over the course of several seasons. Or perhaps he had accrued the extra muscle, whilst carrying the clan's possessions. Whatever the cause, the effect was striking. Sunny was no longer a gangly adolescent, mismatched, with an image akin to a dog on stilts. He was almost butch. He commanded the space around him. And so, when he had stomped about, the effect had been alarming.

Still the silence lingered.

Only when the baby cooed, *"Aah-ooh, aah-ooh"*, did Serenity lift his hand in a somewhat tentative fashion; raising it a little, pausing, allowing it to descend, raising it a little more, before extending it above his head. Sunny supposed he had something to say. But Serenity remained silent, setting an example for the others to follow.

Aura lifted her hand. Pilgrim lifted hers. Harmony and Buffalo went next.

Hands rose, like bubbles in a brook. Yet no-one felt a need to speak; not to ask a question, propose a vote, or declare its result.

Sunny was dumbfounded:

"Dawn: If Dusk agrees, then surely you must object?"

Dawn shook his head.

"Okay... Very well... Dusk: Dawn here supports

this motion. So you must wish to oppose it?"

Dusk did not.

It was all too much to bear.

"Sacred loincloths!"

Still that silence lingered; not so much wafting, as undulating; up and down, quiet and quieter still.

Only when the baby cooed, rumbling the hush, did Dawn decide to respond; speaking to Dusk, rather than to Sunny; uttering a single sentence, which was even more mysterious than the silence:

"Brother: I'm sorry for leaving you to fend off that buffalo alone."

And now Dusk replied:

"Brother: I'm grateful to *you*, for defending me from that creature."

Sunny was so bewildered, he thought he could have screamed. But when he opened his mouth to protest, he discovered that his ability to produce noise had been stolen by an irresistible force, which he could not identify, no matter how hard he tried.

***

Sunny would have left before daybreak, had it not been for this extraordinary exchange. But it had bugged him so much, he felt compelled to get to the bottom of matters, before he embarked on the mission.

At least, this is what he told himself. And, in part, it was true. But he also had another, rather less worthy motivation: Sunny was a bundle of nerves; fearful of the dangers which might lie in wait, and grateful for the excuse to delay his departure.

He had barely slept, tossing himself awake at regular intervals throughout the night, asking himself: "Is it worth the risk? If I'm caught, I'll suffer a punishment, like Songbird's daughter. I might be murdered. And for what? A little food? We've survived this long already. Surely, we can survive a little longer."

The plan had made sense the day before. But Sunny had made a rudimentary error: He had allowed his words to escape through his mouth, before they had the opportunity to reach his brain. A sensible person would have pondered their plan, considering the pros and cons. They would have only proposed it to their peers once they were fully committed. But Sunny had done no such thing. He had been rash. And now he was dithering; delaying his departure for as long as he could.

He went in search of Dusk. Then he spoke with Dawn.

He pieced their stories together...

As Sunny had long since supposed, those two men were not jilted lovers, who had come to blows over a woman. They were prolific hunters who had bitten off more than they could chew.

One day, when they were even younger than Sunny, they had spotted a buffalo within striking distance of their camp. Intoxicated by adrenaline, and by the heady whiff of glory; they convinced themselves that they had to act, to protect their home, lest it be attacked by that fearsome creature.

The two youngsters snuck up on the buffalo, intending to launch offensives from either side. But Dawn panicked. He caught sight of the buffalo's eye, which seemed to be dripping with blood. He hesitated, for the briefest of moments, leaving Dusk to attack alone. The buffalo struck back; turning, lunging, sinking its horn into Dusk's thigh; inflicting a wound which could be seen to this day.

Here their stories diverged...

Dawn believed he had responded, albeit a

little late; attacking the buffalo, and forcing it to flee before it could land a fatal blow. He apologised for the delay. But he believed his bravery had more than compensated for his hesitation. He had saved Dusk's life. His friend should have been grateful.

Dusk recalled a different story. In his mind, the buffalo had only fled because *he* had stood back up, and speared that animal himself; cutting its ear, causing it to wince, and convincing it to bolt. He had survived that attack without any help from Dawn.

The truth was impossible to know. Both men were committed to their own version of events, and nobody could persuade them to tolerate the alternative point of view.

Whenever Dawn claimed that he had come to Dusk's rescue, it made matters even worse. It was bad enough that Dusk had been abandoned. But his erstwhile friend would not even admit to his misdemeanour. He had made up a story to protect his pride! The man was taking him for a fool.

And whenever Dusk claimed that he had defended himself, it offended Dawn. Dusk should have had the decency to acknowledge his bravery, even if it was a little delayed. He had saved the man's life! He deserved a simple "Thank-you".

They never reached an accord.

In the end, they stopped discussing the matter. It was less painful to ignore the dispute, than to pick at a festering wound.

The older generations made their pilgrimages to the ancestral forest, taking their memories with them. And Sunny's contemporaries were forced to use their imaginations to fill the gaps; telling each other that Dusk and Dawn had come to blows whilst competing for the attention of a beautiful woman.

This story was clearly a sham, but it was all they had.

Only now, Sunny knew better.

And only now, could Sunny understand their previous comments.

Dawn had said: "Brother: I'm sorry for leaving you to fend off that buffalo alone."

And Dusk had replied: "Brother: I'm grateful to you, for defending me from that creature."

Neither man had sounded particularly convincing. Dawn must have still believed that he had saved Dusk, who must have still believed that Dawn had left him to die. But they had been pushed to the brink of starvation. Sparrow, a man like them, had only just died of *hunger*! If they did not put their differences aside, a similar fate was sure to befall them all.

And so they had swallowed their pride, and said the things that they had been waiting a lifetime to hear; even though they did not believe a syllable they were saying, let alone an entire word; and even though it caused them a great deal of discomfort.

Their statements had the desired effect. They united the clan. They helped to quell Sunny's doubts. And they gave him the conviction he needed to proceed.

If Dusk and Dawn could make up, after all these seasons; if they could agree to the mission which Sunny had proposed, without the hint of a disagreement; then it must have been essential. These men never agreed on *anything*.

This was Sunny's time.

*He* was the buffalo hunter now.

***

The air was light and heavy. It pressed down upon Sunny's shoulders, and prevented his feet from touching the ground.

He had arrived on the fringes of the Wogies' camp, with two companions by his side: Buffalo and a girl named *Butterfly*; an adolescent who went to great lengths to mute the compassion which lurked within her eyes, coating them in ashes and condescension.

Sunny had insisted on performing the raid alone; a request which was met with vociferous opposition. They were a collective, so his peers declared; they were duty-bound to stick together. But Sunny had been persistent, saying this idea was "Suicidal"; that it was not worth endangering the entire group, when a lone individual could shoulder the risk, and the benefits would remain the same. He refused to back down. And, in the end, he got his way.

Sunny had only brought Buffalo and Butterfly to act as porters.

He left them among a patch of trees, promised to return once he had gathered their food, and told them not to follow him under any circumstances.

He said his goodbyes and headed into town, thinking of nothing but the task at hand.

It came as quite a surprise, therefore, when he realised he had veered off track. He was inside

Songbird's home, as was becoming a bit of a habit. But he could not be sure how he had arrived there.

There were some new items in this place: Something large, which Songbird would later call a "Table", and four smaller items, which she would refer to as "Stools". But Songbird was missing. She only returned after a tinny sound had reverberated six times, explaining:

"That ding-dong machine has enslaved the lot of us, even the Wogies. It chimes seven times in the morning, and we must all rush off to work. We can only leave when it chimes another six times in the evening. It's the most stubborn of chiefs. Protest, argue, fight, run for your life... Still it chimes! *Ding dong, ding dong, ding dooly dong*! And still the people obey."

Sunny was certain this was a joke. People might make things, or hunt, or gather, or fish; so long as there was an actual need. But you would have to be crazy to do something simply because you had heard a noise, or because it was a particular part of the morning.

Yet it was not a particularly funny joke. It made him frown, but it did not make him want to giggle.

Songbird *did* chuckle, however, when Sunny explained the plan.

"Ha!" she cried. "You're just going to walk into a store, gather enough food to feed a clan, and be off on your merry way? The who, the what and the why! You know they'll catch you? You know they'll *punish* you, like they punished my baby girl?"

Sunny supposed she was right. He had been having similar thoughts himself. And so it did not require much persuasion, to convince him to wait until the darkest part of the night. Songbird said the mission would still be fraught with danger. A vicious gang, who called themselves the "Nightwatchmen", would be out on the prowl, searching for people like Sunny. But it would still be safer than proceeding in the daylight, in front of hundreds of prying eyes.

Songbird prepared dinner as they waited; chopping onions, tossing them into a pot, adding mustard seed and chicken. Wisps of white steam meandered upwards; aromatic, sticky and cerebral.

They got to talking...

Sunny asked about Songbird's daughter, and was alarmed to discover that she had been taken away. "Not to be punished or enslaved. But to attend something the Wogies call a 'Boarding school'."

According to Songbird, native children were being snatched from their mothers, and taken to that distant place. They were being made to cut their hair, wear Woggy-style cloths, eat with something called a "Fork", and worship Chief God. Apparently, this was a *good* thing. "Kill the savage," they said, "And you'll save the man." Those children were being taught to speak the same language, adopt a singular culture, and pass identical "Exams". Songbird had heard that they *were not* being taught to read and write, because the Wogies wanted to "Keep them in their place." And she had heard that they *were* being taught to read and write, because the Wogies wished to "Raise them up." She did not know what to believe.

Sunny knew exactly what to believe: He wanted to challenge the idea that *they* were the ones who needed to be "Raised up". But Songbird had already changed the subject, explaining what had happened to their indigenous art...

Each tribe in the region had their own artistic

style; creating sculptures, carvings and pendants; carrying these items wherever they went. Some possessed artworks which were hundreds of generations old; communal heirlooms, which provided a bridge between them and their ancestors. According to Songbird, the Wogies had said these were "Heathen artefacts". They had claimed they were against the will of Chief God, stolen them, smashed them, and thrown them onto a fire.

Again, Sunny wished to question these events. And again, he was denied the opportunity. Songbird had moved the conversation on; explaining that the Wogies had also destroyed their *instruments*. Native music had been banned. The Wogies had introduced their own style of music, but Songbird was not a fan:

"That screechy racket makes me want to bite off my ears and eat them."

***

Songbird's monologue continued until after the sun had set. Sunny supposed it was cathartic. Left here alone, without her daughter, Songbird must have felt a need to unload her thoughts. She had performed her soliloquy to Sunny, because he was the first person who had deigned to listen.

He was wrong. Songbird *did* have a companion; a native man, who entered without uttering a word, soon after the bell had chimed another seven times.

As soon as his buttocks landed on a stool, a meal landed before him; placed there by Songbird, who had timed this routine to perfection.

The man began to eat, using a knife and fork, without even looking up.

He was rather startled, therefore, when Sunny said "Hello".

"Ah gazump. What on God's green earth?"

The man's torso recoiled, instinctively, but his feet were unable to follow. This caused his stool to tip back, and his chin to tip up; revealing the full scope of his expressionless face. It was an unreasonably normal kind of face. No feature was too pronounced. His nose was neither too big nor too small. His lips were neither too fleshy nor too thin. For all the logic in the world, his features should have merged to produce the archetype of a beautiful face. Yet they did not. They were too uniform. It was as though he had been painted by an artist who lacked imagination. His face was plausible, as far as faces went. But it did not look realistic.

Sunny had to squint, to be sure he was speaking to a real person; not an ancestor or a spirit; not a Woggy who had donned a disguise, or a woman who was wearing a mask.

"Hello... Are you... Umm... A *person*?"

"A person? Oh, fiddlesticks. How very rude of me. Yes, young gentleman, I'm Mister Jacobson."

Sunny had never heard of a "Jacobson".

"I say, that's my moniker nowadays. You can call me Starlight... Actually, you'd better not call me that! Call me Jack."

"Jah... Jah... Jack? Jackfruit?"

"A pleasure to make your acquaintance. And with whom, may I ask, am I speaking?"

"Err... I mean... You may ask."

"*Haha*! What rollicking banter! My oh my. Do pray tell, young sir. Your name, dear chap. Your name."

"Oh. I'm Sunny. But you can call me... Err... Sunny."

"Yah, yah. I thought as much. You're still using your savage name?"

Sunny attempted a nod, which was only

partially successful. His head moved upwards, but it got stuck and refused to return. Sunny had never considered his name to be a "Savage name". It was simply his name; the only one he had ever required.

"Yah, yah. It takes some getting used to. Like with Katie and myself. We're family now."

"Oh... Who is 'Katie'?"

"Why, who the deuce do you think has been hosting you all the while? My fellow, *this* is Katie."

Jack pointed his finger at Songbird, who responded with the faintest of shrugs.

"Young Sunny. Actually, no. That doesn't quite cut the mustard. Let's call you 'Steve'. Okay? Splendid! Ra!... *Young Steve*: Do you know about 'Family'?... No?... Okay, let me see... Yah. In savage times, we lived among our clans. Ghastly things, where no-one knew their own father... Well, not anymore! No, no, ruddy well no! If one doesn't know which children are their own, how in Jesus and Joseph's name can they pass their possessions onto their offspring? One might work their entire life, building up a nice little portfolio, die, and then *puff*! It's all gone up in smoke. And one wouldn't want that, would one?

Heavens, no! So you see, Master Steve, it's devilishly important to commit to a single woman, and ensure that she commits to you. That way you can be certain that her children are your children, and that your property will be passed onto smaller versions of yourself."

Sunny could not understand why Jack cared so much about what might happen to a few material objects, once his spirits had travelled to their ancestral forest. But the arrangement seemed to please Jack, which he supposed was an end in itself.

Still, this did little to explain why *Songbird* had agreed to this arrangement.

"What's in it for you?" He asked his friend, who had retreated into the shadows. "I mean... You know which children are yours."

Songbird raised her eyebrows and opened her mouth. But her words coagulated in her throat, forming a blob of mucous and spite.

She took comfort, embraced by the neutrality of silence, up until the point at which she caught sight of Sunny. Accosted by the compassion in his eyes, her words began to melt. They turned to steam, ascended, and escaped through her lips:

"I thought I could re-gift... *Repay* the mortgage, by making those pots. But the Wogies added 'Interest' to that debt. I have to gift *more* than I owe. And the merchants reduced my wage. I get gifted... I get *paid* by the 'Hour' now. That's the period between each set of ring-a-dings. And there's not enough of these hours in a day. They really ought to make more.

"So, I was going to lose the house. But then Starlight came to the rescue. He gets gifted more money than me, for working with oxen. We pool that money, and use it to re-gift... To *repay* the mortgage."

Sunny rattled his brain:

"But *you* used to raise oxen yourself. You gave me one, back when you were free... Why couldn't you raise them here, instead of making pots?"

"That's men's work now."

"What's 'Men's work'?"

"Work for men."

"Oh."

"Men work *outside* the home. They come into regular contact with the chiefs. But most women stay at home, or close to home. They aren't seen, they have less influence, and so they get gifted less money. Hmm... They must get themselves a man, to get the money they need to survive."

"Oh, I see. Women have to enslave themselves to men because of money?"

"No."

"Because of cargo?"

"No."

"Then why?"

"I'm not a slave to any man!"

Sunny would have replied, had he not been struck by the change in Jack's appearance. If he was more attentive, he might have noticed the way in which Jack's eyes had become deeper, darker, and more dismal. But the change had been so gradual, and Sunny had been so engrossed in his conversation with Songbird, that he had not spotted the transformation.

If anything, Jack's features looked even more nondescript than before. His lips were even more average. His nose was even more central than seemed good for his health.

"No!" Jack shouted. "Excuse me... No, Master Steve, you're mistaken. Indubitably! *You're* the real slave. You're enslaved to your base instincts; fornicating with anything that moves, without good old-fashioned self-control. You're enslaved by the present, without a thought for the future. You're a slave to destiny. You don't clear your own path. You're a slave to the darkness. You haven't stepped into the light."

Sunny could tell he had caused offence. Jack's breath felt hot upon his cheek. But he had no idea what he had said to spark such indignation.

"I'm sorry... I didn't mean to... I just want to understand: Songbird... *Katie* made clan... Made *family* with you, so she could keep this hut... This *house*. And you made family with her, so her *children* could keep this house... Have I got that right?"

"Good heavens, no! Actually, yes. Yah. But no! Ruddy well no!... Master Steve: Katie and I married for *love*. For love, old chap. The most beautiful of God's creations. We married because marriage is a sacrament that honours the Lord."

"Oh."

Sunny was lost, but he tried not to let it show. This Jack fellow looked like a native, but he spoke like a Woggy. It was a combustible mix, which had to be treated with caution:

"Please enlighten me. I'm just an ignorant savage, after all... So, these muggled... These *married* people... They protect each other? Like clans-folk? Like members of a tribe?"

"Actually, yes. Yah. Families are like little tribes. But one relies upon *the state* for protection."

"The 'State'?"

"Indubitably, old sport: The king. The queen. Politicians. Civil servants. Judges. Police. Armies. Laws. Rights. Prisons. Territory. Borders... The state! The bedrock of civil society."

"Oh."

Sunny had been besieged by a barrage of grunts, which he supposed were probably words. They certainly sounded like words. But they weren't like any words *he* had ever used.

"And taxes! Like the one announced today... Katie, sweetheart: Did you hear of this spiffing new idea? This *Moralising Tax*? It's a bit different to the previous tax. The one which reimburses the master race, for the expenses they incurred whilst civilising this land... Yah... This will be *our tax*. It'll raise the funds *we need* to be self-supporting. To stand on our own two feet, so to speak; building *our own* highways, bridges, schools, and so on and so forth."

Sunny was confused:

"Tah... I'm ever sorry. You lost me at tah..."

*"Taxes*?... Oh, golly gosh! Of course, *you* don't have taxes. You're not civilised. How terribly presumptuous of me to forget... Now, taxes are a sort of fee. One pays taxes to the state for one's own protection."

"Pay?"

"Yah. One gifts money."

"So, hang on... The Wogies make money. Then you have to make real stuff, with an actual use, just to get those beads. Then you have to give those tokens back, to protect yourselves from... From whom?... From the Wogies?"

Jack's face was unintelligible; a more aggressive shade of its original colour, with slightly more placid features, which were slightly less defined. He was clearly emotional. But it was hard to tell if he was reacting positively or negatively.

Sunny adopted an inoffensive tone:

"I thought you gave the Wogies the money *they made*, in order to get back some of the things *you made*."

"Yah, yah."

"But you also have to give them *taxes*, so they can get the things they want to make for themselves?"

"The things they want to make *for us all*! We all pay, and we all benefit."

"Oh... So they need this money, to make things which benefit us all?"

"Exactly."

"But they make this money themselves?"

"Yah."

"So why don't they just make some more money, and then use *that money* to make the things which benefit us all?"

"Excuse me?"

"Why do they need a tax? Why do they have to take money from people like you, when they can make *new money*, and avoid all the hassle?"

"Ah! Old bean, why I do believe I've caught your drift. Yah, yah. I say, this is exactly what the savages need to learn. Nail on the head. Bravo!

"The clue is in the name: The *Moralising Tax*. It's educational. It's designed to teach the value of an honest day's work... It's genius, when you think about it: Even the most primitive farmer, in the furthest-flung corner of the bush, can harvest and sell a crop; garnering the money they need to pay their share. So long, that is, that *they work hard*, throughout the year; tending the fields which the ruling classes have been so generous to bestow upon them... Although they must sell their crops when prices are low, which is a dreadful shame, because they can end up selling *too much*. And then they must buy food to eat, when prices are high. But one digresses... Yah. Those fellows can always apply for a loan. They can always find work on a plantation. No-one needs to starve. There's always a way, old mucker. There's always a way... Now, the point is a simple one, Master Steve: There's always a way to pay, so long as one is righteous. So long as one works hard. And we'll all benefit from that hard work in the end. I say, just look around you. We live in a house! A house, old bean. A house! We eat meat two times a week.

"We're going places. We're creating a consumer culture. New products. New habits. Everything new! Everything better than before. With luxury items for the first time in our history. With imported goods, which bind us to the fatherland. Yah! Yah, yah, yah! Everything interconnected. Everything a part of God's plan."

***

It took almost three "Hours" for Jack to speak himself unconscious.

His head flopped onto the table, mid-sentence, and his body embarked on a curiously mediocre form of sleep; a rest which was not too deep, and not too light, but somewhere in the middle. Jack's slumber was only interrupted by the occasional blast of sleep-talk. Every now and again, he shouted a random word, like "Work" or "Savage". But he did so in the most moderate of fashions; in a manner which was far too restrained to shake him from his slumber.

Sunny had barely uttered a word. It would have been rude to interrupt the man, whilst he was having so much fun. And it would have been foolish to mention the mission. Who knew how this man would react?

He got more sense from Songbird, whom he took to calling "Katie", purely as a tease.

Songbird let her feelings be known, soon after her husband fell asleep; saying that she would rather not be a part of this "Blasted marriage", just as she would rather not be a slave to that "Tyrannical clock". But what choice did she have? The alternatives were worse.

Songbird admitted that she had known of the old tax, when Sunny had visited before. She had never raised the subject, because Sunny had never asked. Sunny protested: How could he have asked, when he never heard of such a thing as a "Tax"? But Songbird was unfazed: "Not my jungle," she stated. "Not my trees."

The two friends covered old ground: They discussed Songbird's daughter, the house, work, money and debt. Then they returned to the subject of taxation.

Songbird said that the natives who had accepted land from the Wogies, had been forced to pay tax, *as well as* their tithe. They feared the punishments they might suffer if they defaulted. But those clans had resisted the consumer culture the Wogies were attempting to impose. They always turned up on time. They gifted the correct amount of tax and tithe. But they refused to buy the Wogies' cargo. If they still had some money, after they had paid their fees, they exchanged it for goats, which they sacrificed to their ancestors; burning those goats to ashes in front of the Wogies' eyes. It was a small act of defiance. But enabled them to maintain their self-respect.

Songbird grew more condescending as the night wore on, claiming:

"These pale-faced motherless daughters! Don't they know, the frog doesn't drink up the pond in which she lives?"

And then:

"Chief King! Chief God! Chief Taxman! Chief Merchant! Chief Magistrate! Chief Money! Chief Mortgage! Chief Chief!... These Wogies have far too many chiefs!"

And finally:

"Money this, money that. Only when they've cut down the last tree, poisoned the last river, and caught the last fish; will they realise they cannot eat their money."

***

The clock chimed twelve times.

Sunny rose to his feet.

"Ha!" Songbird proclaimed, before hushing herself, checking on Jack, and continuing in a whisper: "It sneaks up on you, doesn't it? You think the bell is a tyrant. But you obey its commands, without realising what you're doing."

Sunny could not disagree. The bell *had* inspired him into action, whether he liked it or not. And, now he was standing, he had no good reason to sit.

"You should leave," he demanded. "Come and live with my clan. Choose freedom. Choose a world without bells, money or tax."

Songbird's response was awash with contradictions. Her face screamed "Yes". Her shoulders jumped, as though to propel her into motion. But her words were a miserable grey:

"Even if you make it out alive, the Wogies will discover what you've done. They'll give chase. They'll come for you *and your clan*... Quite frankly, I'd rather take my chances here."

Sunny tensed a cheek.

"Okay," he concluded. "But you're always welcome. Our land is your land."

"The same."

They rubbed noses and parted ways.

***

The passageways smelled different, now they were shrouded by an invisible shade of darkness; purified by an absence of light, but sullied by the smoke which was wafting out of the remnants of a thousand snuffed-out fires. Sunny could not see the buildings, but he could feel their presence. They seemed to be tiptoeing towards him, pressing his ribs; inspiring him to up his pace, skip, and then jog.

He scampered in the direction of a glistening light, without stopping to consider its source. It was only when he was standing beneath its shadow, that he realised it was emanating from the very same instrument which had been accosting his ears; ding-donging once an hour. It was a shiny contraption, which reflected the moon's amber light.

Even when it was silent, that thing possessed an irresistible power! It was sinister, malevolent, and to be avoided at all costs.

Sunny vowed to keep his distance. He backed away, turned, and broke into a trot. He did not even consider the direction he was heading, only that he was heading *away* from that bell.

He reached the opposite side of the square.

The mud here was knuckled with stones, which seemed to be arranged in lines; like backbones buried in earth. It felt both strange and familiar; caressing Sunny's feet, but biting his soles.

The air was excessively thick.

A light glistened. At first, Sunny supposed it was that pesky bell. But no. This light was haphazard. It flickered and blazed. It was large and distant, or small and somewhere nearby. It was moving towards him, or away from him, or not moving at all.

Of one thing, Sunny was certain: This was a bad omen. In all likelihood, that flame was illuminating the way for the kind of person who might attack him without a moment's hesitation. It represented a threat, which had to be avoided.

Sunny's heart went "Pop", pounding the lungs on either side. Then it plummeted, returning to its natural position, even though it had never ascended. It defied reason. But it did not have to make any sense. Sunny had already noted the lesson. And now he was taking heed; lightening his step, holding his breath, bowing his head, and diving into a store.

His head crashed into the door:

Clack! Ouch! Shush.

The sound had not been overly loud, but it jarred with the prevailing silence. Anyone who was awake, would have been alerted by the suddenness with which the door had clanged, and by the speed with which it had been hushed.

Sunny's stomach erupted. If that organ had not been secured in place, he was sure it would have broken into pieces and sprayed in every direction.

He felt pressured into acting with haste, before he was seen by whoever was carrying the torch. But this was counterproductive. His fingers moved too quickly for his brain; fumbling where they should have caressed; jangling with noise, when they were supposed to proceed in silence.

Sunny forced himself to take a breath. He allowed his mind to cool, and his pupils to dilate, before continuing with the task.

It did not take long for him to deduce the issue: The door had been bound by an inflexible hoop. When Sunny had tried to enter, that hoop had smashed against the frame, creating that dreadful sound.

That ordeal was behind him now. But his situation had not improved. There was no way of entering this store, without kicking down the door; an act which would have bellowed across the camp, alerting the Wogies, who would find him and shoot him down. He was almost certain that he was about to be captured. He could sense his adversary's breath, blowing against his neck, just waiting to be joined by a mouth, a face and a body.

He slunk away from the light, bent double, inhaled and exhaled. At first, there was just one thing on his mind: Escape. But then he recalled the mission; poor Uncle Sparrow, Hope's precious baby, and all his starving peers. He gulped, turned inwards, tried the next store, and discovered that its door was also bound. He tried a third store, with much the same result.

It was most peculiar. His kinfolk erected a store whenever they built their Small Camp. Their tribe had a much larger store, which was overseen by a Women's Council. But their entrances had never been bound. Everyone was welcome.

If Sunny had more time, he might have stopped to consider just *why* the Wogies had sealed their doors. It was such an alien concept, that to understand it would have required a great deal of thought.

But Sunny did not have the luxury of time.

He found a gap between the second and third stores, turned sideways and squeezed inside. It was a claustrophobic space, too narrow to be an alley. He had to inhale to get through the tightest portions. He almost choked, stifled the noise, and almost choked again; allowing himself to wheeze, before sidestepping through to the other side.

It was so dark, Sunny had to see his way

through touch; caressing the wall, in search of an opening. He stroked that structure from left to right, and from right to left; repeating this process, and repeating it again.

His efforts were in vain. There was no entrance to be found.

On the precipice of defeat, Sunny struck upon an idea: This wall was made from overlapping strips of wood. If he could remove a few, he might be able to slither inside.

He was unable to get a grip. He shuffled along to the end, where a corner was exposed, and tried again. This time, he had a little luck. He was able to prise his nails beneath the plank, but he lacked the strength to lever it open.

He was close to despair. He had risked his life to be here. He could be captured at any moment. Salvation lay on the other side of this wall. And yet their food remained elusive. It was enough to fry his blood.

He paused to think: Could he kick the wall open? The wall looked too strong, and his kicks would be too noisy. Could he burn the wall? He had been making fires all his life. But the smoke would alert the Wogies.

No. He had been right before. He should test

the doors, search for other openings, and attempt to prise open the wood. These were the only sensible options.

He felt his way beyond this store, beyond another narrow gap, and along the rear of the second store. Again, he explored that structure. Again, he tried to break open the wood. And again, he was driven to despair.

He found a loose strip of wood. And then he found a semi-circular hole, where the grain had curved asunder. Laying on his back, he inserted his toes into the opening, pressed his heels against the plank beneath, and pulled the top of his foot back towards his body; levering those planks apart.

The wood creaked.

Shush!

Sunny scolded the wall, before trying once again; going a little slower, and achieving a modicum of success; loosening the plank, but only by a small amount. He repeated the process until it came free at one end, but not the other; creating a smallish gap.

It was a start, but he had a long way to go.

Despairing of what he was about to do, but unable to think of a better alternative; Sunny cursed himself, cursed the ancestors, got down on his knees, and began to nibble the wood. He emerged with a mouthful of splinters, wiped his tongue, picked his teeth, questioned his sanity, and questioned the sanity of nature. Then he began again afresh. He could see that his efforts were having an effect, but his progress was painfully slow.

Sunny would have lost track of time, had he not been serenaded by the bell. By the time it chimed once, he had chewed his way through the first plank. He had cut his lip, but it had not begun to bleed. By the time the clock had emitted another two dings, and another two dongs, he had chewed through both ends of two planks, and removed the sections between. His tongue stung with the serrations, and his lips were pink with pain.

He was ready.

He braced himself, held himself slim, asked Mother Nature for her assistance, thought of Hope, thought of his mother, and forced himself through.

The gap was wide, but not especially tall. His head slid through, when he rotated it to the side. But when he turned it back, he felt certain he had locked himself in place. The Wogies would come, see that he was trapped, guffaw, tickle him, pinch him, cut him loose, and perform the most painful "Punishment" they could concoct. It was sure to be a gruelling ordeal.

He had to press each of his ribs in turn, popping them through the opening, before he was able to slither through.

He tumbled head-first towards the ground.

It was even darker in here than outside. It was as though the walls were reflecting the darkness back onto Sunny, with double the intensity, and none of the starlight or moonlight.

He closed his eyes. If anything, his vision became *brighter* than before. He opened his eyes, closed them, opened them, and completely lost track of his senses; struggling to recall if his eyes were open or closed, and concluding that it did not make much of a difference.

He reached out, grabbed at thin air, stepped forwards, took another step, and touched upon a shelf. His hands meandered around in a spider-like fashion. His fingers scurried in one direction, and then another; finding nothing, and finding something; something organic, something crispy and... It felt like food! Could it be a leaf?

Or a vegetable? Sunny's brain expanded. It would have pushed against his skull, had his skull not inflated as well. He grabbed that furry substance with more gusto and bustle than he had intended, pressed it to his face, rubbed it into his nose, rubbed it into his eyes, and inhaled its musky flavour; shunting it into his mouth, and chomping down with rapacious zeal.

His body understood before his mind could process the information, spraying bolus into the void. Sunny could not quite believe what he was doing. Why was he wasting this precious food, when his kinfolk were on the brink of starvation? What had he become?

He was left with little choice but to listen to his tastebuds, which were delivering the message his subconscious had been trying to ignore: This was not food. This fluffy substance had no nutritional value.

What was it?... It could not be... It had to be... But no... But yes... It was not... It was... This leaf was... It was *cotton*.

Sunny was desperate to avoid this reality. His fingers were already scuttling along the next shelf, and the shelf after that; searching for something different. But the longer he searched, the less he could avoid the truth: This was the first store he had visited with Hope. That giant hanger, which contained nothing but rubber and cotton. There was no food in here. His efforts had been in vain.

Sunny supposed he must have known this was a possibility, whilst he was making his way inside. He had been in denial. But there could be no denying the truth: He had exerted all that effort, he had risked the Wogies' wrath, and he had not achieved a thing.

He could not bring himself to retreat. Even though he presumed it was futile, he still explored the other shelves. Perhaps something had changed. Perhaps this place was now used to store food, *as well as* rubber and cotton. Perhaps someone had stored a small amount of food in here, for want of space elsewhere.

Alas, Sunny's optimism did little to overcome the blanched reality of his situation. He was not going to find food in this place, no matter how much he searched.

But Sunny was pretty sure that the next store, which he also visited with Hope, *did* contain some food. Before he had tried on a pair of foot-cloths and held up an axe, he had spotted a few legs of meat, which were hanging from the rafters in that store, and a row of sacks, which were filled with a kind of grain.

Now his spirits were raised. He almost ran. He almost tripped, almost slipped, actually stumbled, and crashed to the ground with a thud. But the pain, which trickled up his legs, did nothing to dent his fervour. He bounced back up, just as soon as he had landed. He bounded across the store, dove towards the wall, pushed himself through the gap, wedged himself stuck, wriggled around, became *more* stuck, pushed harder, scraped his flesh, and emerged on the other side.

He wasted no time, sidestepping along that wall, leaping across the void, and feeling his way across the back of the neighbouring store; searching for a loose plank, or a gap in the wood. He was so engrossed with this endeavour, that he responded with a swallowed gasp, when he touched something which felt peculiar. His pulse quickened to an incalculable rate. It almost stopped. Then it returned to its previous briskness.

Sunny had become so accustomed to the feel of these wooden walls, he was affronted by the presence of a different material. He did not ask himself: "What is this?" Rather, he asked: "What is this doing *here*?"

He flicked that aberration. He pinched it. He butted it with his nose.

Only when he had finished, did he stop to investigate the substance; seeing it with his palm, feeling his way to a conclusion.

No! Sunny could not believe it. He had wasted all that time and energy, chewing through the wall of the wrong store. And the store which contained food, had a window! Sunny did not know whether to celebrate the fact that it might be easier to enter this place, or curse himself for his lack of judgement. Why had he not investigated this building before? His nerves had laid waste to his senses.

In the end, he felt both joy *and* despair. Those emotions waged war in his stomach; swirling around, mingling with his bile, merging with his blood; leaving him queasy, wheezy and raw. He doubled over, clutched his belly, regulated his breathing, and allowed himself to smile.

The window itself was similar to the one he had seen in Songbird's hut. It was made of a substance she had called "Glass"; a strange, translucent thing, which repelled the rain, but admitted most of the light. Sunny supposed it might be easy to break. It was awfully thin. But, then again, you never could be sure with these strange, Woggy contraptions.

He gave it a tap, which produced a tinny sound. He supposed it would create an even louder noise, if he attempted to push it through. But, try as he might, he could not think of a better plan.

He took a deep breath. Was he really going to do this? Of course! He had not come this far, just to pivot and back away.

He squatted down and began to crawl; searching for a suitable object, without knowing what that object might be. In the end, he was unable to find anything other than a handful of rocks. He could use those to break this glass, but it would be far too noisy for comfort.

He reassessed the situation, and came up with a better plan...

He removed his loincloth, and stretched it across the glass. He collected the pieces of wood, which he had removed from the previous store, and used them to pin his loincloth in position. Then he took the smallest stone and tapped it against the leather; applying just enough force to fracture the glass, without jostling the shards from the pane.

The loincloth did its job, muffling most of the noise.

Sunny took his time, cracking the window's perimeter, before fragmenting the central section. When the glass was shattered throughout, he pushed the middle, to little effect. He pushed a little harder, perhaps a little *too* hard, and felt the glass implode around his wrist.

A shower of crystalline droplets fell through on the other side.

Sunny had done a decent job. The largest pieces of glass were no bigger than his thumb. But he had not done a *perfect* job. The glass still fell from chest-height, landing with a chime and a jangle.

He ducked, instinctively, before scampering away; hiding in the gap between stores.

He waited until he felt safe, waited a little longer, and only emerged once he was certain that no-one was coming.

He placed his loincloth over the shards which lined the bottom of the window, pushed the wood into the serrated glass on either side, and heaved his body through the void; landing on his hands, and rolling forwards across the ground.

He exhaled with relief, almost giggled, almost laughed, and smiled in a hysterical fashion. Then he recoiled in terror and shock. His heart pounded so hard, he thought it must have ascended into his throat. His throat *had* bulged, but that was because he had gulped down too much air. It felt as though all his blood had rushed towards the small zone between his shoulders. That region felt dense. But he could not feel anything below his ribs.

There was a reason why he had reacted in such a manner...

By his feet, curled up in a foetal position, was the person he and Hope had met the previous time they were here. The man who had stormed into this store, stopped, laughed at Sunny, told him he was holding the axe the wrong way around, and suggested they depart, because "Once they've got you, there's really no escaping."

Sunny had pondered that meeting on several occasions: Who was this man? Was he defending *him* from the Wogies? Or was he defending the

*Wogies' cargo*? Sunny could not tell if this fellow had been mocking, threatening or protecting him. He could have been doing *all* these things. It was impossible to say.

Right now, Sunny could not even be sure if this man was actually asleep. Sunny had been relatively quiet, but he had still made a little noise. His actions had produced a deluge of glass, which had hurtled towards the man. That person appeared to be asleep. He was whistling into the darkness, and biting off chunks of air. But he might have been faking. He might have been waiting for the perfect moment to pounce.

Sunny thought better than to wait and see. He climbed back through the window, crouched down out of sight, spied on the man, and only returned once the clock had chimed again. If this man could sleep through such a noise, Sunny supposed he could sleep through the sound of a breaking window. Perhaps he had grown accustomed to the cacophonous melodies of this town. Perhaps he had always been a deep sleeper.

Sunny returned through the window, tiptoed through the back room, gathered all the cured meat he could carry, retraced his steps, and passed that food through the window. He repeated this process a second time. On the third, he returned with a sack which contained some yellow kernels, and a second sack, which contained something that Songbird had called "Rice".

He clambered through the window, picked up three slabs of meat, and hurried back to meet Butterfly and Buffalo.

*** 

Sunny completed two missions. He reunited with his companions and handed them the meat he had gathered, before returning to fetch some more.

If anything, they were more relieved to see *him*, than the food he had foraged. They had grown increasingly worried, the longer he remained away; fretting over his safety, and the safety of their clan. They only inspected their food after they had hugged Sunny, checked that he was real, hugged him a second time, rubbed his nose, nuzzled his cheeks, hugged him a third time, and then a fourth.

Sunny thought that Butterfly might have been concerned about the weight of the food he had asked her to carry. But he could be entirely sure. She had not emitted a sound.

Buffalo was not nearly so aloof.

"It's enough," he insisted. "We can carry this between us. It'll last us for almost an entire lunar-cycle, if we pad it out with leaves."

But Sunny, high on adrenaline, was in no mood for a compromise:

"We don't need to 'Pad it out'. I've gathered some grains. It won't take long to fetch them. And then we'll be able to survive for *several* lunar-cycles."

Sunny was compelled as much by stubbornness as by reason. He had overcome so many emotions, he felt it would have been foolish not to maximise the returns, now that the worst of it was over. He just had to make one final trip, and the rewards would be substantial.

"Go ahead... No, sister, brother: I insist. The others will be worried... If everything goes to plan, I'll catch you up on the way. If not, I'll meet you at the camp... That's correct. Don't worry about me. I'm telling you: Go! Be gone!"

Sunny shot them a glare which was so red, so piercing, it inspired his friends to pat their sides, to check if they had been burnt.

They did not say a word. Buffalo was too

meek to argue, and Butterfly was too shy. They had a mission to complete. Sunny could do whatever he liked.

***

Sunny was in a mood which verged on the cavalier; breezy, carefree and proud. He had even caught himself whistling, as he passed by Songbird's home. He had muted his lips, the moment he became aware of his bluster. But he could not stop himself from smiling at the brazenness he had displayed.

He skipped down lanes, and cantered around corners. His feet skimmed the surface, caressing the wisps of mud; guiding his body, as it slunk through the darkest patches of air. He was no longer thinking of the sleeping man. He had forgotten about that eerie flame.

He crossed the square, slid sideways through the gap, located the remaining food, crouched down, gripped the sacks, and eased himself up.

He was surprised to discover that he had not, as he had supposed, returned to a standing position. He was still squatting. The sacks were still on the ground.

It was strange. But it was not insurmountable.

He clenched his cheeks and began again, with

much the same result. He supposed the sacks were too heavy to lift. But this did not adhere to reason. He had carried them here before.

He tried a third time, and a fourth, before jumping, but remaining in the same position. He had been startled by a voice that was so unforeseen, it felt ten times more vicious than it sounded. But he was unable to rise, because he was being held in place by an insurmountable force: Two hands were grasping his shoulders.

"Blah, blah blah, blah-di-blah, blah blah..."

Sunny could not understand a word. At first, he was relieved. The mission had been thwarted. But it had been thwarted by a child or a fool; a person who was incapable of coherent speech. He gulped down three lumps of air. And only then did he recall where he was, and what sort of people had occupied this place. He had not been accosted by a child, nor by a fool, but by a Woggy; the most fearsome creatures their tribes-folk had ever encountered.

In a single sudden movement, he twisted his torso, and launched himself to the side; producing a horizontal thrust, which he hoped would propel him beyond the reach of his assailant.

He landed face-first in the dust.

A foot had been hooked around his ankle, just above his scar; holding his foot in position, as his body flew into the void. Now his face was kissing the ground. Dirt was filling the gaps between his teeth, a knee was pressing his spine, and two hands were pinching his shoulders.

"Didn't you hear? We said you'd be given a fair trial. Justice *will* prevail. Stay calm. Inhale. Justice *will* prevail."

Sunny frowned, even though he knew that no-one would see.

"Oh... You said all that?"

"Ah, yes. I thought as much... You don't understand the Civilised Language."

Sunny tried to shrug, failed, and reluctantly said "No".

"That'll explain it... We were just saying that you're going to come with us. We'll put you in a cell overnight, and you'll stand trial tomorrow."

"What's a 'Cell'?"

"A prison... Err... A hut from which it's impossible to escape."

"Oh... So you're kidnapping me?"

"'Kidnapping'? *Hah hah! Hee hee!* No, my cousin. We're *arresting* you."

"Oh... This 'Arrest'?... Is this the Woggy word for kidnap?"

The speaker paused to think of a suitable response, giving a second person the time he needed to light a torch. For some reason, beyond the bounds of logic, Sunny had supposed that he had only been assaulted by a single individual. He had not considered that the two different voices might have come from two different mouths; even though one was high-pitched, the other low; even though the first had spoken Woggy, and the second had spoken in a dialect which was similar to Sunny's. Nor had he realised that the force used to restrain him had been so great, because it had been applied by two different pairs of hands.

The lull in conversation allowed his reason to catch up with his mind, which had been careening out of control; fuelled by a heady cocktail of shock, fear, adrenaline and bile. It seemed obvious to him now: The man with the torch was the nightwatchman; the man he had been trying to avoid. The second man was the store's attendant. He must have woken from his slumber, spotted the broken glass, gone to find help, returned with the guard, and hidden with him in the shadows, whilst waiting for Sunny to return.

Now he was speaking again:

"No, no... 'Kidnap' is when you seize a person for no good reason. 'Arrest' is when you... When the *state* kidnaps... When they *capture* a person because they've committed a wrong."

Sunny was puzzled:

"But I've not 'Committed a wrong'. *You're* the ones who assaulted *me*; shunting me to the ground. You're the ones who are hoarding all our food. I'm telling you: You should be 'Arresting' yourselves."

The nightwatchman gave a long reply, which the attendant attempted to translate; abbreviating his partner's speech by such a large degree, that Sunny paused before he offered a response, because he was almost certain there was more to it than this:

"My friend says you're wrong about what you called an 'Assault'. Such things aren't assaults when they're committed by the state. The state has a monopoly on violence."

Pause.

"A 'Monopoly'?"

"The state's representatives are permitted to

attack... to *restrain and punish* the people. But the people do not have permission to attack the state."

"Oh... That doesn't sound fair."

"Now, he says you've committed what's called a 'Theft'. You took something that didn't belong to you, without the owner's permission."

"Oh... But I only shared some food. And food belongs to the hungry... And I was hungry. So it *did* belong to me. I had a right to gather it up."

Sunny could not see how his assailant had responded. His forehead was pressed into the dirt. Yet he was fairly certain that the attendant was smiling. He could hear the sound of a smile, which reverberated through that person's speech; accentuating the last syllable of every word, and heightening his pitch each time he launched a sentence:

"Ah! What savage logic! 'From each according to their ability, to each according to their need'. *Hah hah! Hee Hee!*... My cousin: Civilised people don't think in such a way."

"Okay... But if these 'Civilised people' had needed this food, they'd have eaten it already. And yet they haven't. They've left it here to rot... Why shouldn't we eat it? Food is meant to be eaten."

"No, no. Starving people can't just take unwanted food. That's *theft*."

"But it's *our* food. It grew on *our* land... We only want to share it."

"My cousin: You can tell that to the judge on the morrow. You can plead your case to him."

# AN OLD FRIEND

"Brother-o: Do you know what I'm holding in my hand?"

Sunny attempted to look. But he was blinded by the light, which was gushing through the door, saturating this jail; a subterranean tunnel, with cells cut out of the rock on either side.

He tried to shake his head and say "No". But he could not be sure of the effect. His head barely moved, and his "No" was little more than a whisper.

"Ah! Brother, it's a fact: This is a 'Key'. The key-o that can conquer this lock."

Sunny's brain did not respond in the normal fashion. It deconstructed his thoughts; detaching the adjectives from their nouns, and preventing the pronouns from agreeing with their verbs:

"Key-o, he bringing, warrior... Strange, he sound, man familiar... Face, he look looking, mine."

He shook his head with nauseous rapidity, in an attempt to unjumble his thoughts.

He recognised the man's accent. It was both strange *and* familiar; as warm as could be expected from a member of the Eagle Clan, with the elongated "O" sound which only they used. Yet his tone was a little too crisp. This man sounded more like Father Ralph than Sunny's kinfolk.

Sunny tilted his head, to see what sort of person could possess such a voice. Was this a friend or a foe? A member of their tribe, or citizen of this town?

The light pierced his eyes. It shone through that man, transforming his body into specks of glitz and dust.

Sunny scrunched his eyes, squinted and blinked. Nothing changed. Then the man's body began to reform, particle by particle; absorbing the sun's rays and beams. First, he was a shuddery outline. Then he was a silhouette. He developed a tone and a third dimension.

This man's facial hair was similar to Sunny's. It stretched down from his sideburns, and reached around his mouth, without filling the spaces between. His shoulders were the same width as Sunny's. They had the same roundness. They connected with his arms at all the same points. His body *was* remarkably familiar. But he wore it in the manner of a Woggy. He stood a little taller, a little brasher; making a concerted effort to lift his shoulders. He wore the same type of cloths that the Wogies always wore.

"Brother-o! Oh brother! So many seasons without the sunshine of your face. And now our stars collide. Old Hunter, with this key. And young Sunny, behind these grisly bars."

It was Hunter! Sunny had been a fool not to realise it before.

Hunter's statement had been true. Sunny *was* behind bars. He had been in this dungeon for what felt like half a day. Although he was unable to say for sure. There were no windows. One could not follow the path of the setting sun or rising moon. The light which entered, when Hunter had opened the door, suggested it was early afternoon. It was probably the first afternoon since Sunny had been arrested. But it could have been the second or third.

Sunny was, he had to admit, a little discombobulated. Hunger was almost certainly a factor. And inexperience was a factor too. He had never been underground. He had never encountered a set of bars.

"Will they murder me?"

"Probably not. Why waste a big wise man like

Sunny?"

"Sorry... 'Waste'?"

"They don't waste resources in the New World. Not without a reason. These are the facts: The Sons of Empire might *execute* a man, to set an example to his clan. They might kill him, if they consider him a threat. But you? Brother: You don't seem like much of a threat."

"Oh."

"No, they wouldn't want to waste a fine resource like Sunny."

"A 'Resource'?"

"A labourer."

"A... You mean... You wish to enslave me?"

"Me? Heavens, no! The *traders* might want to enslave you. There's good money to be made from shipping off a strong lad like Sunny."

"'Shipping'?"

"Putting you inside a giant canoe. Paddling you across the seas. Taking you to a distant plantation."

"Oh... I think I'd rather be... Umm... What did you call it?... 'Executed'?"

"That can be arranged. But I can do better. For my very own little brother? Why, I wouldn't want you to be enslaved *or* killed."

"Oh."

"Oh, Sunny-o, oh! Why do you think I brought this key?"

"To mock me?"

"Brother!"

"To move me?"

"Come! You're breaking my heart."

"I don't know."

"*You don't know*? Sunny! Wow! Haven't you learnt a thing? After everything I've done?

"I warned you. I told you, 'The Sons of Empire are coming. They will see and they will conquer.' I told you to flee, to 'Make a new life for yourselves, in the deepest depths of the bush.' I offered you medicine and blankets. I even gave you a gun; the sort of gift that no other clan has ever been offered before.

"Brother: You're my very own flesh and blood. *Family-o*. And one doesn't kill or enslave one's family. How could you think such a thing? Factually! It pains me inside.

"You might not agree with my lifestyle, or with every little thing I've ever done. But you shouldn't doubt my intentions... Sunny: These matters aren't so wet and dry. I tried to save you before, and I'm here to save you again. These are the bones of the matter."

Sunny repressed a frown. The Hunter he remembered was no saviour. He was an exiled Uncle Crow; someone who had imposed a debt, and then used that debt to blackmail him; threatening to expose Sunny, for sharing a gun, if he did not support his motions.

"You're here to... To 'Save' me?"

"This is an indisputable fact! I came as soon as I heard the news. A young man had stolen enough food to feed an army. Wow! Just wow!... I asked myself: 'Who could that possibly be?' And I could only think of a single person: Brother Sunny. Sunny the impetuous. Sunny-o... Factually: I had to stop what I was doing and come here right away."

"Oh."

"'Oh' indeed! I thought to myself: 'I cannot allow a brother to rot in jail. I cannot stand by whilst he's enslaved. What sort of man would I be?'"

"Oh."

"I thought: 'I must save this big wise man. I must come to his rescue, before it's too late.'"

"Oh."

"And so here I am!"

488 | OTHER WORLDS WERE POSSIBLE

"To save me?"

"To save you-o!"

"Oh."

"Well? Do you wish to be saved?"

"I suppose."

"You *suppose*?"

"I mean, yes. Of course."

"Ah! Of course, brother Sunny, of course. Let's make like lightning and bolt."

Hunter inserted the key, turned it through ninety degrees, allowed the door to swing open, waited for Sunny to emerge, followed him up the steps, and led him into the light.

***

His peers were struggling to believe the news: Sunny had been kidnapped. And then he had been freed. And it was *Hunter* who had freed him.

Hope thought it was a joke:

"You're freezing our piss!... We might've believed you, had you told us you'd escaped. We might've believed you, had you told us you'd evaded capture. But do you really expect us to believe that they seized you, and then they freed you, and they didn't even perform one of their protections... Their *punishments*? Eh? They thought you were Mister Too Ugly To Fuck? Mister Too Worthless To Sell?

"Humph! You're taking us all for goats."

Aura also thought that the story was too good to be true:

"I don't know what they're up to, but I don't like it a bit. They've got something hidden up their loincloths, that's for sure. Something gruesome. No, it all smells rabbity to me. I'd rather trust a horny cuckoo than one of those no-faced ghouls."

Serenity, however, was prepared to give Hunter a chance:

"Sistren: What more could you possibly want? This brother warned us. He gave us guns. He offered us blankets. And now he's rescued Sunny from the bowels of the earth.

"In the name of our sweet ancestral mothers: He was a friend and an ally all along. Are we really so blind, that we refuse to see? Or so stubborn, that we refuse to acknowledge the error of our ways?"

Serenity's remarks were well received. Serenity's remarks were *always* well received. And he had only stated the facts.

His speech appeared to sway the group;

inspiring a murmur of consent and a rumbling of nods.

But Harmony was unconvinced:

"He offered us blankets? *Blankets*?... Aunties and uncles, sisters and brothers: Don't you remember what Sunny told us?... No?... Come on, think a while... Yes? You remember it now? Those blankets were riddled with plague. *Plague*! The clans who took them, no longer exist in the mortal realm. The clans-folk who survived, had to approach the Wogies and beg them for the cure. They've been slaves in that frown, that clown, that *town* ever since."

Almost everyone reacted in the same manner: They shuffled backwards, away from Sunny.

Sunny had never felt so shunned in his life.

"Err..." he replied. He felt compelled to supply an answer, even though no question had been asked. "Yes, I suppose our sister has a point."

But if he had thought his modesty would endear him to the group, he was about to be disappointed.

"They gave Sunny Bon Bango a disease!" Harmony continued, whilst bulging her eyes and chomping her teeth. "They gave him the lurgy. Then they sent him here to infect us."

Everyone turned to face Sunny, who lifted his shoulders and replied in a tepid tone:

"I don't feel ill... They didn't touch me, once they'd put me in that hell... That cell... They didn't give me any of our food or water."

"It's the blankets, Sunny Bon Bango! The blankets in the... In the whatever you called that place."

"I'm telling you, sister: There weren't any blankets."

"Then whatever. I don't know. You do look rather ugly."

"You think I always look ugly."

"As ugly as a warthog's scrotum. But still, your nose is covering half your face. And it normally only takes up a quarter."

Sunny grabbed his nose; attempting to squeeze it back into position, even though it felt the same as normal.

Serenity cleared his throat:

"Ahum."

He rose to his feet, waited to see if Harmony had anything to add, and then turned to address the group:

"I understand your fears, about Hunter *and* Sunny. These are emotional times... If you're worried, we can always ask Sunny to quarantine himself on the fringes of our camp. Although he's already shared a meal, and nuzzled our cheeks..."

Serenity was about to propose a vote.

But Sunny had already begun to speak:

"I'll quarantine myself! If it'll set your minds at ease, then I'd be happy to oblige... At the end of the sunset, when all is hunted and gathered, I think we could do with a sentry. Yes, that's it: I'll take a spear and magic spear, and I'll go be a meerkat over there."

***

His peers had been awaiting Sunny's arrival...

When Buffalo and Butterfly returned, their clans-folk had run to greet them. Seeing their friends, and seeing their haul, they did not suppose that anything was amiss.

But by the time the sun had reached its zenith, they were hit by a sense of discomfort, which became more bilious, and tasted more of grapefruit, the longer Sunny was away.

They performed ghost dances, imploring the ancestors to deliver him to safety.

Sunny's mother chewed her nails, which was unusual, since she *never* chewed her nails. But, then again, her son had never gone missing, amongst a strange and frightful people. Desperate times, inspired desperate reactions.

She was not alone. A few of the youngsters followed her lead; attempting to chew their toenails, once they had finished with their fingers and thumbs. Serenity paced around in circles and squares. Hope twirled her hair; braiding it, un-braiding it, twisting it one way, and then twisting it back the other.

When Sunny did finally appear, his peers' relief was so evident, it manifested itself in physical form. They exhaled as one; producing a breathy cloud, which lingered, solid and white; scrambling their vision, before dissipating into translucence.

The clans-folk froze, unfroze, bolted, and squeezed their brother tight. They sat him down, fed him, encouraged him to speak, bombarded him with questions, spoke of their worries, and aired their doubts.

It was the briefest of interludes. He had arrived, Harmony had suggested that he might be carrying a disease, and then he had departed; subjecting himself to a quarantine, in what felt like a blink of an eye. His mind was giddy. But he was safe. The clan had food. And that was what mattered.

***

Bang!

Sunny had not fired a gun for the better part of ten lunar-cycles. He had not heard a gunshot since Serenity had shot a goat, back at the tribal camp. The sheer noise of that thing was enough to make him jump.

Sunny landed with a thud. His head stopped shaking, and his vision stopped spinning.

He could not help feeling that the gunshot had not been particularly loud. Yet it had *felt* far noisier than it sounded. It was a bizarre sensation. His ears had betrayed his emotions.

Then again, he was not really responding to the shot itself. He was responding to the ghastliness of his action. He had fired a shot, intending to kill another person; someone who might have had feelings; someone who probably had a mother.

How could he do such a thing?

To protect his people! That was how.

Yet despite such logic, his behaviour still evaded his comprehension. The first time Sunny had killed an animal, a rabbit he had caught in a trap, he had cried and cried and cried. He had hesitated before wringing its neck, closing his eyes so hard they began to blister. He had been so devastated by the mortality of that act, he had refused to eat meat for twenty-seven days.

The residue of that sensation had drained away. He had not experienced anything like it, until now...

His ribs felt like they were being crushed. His lungs felt like they were being squeezed. He might have frozen, had duty not been calling his name.

His shot had missed his target; whistling past that man's shoulder, and disappearing into the unseeable beyond. But that Woggy, who Sunny thought he recognised, remained a threat. That man had been spying on the clan from behind a pile of boulders. Sunny did not know what he intended to do; why he was neither advancing nor retreating. But he was clearly a menace. Why else would he be holding a gun?

Sunny selected another shot, wrapped it in cloth, added powder, rammed it down the barrel, and cocked the hammer. He had only brought three shots in total. If he missed a second time, the pressure would be immense.

There was no way he would be able to return to his peers. The intruder would shoot him down.

Whoosh!

A metallic ball thwacked the branch above Sunny's head, embedding itself in the bark. Splinters fell like weightless rain; glistening in the sepia light, sparkling, meandering left, floating right, not really falling at all.

If Sunny had any doubts, they vanished with that shot. This was war. One of them was going to die.

Sunny was hiding inside a small cluster of trees. But this place was far from a fortress. The mature trees had been felled, and only the smaller trees remained. Their leaves were large, but their branches were sparse.

Sunny had been squatting. Now he was on the ground; floored by the asphyxiation he felt when he pulled the trigger, and flattened by the fear which had overcome him when his adversary fired back.

He was better off down here, he supposed; belly to the earth, camouflaged by pebbles and sand.

He steadied his arm, and gazed down the length of the barrel. He looked left and right, up and down, but he could not locate his target.

Whoosh!

Sunny could not see where that shot had landed, but he presumed it was nowhere near. This settled his nerves. Yes, it implied that the man had plenty of shots. Why else would he waste them so freely? But he was a terrible marksman. Or he was unaware of Sunny's position.

Whoosh! Whoosh! Whoosh!

The first two shots missed by a distance. But the third hit the earth, a few body lengths in front of the trees; puffing up dust, and skimming a pebble towards Sunny's head.

He batted that projectile away, exhaled with relief, and then panicked. What if the man had seen him? What if he adjusted his aim?

There was no time to waste. The intruder had also given himself away, whilst standing to shoot. He had ducked back down. But Sunny could still see some wisps of his hair, which were billowing in the breeze, and his shoulder, which was plugging the V-shaped gap between two boulders.

Sunny fired.

Ouch!

The man's cry muted the sound of the shot. It was a piercing yowl, which silenced the wind. And it was a crestfallen cry, which spoke more of disappointment, than any actual pain.

His body slunk to the side.

Sunny almost rose. He almost bounded forwards; compelled by an urge to stand above that man, lift their clan's spear, and strike a fatal blow. If he had shot an animal, he would not have shown such restraint. He would be looming above it already. The spear would be crashing down.

But this man was not an animal. He had a gun. Who knew what other weapons he might be hiding behind those rocks?

Sunny reloaded the rifle, took aim, steadied his hand, shuddered, and placed the gun back down on the ground. He allowed his face to caress the earth, took the smallest of breaths, composed himself, took aim again, and squeezed the trigger.

The Woggy rolled onto his side.

***

"CHICK-I-LICK! SUNNY, CHICK-I-LICK!"

His mother's screams came as quite a surprise.

Sunny's kinfolk had been known to argue for days. They mocked their peers on a regular basis. But they did this in the calmest of fashions; controlling their breathing, and speaking at a steady rate. They almost never screamed. And this was no ordinary scream. It was piercing enough to set fire to Sunny's blood.

"Oh, I am sorry, chick-i-lick... We thought you'd been shot. We thought a Woggy had... Oh ancestral spirits! I can't even bring myself to say it."

Sunny did not respond with words.

He walked, then skipped, then bounded towards his mother; jumping into her arms, hugging her, and accepting the barrage of nose-rubs which came his way.

He checked his nose. Then he explained the situation, concluding:

"That man must've followed me here. But as for why he loitered behind those boulders? Well, I'm as lost as a fish in a jungle."

Serenity scrunched his lips.

"This intruder is over there?"

Sunny nodded.

"Dead?"

Sunny shrugged.

"Let's investigate."

***

Serenity led by example; distributing the spears, before walking ahead of the group. Not everyone followed. Some were too young, old or weak. Others were paralysed by fear. But eight people did heed Serenity's call, of their own volition, and nobody attempted to stop them.

They leaned over the stranger, forming a pyramid which muffled the light.

One shot had struck the man's shoulder, and the other had hit the top of his opposite bicep, all but paralysing his arms. But Sunny had missed the vital organs. The man was a shivering mess; unmistakably conscious, and unavoidably subdued. His crotch was moist. His eyes were perturbingly hard.

Judging it safe, they beckoned towards their peers.

Health came running. She removed her loincloth, strapped it around the man's shoulder, and pulled it tight.

The response was mixed. Some people smiled or nodded. Others began to tut. A couple of people did not react at all.

Butterfly spoke as modestly as she could,

doing her best to disguise her shock:

"Dear Auntie: What... What are you doing?"

"I'm stemming the bleeding."

"But if he recovers, he'll devour us all. Why do you wish to save him?"

Aura and Health replied together:

"So we can kill him again as a clan."

"So we can hurt him when he can feel it."

Individually, these comments made sense. But Aura's words piled upon Health's, jumbling them up, and rendering them incoherent.

The clans-folk had to scratch the insides of their ears, to make sense of what they had heard. And even then, they struggled to decipher these remarks.

Sunny had no idea what either Aura or Health had said. But he was almost certain that Butterfly was correct. No good would come of this act.

"Dearest Aunties, I don't think you understand. I'm telling you: If we heal this man, he'll commit a 'Punishment'."

Neither Health nor Aura replied. And yet they demanded an explanation; with their brows, which furrowed beyond recognition; and with their eyes, which vibrated with curiosity.

"I recognise him... I didn't wish to say

anything before, until I was certain... But there can be no mistaking the truth: This one... He's one of the men who did the punishment on Songbird's daughter. He did unspeakable things. He... Do you want him to do that to us?"

Serenity closed his eyes.

"Sunshine: This is the reason we must save him. We must bring him back to life, so that we can kill him again together. Then we must revive him a second time, so we can kill him a third time, and then a fourth."

Serenity's words soothed a few of the people who had been astonished by Health's behaviour.

But it did little to placate Dusk.

"I'd rather eat the thing! I'd rather drink down all its fat."

Everyone turned to face that elder, supposing he might recount a story, from a time of war and famine, when his peers had been forced to perform such a gruesome act.

But Dusk just shrugged; raising his shoulders, and parking them aside his head.

"It wouldn't be like eating a human. These people aren't human. I'm not even sure they're real. And its meat would last us a day."

The group turned to face Dawn, expecting

him to argue. Compelled by the force of habit, Dawn did open his mouth. He was about to say "No". He almost launched a verbal tirade; claiming this was a trap, that this man had been poisoned, and that eating him would kill them all.

He restrained himself, allowed his face to soften, and suggested a compromise:

"Why not raise him to life, to please Aura? And *then* eat him to death?"

"You mean... Eat him whilst he's still alive?"

"One part at a time."

"That's macabre."

"It is."

They lifted the spy and carried him towards the fire.

\*\*\*

It did not take long to finish the job...

Aura used a spare loincloth to bind the second wound, before using a third one to dress herself. It was still not enough. Her patient, who had lost a copious amount of blood, was flitting between consciousness and the abyss.

The group had left their sniffing salts with the Dog Clan. So they were forced to improvise; lifting their victim above the fire, holding him in place, and waiting for him to inhale the smoke.

He coughed himself awake, producing a greenish kind of snot, which had the consistency of mashed bananas.

His eyes flickered with the advent of recognition; able to understand that he had been saved, but unable to figure out *why*. When he looked left, he did so with curiosity; keen to discover what might be about to happen. But when he looked right, towards Sunny, he was overcome by a colourless shade of fear.

Bluebird, Hope's mother, had already filled their pot with water and placed it above the fire. It had not begun to boil. But Kitten was in no mood to dally. She took the stranger's hand, which was too limp to resist, and plunged it into the pan.

"Aaagh..."

The stranger attempted to stifle his scream. This was not because the water was still cool. He could no longer tell hot from cold. It was because he wished to disguise his pain; to appear defiant in the face of his tormentors.

In this, he failed. He lacked the strength to censor himself; screaming for much longer, and with far more devilment, than he had intended.

Even if he had not made such a racket, he would have been betrayed by his façade. The man had become a mirage; so pale, and so gaunt, that it was easier to look through him, than to distinguish his actual shape.

Kitten donned a twisted smile, puckered her lips, and nodded at a small girl; who took a handful of chillies, and rubbed them across his skin.

"For flavour," she explained.

The man gulped.

Kitten looked him in the eyes, winked, and then smiled with passive violence; fixing her eyes in place, whilst Bluebird added the chillies to the broth.

The children formed a circle around them all, locked arms and performed a dance, singing:

*Five little ducks went out one day,*
*Over the hills and far away.*
*Mother Duck said, "Quack-quack-quack",*
*But only four ducks came back.*

They repeated this song five times, until "No little ducks came back." Then they turned to face the Woggy, in the most haphazard of fashions; giggling and rubbing their bellies.

Kitten also giggled. Only her laughter was not

so childish. It was a mouthy guffaw; one which permeated her gums, and allowed the air to rattle around between her teeth.

"Little ducks are yummy... But not as yummy as Woggy hands!"

By the time she had finished speaking, she had grabbed hold of the man's wrist, and plunged his hand into the water, which had just begun to boil. The man did not notice straight away, and so he offered no response. But this soon changed. His eyes pulsated; more through fear than pain. And he attempted to remove his hand.

His efforts were futile. He lacked the strength to resist. And another two women were holding him in place. Two children were propping them up.

He inhaled the soup, which smelled of himself, and wailed:

"What... want... you? What... you people... want?"

Kitten frowned. She felt she had been asked the most obvious question in the world. Something akin to, "Why do you breathe?" or "Why do you drink?". At first, she did not believe it deserved an answer. Then, supposing that something must have been lost in translation, she had a change of heart. She opened her mouth so wide that her tonsils were visible. And she adopted the voice she used whenever she spoke to an infant:

"Why, we want to eat you, of course. We want to eat the Woggy, so we can absorb the Woggy powers, become Woggy-strong, and repel you nasty invaders."

The man would have turned ghostly white, had he not lost his colour already. As it was, his appearance barely altered. His eyes were still pulsating. His hand was proceeding with its vain attempt to escape.

The meeting place was fragrant now. You could taste the stock, which floated atop ribbons of air; thick, warm, sweet, leathery and human.

Bluebird removed the man's hand, banged it down on a rock, collected a sharpened stone, and used it to slice through the skin. The man did not react at first, refusing to believe what was happening. Then, he fainted. The women had to lift him over the smoke, to revive him, before Bluebird resumed her task.

He whimpered:

"Have... forgotten... you are?"

It was impossible to tell if he was struggling to speak because of the pain, because he had lost so much blood, or because he was not yet fluent in their language.

"We watch... Err... study... *We study you*... You no... spank... own children... *You don't spank your children*... Good God... woman... come senses... come! Behave... act... normal."

Serenity was the first person to unscramble these words, and the first to respond:

"Spank our children? Upon our sacred ancestral mothers! Who would do such a thing? Sweetest cousin: We aren't brutes. We'd never hurt *one of our own*."

"You... no... spank. But... cut... hand! You... eat... *people*?"

"By the good earth! *Ho ho ho.* We don't remove our own hands. We'd never eat ourselves!"

The man did not reply.

"Our welcome guest: Please allow us to explain. Our habits must seem awfully peculiar to you, in much the same way as your habits seem so outlandish to us... Now then, we don't believe the earth is ours to own and exploit. We consider the earth *a treasure*; a gift to be preserved for future generations... Whereas you and your sisters... Sweetest cousin: You threaten everything we hold dear. You're waging a war on all the children who're still waiting to be born; stealing and destroying their birthright... Please try to understand: We aren't *spanking* you. We're only *neutralising* you. We're protecting our unborn descendants."

The man did not reply.

"You should be happy. We're sending you to your 'Heaven'. If it's as good as you say, if it's better than the real world, then you should be eager to get there alive."

"You... me... punish! I... no... do... wrong. I... *obey*... law."

"Sweet stranger: We don't know of this 'Law'. And this is no 'Punishment'. We're not a brutish people, who have to resort to violence to stop our sisters from doing harm. We don't need to be forced to do good. We aren't so wild as that... This is a 'Protection'. We're *protecting* the children of a thousand generations to come; protecting them from this wave of Woggy violence."

"Stop!"

"Why?"

"Why?"

"Sweet stranger: Why should we stop?"

"Information... I... have."

"Go on."

"Not... you... here... safe."

Serenity gestured for the man to continue.

"I... follow... no... alone. Come... me... with... man. Stay... me... to... watch. If... move... *If you move*... then... me... follow. Me... report... new... location."

Serenity nodded.

"Other... man. He... help... go... for. Man... soon... again... come. Come... here... with... horses. Come... here... with... men. Come... here... with... guns."

Serenity raised his eyebrow.

"Stop!... Please!... Stop!"

The group convened a meeting.

***

The votes had been unanimous...

Everyone agreed that they had to move. If the Woggy militia was on its way, it would have been suicidal to remain.

Everyone agreed that the clan should split in two. The first group would head east, leaving a couple of members with each clan they passed.

The second group would travel in the opposite direction.

It had not taken long. Half their peers had already left; a bittersweet moment for Sunny, who had been forced to split from Hope.

"I'm telling you: I promised to mother your baby," he had insisted, sucking back the tears.

But Hope had been firm:

"It doesn't matter. Even if you came with us, you'd end up with a different clan... And anyway, your niece is going to need you."

"Niece? I don't have a niece. I..."

"Just look at Harmony's midriff."

"Oh."

The conversation had passed by in a flash. Hope had already jogged off, baby in arms, to catch up with her mother and siblings. Sunny was standing with the other half of their clan, who were itching to leave themselves. But he felt utterly alone; sucked into a vacuum, from which he was unable to escape.

He could not abandon his mother and sister. But he did not have it in him to abandon Hope's baby. Torn, his body pulled one way, and also the other. An invisible force stretched his skin beyond its limits; squishing his stomach, and squeezing his bowels.

But there was no time for self-pity.

The earth quaked beneath his feet. At first, he thought it must have been a symptom of his own imagination. Surely, it was *his legs* which were moving. The earth did not wobble.

A smattering of leaves fluttered down from their branches, swaying this way and that.

A few pebbles shimmied across the earth.

Sunny's perception warped. He no longer knew what was real, what was imagined, or how he was supposed to tell the difference. Could the ground actually be moving? For real?

The vibrations did not abate. If anything, they became more pronounced; accompanied by a thunderous rumble, which grew louder and louder, to the very point of muteness. Everything turned so dark, Sunny had to look up, to check that the sky was still in position. And the smell! The sweetness was sucked from the air; replaced by the aromas of vinegar, molasses and leather.

Their group had been surrounded.

It seemed so obvious now: It was the Wogies' horses who had made that noise. The ground had vibrated, because it had succumbed to the pounding of their hooves. More than fifty

Wogies were looming high, sitting atop those creatures; polluting the air with their stench, and darkening the light with their shadows. They looked like silhouettes; sitting on silhouetted horses, holding identical guns.

Sunny turned his head, allowed his body to follow, and attempted to decipher each face. Here was a man with manicured whiskers, which grew sideways, before curling upwards at either end. Here was a man with a currant-shaped wart on his nose. Here was the nightwatchman.

Sunny had to scrunch his eyes, before he could process what he was seeing. The nightwatchman... One of his kidnappers... He was! He could not be... But yes, he really was! The truth could not be denied: The nightwatchman was one of the Desert Wogies. His kinfolk had saved his life! And this was how he responded? It defied all explanation.

Sunny continued with numbed disbelief...

He saw a man who had wrapped his face in cloths. He saw a man with an impossibly large forehead. And he saw a man with no hair.

They were all men. But this was hardly surprising. Sunny had never seen a female Woggy. He could not be sure if they existed.

Sunny panned around to a young man with mismatched cheeks. He moved on to an elder with uneven eyes. And then he spotted someone he recognised. Someone with a sparkling tooth. Someone with the same facial hair as his own.

No, it could not be.

Yes, it was!

"Hunter?"

"One and the same, my brother. One and the same."

Sunny lifted his gun.

"Ah, ah, ah... Don't be so hasty. We've come here in peace."

Sunny did not pull the trigger. But neither did he lower the gun.

"How could you?"

"How could I?"

Sunny nodded.

"How could I *what*?"

"How could you betray your own people?"

"My people-o? My people are here, by my side."

Sunny frowned.

Hunter continued:

"*This clan.* You think I've 'Betrayed' *this clan*?... Oh brother! This clan sent me into exile.

Everything I ever did, I did it for them. I brought them so much meat. More than anyone had ever brought them before. And did they say 'Thank-you'? Did they smile? Did they show a little respect?... No, brother, no!... Do you know what they did? They banished me! Wow! And when I returned, laden with gifts, they banished me again!

"Brother-o: These people aren't my clans-folk. It's an undisputed fact! Clan doesn't banish clan.

"Look around. *These men* are my 'Family' now. Fellow citizens. Subjects of the state. The Sons of Empire!

"And look at me! Just look at me, in these marvellous clothes. Here on this horse. Here with this gun... I'm not betraying my people. *These are my people*. And we've come to civilise you savages."

Everything was beginning to make sense: Hunter had only released Sunny so he could follow him, locate the clan, and kidnap them all together.

What had Sunny done? Why had he been so trusting? So naïve? He should have realised Hunter's plan. He should have led his captors astray; sacrificing himself, to save the rest of the

516 | OTHER WORLDS WERE POSSIBLE

group. But no. Half the members of their clan were about to be murdered, and he was to blame.

He wished the earth would swallow him whole.

He touched the trigger, but did not squeeze. His finger reverberated; caressing the trigger, before ricocheting back the other way. He supposed the gun might fire at any moment. But he could decide if this was a good thing or not.

"Brother-o. Oh brother. If you shoot, we'll return fire. We'll shoot every member of your clan. And we'll force you to stand there, watching on, as the blood trickles out of their bodies."

Bang!

Sunny's head turned heavy, and his finger pulled tight.

He could not be sure if he had intended to fire that shot. But he knew *why* he had fired: He was unaccustomed to threats. Hunter may have threatened *his kinfolk*, when he was attempting to impose the Wogies' blankets and guns. And Father Ralph may have threatened their *tribe*, whilst addressing the Tribal Council. But they had done so in an abstract fashion; warning of the terrible things which *might* befall them, *sometime in the future.* No-one had ever singled-out Sunny, looked him in the eye, and said: "If you perform this act, you'll be made to suffer *right now, in this specific way.*" The sheer indecency of it had overwhelmed him. It was not just his finger that had tightened around the trigger. *Everything* had tightened: His muscles and his organs, even his capillaries and veins. His lungs had compressed so much, he had almost forgotten to breathe. His heart had clenched so abruptly, it was a wonder it was able to function.

The trigger released the spring, which jolted the hammer, hit the flint, ignited the gunpowder, and propelled the shot.

Sunny watched that metal ball as it flew through space and time; creating a vortex of air, which rippled with visceral light.

He could see the Wogies' reactions. One man closed his eyes. Another gasped. A third man repressed a smile.

Hunter ducked, and the shot flew over his head.

Perhaps it would have missed, even if had he not reacted. Perhaps it would have hit its target.

No! What was Sunny thinking? A person could not dodge a flying shot. He must have missed. Had he meant to miss? He had not even meant to fire. But he had. And now he would be made to suffer.

Hunter swung a leg over the horse's back, and disembarked in a single fluid motion. He landed with his back to the horse, turned inwards, and sauntered across to Sunny.

A smug, Machiavellian grin was smeared across his cheeks.

"Sunny, oh Sunny. You had one shot and you missed. One shot! You had to make it count. There's no room for error, when one only has a single shot."

Hunter tutted to himself as he progressed; taking languid steps, to prolong his theatrics. Every now and again, he stopped tutting, and shook his head; as though both actions could not be performed together. He paused, looked around, shook his head, took a couple more steps, and then stopped for a second time; tutting, veering off towards their mother, pivoting back, shaking his head, and moseying across to Sunny.

He removed the gun from his brother's grip.

Sunny saw no reason to resist. The Wogies would have shot him dead, had he attempted to reload that weapon.

"Brother-o: Would you care to follow us home? To step into a brilliant new life, in a bold new world?"

It was a rhetorical question. Sunny was not expected to answer. Nor was he given the chance to reply. When Hunter had begun to speak, around half of his comrades had climbed down from their horses. By the time he had finished his question, those men had grabbed hold of Sunny's peers. Now they were attaching leg-cuffs to their ankles, and connecting chains to those cuffs; binding the clans-folk together.

They connected the chains to a couple of horses.

"Giddy up! Tallyho!"

The horses shook their heads, warbled their lips, sprayed saliva to both sides, and trotted back towards the town; leaving their prisoners with little choice but to jog behind, lest they fall and be dragged through the scree.

# THE END OF HISTORY

The dampness hung in mid-air.

It was probably morning, but it could have been the afternoon. They were back in this underground jail, shrouded by darkness, unable to see their hips.

"Hello."

It took a while for Sunny to realise that it was Serenity who had spoken. He had almost forgotten that Serenity had remained with their half of the clan. It must have been the stress. He was struggling to recall who was here, and who had fled with Hope.

"Hello," his mother replied.

"What's the plan?"

"We don't really have any options."

Serenity paused to think, before striking upon an idea:

"How about a story?... Yes... Okay... Once upon a time, a clan of goats decided to climb their favourite cliff. On their way, they were ambushed; surrounded by a pack of buffalo-people. You should've seen those creatures! They stood upright, on legs like yours or mine. But they had torsos like the ones you might find on a buffalo... Now, those buffalo-people hadn't eaten for days. You could hear their bellies rumble. You could smell their thick saliva.

"Upon the good earth, those goats were almost certainly going to die. What could they do? The buffalo-people had powerful arms and crazy teeth. You know the type: Pointy, serrated and sharp. But the goats were weak. Those buffalo-people were compelled by hunger and desperation. The goats were covered in the juiciest meat you've ever tasted."

Serenity stopped. Nobody could tell just *why* he had fallen silent. It was too dark to see what expressions or gestures he might have been making. But it was impossible to ignore the silence, which rattled around the tunnel, rebounding off the walls and bouncing off the ceiling.

An anonymous voice pierced that oppressive silence:

"What happened?"

"I don't know. Sistren: I have to admit that I was inventing the story as I went. I need a few moments, to think up a happy ending."

"I know! I know!" A young child shouted with glee. "I know what happens! The goats get really,

really big. They grow teeth which are more massive-er than a shark's. And they roar so loud, the cliffs all fall to species, come tumbling down, and squash those naughty buffalo-people. Then the goats go and eat some moo grass."

The silence was as brief as it was warm; heated by the onslaught of laughter, which reddened the most solemn of cheeks.

Serenity's words danced atop the fading rhythm of that laughter:

"*Ho ho ho.* Yes. Wouldn't that be lovely? And we should implore the ancestors to make it happen. Come on... Altogether... Yes, that's good... Keep meditating... Channel your collective spirit...

"Sisters: I do think that we also need a backup ending, just in case the ancestors can't help. They'll do their best, but they aren't almighty... How about this? One of the goats surrenders themselves on behalf of their clan. 'Sweet buffalo-people,' they say. 'We can see you're hungry. But a single goat will satisfy you for many days to come. Please just eat one of us, and allow the rest of us to live.'"

Sunny felt the eyes of his peers turn towards him, supposed this was nothing more than paranoia, and opened his mouth to speak.

But his mother was already responding:

"Ancestors, oh ancestors: The buffalo-people would never agree to such a deal! Not in a million seasons... And even if they did, a single goat couldn't possibly satisfy their hunger. Have you even seen a buffalo-person? Have you seen the size of their stomachs? The blood in their eyes?... No way, fountain spray! Once they've started, there'd be no stopping them. They'd come back for another goat, and then another, until all the goats were gone."

Perhaps her peers agreed. Perhaps they did not. Sunny was not concerned with their opinions. He had recovered his ability to speak, and he was determined to be heard.

"It's a flawed plan," he asserted, a tad more bombastically than he had intended. "But if it's the best plan we've got, then it's worth a try. I'll offer myself to the Wogies, just as soon as they return. I'm the reason we're here. I should be the sacrificial goat."

Nobody disagreed.

*** 

The door swung open, and then it closed; admitting a torrent of light, which blinded the clans-folk, before engulfing the jail in darkness.

Silver sparkles flitted across their eyes.

"Family-o! Uncles and aunts: Welcome to your humble abode."

A pitter-patter of footsteps tickled the ground, accompanied by a succession of xylophonic rings; the sound of a finger being flicked along the bars.

"Chick-i-lik?... Is that you?... Hunter?..."

Their mother's voice was a melee of contradictions. She sounded sure and unsure, hopeful and anxious. Her words frothed with love, fear, uncertainty, longing and foreboding:

"We never did get to talk, the first time you returned, and I'm not entirely sure why. I've been biting these teeth ever since, damning the malevolent force that kept us apart."

The bars stopped ringing.

"Ah! Mother-o! So, you've finally found your tongue?"

Hunter tapped his foot:

Tap-tap, tap-tap.

"You didn't speak up, back when I was banished."

"Oh, lovely: We were also invited to experience a period in exile. But we were welcomed back with open shoulders. You'd have been welcomed too, if you'd returned with your eyes bowed, and begged for the clan's forgiveness.

"Do you know why you were banished?... It wasn't one of these Woggy *punishments*, born of maleficence and spite. It was a *protection*; a lesson in humility, which came from a place of love.

"Don't you think I prayed for your return? I beseeched the ancestors with every spirit in every joint. I performed five ghost dances a day, every day, solstice after solstice. I dreamt of the moment when you'd appear, with that soft skin, which I used to tickle, and with those eyes, which followed me around and around.

"A mother's love is eternal. Beat her, insult her, sell her into slavery. It doesn't matter. She'll keep on loving her baby... Chick-i-lick: I never stopped loving you."

The silence which followed was just long enough to be theatrical, and just short enough to reveal Hunter's impatience.

"Love? Soppy, soppy love? Love is a weakling's disease. I don't burden myself with 'Love'. You can save your love for your favourite child: *Sunny dearest.* The son you didn't abandon. I've got clothes, a house and a horse. Why would I need your *love*?"

Their mother's reply was muted. She had already chosen her words, even before Hunter had begun to speak. They seemed superfluous now. But they were emerging from her mouth, uninvited, as though they had taken on a life of their own:

"It's not too late to return to the clan. It's not too late to unburden yourself of your sins; to apologise and show some remorse."

Hunter did not respond to his mother. He projected his words in the *opposite* direction, adopting a grandiloquent voice:

"Now..."

Sunny interjected:

"Hunter!"

He clenched his lips, ingested his volume, and proceeded in a bureaucratic tone:

"You want blood. You want revenge..."

Sunny pinched his throat, to symbolise a desire for vengeance.

"And we don't judge you for these things. The rains will always fall. We only ask that you *take me*. Murder *me*. Do whatever you want with *me*.

But let the others go. Whatever the spectacle you crave, whatever sacrifice you feel compelled to make to Mother Nature... To *Chief God*... You can satisfy it with just a single person. I tell you: There's no need to hurt anyone else."

Sunny could hear the sound of something tapping against bone. Perhaps Hunter was chattering his teeth. Or perhaps he was flicking his forehead.

"Ah! It's very kind of you to offer. Yes, we might kill you after all. Wow! What a splendid idea. Perhaps I'll fire a shot *at you*, and *you* can see how it feels... But I don't think you're in much of a position to bargain. Why, we might kill you all. Factually! We could turn it into a feast day. A celebration of the end of the savage."

That tapping resumed afresh.

"No, I'd like to think I've done my part... What, you didn't think I'd noticed?... Bother-o, oh brother! Come, come. Don't take me for a fool. I saw that your numbers were depleted. Half your members had fled, and I didn't utter a word... Yes, I'm a jolly good chap, all things considered. Just think of the lives I saved!"

There was no tapping this time. Sunny supposed that Hunter was probably nodding.

Perhaps he was thumping the air, or performing some other gesture.

"But you, brother-o. Purloiner of our mother's heart. Usurper of hut and home. You? What have you ever done for us? Have *you* saved half this town? Why, no! You've *stolen* from this town. You've tortured an innocent citizen. You've shot at a brave, heroic soldier... No. We aren't anything alike, you and I. You still live in the darkness. I've walked into the light.

"Now come, Brother Sunny. You have a date with justice."

***

Sunny was standing with his back to his peers, facing a man who was wearing a cloud on his head. No, that was not it. Sunny could not tell what *it* was. It consisted of several rows of curls, which were probably made from an animal's fur. That thing covered his hair, and hung down beside his cheeks. It looked so ridiculous, Sunny had to repress his laughter each time that person spoke. He had such a grave gravelly tone, and such a grey earnest face. This baffling piece of headwear juxtaposed with the rest of his persona.

Perhaps these brief flashes of hilarity served a

greater purpose...

There could be no escaping from the seriousness of Sunny's predicament. It had not sunk in before, when he had spoken of sacrificing his life, as though it were an abstract idea; something that *might* happen to another person, at another time; but not to himself, and not at that very moment. Sunny had been numbed to the reality of their situation. It was a coping mechanism, he supposed. But the anaesthetic had worn off, as they made their way to this courthouse; forming a procession; marching past the gathered townsfolk, those wooden and whitewashed walls, that churned up mud, those stores and those saloons. The fresh air had reinvigorated his senses, freeing his mind for a fraction of an instant, before landing a blow to his bowels. He had seen his mother's eyes, which were bloodshot and teary. And he had realised that *he* was to blame. He had led her into this trap, and he had offered up his life. No mother deserved to witness her child's death. That was torture. *He was torturing his mother.* His shame consumed him; pressing down on his shoulders, with ever-increasing force; making each step a little harder than the one which had come before. He felt that he was shrinking; that the world was impossibly heavy, and his body was hopelessly soft.

But then he saw this serious man, with that silly headdress, and he allowed himself to giggle. It was churlish. It would do him no good. But it was a ray of sunshine on a greyish day. He deserved the light relief.

***

It seemed that Sunny was the only person who would be standing trial. Hunter *had* accepted their request. Sunny might be murdered, but his kinfolk would be spared. Yes, that had to be it. Hunter did have a good side after all. He might cloak it in condescension. He might disguise it with indifference. But he still cared for his kith and kin.

Or maybe Sunny was wrong. Maybe the Wogies *were* going to perform a punishment on them all. He was just the first in line.

They were gathered inside the cross-shaped building, on the pews which had just been installed. Sunny's clans-folk were sitting on the front two rows, bound and chained. Their captors were sitting on the opposite side of a central aisle. Chief Judge was standing on a platform, high above them all. And a few hundred onlookers were crammed in behind; squeezing onto the other benches, sitting atop the unfinished walls, and spilling out into the town square.

The noise was cacophonic. Everyone was speaking at once; in love with the sound of their voices, and determined to make them heard.

The smell was spicy and rank.

Here was a "Family" unit; a mother, "Father", daughter and son. They looked like natives. But the women were wearing pink body-cloths, and frilly head-cloths with giant rims. The men were wearing a mashup of black and white.

Here was another "Father", with two of his sons. They looked like Wogies. But they were dressed in an almost identical fashion. Only their cloths were a much better fit, as though they had been made to measure.

Most of the natives were positioned behind the members of the Eagle Clan, whilst most of the Wogies were behind the captors. Sunny could not tell if this segregation had been enforced. But it did not seem to affect the way those spectators were behaving. Sunny was shocked to note that the natives were even *more* vicious than the Wogies. Their stares were more piercing. Their tuts were more pronounced.

These people belonged to this land! They were just like them! They should have been on *their* side!

Perhaps it was a figment of Sunny's imagination. Perhaps they *had to* act like that, to avoid a punishment. Songbird was also tutting in an aggressive fashion. But at least she gave him a wink, once she had checked that no-one was watching.

"Do you consider this a laughing matter?"

Sunny must have failed to suppress a giggle. For Chief Judge's reaction had been instantaneous. He had straightened his back, turned a dark shade of crimson, and blurted out this question; which Father Ralph had translated.

Sunny refused to answer. He *did* think the judge's headpiece was a laughing matter. But he supposed it would rile that dangerous man, if he were to say such a thing out loud.

"How do you plead?"

"'Plead'?"

"Guilty or not guilty?"

"What are these things?"

"Do you admit that a wrong has been done?"

"Oh yes. Many wrongs."

"So, you plead *guilty*?"

"If you say so."

"You admit to theft, jailbreak, two counts of attempted murder, and one count of gross bodily harm?"

"Absolutely not!... I believe... I believe you're utterly confused. You must be talking about the times I *shared* our food, *escaped* to freedom, committed two acts of *self-defence*, and participated in a *protection*... These weren't 'Wrongs'. Mother Nature, no! These were duties... I tell you this: The *wrongs* were performed by the brothers to the left. These heartless goons, who ambushed us, kidnapped us, and buried us beneath the ground. They were done by the brothers who took our land and food; who refused to share the things they'd borrowed... Murdering our ancestral forest was a *wrong*. Depleting our watering hole was a *wrong*. Your greed, hoarding and violence are all *wrongs*. Your punishments are vile and wrong. Your enslaving of innocents is wrong. Your disease-laden blankets are wrong. Your imposition of money, work, schools, time, tax, ownership, monogamy, patriarchy, jails, Chief

King and Chief God is the greatest of all possible 'Wrongs'. Indubitably! *This* is what I 'Plead' and what I 'Guilty'."

Father Ralph glanced at Chief Judge. He shrugged. But he refused to translate this tirade.

"It's for your own good," he reasoned. "His honour would react badly, if he knew you were speaking ill of *his people*."

Sunny could not tell what "Good" this might achieve. If Chief Judge could not understand how their clan had been wronged, he would struggle to empathise with their plight.

"So, you're pleading guilty?"

"If you say so. I'm unfamiliar with this word."

"Guilty?"

"These men have done wrong. You Wogies have done many wrongs. You've done more evil than anyone we've ever encountered... We just want to live the lives we've always lived."

"Guilty?"

"I'm telling you this: If you must, then take me. Do whatever you want with my body. But let the others go."

Sunny silenced himself a little too abruptly, such that a hum continued to buzz atop his lips, even though he was clenching them together.

It was not the first time he had made such a remark. But his words felt different now. They were lumpier. They tasted of uncooked fat and charcoal. This time, *his words felt real*. He was telling another person to make him suffer; to end his life, when he had so much living to do.

He succumbed to a dizzy kind of ambiguity. He was pulled one way by his duty to his kinfolk; by the knowledge that he was doing the noble thing, attempting to save their lives. And he was pulled the other way by his duty to life; knowing that he could make the ultimate sacrifice, and it might not make a difference. The dizziness washed through him. His feet became rickety, his legs wobbled, and his vision became a blur.

"Take me," he repeated. "Sacrifice me. In the name of all that is natural and pure: Let the others go!"

"Let them go? They cooked a man's hand! One doesn't simply cook another person's hand, and then just 'Go'."

Chief Judge looked to Sunny, his kinfolk, the kidnappers, and Father Ralph.

"Any further comments? Any other wild requests?"

There were no further comments.

"Jolly good."

Chief Judge cleared his throat and launched his closing remarks.

Father Ralph translated:

"In the case of Sunny Eagle versus the State: The facts of this case, in all their painful details, are essentially undisputed. They've been rehashed most carefully by Mister Jones Q.C., leading counsel for the Crown."

Chief Judge tipped his forehead towards one of the kidnappers.

Sunny had not noticed that man before. He was rather nondescript; with a greyish face, which muted his features, and a shrunken manner, which blended him into the background. Perhaps this man had "Rehashed" the "Painful details" of the case. But he had not done so in Sunny's presence. He might have addressed the court before Sunny arrived. Or he might have spoken to Chief Judge in private. It seemed unlikely that Sunny would ever know.

"Will the defendant please stand?"

Sunny was already standing.

"Sunny Eagle: You wilfully damaged private property, showing no concern for its owners. You stole food which didn't belong to you. You hoodwinked yourself away, whilst under the state's protection. You shot at not one, but *two* members of His Majesty's Royal Guards. You were party to the torture of one of these guards... You don't deny your crimes. Credit should be given for your plea... But you've shown no sympathy towards the people you've hurt, no remorse for your indiscretions, and no understanding of their wider consequences. It's not only a matter of the suffering you've caused to your victims. It's the terror you've sown in your wake. It's the average man on the street; unsure where to look, or where to turn; who must live in constant terror, fearful of other extremist groups, and other terrorist attacks."

Father Ralph gave Sunny the sternest look he could muster, clenching his brows and puckering his lips:

"The consequences are stark...

"On the count of attempted murder: You've been found guilty, and shall be put to death. On the count of terrorism: You've been found guilty, and shall be put to death. On the count of treason: You've been found guilty, and shall be put to death. And on the charge of torture: You've been found guilty. You shall be made to endure the same ordeal that you inflicted on the plaintiff.

"I've taken into account your other offences: Theft, vandalism and jailbreak. And I've reached a decision *not* to impose an additional penalty. Let this be a lesson to you and your people: We're unflinching in the pursuit of justice. But we're fair, and we're forgiving. We have a compassionate side, which you'd do well to emulate.

"You have no right to appeal."

Chief Judge attempted to bang the device he had been waving as he spoke; a wooden contraption, with a lithe handle and tubular head. But he only managed to swing it through the air. He turned, somewhat ruffled, and stepped on his long black cloth; almost tripping, and almost coming undressed. He grabbed hold of a pillar, to regain his balance, before banging the device on that pole; producing a vulgar clang.

"Take the defendant down!"

***

Sunny had been marched to a platform in the town square.

Almost everyone had followed, filling the

space in front of that stage. A gaggle of chiefs were standing on either side of the platform. Hunter was positioned behind Sunny's back. And the spy was sitting on a chair.

Sunny felt a twang of sympathy for that man. The bandages around his shoulders were bound so tight, they had squeezed him out of shape. His hand was also bandaged. And his eyes were a confusion; sharpened by disdain, sparkling with bloodlust, but dulled by the darkness of depression.

Sunny felt a twang of sympathy, but he did not feel any *remorse*. That man had also shot at him. He was the enemy; a marauding, pillaging, ransacking fiend; someone with no respect for nature or tradition. If anyone deserved to die, it was the spy, and not Sunny.

Sunny panned across the audience; gazing down upon the Wogies who were jostling for position at the front, and the natives who were crammed into a pen on one side. Behind them, the mob was moseying about; chewing luminous cobs, picking their teeth, spitting out the chaff, and throwing the remains asunder. Beer Men were running between the crowd and their premises, taking orders and delivering drinks;

turning a tidy profit. Children were polishing shoes, hawking nuts, and picking pockets. One man was selling rattles. Another was selling horns. God Men were selling benedictions. Beggars were pleading with blackened palms.

Sunny paused to stare at a *female* Woggy. Such creatures did exist! Although that woman did look a tad peculiar; like most of the male Wogies, only with a little less facial hair. She was also *doing* something peculiar; planting her lips upon a man's face, and inserting her tongue into his mouth. The horror! Sunny supposed she must have been eating that man's insides.

It was little wonder that the Wogies had fled their homeland. They were trying to escape from their women! Sunny could not help but feel grateful to the likes of Hope, who had never tried to eat him.

Behind that woman and her victim, Sunny could just about see his kinfolk, who were being forced to watch; separated from the rest of the throng, surrounded by an armed gang. They had not been tried, which was a relief. But they were still in shackles and chains.

Sunny could not locate the youngsters. Perhaps they were too short to be seen. But he had a niggling suspicion that they had been carted away to one of the Wogies' "Boarding schools"; those child colonies, where they would be groomed to think like Wogies, do Woggy-style work, and worship the Woggy's God.

A single tree still remained in this square; an evergreen with a bulbous crown. Its very existence was strangely reassuring; a reminder of Mother Nature's presence, and a not-too-distant past, when they lived on this land alone.

Sunny felt its cool embrace. He inhaled its scent; honey-laced and moreish.

Sunny assumed that the Wogies could not smell that aroma. For if they had experienced its sentimental tang, their spirits would have softened, their eyes would have watered, and they would have been rendered incapable of violence. But it was such a subtle aroma, thinner than the air. It was all too easy to miss.

How had it come to this?

Surely this was not the end. Surely the tribe would unite, form an army, stage an invasion, overpower the Wogies, and set their people free.

Yippee! Here we go!

For the sweetest of moments, Sunny supposed those cheers were for him. Yes, that had to be it! A tribal army had come to liberate their clan.

What a fool he had been. The natives and Wogies were cheering *together*. But they were not cheering Sunny. They were cheering the hangman, who had performed a theatrical bow.

That person did not appear altogether human. For sure, he had a face, with a nose and a mouth, as you might expect to find on a regular person. And yes, he had arms, shoulders, a torso, and a pair of matching legs. These body parts were all put together in the normal fashion, although his limbs did bulge at their sockets, as though they had been shunted into position with far more force than was required. And yet something was amiss. His eyes were not quite alive. They were too sunken, too dark; a little too small or large. His face was too gaunt. There was a mound of skin, on either side of his mouth, but it would have been a stretch to call them "Cheeks". There was no depth, no softness. It was impossible to imagine a smile on his face. It was impossible to suppose that this man had lungs, which enabled him to breathe, or a heart, which pumped blood around his body.

But he did have the crowd's approval:

Yippee! Here we go!

The human-esque creature made another theatrical swoop, swooshing his arm out to the side. He held it at a right angle to his chest; allowing a black cloth to hang down, wing-like and square.

He opened his palm, to present Sunny to the crowd.

Boo! Terrorist! Off with his head!

Sunny spotted Songbird.

He mouthed a question:

"The children?"

"School."

"The adults?"

"Slavery."

"On a... Err... *Plantation*?"

"Here. Removing ancestral forests."

A steaming pot of water was placed by Sunny's feet. He recognised that vessel, glanced at Songbird, and saw her tense a cheek.

Sunny was not offended. It was strangely reassuring to know that his hand would be boiled in a pot which had been made by someone he loved. He understood that the experience would be just as painful. But he felt comforted by the idea that he was being assaulted for honouring their tribe's traditions, in a place which had always been their home, beneath this native tree, using a pot which his friend had made. The Wogies could squat upon this land. They could exploit it, ravage it, and turn it into a wasteland. But they would always be surrounded by things which were not theirs, which would never be theirs, which they would never understand, and which would never love them back.

Fingernails pinched the skin beneath his shoulders; digging in beneath the bone, and shunting him onto his knees.

The hangman, now just a blackish blur, gripped hold of Sunny's arm.

Sunny did not resist. He allowed his hand to be plunged into the scalding water, as the crowd hollered, and as the air turned sticky with noise. He was determined to act with grace; without a simper or scream. And in this, he was partially successful.

Then he spotted Chief Judge, and that cloud-like monstrosity on his head. Sunny could not help but giggle, then chortle, then guffaw.

His laughter and screams merged into a single, diabolical noise. Sunny looked possessed;

as though he was enjoying his pain, and was pained by his joy. He was both agonized *and* numb, ecstatic *and* detached; an impossible combination of things, which had no real right to exist.

Blood vessels appeared in his eyes, accelerating outwards in zags and bolts. His hair frizzed with static. His cheeks spasmed with ecstasy and pain.

His hand was removed from the water, and Sunny exhaled. The worst of it was over. His ordeal was nearly done.

But the hangman did not appear ready to move on.

A second pot was carried onto the stage, fresh from the fire. It looked much the same as the first pot. Only this one was slightly bigger.

The water was thick with steam.

Sunny was unsure what was about to happen. Chief Judge had said he would be treated the same way that his kinfolk had treated the spy. His hand had already been boiled, and now it had to be cut. There was no need for a second pot.

He felt a force press down upon his shoulders, driving him forwards and downwards;

dunking his head into the pot. Perhaps Sunny screamed. He could not be sure. The water had rendered him mute; forming a wall through which no sound could possibly pass.

The pain was real. Or then again, perhaps it was not. It hurt so much, it did not really hurt at all. His skin was on fire. His fat was melting. His face was sliding from his skull. But his nerve endings had burnt on impact, and he had lost the ability to feel pain.

His vision blurred into tufts of white upon silver.

He retained the ability to smell, although it took him a while to identify what he was smelling. It was not that the scent confused him. He recognised the tang of boiled meat and burnt blood. It was more *the way* those aromas hit him. They did not waft up his nostrils, in the manner to which he was accustomed. His nostrils and lips had melted, gluing themselves together. Rather, those odours seemed to be emanating from *within* his nose. He was smelling *his own* insides, his own decomposing body, his own molten flesh.

It smelled delicious.

Was that wrong? Was it wrong to enjoy one's

death? Surely, a person could allow themselves a little pleasure, once their end was all but assured.

His head was yanked from the water.

He tried to breathe; pulling his lips apart, leaving shreds of skin in all the wrong places; jagged, bloodless and raw.

He bit off a chunk of air, which caused him to endure the most outlandish sensation; a perfect blend of agony and endorphins.

All was so white, it was black.

He saw something now. Someone he recognised was riding towards him, standing atop the largest buffalo he had ever seen. It was Hope! Of that, there could be no doubt. Her arms were thumping the sky. The buffalo's hooves were pounding the earth, throwing up puffs of ash and smoke. And now that smoke was fading. And now his vision was clear. Hope was not alone. She was accompanied by a thousand other natives. No, there were *two thousand*. No, there were *ten thousand* natives, riding atop ten-thousand buffaloes. Here was the other half of their clan. Here were Beetle, Protectress and Bear. Here were the Dog Clan, and every other clan in their tribe. Here were the neighbouring tribes. They had united, for the first time in history. They were riding together; waging war on the Woggy hoards.

All was so white, it was black.

Sunny could see that army approach. He could hear the ground vibrate. He could feel the buildings tremble.

This would soon be over. The Wogies would be vanquished. His people would be free.

"For the crimes of attempted murder, terrorism and treason: You, Sunny Eagle, shall be hung until you're dead."

He was being lifted; supported under his armpits, and dragged up onto a step.

"Hung until you're dead."

The tribal army must have been close. Sunny could not see them. But he was certain they would arrive at any moment.

"May the Lord, in his love and mercy, help you with the grace of the Holy Spirit."

All was so white, it was black.

"May the Lord, who frees you from sin, save you and raise you up."

Something was placed around Sunny's neck.

"Praise be unto the Lord!"

The tribal army appeared. They were in this

very square.

But wait...

It was not an army at all. It was a single person: Hope's baby girl. She had transformed into a giant; taller than a mountain, and wider than a cloud. She was holding a bow, loaded with ten-thousand arrows. She was lofting it above her head. She was taking aim.

"God is love!"

The world was removed from beneath Sunny's feet.

He could feel himself fall, in the slowest and quickest of motions.

And he could hear a familiar voice:

"Brother-o. Oh brother! What fun we could've had. We could've worn silk and pearls; eaten pastries, muffins and crumpets. We could've travelled the world by train. Yes, brother. Our masters are bringing us *trains*! I've seen them myself, in the Faraway Lands, where people never die. And now we'll have them here. Trains! Wow! Trains!

"If only you'd stayed alive. There'll be trains on this colonial land. Wow! What a wonderful, wondrous gift!"

# FREEDOM!
## THE CASE FOR OPEN BORDERS

"A manifesto of hope" – **New Edge Times**

" A worldwide journey" – **Midwest Book Review**

"Logical... Well-researched" - **Readers' Favourite**

Once upon a time, we were free to go wherever we chose. It wasn't so long ago. The history of humanity, is a tale of constant motion.

People are supposed to move about. We have imaginations which encourage us to dream about life in other places, bodies which are built to roam, and hands which can make an array of vehicles. A few of us even possess the "Wanderlust Gene", which encourages us to take risks – to sail across unchartered oceans, and launch ourselves towards faraway planets.

Some of us are forced to relocate. Lots of us choose to migrate. A few of us belong to nomadic communities.

But if one thing is clear, it's that mobility improves our societies. Emigrants send back billions in remittances – helping to reduce poverty, and inspiring their peers to upskill. Immigrants do the work that their hosts are unwilling or unable to perform. They sustain economies which have ageing populations. They establish industries, invent products, create jobs, increase wages, fuel growth, pay taxes, and enrich our cultures – enhancing our music, arts, sports, languages and cuisine.

It's time to celebrate movement! It's time to demand our freedom! It's time for open borders!

This book explains why – making the historical, scientific, economic, cultural, political and philosophical cases for free movement.

# DEMOCRACY
## A USER'S GUIDE

**THEY SAY WE LIVE IN A DEMOCRACY. WE ARE FREE AND WE SHOULD BE GRATEFUL.**

But just how "Free" are we? How democratic are our so-called "Democracies"?

Is it enough to simply elect our leaders and sit back, helpless, as they rule over us like dictators? What good is selecting our politicians, if we cannot control our media, police or soldiers? If we must blindly follow our teachers' and bosses' commands, whilst at school and in the workplace, is it not a little naïve to believe that we are the masters of our own destinies? And if our resources are controlled by a tiny cabal of plutocrats, bankers and corporations; can we honestly say that our economies are being run for us?

Could things not be a little bit more, well, democratic?

Indeed they can! "Democracy: A User's Guide" shows us how...

Within the pages of this story-filled book, we shall visit Summerhill, a democratic school in the east of England, before stopping off in Brazil to check out Semco, where workplace democracy is the name of the game. We will travel to Rojava, to explore life in a democratic army, and head to Spain, to see why Podemos is giving liquid democracy a go. We shall travel back in time, to see democracy at work in hunter-gatherer societies, tribal confederacies, the guilds and on the commons. We will consider the case for participatory budgeting, deliberative democracy, collaborative hiring, community currencies, peer-to-peer lending, and much much more.

The message is clear and concise: Democracy does not have to be a pipe dream. We have all the tools we need to rule ourselves.

# INDIVIDUTOPIA

"Gloriously colourful" – **The Canary**
"An exciting tale" – **The Dallas Sun**
"A must read" – **The Bay Net**

**Beloved friend,**

The year is 2084, and that famous Margaret Thatcher quote has become a reality: There really is no such thing as society. No one speaks to anyone else. No one looks at anyone else. People don't collaborate, they only compete.

I hate to admit it, but this has had tragic consequences. Unable to satisfy their social urges, the population has fallen into a pit of depression and anxiety. Suicide has become the norm.

It all sounds rather morbid, does it not? But please don't despair, there is hope, and it comes in the form of our hero: Renee Ann Blanca. Wishing to fill the society-shaped hole in her life, our Renee does the unthinkable: She goes in search of human company! It's a radical act and an enormous challenge. But that, I suppose, is why her tale's worth recounting. It's as gripping as it is touching, and I think you're going to love it...

**Your trusty narrator,**

**PP**

# MONEY POWER LOVE

"Breathtaking" – **The Huffington Post**
"Picaresque" – **Scottish Left Review**
"Unputdownable" – **The Avenger**
"Strangely kind" – **The Tribune**

Born on three adjacent beds, a mere three seconds apart, our three heroes are united by nature but divided by nurture. As a result of their different upbringings, they spend their lives chasing three very different things: Money, power and love.

This is a human story: A tale about people like ourselves, cajoled by the whimsy of circumstance, who find themselves performing the most beautiful acts as well as the most vulgar.

This is a historical story: A tale set in the early 1800s, which shines a light on how bankers, with the power to create money out of nothing, were able to shape the world we live in today.

And this is a love story: A tale about three men, who fall in love with the same woman, at the very same time...

# THE LITTLE VOICE

"The most thought-provoking novel of 2016"
**The Huffington Post**
"Radical... A masterclass... Top notch..."
**The Canary**
"A pretty remarkable feat"
**BuzzFeed**

**Dear reader,**

My character has been shaped by two opposing forces; the pressure to conform to social norms, and the pressure to be true to myself. To be honest with you, these forces have really torn me apart. They've pulled me one way and then the other. At times, they've left me questioning my whole entire existence.

But please don't think that I'm angry or morose. I'm not. Because through adversity comes knowledge. I've suffered, it's true. But I've learnt from my pain. I've become a better person.

Now, for the first time, I'm ready to tell my story. Perhaps it will inspire you. Perhaps it will encourage you to think in a whole new way. Perhaps it won't. There's only one way to find out...

**Enjoy the book,**
**Yew Shodkin**

# OCCUPIED

"A unique piece of literary fiction" - **The Examiner**
"Darker than George Orwell's 1984" - **AXS**
"Candid and disquieting" - **Free Tibet**
"Genre-busting" - **Pak Asia Times**
"A must read" - **Buzzfeed**

**SOME PEOPLE LIVE UNDER OCCUPATION.**
**SOME PEOPLE OCCUPY THEMSELVES.**
**NO ONE IS FREE.**

Step into a world which is both magically fictitious and shockingly real, to follow the lives of Tamsin, Ellie, Arun and Charlie; a refugee, native, occupier and economic migrant. Watch them grow up during a halcyon past, everyday present and dystopian future. And be prepared to be amazed.

Inspired by the occupations of Palestine, Kurdistan and Tibet, and by the corporate occupation of the west, 'Occupied' is a haunting glance into a society which is a little too familiar for comfort. It truly is a unique piece of literary fiction.

# INVOLUTION & EVOLUTION

This is the story of Alfred Freeman, a boy who does everything he can; to serve humankind. He feeds five-thousand youths, salves-saves-and-soothes; and champions the maligned. He helps paralytics to feel fine, turns water into wine; and gives sight to the blind.

When World War One draws near, his nation is plunged into fear; and so Alfred makes a stand. He opposes the war and calls for peace, disobeys the police; and speaks out across the land. He makes speeches, and he preaches; using statements which sound grand.

But the authorities hit back, and launch a potent-attack; which is full of disgust-derision-and-disdain. Alfred is threatened with execution, and suffers from persecution; which leaves him writhing in pain. He struggles to survive, remain alive; keep cool and stay sane.

'Involution & Evolution' is a masterpiece of rhyme, with a message which echoes through time; and will get inside your head. With colourful-characters and poetic-flair, it is a scathing critique of modern-warfare; and all its gory-bloodshed. It's a novel which breaks new ground, is sure to astound; and really must be read.

Printed in Poland
by Amazon Fulfillment
Poland Sp. z o.o., Wrocław

34412595R00316